DAMNATION MARKED

THE DESCENT SERIES

⌀

S.M. REINE

RED IRIS BOOKS, 2012

BOOKS BY
SM REINE

THE DESCENT SERIES
Death's Hand
The Darkest Gate
Damnation Marked
Dire Blood

THE SEASONS OF THE MOON
Six Moon Summer
All Hallows' Moon
Long Night Moon
Gray Moon Rising

DAMNATION MARKED
Copyright © SM Reine, 2012
Published by Red Iris Books
   ISBN-13: 978-1-937733-13-1
   ISBN-10: 1-937733-13-0

SM Reine
Website: smreine.com
Email: smreine@gmail.com
Twitter: @smreine

Interior and cover design by SM Reine.

As always, thanks to my editing team: Rory Hume, Emily LaDouceur, and Ashley Davis. And an extra big thank you to S&R for all the ocelots, monkeys, and tiny giraffes.

PART ONE

MERCY

A great Tree stood alone, isolated within a gray void. It was wider than a city and taller than the clouds in the sky, and a garden was trapped between its winding roots.

Bridges of white cobblestone led from one root to the next, and a silent stream frothed underneath. The Tree's branches stretched into the endless expanse of nothing, glimmering with broad leaves and bioluminescent blossoms. Empty stairs wound along the outside with spikes buried in the aromatic bark for support, and one gold-skinned apple dangled from the highest branch—too high for anyone to reach. The rest had been carefully extricated from the dimension.

Even eternal flora required occasional tending, and their care fell somewhat ironically to Samael. His specialty was death and his preference was to avoid the garden completely, he couldn't stay away forever.

Samael passed through the gate, alighted on the plain, and folded his wings behind him. The feathered tips dragged along the grass like an overly long cloak.

As soon as he stepped away from the gate, its mighty humming was replaced by indomitable silence. He knew the stream was nearby, somewhere beyond the crumbling garden walls, but it did not babble. There was no wind through the branches, and no squirrels in the bushes. Nothing dared make a sound.

Samael sought the door into the garden. The entrance liked to move occasionally, and he walked around the gray stone wall for some time before finding it. He was careful to ignore the void behind him as he searched. Gray nothingness hung beyond the precipice of the roots, empty of stars or sunlight, and he did not want to see it again.

He located the door some minutes later. The garden's entrance was twice his height and had no visible seam until he

SM Reine

pressed his hands into the stone. It had been years since anyone had visited, so he had to tear away ivy to enter. The creepers curled around his hands, hungry for his warmth. He flicked them to the grass.

The marks on the bezel flared, and Samael entered.

Inside, the flowers were in full bloom. The river spilled cool water over its banks, as if filled with melted snow, and the grass was lush and springy beneath his bare toes.

He walked down a grassy path bordered by rosebushes, which reached for him with thorny fingers. Branches creaked softly as though muffled by fog. He paused to pinch a few of the buds off with his fingertips, and the roses sighed with relief.

Samael brushed his hands over each plant, occasionally stopping to stare at a weed jutting out of the earth. His gaze was death, but it took his hardest glare to kill those unwanted flora. They were black and thorny, born of ill thoughts and deeds, and they oozed ichor when snapped.

The air grew ever more silent and reverent as he spiraled inward, tracing the dark valleys and scaling the arching bridges toward the Tree. Samael tried to ignore the windows carved into the trunk as he passed, and continued to tidy the tangles of weeds and prune ambitious bushes.

He reached a platform built onto a low branch and stopped to strip creepers off the bark.

That was where he found the girl.

She didn't acknowledge him at first, and he likewise tried to pretend he did not see her sitting on the gray stone bench overlooking the garden. Unlike the flowers, she didn't need to be tended by Samael—someone else had that job. He was confident she would be well fed, groomed, and kept in perfect condition. All the children were, at first.

But her name and identity had been stripped away as soon as she had passed through the gate, and with them would have gone her mind. What remained of her consciousness would have been worn like rocks battered under a river of time. Samael had seen it happen a dozen times.

He kept his eyes down as he killed a sprig of thorns buried within the Tree's bark, but he could not help but peek at the newest child as he worked.

This one was physically unlike the others. She was not fragile, nor doll-like. She had not been selected for her beauty. Her nose was a little too strong, her eyes a little too far apart, her freckles too numerous. Someone had brushed her hair out into a long, coppery sheet of curls down her back. The filmy white gown hid her figure beyond the hint of developing hips. She had been walking through the garden for years. Her eyes were empty.

But Samael was entranced by her—as he always was by the children and wives—and it was difficult to focus on his work.

He kneeled by a patch of growing weeds and dug his fingers into the bark. The weeds bled sticky purple and smelled of iron as he broke the stems, burning his fingers.

The girl rose from the bench, and Samael couldn't resist the compulsion to look up.

Visions flitted around her head. The occasional flash of metal and a spill of crimson swirled through the child's mind, and it gave him pause. Those were not ordinary thoughts for such a young girl.

He paused in the middle of his task to watch waking dreams flash over her.

She was thinking of murder. Demons. Hunters and prey and darkness.

He ducked his head and returned to weeding. Even with his eyes averted, he was acutely aware of her presence—she was electricity, magnetic and inviting, and his heart beat too fast in his chest.

Motion caught his attention. The girl lifted her hand to touch a branch. He saw the mark of their Lord on her palm first, and realized that she was holding something second.

A piece of apple.

Oh no.

He dropped the weeds and straightened. "Put that down."

She turned her empty gaze on him. Her eyes were unfocused and white around the pupil.

She brought the slice of apple to her mouth, closed her broad lips over the fruit, and bit. Juice oozed down her chin and dripped onto her dress. The apple's meat was gold, but it stained the cloth like blood.

Her jaw worked. The bite slid down her throat.

The child's irises unfogged.

She had hazel eyes. God help him.

Intelligence appeared next, all too quickly. She must have been eating the fruit of the Tree for days for such a small bite to have such a drastic effect. How long had she been aware that she was in the garden? This was wrong, it was all wrong.

The child considered Samael, from his expansive wings to the hair that fell to his elbows. "Help me," she said, breaking the muffled silence. It was not a plea. It was a demand.

She was radiant and fierce and filled with fire. Samael realized, with sudden surety, that someone had made a terrible mistake in sending her to the garden.

He glanced around to see if they were being watched. Their Lord was certainly there—He was always *there*—but omnipresence didn't mean that He was always paying attention, especially in recent years. "You shouldn't speak." Samael's soft words faded into the groans and creaks of the growing Tree.

He backed up as she approached him. Her steps were swift and sure, and his back bumped into the Tree.

Her hands gripped his sleeve. Blood smeared on white linen. "I can't be here." Her voice was like a fist clenching deep in his heart. "Have mercy."

The word hung between them. *Mercy.*

Samael was torn between adoration and fear. He was her servant—they all were—and he couldn't ignore the request. But their Lord would be furious that they had spoken, and helping the children was *definitely* forbidden.

All he could think to ask was, "Why?"

Her eyes blazed, as if the question were an insult.

"My name is Elise. I need to get home."

He closed his eyes and shuddered. *Elise.* A name, she had a name. Such sweet sin. He loved her as soon as the word passed her lips, and Samael knew he was damned.

"Yes," he whispered. "Of course."

July 1998

Piotr Blodnieks did not look like he was the best at anything. He had a gentle smile, soft features, and a tiny beard under his bottom lip that resembled a paintbrush. His narrow shoulders and sharp joints made him appear awkwardly and gangly instead of lean and fast. At twenty-one years old, he hadn't yet grown into his adult muscles.

Regardless of appearance, Piotr's name was stamped on Hell's history books as the greatest living kopis. He was best known for singlehandedly slaughtering a centuria of demons in the Ukraine. And nobody would ever know it by looking at him.

Nobody aside from the dozen kopides he had just beaten in a sparring match, anyway.

Hamengku groaned on the ground, cradling his shattered knee, while Piotr wiped blood off of his hands with a white towel. "Will he be okay?" he asked his friend, Malcolm, in Russian.

Malcolm helped Hamengku to the sidelines. "Oh, certainly, given a couple weeks of healing." He switched to his native English. "Isn't that right?" The loser glared at him without a hint of understanding in his eyes. Most people waiting around the fighting ring didn't share a common language. "Right! No hard feelings, then? Who's next?"

The kopides who had lost their sparring matches muttered amongst themselves. The other men only shifted uneasily.

Two weeks prior, they had all been summoned to an empty warehouse in Wales by a delegate from the Council of Dis. Over three hundred invitations were sent out, and thirty men arrived to compete for the line of succession. But no one could defeat Piotr. He was, in Malcolm's words, "a bloody machine." The Council's delegate—a petite witch with curly brunette hair—had supervised the fight from her seat on a nearby crate, and she looked bored.

She wasn't the only one who was getting antsy. The shared bravado rapidly dwindled as Piotr felled one kopis after another.

"Oh, fine. Let me try," said a man named Brandon when his friend, Shawn, nudged him forward.

They cleared the floor again. Malcolm mopped up a puddle of sweat with a bloody towel, then stood back.

Piotr and Brandon exchanged blows. The air was filled with the sounds of knuckles meeting face.

Malcolm hollered, and his cheers encouraged the others to join him.

Nobody noticed the side door, or the two people who entered and stood at the back of the crowd.

The fight was short. After a few minutes, Brandon backed off with blood streaming from a cut in his forehead, and held up his hands to indicate that he was done. The other men booed. "You're too fast, man," Brandon said. "I've got to catch a flight tonight. I don't want a concussion."

Piotr turned a confused look to Malcolm, who translated. "Looks like you're stuck being undefeated, mate. Better hope you're immortal!" He laughed and clapped the greatest kopis on the shoulder. "It's hard being at the top!"

A quiet, confident voice broke through the laughter. "I'll fight him."

One by one, the kopides turned around to search for the speaker, and their eyes fell on the pair at the back of the room.

The first was a man over six feet tall, dark-haired and blue-eyed, who seemed like he would have preferred to be anywhere except the warehouse. He rubbed his hand over his eyes with a low curse.

His companion was a full head and shoulders shorter. She was lean with muscle, and her red-brown hair was chopped so short that she could have passed for a boy if not for her breasts.

She was also—clearly and undeniably—the one who had spoken. She was the only woman in the room aside from the Council's witch.

"Aspides don't fight," Malcolm said.

The girl pulled off one of her motorcycle gloves and bandaged her knuckles without responding.

"She's not an aspis, you idiot. Does she look like a witch?" snapped the man at her back. He raked a hand through his hair. "Dear Lord, Elise, do you really think…"

Piotr came to stand beside Malcolm, as did Brandon and Shawn. They formed a wall of muscular bodies.

The tall man trailed off.

Malcolm folded his arms. "Human girls aren't eligible for these fights, either."

Elise's eyes flicked from one person to the next, and she planted her hands on her hips. Her biceps were as well defined as the line of abs that peeked over her jeans. "I'll take all of you."

The men laughed, but their laughter had grown uneasy.

"What's going on?" Piotr asked in Russian.

"I think she's a kopis. She wants to fight you." Malcolm switched back to English. "You realize what you're volunteering for, right?"

She stepped into the ring.

Piotr surveyed her as she lifted her fists and spread her feet in a wide stance.

"I'll fight," he finally said. No translation necessary.

14

Rules were rules. The sparring match was not a group fight, even if she had made the offer. Everyone backed off and spread out.

Piotr and Elise studied each other. He had several inches on her, but she was more muscular. "Well? What are you waiting for?" Brandon asked from his seat on the sidelines, gauze pressed to the injury on his face.

Piotr made the first move—a feint to the right.

It triggered a flurry of motion. Elise parried, ducked, and hit back.

Unlike the fight against Brandon, neither of them restrained their blows. It only took about ten seconds for Piotr's fist to meet Elise's face, break her nose, and send blood pouring down her lips.

"Hey!" Malcolm shouted over the cheers of the other men. "Careful! She's a—"

Elise's friend silenced him with a shake of his head. "Give it a moment."

The fight was fast and brutal. But at some point—somewhere between Elise's broken nose and Piotr's broken hand—the tempo of it changed.

The girl went from defensive to offensive. The greatest kopis started blocking more than he attacked.

Finally, Elise jumped onto Piotr's back, hooked her arm around his throat, and squeezed.

He did everything he could to shake her off. He tried to flip her over his shoulders, but her legs were wrapped too tightly around his midsection. His fingers weren't strong enough to pry her arm free, either.

Piotr slammed her into the crates, and she only grunted.

Finally, he dropped to the floor to crush her against the cement with his weight. But still she hung on.

After a minute, his beating fists grew weak.

15

Then his eyes unfocused and he stopped fighting back.

She gave it a good thirty seconds more—during which everyone watched in stunned silence—and then let go, shoved his limp body off of her, and stood.

Malcolm rushed to his friend's side. "Jesus, Mary, and Joseph!"

He slapped Piotr's cheeks lightly, and then much harder, but the man was thoroughly unconscious and didn't react. His broken hand was turning into a swollen purple mass, and his opposite elbow was bent in the wrong direction.

She had done more than win the fight. She had disabled Piotr for the next week.

Elise wiped blood off her upper lip, probed the bridge of her shattered nose gently with two fingers, and grimaced. Then she walked out of the ring. She didn't seem to care that people were watching her, or that winning a match against Piotr meant she would be the greatest kopis when he died.

"Have a good afternoon," the tall man called to the crowd as he hurried to follow her out of the warehouse.

The witch from the Council of Dis made a note on her laptop, closed the lid, and nodded to the men staring slack-jawed. She climbed into the waiting sports car and drove away.

Brandon shook his head. "American girls."

"Bloody hell," Malcolm said. "I think I'm in love."

February 1999

When Piotr died, Malcolm had a hell of a time tracking Elise Kavanagh down to tell her about it. Every kopis he asked had seen her at some point, but she was gone every time he arrived at one of the places where they had been sighted.

He ended up having to hire a prophet to search for her remotely. Even then, she was gone from Bruges by the time he got there. A demon did report getting beaten by her outside a monastery the night before. It was the closest he had gotten to Elise in weeks.

Malcolm finally located her on the steps of a cathedral three days later.

The grounds of the monastery were layered in snow. Icicles hung from the branches of bare trees. High stone walls faded into foggy steel sky.

It was chilly enough to drive most people indoors, but Elise still wore fingerless motorcycle gloves and a pair of jeans with a hole in the knee. Her fur-lined jacket was more patches than leather. She carved symbols into the blade of a falchion resting on her thigh.

"Hey there, beautiful," Malcolm said, flashing his most winning smile. "You are not an easy woman to find. I don't know if you remember me, but—"

"How did he die?"

His grin faltered. There was only one "he" that Malcolm could imagine that Elise could be talking about, but there was no way she could have known about it yet. Piotr's death had been kept a secret pending notification of the new greatest kopis.

"I was at the sparring match last summer," he went on, like she hadn't spoken.

She blew fragments of metal off her sword and tilted it to catch the light. "Yeah. How did he die?"

So she did know.

"Baphomet repaid him for what happened to her centuria. Snapped his neck. So that means you're up next."

Elise continued carving as though he wasn't there.

He stood back with his arms folded to study her. She looked meaner than he remembered. A bandage covered half of her forehead, and the hunger made her appear older and angrier. He liked angry women.

"We should have a drink to celebrate. I've got a car waiting. It would be much more comfortable than sitting in the snow." His proposition was made only fractionally less suave when he blew into his hands to warm them. He couldn't feel his nose.

Her hand paused on the blade, and her look could have frozen the ocean. "Wasn't Piotr your friend?"

Malcolm shrugged. "Ancient history."

She got to her feet and drew a second falchion from her back sheath, holding both like they were extensions of her arms. Her stance screamed *I will stab you*, and his grin widened.

"You should go," Elise said.

"Don't you want to hear about the selection process? I could tell you all about it… while we get a beer."

She said nothing.

"The delegate from the Council of Dis was too scared to give you the news herself. I'd love to hear how you made such an impression."

She remained silent.

Malcolm sighed. "How old are you? Twenty? Twenty-one?"

"Seventeen."

She was younger than he had expected. But hey, that was legal in most countries.

"Seventeen! You are much too young and much too beautiful to be that serious. Come on, now! You might be the first lady to be the greatest kopis. Don't you think that's exciting? Don't you think we should celebrate?" He faked a playful punch at her arm.

That hard edge softened in her eyes. He thought she was going to respond, but someone else spoke first.

"What are *you* doing here?"

James Faulkner strode from the doors of the cathedral, bundled in a woolen pea coat and earmuffs. A wooden pentacle dangled from a chain at his neck. Pages protruded from his pocket.

Malcolm took a step back to appraise the witch. He'd asked around a bit—or a lot, actually, in kind of an obsessive way—after meeting them at the sparring match, and rumor had it that James was one of the most powerful witches in the world. "I was letting Miss Kavanagh here know about her new status as the greatest kopis."

His brow drew low over his eyes. "What?"

"The last 'greatest' died. *She's* the greatest now. Does that go over your head? Should I spell it out more clearly?"

"Oh, hell." The witch glanced around the monastery grounds like he expected an attack.

Elise sheathed both of her swords. Somehow, she seemed equally dangerous unarmed. Malcolm could have just pounced on her.

"I'm going to pack," she told James.

Malcolm jumped in. "Leaving so soon? You can't go anywhere until you promise to have a drink with me. I have got to hear your story. Not now, maybe, but soon. Please?"

The corner of her mouth twitched. "Fine."

"Elise—" James began.

She had already turned to leave. Malcolm jumped in front of her. "I'm going to hold you to that." Then he swooped in and planted a kiss on her lips, seizing her face in both hands so she couldn't escape.

He danced back with a laugh as her right hook swung harmlessly in the air.

"See you around," he called as he jogged away. Elise glared at him with pink cheeks as James gaped.

But she almost smiled, too. Almost.

PART TWO

A CREEPING
SHADOW

I

November 2009

Rick used to make a living selling medicine to plague doctors.
He once watched a patron stuff his beak with camphor, rose
petals, and laudanum using gloved hands, while explaining that
the aromas would spare him from miasmatic air. The doctor
had spoken with confident authority, and Rick believed him.
It seemed to be as good an explanation for the plague as
anything else.

The doctor slid the mask over his face, donned his fedora,
and departed to treat the dying.

A few weeks later, Rick passed a pyre of bodies and saw
his former customer at the top of the pile. The doctor's neck
below the mask was riddled with buboes. His robes curled with
flame. The mask's long beak was cracked.

It was about then that Rick realized that humans were
deeply stupid creatures.

He avoided Earth for a few hundred years after that. The
market for human trinkets was good in Hell at the time,
considering that there was no reliable way to travel between the
dimensions, and he eked out a decent living.

The next time he set foot in a mortal city on the planes of
Earth, those deeply stupid animals had somehow created heavy
machines that could drive at unimaginable speeds, and they
allowed *anyone* to do it. It was lunacy. Or idiocy. Or very
possibly both.

He wanted nothing to do with them.

SM Reine

But his passport had expired, so it was too late for Rick to go back to Hell. He picked a town, bought a shop, and hadn't left it since—not once.

Rick watched through the window as his newest assistant accepted a shipment, gnawing on his claws with jagged teeth. Jerica was taking her sweet time signing for those crates. She was a nightmare too, though much younger than Rick, newly substantiated and still marveling at the wonders of her corporeal form. She seemed to enjoy using it to flirt with the delivery driver.

What if that blasted truck rolled over and killed her? It had been hard enough finding one assistant. He didn't want to find a replacement, too.

The shopkeeper kept an eye on the empty street as Jerica continued to talk with the driver, who didn't seem concerned about the possibility of being killed on the sidewalk, either. She pointed at the boxes, then tipped her head back and laughed. Laughed!

Rick couldn't watch. He just couldn't. It was too much for his constitution to handle.

He returned to the counter of his drugstore and took a shot of cactus juice to settle his cramping gut. It tasted like ass, and Rick knew ass. They considered human anuses to be a gourmet treat in Hell. The cactus was definitely worse. But it did good things for his stomach.

Moving away from the window didn't keep him from worrying over his assistant. He could watch Jerica on the blurry monitor hanging over the locked case of condoms. And watch her he did. Rick worried about that girl.

Eventually, after what felt like hours, the bell over the door chimed. His nightmare assistant backed into the shop carrying one of the crates on her shoulder.

"What is this? It's heavy." Jerica crouched to set it on the cracked linoleum.

He wrung his hands. "Do you think you took long enough?"

"What, are you having a rush of business in here?" She popped a bubble of gum and sucked it into her mouth again. "Relax. Being nice never hurt anyone."

"You would be surprised," Rick said darkly, thinking of plague doctors and blackened extremities. Jerica moved to open the crate, but he slammed a hand on the wood to stop her. "What do you think you're doing?"

"Checking the shipment. Don't you want to make sure we've got everything?"

"Not up here, where we can be seen through the windows," he hissed. "Downstairs!"

Rick took the first crate to the basement while Jerica retrieved the other two.

The space beneath his shop was dim, narrow, and had a low ceiling. He still occasionally smacked his forehead on the beams, even after seventy-five years. His desk and reclining chair occupied one corner; the rest of the floor was filled with boxes of inventory.

He kicked a space clear for the crates and directed her to stack all three on top of each other. Then, and only then, did he lift the lid on one to examine the contents. It was filled with egg cartons, each of which protected twelve small, glowing cubes.

"Lethe?" Jerica asked, sounding wholly unimpressed.

"Mind yourself. This is a special order."

She jutted a hip. With her asymmetrical haircut, scalloped tunic, and cocky stance, she looked more like an abstract geometric painting than a teenage girl. "Rick, man, you know I love you…"

He smashed the lid onto the crate again. "Ha."

"…but anyone making special orders of lethe is not someone you should be dealing with. I mean, drugs? *Demon* drugs? You know what this stuff does to people?"

"It does nothing to *people*," he said, unfazed by her attempt at showing concern for him. "Only demons. I don't question the orders, and neither should you."

A quick scan showed that every cube was in its proper place, and in good condition. Rick still had an intake bracelet somewhere, probably at the bottom of his laundry pile. Maybe the client would want to drop a couple together. He hadn't been on a trip in a long time—literally or figuratively.

His assistant watched him replace the lids with disapproval. "Rick…"

"Get on out," he said, shooing her upstairs. He locked the basement door behind them. "Go on. Get."

She sighed. "Maybe I should stay and help you with this."

"Your shift ends in fifteen. I'm not paying overtime. I told you, get on out."

"You don't have to pay me."

But he pushed her toward the door, and she could hardly fight against him. Especially when he exerted the strength of millennia against her dozen or so years. "Careful on your way home. Stay out of the streets. And watch for those cars!"

Her lips stretched so wide from ear to ear that he could see the wad of gum pressed between two yellowed molars. "Nobody's going to run me over on the way. But if you're really worried, you could walk me home."

"You're funny. Just so fuckin' funny."

He shut the door in her face, but considering it was a glass door, it didn't do much good. He saw her mouth moving on the other side: *Be careful. Okay?*

Then Jerica faded into the shadows, slipping across the street without touching the pavement, and reappeared under a streetlight. She waved at him before dancing into darkness once more.

Rick sat on his stool behind the counter and found his paperback under a folder of ledgers. Since he didn't sleep, all he had was free time, and Rick read a lot. Despite being dumb animals, humans were good with stories. He was in the middle of "The Billionaire's Busty Bride." The pages curled under his long fingers.

Soon, he was so absorbed that he didn't look up when the bell over the door jingled. Footsteps shuffled in.

"Leave your bag outside," he said, licking his thumb to turn the page. "No backpacks."

The silence that followed his order had weight to it. Rick glanced up. The customer was a tall guy in a leather jacket with a spiked iron band wrapped around his forehead. He was ugly, even by a nightmare's standards: smashed nose, sausage lips, lined face. Flecks of dried blood were peeling off his leathery skin like he hadn't washed his face since his last meal of manflesh.

Zohak slammed his fists on the counter. "Where is it?" He had been on Earth for months, but his accent was miserable. Everything was still pronounced in the back of his throat, like he was about to spill out a tirade of Hell's native tongue.

Rick folded the corner of his page, closed the book, and stuck it under the cash register. "All right, all right." He shuttered the windows to block out the night. "This way." Zohak lumbered down the stairs to the basement. His weight made the whole building creak. "No company this time?"

The demon-king glared over his shoulder. "I trust no one."

"That wasn't the story last time I saw you."

"My fiends hadn't been slaughtered last time." Bitterness dripped from his growls.

Rick knew a subject he shouldn't touch when he heard one. It didn't matter if Zohak had his legion anyway. Only if he had money.

They opened the top crate. A silvery-blue glow splashed over their faces, highlighting the furrows on Zohak's face. The demon-king's eyes raked over the inventory.

"Is this all you have?"

"It's all you ordered. Three stacks of lethe."

Zohak towered over the nightmare, clenching his hands and baring his teeth. "I ordered five!"

Rick wasn't impressed, but he *was* prepared. He whipped the ledger out of his back pocket and held it up. "Three stacks."

The demon king deflated a little. Actually, he deflated a lot. He quivered, and his broad shoulders sagged. For an instant, an oily sheen obscured his red irises.

He moved to put the lid back on the crate, but Rick stopped him. "Payment?"

The king blinked, and the oily veil vanished from his eyes. "This one is on…" Zohak searched for the word. "Credit."

Rick flapped the ledger. "No. It's not."

"I must sell this before I can afford to buy it."

"What about the last batch you flipped?"

Zohak seemed to struggle with the words, but not because of the language barrier. "I… lost it."

And with that, the overhead light bulb flickered.

A strange energy rolled through the basement, and Rick closed his eyes to focus on it. Weight pressed between the space where his shoulder blades should have been. It tasted like ancient papyrus, like the clouds in the sky, and he tried to swipe it from his tongue.

"Wait here," he said, leaving Zohak with the inventory to head upstairs.

The intensity of the energy grew as he ascended. The air buzzed as though a low electrical current were vibrating through it.

Rick lifted the blinds. One by one, the streetlights dimmed and turned off, marching in a line from the end of the block toward his shop.

His security system beeped, drawing his attention to the monitor. The camera mounted outside his shop flickered, snowed, and cut out. Then the "Open" sign in the window turned off, followed immediately by the lights inside.

A power outage? The clouds were heavy with the promise of snow, but a single flake had yet to fall, and the air was completely still.

Tendrils of dread began creeping over him. "What in the seven hells?"

He willed his corporeal form away, focused on the window, and reappeared beside the warped glass with a thought. He peered into the night.

There was someone moving on the street. A woman.

Rick locked the door and stepped back. "Zohak! Incoming!"

The demon-king already stood at the top of the stairs, and his eyes blazed with red fire. Rick didn't recognize the woman approaching on the street, but apparently he did.

It only took a moment for her to reach the entrance. Her hair was in a thick braid over one shoulder. There were straps at her shoulders, as though she wore a backpack. A college student?

The back door creaked, slammed, and Zohak was gone.

Rick phased to the counter. Grabbed his crowbar.

The woman rattled the door—locked. She raised her booted foot and slammed it into the glass. Shards rained onto the linoleum.

Rick shook his crowbar. "I'll call the police!"

The woman reached behind her, and he realized belatedly that she wasn't wearing a backpack at all. She had a spine scabbard with two swords. The one she drew had a short blade, barely longer than her forearm, and occult symbols etched into the metal.

Rick had heard of that blade, and the woman who wielded it. They called her the Godslayer.

No wonder Zohak had run.

She used it to beat away the remaining glass and ducked through.

"Didn't you hear me?" Rick said, with somewhat less steam than before. She wouldn't be impressed by the police. Rumor had it that they had tried to arrest her once, but she killed half the force, bewitched the others, and escaped without a mark on her permanent record.

The Godslayer straightened and shook glass out of her hair. So she wasn't ten feet tall after all. Her eyes weren't filled with angelfire, either. She looked... human.

"Where's Zohak?"

He sent out a tendril of energy to sniff at her mind, but there was no hint of normal, brittle human emotions. It was like trying to penetrate a brick wall with a toothpick.

Rick wavered. Surviving in Hell for millennia had left him without a hint of pride. And Zohak hadn't paid for his goods anyway.

He dropped the crowbar. "Out the back door. Just leave me be!" Then he threw himself behind the counter and covered his head.

That should have been it. The Godslayer didn't want puny Rick—merely a nightmare, a petty hellborn immigrant of no great consequence—but she rounded the counter and seized him by the arm regardless. Her gloved fingers dug into the place a human would have had a bicep.

"You're coming with me."

She strode to the back door, kicked it open, and Rick realized what she was about to do an instant before he crossed the threshold. "No!" he cried, struggling in her grip. "I can't—stop!"

His feet hit pavement, and he could barely breathe. Electrical lines ran through the air over his head. Dear Lord, what were those animals *thinking*? And there was a car parked in the alley, so who knew when it might start to roll—

The Godslayer, of course, was unimpressed by this human madness. And she wasn't slowed by dragging a nightmare, either. She lifted his featherweight body from the ground and strode after Zohak.

She dropped Rick at the mouth of the alley. He tried to scramble back toward his shop, but she kicked him to the ground. Her boot sank into his spongy gut and left an imprint of the sole.

His back hit the car's tire. It didn't hurt, but he gave a strangled yell. "Please, *please*, I can't be outside!"

"Where does Zohak den? Point me."

Rick lifted a quavering finger, silently praying that she would leave him to return to his shop if he told her where Zohak lived.

But she seized an ankle and pulled him along with her.

She forced him to give directions all the way to the empty tattoo parlor Zohak inhabited. She even took him across the street—black pavement, orange lines, traffic lights, cars! He almost passed out.

They reached the back of the parlor shortly after the demon-king. Zohak scrambled over the chain link fence, and the Godslayer finally dropped Rick to follow.

She scaled it in two short motions, vaulted the top, and landed on top of Zohak. He grunted as they both fell to the pavement.

Rick searched wildly for another exit from the alley. Anything to get him home without crossing another street. But he was trapped, so he pressed against the wall, drew his knees to his ears, and prayed to long-dead gods for help.

He watched as the Godslayer and Zohak exchanged blows on the other side of the fence. Her strikes were fast and brutal. She went for the soft spots on his face, and when he exclaimed with pain, she ripped the crown from his head and flung it into the wall.

Fury blackened his visage. He threw her into the back door of the tattoo parlor and grabbed his crown.

For an instant, Rick could see nothing around the back of the demon-king, and then he heard a wet *crunch*, a feminine cry, and a guttural laugh.

Blood splattered on the asphalt inches from Rick. Mortal blood.

So she *was* human.

"Stupid," Zohak said, hand clenched around her throat. "You should have known by now not to face me alone."

Her voice was strained when she replied. "I'm not alone."

The streetlights flickered. Turned off.

A massive shape hurtled out of the night sky and slammed into the pavement.

The shockwave rushed through the alley, expanding the air inside the dumpsters and making their lids bang open against the walls. Grates rattled. The smell of rotting produce filled the air.

Rick gagged, but not from the smell. He gagged on the energy. His throat closed as that crushing pressure weighed on him, his vision darkened at the edges, and he realized that at least *some* of the rumors about the Godslayer were true.

She had an angel bodyguard.

He was tall, willowy, and ageless, with coppery hair to his shoulders. Luminous blue eyes turned on Zohak as the angel straightened. Downy feathers drifted to the asphalt.

"Took you long enough," the angel said with a delicate snort. He addressed the Godslayer. "Are you okay? You're bleeding."

"Don't worry about it, Nukha'il."

He inclined his head. "How can I help you?"

"Hold Zohak down."

The demon-king's eyes went wild. He darted for the fence, but the angel grabbed the back of his shirt and threw him into the Godslayer's waiting arms.

She pinned him against the wall with a hand to his throat and her sword digging into his stomach. Nukha'il didn't have to do anything. His presence was threat enough.

"How many times did I tell you to leave my city?" the woman asked.

"*Bistak*," Zohak replied.

She shoved him to the ground and used her weight to pin him. Her bicep bled where he had injured her. Barely a scratch. "Tell me where your fiends are, and I'll have Nukha'il escort you out of the city—out of the *country*."

"They are dead. You killed them."

She punched him with the hilt of her sword, and his head slammed against the pavement. One of his horns chipped. "Where are your fiends?"

"Dead!"

33

"He's telling the truth," Nukha'il said. "He believes you killed them."

Her sword wavered. "How did they die?" she asked Zohak, and her voice wasn't quite as angry as it had been earlier.

"Deep beneath the city. There's something down there." He whimpered. "Something... *black*."

"Tell me."

"It came from the earth, from the rocks. A shadow with inertia." His voice changed, deepened, as though he were speaking through an echoing cavern. "It came upon us. One by one, it devoured them, and then..." His face twisted. "And then it took me."

Rick had heard the rumors. Creeping shadows, a hungry darkness, a change in the Warrens. Everyone said it was the Godslayer. They said she had unimaginable power.

But she exchanged glances with the angel, and her expression was genuinely confused. She didn't know anything. That information would be worth money—if Rick could get home without dying.

She shook his jacket. "You're lying, Zohak. You have to be. Where are your fiends?"

Zohak responded with a groaning cry. The inky shadow devoured his eyes again. His body shuddered, and his hands reached up to close around the Godslayer's wrists.

The demon-king jerked her hands down and plunged the blade into his heart with a sickening *crack*.

"Whoa!"

She struggled to free herself, but it was too late. A black fog spilled from his chest, creeping up her blade.

With a shout, she dropped the sword and leaped to her feet.

The ichor spread over the sword and fountained over Zohak as he twisted on the ground. His eyes were wide open, and his mouth yawned in a silent cry. He sat up, hands gripping his chest, and tried to get to his feet as the shadow devoured the last of his flesh. A croak tore from his throat.

Rick's heart beat a panicked tattoo. Forget the humans. Forget their technology. Forget their goddamn *cars*.

The nightmare leaped to his feet and ran.

II

"Holy mother of demons, what the hell is *that* thing? Is that a body bag?"

"Clear off the desk, Neuma," Elise grunted, staggering up the stairs to the manager's office in Craven's Casino.

She held Zohak by the shoulders, and Nukha'il had his feet. Even wrapped tightly in trash bags and twine, he was strong enough that they were both sweating with the effort it took to hold him.

Neuma shoved the paperwork to the floor, placed the laptop on the filing cabinet, and watched anxiously as Elise lowered the body to the desk. She wasn't in her stripper costume that night, and might have passed for a normal girl if not for the glowing skin and black eyes.

Zohak arched and roared. He nearly threw himself to the floor. Only Nukha'il's hands pressing into the demon-king's shoulders kept the bag pinned down.

"Ropes," Elise said, "get the ropes!"

Neuma vanished.

Elise ran to the closet behind the desk. The charmed lock didn't open the first time she tried to open it. It didn't respond to the second or third attempts, either.

Finally, she gave it a swift kick and yelled, "Goddamn it, it's me! Open up, you moron!"

Somewhat begrudgingly, the lock clicked, and she opened the closet.

The walls were filled with rows of hooks and dangling tools—mostly torture devices left by the last manager of

Craven's. Her belongings had begun migrating to the closet ever since she had taken over: a few knives with the mark of St. Benedict stamped on the blade, some free weights for when she got bored, and several looping golden chains with dangling medallions.

She took the chains and shut the door, which locked itself again with an offended *click*.

Neuma returned carrying an armful of heavy silver chains. "Will this work? These are the thickest ones I've got. I only had time to run to the play room."

"That's fine," Elise said.

The angel restrained Zohak as the women tied him to the desk, wrapping the chains all the way around the heavy oaken furniture. There were metal rings welded to the floor too— probably for the same reason that David Nicholas had kept torture implements in his office closet. Elise clamped the chains to the rings.

Nukha'il stepped back, and the demon struggled in vain. He was secure.

"Did the ichor touch you?" she asked the angel.

"No, I'm fine."

Neuma bent to pick up the boot knife. The inky shadows had moved to consume the entire blade, joining with the metal and turning it obsidian.

"Don't touch that!" Elise barked, and the half-succubus froze. "Don't touch *anything* black right now. Even if you think it's just shadow." Neuma glanced around the office, and Elise knew what she had to be thinking. The previous manager's aesthetic tastes ran toward the dark. Aside from the tacky casino carpeting, which was patterned with red geometric shapes, *everything* was black. The walls, the furniture—even the tinted windows overlooking the floor of the gaming room.

"Now stand back. Both of you." She eyeballed Nukha'il, who made her palms itch. "Especially you."

He politely backed into a corner, and she closed her hand around the charms.

It had been months since she had attempted an exorcism. In fact, she hadn't done one since she sent David Nicholas back to Hell. And something had definitely changed. It was as though her center wasn't quite so… centered.

She had to try.

"*Crux sacra sit mihi lux,*" she began, voice quavering. She cleared her throat. "*Non draco sit mihi dux. Vade retro, Satana—*"

Zohak heaved and jerked. He was spitting with laughter.

The bastard had spent weeks trying to take over Elise's city, and he kept mocking her after she killed him.

Heat swelled within Elise's ribcage.

There was her strength.

She slammed her fist into his chest, and the charms blazed. "*Crux sacra sit mihi lux. Non draco sit mihi dux.*" Elise envisioned reaching her power into the hole in his chest, beneath the bag and beyond his shattered breastbone. "*Vade retro, Satana. Nunquam suade mihi vana. Sunt mala quae libas—*"

A shadow passed her closed eyelids, as though something huge had blocked out all of the light in the room.

Elise's eyes flew open.

And she saw nothing.

There was no floor beneath her feet, no chains around her hands, no air in her lungs. She was blinded, disoriented. Elise tried to gasp and didn't find any oxygen.

The shadow gripped her throat.

She clawed at it, but there was no breaking from the grip of immense *nothingness*.

And a voice rose from the darkness. It was silky, feminine, and furious.

Exorcise me? You must be kidding.

Pain exploded in the back of her head. Elise shouted—which meant there was air, blessed air—and her forehead was pressed to the ugly red carpet.

Her vision cleared. She had been thrown clear across the manager's office and was crumpled on the floor by the door.

She couldn't see Zohak's body on the desk because Nukha'il had thrown his wings wide, filling the entire span of the office.

Neuma was screaming. Once she could breathe, Elise snapped, "Shut up!"

The bartender clapped her mouth closed, smothering her cries with both hands as Elise struggled to her feet. The chains burned with heat, and she flung them to the carpet. The instant they touched the ground, a fire sparked.

Elise stomped the flames out before they could spread, and Neuma ripped the extinguisher off the wall. A white cloud of flame retardant chemicals blasted over the chains.

"Elise!" Nukha'il called. "You need to see this."

Neuma remained poised with the fire extinguisher, eyes wide and chest heaving. Elise edged around Nukha'il's wings. Her palms burned, and there was no way to tell if it was from the charms or the power of his angelic energy. But she forgot all about it once she saw Zohak.

He had stopped thrashing. The ooze had melded with his skin in much the same way it had with Elise's knife, and he was frozen in obsidian.

His mouth was spread in a frozen cry. His eyes had been sucked into his skull, leaving empty pits.

"What did you do?" she asked.

Nukha'il's eyes widened. "Nothing. I thought you did this."

Elise recalled the voice she had heard from the darkness. *Exorcise me?*

It was suddenly too hot in the office. She wiped sweat from her brow. "Damn."

"I think I missed something," Neuma said, voice shaking. "Weren't you going out to find Zohak and get rid of him, for good this time?"

"We just did."

Nukha'il folded his wings against his back and stepped aside. Considering his impressive wingspan, they could be folded down comparatively small, and they vanished completely with a moment's thought. He looked like any other man who was well over six feet tall, androgynous, and ageless, with blue eyes that glowed in the dark.

Neuma clung to Elise's shoulder and got on her toes to peer into the garbage bag. "That doesn't look like him."

"It's him," Elise said. "What's left of him."

The bartender dropped the fire extinguisher and inched forward. "What killed him?"

"I did. I stabbed him in the chest with one of my falchions."

"Oh," she said.

Elise located a knife and sliced open the trash bag over Zohak's gut. The shadow didn't spill forth and consume her knife a second time.

Elise tapped the point of the knife against his stomach. It sounded like stone.

"We need to get rid of this."

Neuma blinked rapidly, trying to process the order. "Shouldn't we... investigate? Do an autopsy?"

"No," Elise said, and it came out more forcefully than she intended. She kneeled and unclipped the chains from the rings in the floor. "I've learned everything I'm going to from Zohak.

Someone needs to take him out of the city and drop him down a mineshaft—a *closed* shaft, preferably, that doesn't lead into the Warrens."

"So shall it be done," Nukha'il said.

She shook her head. "Not you. Neuma, could you find a volunteer?"

"Sure thing."

The stripper scurried downstairs again. As soon as the door shut, Elise stopped undoing the chains.

She drew her sword.

When the shadow had spilled from Zohak's chest in the alley to devour her falchion, she had wrapped it in trash bags and jammed it into her spine sheath for later study. Now she held the sword in both hands without unwrapping it. Elise wasn't sure what would be worse—if she opened it and her sword was destroyed by the same obsidian that had taken Zohak, or if the shadows were still seething.

She hefted its weight in her hands and swallowed hard.

Nukha'il noticed her silence. "Is there a problem?"

"No."

Elise climbed to her feet, opened the closet after a short argument with the locking charm, and set the sword on a suitcase inside. Her back felt unbalanced with only one sword. It wasn't the first time she had lost a falchion, but after months of using the pair together again, she hated to lock one away.

She shut the door. Her fingers were shaking, so she shuffled through the desk drawers and came up with a half-empty pack of cigarettes and a lighter.

It took two tries to get a flame. She sucked hard on the cigarette and sighed out the smoke.

That was all she needed—just a taste. If David Nicholas had seen her smoking his leftover cigarettes, he would have thought it was the greatest joke ever. He probably would have laughed himself to death.

Good thing he was already dead.

"You know that could kill you," Nukha'il said.

Elise ignored him and stubbed it out in the ashtray, which was filled with barely-smoked cigarettes. All hers. She stuffed the box in her pocket.

Back to business.

Elise continued releasing the silver chains. "I need you to go into the Warrens. You have to go to the gate."

That got his attention. His hands stilled on a clamp on the other side of the desk.

"Why?"

"Because you're the ethereal delegate and it's your job, that's why," she snapped. "Zohak said that there's something underneath the city. I need to be sure that the gates are still safe. Still secure."

"Very well," Nukha'il said with an edge to his voice that hadn't been there before.

He had remained in Reno to ensure the safety of the gates, so they had been working together toward those ends for over a month. But neither of them had found occasion to go that deep into the Warrens. In fact, they had both been doing their very best to avoid them.

She opened her mouth to speak again, but her ringing phone interrupted her. She glanced at the screen.

It was James. Of course it was James.

Elise pressed the button to deny the call and scrolled through the history. He had already tried to reach her three times since midnight. Nothing like a failed attempt at an exorcism to wake up her aspis.

"What if the gate has already been compromised?" Nukha'il asked, drawing her attention back to the task at hand.

What if the gate *had* been compromised? What could an infectious shadow do to an ethereal city suspended in a second dimension over her territory?

Elise grimaced. "Just go check."

By the time Neuma found "volunteers" to discard Zohak's body in the desert—which happened, in this case, to be two very nervous basandere—dawn was approaching, and it was much too late for Elise to try to get any rest.

For weeks, her nights had been dedicated to unearthing the roots that Zohak had embedded in her territory. He had trafficked drugs, used his fiends to bully other demons, and had managed to destroy one of Craven's subsidiary restaurants on the south end of town.

Tracking him meant hitting the streets for hours on end, every single night. It meant that she hadn't slept more than two hours at a time since September. It meant that she could rest, now that Zohak was dead.

So why did she feel so unsatisfied?

Elise loosened her fraying braid, retied it into a ponytail, and threw on her jacket before heading out onto the streets for a jog in the dim blue light of false dawn.

That was the time when she liked the city the best. Most demons had crawled into the Warrens to sleep for the day, and it was before shifts changed for the human casino workers. All that Elise faced on her jog was empty streets and blissful silence.

The guard she had posted at the front door of Craven's gave her a polite nod as she passed. "Good morning, ma'am." Sharp teeth flashed between his lips when he spoke. He was a real teddy bear, but he *looked* scary as hell, and he was meant to deter Zohak from sending fiends through the front door.

Elise paused. "Go home, Ed. Enjoy the day."

She didn't have to tell him twice. His shark-like mouth split into a grin, and he loosened the top button on his Craven's-branded polo shirt. "Thank you, ma'am."

"And stop calling me that," she yelled over her shoulder as she jogged away.

Even at five in the morning, the casinos hadn't turned off their lights, so gold and green and red strobes splashed on the sidewalk beneath her pounding feet. She dodged patches of black ice as she crossed the street and headed down to the river, which was never quite empty. Not since the economy had crashed and dumped the jobless onto the streets. They made their camps on the path that ran the length of the Truckee.

Elise slid down the embankment to the trail, careful not to disturb three men sleeping under heavy jackets and reflective blankets.

She didn't see the trail beneath her feet as she ran. Her mind was back in the manager's office.

Exorcise me?

Zohak wasn't the only demon that had visited the city with unsavory intentions. Everyone knew that there was no overlord left in Reno. Elise had been forced to quash a few other uprisings, none of which had been very effective.

Was the shadow another demon moving in to conquer? And what the hell was she supposed to do about an enemy that could take out Zohak's army of fiends, and was impervious to exorcism?

The morning didn't seem quite so bright after that.

She continued running until the path narrowed and the sun rose. Elise angled herself to return downtown.

North of the city, in a suburb built around golf courses, James was falling asleep again. He had been sitting awake in his kitchen since she had rejected his calls, but his head was drooping. James hadn't been sleeping well, either. She knew this for a fact because she often saw his dreams. He dreamed of the same things she did—pillars of towering white bone, cobblestone streets, and a blond woman with a gunshot wound in her forehead.

Sensing her attention, he yawned and spoke aloud, his gaze fixed on a cup of tea. She heard his voice as though he stood beside her.

"Are you okay?"

She replied silently. *I'm fine.*

"Do you need help with anything?"

No.

"What are your plans for the day?"

She sighed. His persistent attempts to have a chat were wearing down on her.

It wasn't that Elise didn't want to see James—she did. Really. But he had a way of steering the conversation toward Betty, and wanting to address Elise's "feelings," and she could only put up with so much of that before it became too much. And she wasn't going to talk to him in the house he shared with Stephanie.

I'm busy, Elise said shortly, and then she blocked him out.

Sirens wailed in the distance, breaking the stillness of the morning.

An ambulance roared up the street, blew past Elise, and cornered hard. It was followed less than ten seconds later by a police car.

She didn't think much of it until she saw two more police cars approach from the opposite direction and turn down the same street.

Never a good sign.

Elise followed the sirens and found herself in front of Rick's Drugstore.

Or at least, the place where Rick's Drugstore had stood the night before. It had been a tiny shop on the corner of West and Second that should have been condemned for fifty years.

But the shop was gone. All that remained was the tiny alley, half of the sign, and the frame surrounding the door Elise had shattered.

It appeared to have collapsed. It was an old building, after all—everything that had been built around it was newer, stronger, and untouched by the destruction. But when she stepped around the police car to peer over the wall, she could see that it wasn't just the floor and walls that had imploded. The basement had collapsed, too, and the hole it exposed was deep enough to disappear into darkness.

It led straight down into the Warrens.

A police officer blocked her view. "Move along. It's not safe to be here."

"What happened?" she asked as she backed up.

"Sinkhole. Looks like a mineshaft. We have to evacuate the street until we determine whether the substructure is safe."

"There aren't mines this close to the surface in downtown Reno."

He took off his cap and ran a hand over his bald pate. "I said 'move along,' didn't I, sweetheart?"

"Sorry," Elise said, and did as she was told.

III

It had taken three months, but James's home office was finally exactly the way he liked it.

Six constant weeks of burning frankincense and lavender had purged all the preexisting energy from the air, leaving him a clean workspace. Now he had filled two of the walls with bookshelves, which reached from floor to ceiling. He had a permanent altar by the window leading into his greenhouse.

He also carved a circle of power into the floor, so all it took was a touch of salt to prepare for a spell. James even had a cage of mice ready as small sacrifices for the most powerful magic.

And he had charms that could keep everyone—including Stephanie—out of his office.

That wasn't the thing that completed his office, though. It was the futon he placed under the second window, which he had been sleeping on every night for the past week. He could fall asleep doing his research and continue working as soon as he woke up.

He hadn't slept in the bed he shared with Stephanie since he had put the futon in his office. Of course, he hadn't shared the bed with her more than a handful of times since they had moved in anyway, as she worked nights at the hospital.

The rising sun beamed light directly through the greenhouse window, spilling onto his circle of power and rousing James from his restless sleep.

He sat up, letting the book he had been reading drop to the floor. Resting it against his chest all night had broken the spine, and it flopped open on the page he had been reading. The heading said, "Mythologies of the Islamic World," and he had left crooked highlights on two lines before losing the battle against sleep.

James sat on the side of the futon and scrubbed a hand through his hair, heaving a sigh. He reached for Elise out of habit—a quick probe to make sure she hadn't gotten killed while he napped. But there was no response. The wards on his office really were powerful enough to block everything, including his kopis.

He shuffled to his altar and opened a wooden box that was seated between images of the Goddess and the Horned God. Inside, a cloud of colorless magic was beginning to resolve around two gold rings. He reached through the haze to tap one of the bands.

The magic sang up his arm. Almost done.

A teapot's whine broke through the air, muffled by the wall.

He closed the box, stuffed his feet into slippers, and passed a hand over the protective charms on his doorway to disable them. As soon as he crossed the threshold, Elise's consciousness blinked into the back of his mind again. She was still alive. Small miracle.

James yawned as he staggered into the kitchen. The crock-pot that had been cooking steel-cut oats overnight had been turned from "low" to "warm." He grabbed a bowl out of the cabinet and was searching for a spoon when arms wrapped around him from behind.

"Good morning, handsome," Stephanie purred, nuzzling her face into his back. "Long time no see."

When *was* the last time he had seen his girlfriend? One week? Two? "Good morning." He turned to drop a kiss on her upturned lips.

She didn't release his arm as he served the oats. "Have you been doing a new workout at the studio? Lifting weights? You look very good."

He set down the bowl, took off his glasses, and rubbed his eyes. "Pardon?"

"I was just saying how much I want you to take advantage of me," she murmured into his ear.

He responded without thinking about it. "Right now?"

Her nails bit into his shoulders for an instant before letting go. "Not if it would inconvenience you." She stabbed the button to start the espresso machine.

"I'm sorry, Stephanie. I didn't mean to suggest I don't have time for you."

"It's been so long since we've had any private time together. When I'm home, you're always locked in your office, or I'm asleep." She rubbed her hands up his biceps. Fondling his muscles made that angry glare soften. "Clearly you've been finding time for yourself, if not me."

"What in the world are you talking about?"

James angled to study himself in the hallway mirror. He turned to the side and lifted an arm. It was hard to tell under his long-sleeved shirt, but there did seem to be more tone than usual.

He lifted the hem. He had dropped a couple notches on his belt, but had thought it was because he had been too distracted to eat. That didn't appear to be the case. His reflection was hardly a man shrinking from work-inflicted starvation: his stomach was flat, his psoas were more pronounced, and his abs could be best described as "chiseled."

"It must be the new routines I'm doing," he said faintly, but he knew it wasn't true. He hadn't had abs like that since his twenties. And he had only set foot in Motion and Dance twice that month: once to drop off paychecks, and once because

Candace asked him to meet the accountant who was replacing Elise.

Stephanie squeezed his bicep. "Maybe you'd like me to help you practice? These routines must be magic."

"Something like that." He dropped the hem of his shirt. "That reminds me—could you humor a strange request?"

"Of course." A naughty smile tugged at the corner of her mouth. Her fingers drew a line from the cut of his abs down his navel. "It wouldn't be the first time."

"Could you order a karyotype test for me?"

"Drawing blood? Kinky." Her smile faded. "What would you be hoping to find, exactly?"

"An overall profile would do. I'm just… curious."

"Weird curiosity," Stephanie said.

He massaged her shoulders. "I told you it was a strange request, didn't I?"

"You did." She stretched up on her toes to plant a peck on his lips. "Visit me at work tonight. I'll take care of it."

"Thank you," he said.

Their kiss lingered. He found himself glancing at the clock over her head, and Stephanie didn't miss his distraction.

She pushed him off. "Really?" He didn't bother apologizing. She grabbed a small coffee cup, slammed the cabinet door, and poured her espresso into it. "Fine. Go back to working on the almanac. I'm going to shower—I have an early meeting with the board."

"Try to have a good day."

Stephanie sniffed and left.

James returned the oats to the crockpot before ducking into the bathroom and stripping off his shirt. He turned to one side and then the other, studying himself in the mirror. The change was most pronounced in his upper chest and shoulders, where he had never been bulky. He tilted his chin to the side. His neck was thicker, too.

He would be turning forty in February, and he didn't keep weight off as easily anymore. Yet he suddenly could have passed for ten years younger.

"This can't be good," he told the slimmer, more muscular version of himself in the mirror.

His concern was enough to trigger the bond. Elise's consciousness nudged at his.

For an instant, he felt like he was sitting on a barstool in a dark casino cafe. It smelled like coffee and cigarette smoke. She sat at the bar with an empty shot glass and an omelet that hadn't been touched.

Her thoughts drifted past.

What's wrong?

The question irked him. He knew she had been doing *something* the night before—something that made her bring out the exorcism charms—but she had blocked his every attempt to check on her. And she had the nerve to ask if *he* was okay?

"Eat your omelet and mind your own damn business," he said, turning from the mirror and tugging the shirt over his head. He saw a second shot glass set in front of her before their shared consciousness ended, and he couldn't resist making a comment. "Tequila? With breakfast?"

Her annoyance was an electric pinch in his forehead. *Mind your own damn business.*

And then she was gone.

The doorbell rang before he could return to his office. He listened for the telltale footsteps that would tell him that Stephanie was answering the door, but the house was silent.

"Stephanie?" he called. She didn't respond. When he stepped into the hall, he could hear the shower running. The doorbell rang a second time. "I'm coming! Just a moment!"

He ran a hand through his hair to attempt in an attempt to flatten it before opening the door.

The man on the other side didn't belong in James's neighborhood of manicured lawns, white picket fences, and golf courses. He wore a black polo shirt with a white "UKA" logo on the breast, black slacks, black boots, and a black patch over one eye. His hair was buzzed short. He was missing an earlobe and had a pistol in a shoulder rig.

He grinned a familiar grin.

"Jimmy!"

James realized his mouth was hanging open. "I'm sorry. Do I know you?"

"What, don't recognize me after ten years and a thorough mauling?" He flipped up his eye patch. The socket was scarred closed. "Oh, come now. You wound me. And that should say a lot!"

That accent. That irritating friendliness. James dredged a name out of the dim depths of his memory.

"Malcolm?"

***

James dressed quickly and joined Malcolm in his SUV before Stephanie could see the company he had attracted to their neighborhood. The houses on their street were split between young families and retirees, neither of whom would take well to a visit from a man with an eye patch and an exposed sidearm.

"I should probably warn you," Malcolm said as they got on the highway heading east, "I'm not working alone these days."

James frowned at the equipment on the dashboard. There were two monitors: one with a map of the area and blinking blue dots, and the other with scrolling lines of text. "I see that."

Malcolm flipped a master switch behind the wheel. The dashboard went dark. "I'm with the Union of Kopides and Aspides. Heard of us? We're trying to unite all the demon hunters under a single banner, and we are all about the high-tech."

"Yes. I've heard a lot about the Union."

Elise and Anthony had a run-in with the Union at the end of the summer. She definitely hadn't made any friends from it.

In the last real conversation Elise and James had shared face-to-face, she had warned him that the Union would probably show up soon, although she refused to tell him why. Given that she had used very colorful language in describing the Union, he knew it wouldn't be for a good reason.

As if he could detect James's train of thought, Malcolm said, "Hopefully you're hearing positive things."

"Not at all."

He laughed. "The Union's earned a bad reputation. Their preferred methods of recruitment are… shall we say, blunt? But now I'm a commander, and when I'm in charge, we do things the nice way."

"They made you a commander?" James couldn't keep the disbelief out of his voice. "Great show of character judgment."

Malcolm's good eye flashed, but not with mirth.

The Union had moved into an abandoned warehouse on I-80 between Sparks and Fernley. Malcolm had to flash two different forms of identification and swipe his thumbprint to get the SUV through the gate. The compound they entered was a sprawling affair with barbed-wire fences, spotlights mounted on towers, and men carrying guns.

James also had to sign a nondisclosure agreement on a sheet of UKA stationary before he could leave the vehicle. He barely skimmed it before dashing his name off at the bottom. It wasn't worth worrying about the particulars; there was no way the Union's contracts could be enforceable in a court of law that didn't recognize their existence. He had no doubt that they had ways of keeping people obedient—but it wouldn't be through litigation.

Malcolm parked the car and jumped out. James followed him. They were near the river, and the back fence was shaded with trees covered in dazzling golden leaves. The wind carried the bite of winter.

"Are you hungry?" Malcolm asked, striding toward the open garage.

"Not particularly."

"Mind if I get some breakfast?"

He moved on without waiting for an answer.

They walked together through the garage, which housed an entire fleet of black SUVs. There were also two large RVs, each the size of a semi truck. And there was a tarp at the back of the room covering a vehicle that looked suspiciously like a tank.

"This is the fleet assigned to my team. We're ready for anything—all-out war against the local demons, if need be," Malcolm said casually, as if having a tank was no big deal. "We've got a helicopter coming this afternoon, too."

"A helicopter?"

"You know, a flying metal thing."

James tried not to grind his teeth together. "I'm just surprised that you have one."

"Union HQ has placed the highest priority on our mission in Reno."

"And that mission is…?"

He winked. "I'll get to that once I'm not so hungry."

They had constructed walls inside the cavernous interior of the warehouse stacked five floors deep. James and Malcolm emerged on a walkway above the highest level. Most of the

Union's building was underground, and he could look down on it from their vantage point.

James had expected Malcolm to be in charge of a single unit, but he spotted at least two dozen men walking the wings, which totaled at least four units. Not a small operation. "How long have you been here?"

"A couple of months." He silently counted, ticking off his fingers. "Yeah, about eight weeks. Since the end of the summit. Come on, mess is this way."

The path down to the mess conveniently routed through one surveillance room—complete with oversized monitors, computers, and beeping equipment that resembled NASA's ground control—and an armory, where several rows of body armor and guns were hanging in lockers. Malcolm was showing off.

"How did you end up in charge of this?" James asked. "More importantly, how did you establish everything here without attracting notice?"

Malcolm grinned, stretching his scarred cheek below the eye patch. "Who says *nobody* noticed? We have a few government friends. The real trick was avoiding Elise's notice, and she's been too focused on chasing after demon-kings to see us."

"You've been watching her."

"We put some surveillance in the city. Ah, here we go."

The mess hall was an open cafeteria on the topmost level of the warehouse. It was unoccupied at the moment, but a fully stocked snack bar with fresh produce and protein bars stood against one wall.

Malcolm snagged an apple and took a loud bite of it. "Sure you don't want anything?"

"Yes. Thank you."

SM Reine

"Why don't we have a talk back in my office?" He blew through the cafeteria, another armory—how many of those did they need?—and entered a long hallway filled with numbered doors. "This is where the men stay," he explained, leading James down the hall. "It's much nicer than military barracks. See?"

Malcolm rapped his knuckle on a door and pushed it open. On the other side stood a small studio apartment, complete with kitchenette and private bathroom. There was a poster of a woman in a skimpy yellow bikini on the wall, a flat screen television, and a comfortable bed.

A shirtless man paused in the middle of performing pushups without getting up. Sweat glistened on his shoulders and dripped down his back.

"Can I help you?" he asked, craning his head back to glare at Malcolm.

The commander bit off a large chunk of apple, chewed, and swallowed before answering. "Just giving the tour, Gary."

Gary dropped the pushup position, got to his feet, and toweled off his impressively broad chest. Every inch of his torso was covered in a mat of wiry hair. He held out a hand. "Name's Gary Zettel. Are you a new recruit?"

"I don't think so," James said, but he shook his hand anyway. The skin-on-skin contact rang bells in his skull. A kopis.

"This is James Faulkner," Malcolm said, carefully enunciating the name.

It apparently meant something to Gary, because his brow lowered over his eyes. "Pleasure to meet you."

"How do you like working with the Union?" James asked.

Gary snorted. "It's better than the alternative. Can I resume training... sir?"

Malcolm held up his hands as he backed out of the room. "Of course, of course. Don't let me bother you. Jimmy?"

The commander's room was at the end of the barracks, and was laid out like a two bedroom apartment rather than a studio. A large window in the living room opened into the rest of the warehouse.

"You never told me how you ended up in charge of all this," James said.

"It was a recent assignment. I enlisted a couple years ago, when I needed some medical care," Malcolm said, flopping onto his leather couch and kicking his feet up on the arm. He waved at his eye patch. "They were going to take Ireland either way. Might as well side with the men who have money, eh?"

"I suppose."

"They sent me to a training facility in Italy, where HQ is located. Nice place. I did that for a few months, and then they gave me an aspis."

"They *gave* you an aspis?"

"Sure. Bloke named Bellamy. Nice guy. Not as good at magic as you are, but what can you do?" Malcolm finished his apple and chucked the core at the trashcan across the room. It missed. "I know what you're thinking, but it's a good match."

James couldn't resist. "You can't *assign* aspides."

"You can, and the Union does. All that superstition about a kopis and aspis having to be 'best friends for life' is a load of crock. All it takes is two people who can tolerate each other. I wouldn't invite him over for Sunday dinner, but Bellamy's a hell of a drinking partner."

"Forgive me if I'm skeptical."

"Think whatever you want. Bellamy and I have done well enough that the Union promoted us to a command position last year. And when the last bloke in charge of this unit fucked up the semi-centennial summit, they demoted him and gave

57

this mission to me. So here we are now." He swept his arms wide. "I have a bloody *army*. Hard to believe, isn't it?"

James peered through the window. Men were running drills in the halls with dummy guns. "And what, exactly, is the purpose of this army?"

"I'm going to give it to you straight, Jimmy."

"Dear *God*, stop calling me that."

Malcolm's grin said he knew exactly how irritating the nickname was. "The Union's not doing well in the United States. Recruitment has gone much better elsewhere, but things keep getting in the way here. American demons are much more likely to have immigrated recently, much tougher. And they have those fiery, independent personalities. Liberty and justice. 'All for one,' you know. Or something to that effect."

"Is this an attempt at recruitment, then?" James asked, gesturing between them. "Because if this is, then for the record, you're not the person I would have sent to do it."

"No, this is definitely not 'an attempt at recruitment.'" He spoke very firmly. "Frankly, the Union doesn't want anything to do with Elise—and that includes her aspis. Which is why we're sitting down to have a nice chat in my warehouse. As much as we want to improve our numbers, we also want the same thing that you want, Jim."

Jim. If Malcolm wanted a good punch to the face, he was heading in the right direction for it. "You have no clue what I want."

"No? Let me take a guess." He kicked his legs over the side of the couch and stood, pacing across the room. He ticked each point off on his fingers. "You want nothing to do with hunting. No more demons, certainly no more angels, and no more peril." Malcolm glanced over his shoulder. "And you want Elise out of it, too."

James kept his features composed.

In fact, that *was* what he wanted. He and Elise had once shared a dream of peaceful normalcy, and for five years, they had succeeded. Those five years of retirement had been bliss. They had worked hard. Built businesses from the ground up. Made friends, found significant others.

But when Death's Hand had attacked in the spring, Elise had fallen into the business of demon hunting again. It was only supposed to be for that one job. Just one exorcism to save a child in his coven.

Things had spiraled out of control. James was back to retirement... mostly. But Elise had dived back in headfirst.

He realized that he had been lost in thought for several long seconds, and that Malcolm was watching him.

"The Union can't give us that," he finally said.

The kopis studied his fingernails. "We can't, eh? Safety? Security? Freedom from the Reno territory and what lies below?"

"How do you propose doing that?"

"Leave," Malcolm said simply. "The two of you can get out of here while you still have four eyeballs between you and live a happy, mundane life together."

James laughed. "We can't just *leave*."

"There are other places safer than this one." He leaned forward, and his smile was completely gone. "We've found a Haven."

"A Haven? Impossible."

"The Union has been to places you can't begin to dream of, Jim," Malcolm said. His gaze went distant. "Places beyond Earth. Places beyond hellfire, places beyond even *magic*." He sighed. "Can you imagine a place with no gods or demons or witches? A place where people die, and they stay dead?"

"No," James said. "I can't."

"Your imagination is terrible, Jimmy-boy."

"You traveled with us for a few months. You know why that is."

"Indeed I do," Malcolm said. "But trust me—Havens exist, and we've found one of them."

If it was true, it was a tempting offer. *Very* tempting. James raked a hand through his hair.

"Even if that were possible, Elise would never leave. Not with what's in the Warrens."

"But we have the manpower to protect the city. We have the technology—you've seen it yourself. We've refined our techniques. So long as you two are safely tucked away in the Haven—far from the all-seeing eye of your most terrible enemies—you can rest assured that nothing and no one will cross through those gates to find you."

James wasn't sure what to say. He searched for words, and found none. His fingertips felt numb.

Malcolm studied James's face, and it might have been the only time in his life that he was sober and serious at the same time. "I brought you here so you could see what I have. I hope you realize how much we've invested in preparing to secure the area."

"And what's the price of our safety?"

"The Union wants the territory. That's the cost. All you have to do is take Elise and get out of the way."

It sounded too good to be true. And if there was anything James had learned in his years fighting demons, it was that anything that sounded too good to be true usually was.

The kopis didn't wait for a response. He glanced through his window at the floor below and huffed.

"Hang on a minute."

Malcolm headed out of the room and took the stairs to the warehouse floor three at a time. He limped when he moved quickly.

James knew his sudden exit wasn't a coincidence. The commander had left him alone to think, surrounded by the grandeur of the Union's finest technology. He was meant to watch as Malcolm directed a forklift carrying a crate to the storage area. He was meant to notice the camera mounted in the corner, and the computer built into the desk.

He was meant to see the glory of the Union and think about what it could offer him.

Leave with Elise?

God, what a thought.

He wasn't prepared to address an idea that significant. Not on the spur of the moment. Instead, he wandered through Malcolm's quarters and studied his belongings.

It was a true bachelor pad. He had a gun safe, but it was unlocked, and his rifles were propped against the walls like umbrellas. He opened the mini-fridge, expecting to find beer, and was not disappointed. Malcolm's laundry was piled on the counter beside a flat-screen monitor that displayed the weather report, the temperature, and a scrolling ticker of Union news.

None of that was as surprising as the bookshelf next to Malcolm's desk. The kopis wasn't much of a reader. Frankly, James wasn't sure the man was even literate. Yet his shelves were full.

The books were comprised of a matching set of small encyclopedias. He eased a volume off of the bookshelf. It was a slender book, barely thicker than his thumb, and the title on the cover said, "Prophecies of Flynn, Q1 2009."

James flipped through the pages. The pages were so thin as to be see-through, the text inside was miniscule, and every line was numbered, similar to a Bible.

The table of contents in the front was about a hundred lines long. There were very specific titles like, "Semi-Centennial Summit," "Vancouver, Canada," and "The Afterlife Incident."

But there were also vague entries that only had dates or, more ambiguously, were simply titled, "Unknown."

James returned it to the shelf and removed the most recent book, which was labeled "Prophecies of Flynn, Summary of Apocalypse." He glanced at the door before opening the cover.

The first line of the Table of Contents said, "Revelations: An Introduction." When he read the second line, his heart skipped a beat. All it said was, "Elise Kavanagh, Entry 1."

She had twelve entries in a row. And below that, there was an entry that said, "Aspis."

He didn't get a chance to read any further. Footsteps approached on the stairs outside, and James jammed the book in his back pocket.

An instant later, Malcolm reentered. "Sorry about that. Listen, Jim, there's lots of work to be done. I'm going to have to have someone take you home. Do you mind?"

"Not at all." He sounded surprisingly calm, considering how fast his heart was beating.

"Fantastic." He stepped aside to let James into the hall. "You don't have to make any decisions yet. Promise to give it a good think?"

"I think I can manage that," James said.

IV

Elise waited until night had fallen and most of the police had cleared out before returning to Rick's Drugstore. They had cordoned off the entire block, surrounding the shop with yellow warning tape and police cars, so she had to approach from the roof.

She had spent most of the day watching the police work the scene. Or at least, she had watched the police *pretend* to work the scene. In fact, she hadn't seen a single officer approach the gaping chasm that used to be Rick's Drugstore.

That had to mean one of two things: they really were worried about structural integrity, or someone with authority had told them to stay out.

She wondered if the influence was federal. There were unmarked black vehicles among the police cars, as well as bulky pickup trucks with camper shells and tinted windows. Yet nobody moved to investigate the collapsed tunnel. It made her curious. *Very* curious.

Several hours and three half-smoked cigarettes later, her boyfriend joined her on the roof of the parking garage, carrying thick ropes over his shoulder.

"I've got everything you asked for." Anthony dropped the equipment on the roof. At her instruction, he had worn a thick jacket and leather gloves.

Elise ground the last cigarette into the cement before sifting through the pile. In addition to ropes, there were a couple of waist harnesses and other rock climbing equipment.

"Perfect. Time to go spelunking."

She threw everything over her shoulder and approached the edge. Elise stayed close to the building, but the police were all outside of the yellow tape. Nobody was close enough to see her anyway.

"So what's the situation?" Anthony asked.

Elise swapped out her weightlifting gloves for a thicker pair that were made of leather. "That hole opens straight into the Warrens." She tied one end of the rope around an air conditioner cage and secured it with a karabiner.

"You mean, the mines where the demons live? Isn't that about a mile down?"

"Yes." She wiggled into the hip harness. "Flashlight?"

He tossed one to her. "What made it collapse?"

"That's what I'm hoping to find out." She hooked up her Grigri and backed up to the edge of the roof. "You coming?"

She jumped off the edge before he could answer.

Elise let herself drop rapidly in order to keep from being spotted. The roof rose over her head, followed by the shattered remnants of a linoleum floor, and then the wooden boards that had supported the basement.

Darkness swallowed her.

She tightened the Grigri to slow her descent. The glow from the street was already no bigger than a pin.

By the time she stopped her downward motion, she couldn't see anything at all. It was like having velvet draped over her eyes.

Elise turned on her flashlight and gripped it in her teeth. She was spinning slowly in a long stone shaft. One wall was close enough for her to make it out in the LED glow. The rocks looked chiseled, as though by teeth.

Rick's hadn't just collapsed. Something had tunneled through the earth.

"Anthony?" Her voice was muffled and didn't echo.

No reply.

She loosened her grip on the Grigri and began sliding again.

Elise spiraled lower and lower. After a few minutes, a level surface appeared beneath her feet, and she set down on crumbling rock. She was surrounded by debris—some of it linoleum, some of it wood, but most of it stone.

It was late autumn and cool enough for a jacket at street level; deep underground, it was as warm as a Louisiana summer. It was hard to breathe in the heat. She shucked her coat and tied it around her waist. The wound Zohak had left on her bicep stung in the open air.

A whirring noise told her that Anthony was approaching a few seconds before his light appeared. It hung around his neck, illuminating his jaw from underneath.

He landed. "Are these the Warrens?"

"I don't know."

Elise unhooked herself from the ropes and stepped away. They were in a vast cavern. Her light didn't hit any walls. "We must be pretty deep," Anthony said, still clutching his ropes.

The back of Elise's skull tickled, and she scratched her neck. "Hello?" Her call fell flat in the cavern.

Shock jolted through her when a voice responded. "Oh, thank the fires. I thought someone would *never* come."

A girl emerged from the shadows. She was stringy and thin, like a teenager, but her sallow skin belonged to someone much older. Her hooked nose matched her pointed chin, and her eyes were black puddles.

Elise drew her sword. "Who are you?"

The girl held up both of her hands in the universal gesture of *please don't kill me.*

"My name is Jerica." Despite her cautious gesture, she didn't seem impressed by the sword. Piercings sparkled on her nostril and in two places on her bottom lip. "I worked for Rick?"

"How did you get down here?"

She lowered her hands. "I phased." At Anthony's blank expression, she elaborated. "You know… the thing where we pop between shadows. What are you guys? Cops don't carry swords."

Elise sheathed the falchion. "It's not safe down here."

"You're telling me. I can't phase out again."

"Why not?" Anthony asked.

"I don't know. I feel sick as a sunny day—like there's no shadows to phase into. But…" Jerica glanced around at the looming shadows and shrugged.

A chill rolled down Elise's spine. She lifted her flashlight over her head and spun again, trying to catch a glimpse of the cavern walls she knew had to surround them. But the darkness only grew heavier the harder she tried to see through it.

She tried to take a deep breath, but it felt like her lungs wouldn't expand. It wasn't from the powerful heat and humidity.

"Last night, Rick helped me track down a demon," Elise said, keeping her tone measured. "That must have been about two in the morning. Did you see him at all after that?" Jerica shook her head, and the wooden jewelry in her ears clacked. "How long have you been down here?"

"Since the collapse."

"How did you survive?" Anthony asked.

Jerica planted her hands on her waist. "You kidding me? Do you even know what a nightmare is?"

"So you were here when it fell," Elise interrupted.

"Yeah. I was worried about Rick. He had picked up a shipment of—are you sure you're not the cops?"

"Pretty sure."

"Okay. Just checking. He picked up a shipment of drugs. He was selling it to a customer we'd been dealing with for a few weeks. Rick seems like a grump, but he's really a nice guy, so I was worried about him. Flipping drugs—that's not the kind of shit he should be doing."

Elise quelled a burst of annoyance. So that was how Zohak had been getting his supply. Rick must have been good as his job; she had been following shipments for weeks trying to track the flow of lethe. "But he wasn't at the shop."

"He *had* to be there. I didn't see him, but Rick never leaves. Hasn't in a hundred years. He must have been in the basement. But I didn't get that far." She glanced at Anthony and Elise's ropes. "Can we finish talking on the surface?"

"What's down here?"

"Nothing, aside from tunnels that go nowhere. I thought I might find a way into the Warrens if I wandered long enough. But this… this is endless." A quaver of fear finally entered her voice. "I'd really like to finish talking on the surface."

Anthony was quick to reattach himself to the rope, but Elise only glared into the cavern.

The shop had been destroyed before she could return to get answers from Rick—probably by the same thing that had killed Zohak before she could question him. Elise was sick of having her answers ripped out from under her.

She helped Anthony double-check his rigging and waved Jerica over. "He'll carry you up."

Anthony caught the suggestion in her tone. "You can't stay down here, Elise."

She didn't feel like arguing with him, so she cut him off with a hard jerk on his rope. "Nightmares weigh nothing, so all you have to do is hang on to each other. Don't drop her."

Jerica obediently looped her arms around his neck. Anthony gagged at her spongy touch, but she didn't seem to mind. Nightmares naturally repelled humans—she was probably used to having everyone give her a wide berth.

"Shit," Jerica said as Elise wrapped the end of the rope around her legs for extra security. "If Rick's gone... It took *months* to get that job. I could lose my amnesty on Earth."

"You need a job?" Elise fished through her pockets and found a crumpled flier for one of Eloquent Blood's events. "Go here. Ask for Neuma, and tell her that I sent you."

"And who are you?"

"Elise," she said simply. The demon's skeptical expression didn't change. Jerica would have been a lot more impressed if Elise had said "Godslayer," but she preferred to spread it around as little as possible.

The fact that she was ever called that title was meant to be a secret, but it had somehow been leaked to the local demons, and it spread quickly. They all whispered that the woman plaguing their nights was called Godslayer. Not kopis, not overlord—Godslayer. She couldn't escape it.

Anthony seemed torn between his urge to escape and his urge to keep an eye on Elise. Self-preservation won out. He caught her hand for an instant before she stepped away. "Be careful."

She gave him a thin smile. Anthony began scaling the wall with Jerica hanging effortlessly from his back. Elise watched until his light vanished.

She was alone.

At least, that was what she tried to tell herself. If Anthony and Jerica were gone, and the cavern beneath Rick's Drugstore was empty, then she had to be alone. Really.

Zohak's words flitted through the back of her mind: *It came from the earth... A shadow with inertia...*

Elise closed her eyes and counted to ten.

The air was hot, but she could breathe. The shadows were not living. And she was *definitely* alone.

She picked a direction and started walking.

The sound of her footsteps was strangely flat as she picked her way over the rubble, pausing occasionally to stack one rock atop another to guide her back to the place where her rope dangled. After a few minutes, the cavern wall curved, and she walked along it until she came upon a tunnel. It sloped deeper into the earth.

Elise began to descend.

Breathing became a challenge. Water puddled in several places in the tunnel, and it was hot enough that it scalded her legs when it splashed onto her jeans.

The tunnel was narrow enough that she could reach out and touch both sides, but she couldn't see both rock walls at the same time. Either her light was fading, or the shadows were deepening.

The path twisted, turned, and split. Elise followed the right wall, trailing her fingers along the dry stone.

And then the wall disappeared. Her hand fell into empty air.

A whisper rose behind her.

Exorcist…

She spun, raising her light.

There was nothing to see beyond falling dust.

The hair on the back of her neck stood on end. Elise drew her sword again and flexed her fingers on the leather-wrapped hilt.

"Show yourself," she said.

Every other sound fell flat, but her words were carried into the gloom, echoing a dozen times over.

Show yourself. Show yourself…

For a moment, only her own voice filled the tunnel. And again, she heard that velvety, feminine voice call to her.

Exorcist…

Elise clamped her mouth shut.

She stepped back until she found the wall, and gripped a jutting stone. Her racing heart gradually slowed.

There had to be an end to the tunnels. There *had* to be.

She followed the wall back the way she had come, but it took her to an unfamiliar place in the tunnels. Elise didn't see any of her signposts at the junction.

No way back.

She hung to the left and kept going. Elise didn't locate her starting cavern, but she finally found the end of the tunnel, more by mistake than by design.

Her toe caught on a rock, she stumbled, and her hands met a wall of fallen rock.

The tunnel roof had collapsed. The debris sparkled with some kind of mineral in the faint light—probably pyrite, which miners used to call "fool's gold."

Water trickled out of the ceiling, making a steaming waterfall down the collapsed rocks that puddled at her feet. She traced her gloves over the dry rocks, feeling for gaps, and found nothing.

Was that wall the place that the shadows were moving toward? Had they caused it to fall?

Her flashlight flickered.

"No…" She banged it against her knee. It flickered again. "No, no, no…"

The bulb went out.

Everything disappeared—the tiny waterfall, the sparkling rocks, her hands in front of her eyes.

She stopped breathing.

A slithering noise echoed from the deep.

It sounded like… dragging.

The weight built in her chest, crushing her like a giant fist. Elise gasped in the heat.

You are a lovely thing, exorcist, murmured the voice.

It was right behind her.

She whirled—or at least, she thought she whirled. But she no longer had any sense of direction. One hand clutched the dead flashlight, the other clutched the sword, and both were equally useless.

Lovely, yes… but not so terribly lovely. I can't see why he's so enamored with you.

From her right side.

Elise swung, and her sword met with nothing. The velvety voice gave a throaty chuckle.

"Lovely?" she hissed between her teeth. The taste of ash crept over her tongue, thick and cloying, and began to slide down her throat.

She coughed. Gasped. Fell to her knees.

I wonder if he would be so enamored with a corpse.

"Elise?"

Someone else had spoken.

A dim glow reached her eyes, and after so long in darkness, it felt like burning arrows piercing straight into her brain.

The pressure in her throat vanished. She sucked in a hard breath.

"Over here," Elise choked out, and the glow moved closer. It resolved into a figure, willowy and tall.

Nukha'il strode to her side, and with him came pale moonlight. It emanated from the wings folded neatly along his spine and flooded the tunnel.

She never thought she would be so glad to see an angel.

"There you are," he said, his features sagging with relief. "When I found that boyfriend of yours alone on the rooftop…" Nukha'il shook his head, as if his fears were too great to utter aloud. "You look like you've survived."

"Somehow." She wiped her tongue with the back of her hand, but she couldn't get rid of that ashy taste. "Remind me not to go spelunking alone again."

"I would be happy to remind you if you give me warning beforehand." Even though he continued to speak calmly, he managed to make it sound like an admonition.

Elise got to her feet, squinting around for a sign of what might have spoken to her before Nukha'il arrived. She wasn't surprised to find them alone. "What's on the other side of this collapse?" she asked, nudging one of the rocks with her feet. "Does this go into the Warrens?"

"I don't know. I'm not familiar enough with the layout of the undercity."

"Can you open it?"

The corner of his mouth lifted. "With a jackhammer."

A knot of tension in Elise's spine eased—just a fraction. She almost found the strength to laugh. But it quickly died in her chest.

"I'm lost."

"Then it's a lucky thing that I found you." He held out a hand. She shook her head. "Still no? After all this time? I've flown with you before."

"We can walk."

"Suit yourself."

He guided her back to the main cavern in silence. Eventually, she began recognizing her signposts, and she led the way to her ropes. Gripping the fiber was enough to calm her again, as if it were a lifeline.

Nukha'il watched as she harnessed herself again. "My wings would be faster."

She bit back an angry response.

"Did you kill my flashlight?"

His wings drooped with embarrassment. "Sorry. I forget sometimes." Her light flickered to life again. It was ugly and harsh after the gentle glow of his wings.

"Why did you come down here, anyway?"

"You asked me to check into the security of the gate. I thought you'd like to know what I found."

Her hands stilled on the rope. "Has it been invaded by the darkness?"

"Not at all," Nukha'il said, though he didn't sound happy about it. "But I did find something interesting." He hesitated, as though trying to choose his words. "It was a man. He was sitting on the gate's dais when I arrived."

Fear shocked through her. "A man? What was he doing there?"

"I don't know. But he wants to speak with you."

PART THREE

FALLEN

January 2000

Something was killing babies. The disappearances could have passed for coincidence at first, but a pattern quickly became too distinct to deny: infants and small toddlers would vanish from their mothers' beds at night, only to reappear weeks later, bloated and lifeless and miles from the places from which they had been taken.

The killer began in African villages and moved quickly. By the time the children's bodies were discovered, the killer was already gone, leaving screams in its wake.

The kopis in Lesotho thought to cut open one of the bodies and was shocked to find it bloated by gas, without a single organ intact. Even the eyelids, when cut open, revealed empty pockets of air that reeked of brimstone.

Elise was passing through and heard about what was happening. It would have been hard not to—the entire countryside was in mourning. The cries could be heard for miles.

After questioning the local kopis—with the help of a friend who spoke a handful of English words—James extrapolated the pattern.

"The livestock dies first," he explained as they walked the dusty road between villages. He had tied a cloth around his head to protect himself from the merciless sun, but his nose was peeling and crispy. "When there are no more pigs, one child disappears, and then a few more over the week. There is a lull for a couple of days. The locals find the bodies after that. It's too late by then, of course, because the killer has moved on."

Elise pondered this information. "Why pigs?"

"Don't you think the question should be: why babies?"

"Everything eats babies." She kicked a rock along the road with her boot. It skittered and danced over the dirt.

"Maras. Ghouls. Lamias. Waiting to do it until there are no more pigs in town is the weird part."

"We'll have to agree to disagree on which part is weird, I think."

"Fine, Mr. Doesn't-Think-Babies-are-Dinner."

He laughed. "I'll stick to James. Thank you."

Elise didn't smile back. Her brow furrowed with thought as she gazed at distant Masai trees and the huge, leathery forms of the elephants milling beneath them. "Why pigs?"

"I have no clue, but given the pattern's ongoing northward route, we'll likely have a chance to see soon enough."

He was right about one thing: the murders continued north very quickly. But they couldn't seem to catch up. Every time they arrived in a new village, the residents were just finding the dead.

Suspicious eyes followed them as they hurried past farms empty of livestock. They didn't need to understand the whispers to know that rumors of white demons were spreading in their wake. To the locals, their appearance after the deaths seemed too soon to be accident. To Elise, they were frustratingly late.

They were sleeping in a hostel a few weeks later when villagers arrived with guns.

That was when they decided that they were done with Africa.

Elise and James moved to France, which had been picked with the rigorous selection criteria of "soonest flight that doesn't land in Africa." She stayed in touch with the kopis in Lesotho with the help of her friend Lucas McIntyre, who had contact information for most kopides and had better luck finding a Bantu translator.

But the Sotho kopis had no more useful information. Pig farms were recovering, no more children were found as husks, and the killer's trail had gone cold.

Despite renting a lovely apartment on the ocean, Elise soon began spending a lot of time in internet cafes.

"What do you hope to find?" James asked when she returned to their room one night. He was casting fresh wards on their balcony, which would render anything that approached their railing unconscious. There was already a seagull sleeping on the planter.

She kicked off her boots and stretched out on the couch with a stack of printed news articles. "Did you know that China has the highest population of pigs in the world?"

"Does this mean we're making another trip to China?" He drew a chalk line over the doorway. "You know I'm not a fan of China—or that entire side of the continent."

Neither of them were. They had mostly avoided East Asia since James had found her in Russia, just to be careful.

"Not Asia this time. Cairo recently had a big outbreak of disease on their pig farms. They lost thousands of heads." Elise dropped a stack of pages on the side table. "Guess what infant mortality rates in Egypt are like this month?"

"If you know where the killer is right now, then why are we reading news articles?"

"Because it will already be gone by the time we get there. We have to know where it will be next. *Before* it arrives."

James dropped his chalk and sat beside Elise. He flipped through the articles she had dropped. "You're dedicating a lot of time to this."

"Yeah. So?"

"So I don't think I've seen you this interested in anything before. Does this killer sound familiar to you? Is this personal?"

Elise's lips pinched together. "Look at this." She showed him printouts from the bottom of her stack. The infants all had skin in mottled shades of brown and black. The bodies were tiny.

He studied the young kopis while she was distracted. It was easier than looking at the pictures.

Elise wasn't sentimental; they had seen dead children in one of their very first investigations together, and she had been as bothered by it as she was by any other dead human—which was to say, not at all. Her face didn't show any hint as to why these deaths were different.

Not for the first time, he wished he could pry open her skull and read her thoughts.

The seagull on their balcony woke up, took three dazed steps, and flew away.

"What will our next destination be?" James asked

She resumed reading. "I'm not sure yet. I'll let you know in a couple of days."

It turned out they didn't have a couple of days. Pigs began dying in France that very night.

They took the train to a village in Brittany, where a farm's entire stock had gone missing. The day was wet, gray, and miserable. James wandered the fields searching for footprints in the mud, while Elise tried to understand the farmer's complaints through his thick regional accent.

It took an hour for her to rejoin James. Her face was pinched. "He didn't hear anything. He didn't see anything, he doesn't fucking *know* anything. God, what an idiot."

James gave her arm a brief, sympathetic squeeze before crouching by the fence again. He hiked up his pea coat so it wouldn't drag in the mud. "See this?" Elise dropped beside him, leaning her shoulder into his. The wood had been burned.

Yellow residue was left behind in a shape like two crescents. "Does that look like a cloven hoof to you?"

She tilted her head to the side. "Maybe one of the pigs fought back. Left a mark."

"Or maybe our assailant has hooves."

Elise scanned the edges of the farm as the wind whipped her scarf around her face. They were right outside a village, and there were no other farms with pigs for miles.

"We have to be on the streets tonight. It's going to hunt."

They took a room at a hostel. James napped through the afternoon while Elise kept watch on the street outside.

When night fell, they split up to search.

James walked through the darkness alone. A damp, heavy fog overtook the city, so he could see nothing beyond the next street corner.

There could have been anything in town that night, and he wouldn't have known. There was no way to distinguish if his feeling of unease was truly due to eyes on his back, or paranoia.

He didn't come across a single person on the street, but at midnight, he heard a cry—a single, sharp noise that ended as quickly as it had pierced the night.

He spun on the spot, searching for the origin of the shriek, but saw nothing. He couldn't even tell where it had come from. The fog muffled every noise. The glow from a single streetlight radiated hazy haloes into the night, undisturbed.

The night was utterly silent after that.

Elise and James met the next morning near the shore. She was wind-blown, quiet, and disappointed. "Nothing," she said in a grim tone that told him that she had heard the cry, too. They walked back toward their hostel, taking the long route past the docks.

That was when they discovered the bodies.

James's heart sped as he realized what he was seeing in the early morning fog—three tiny shapes, too small to be fully-grown pigs, and too small to be adult humans.

Infants.

"They didn't try to hide the bodies," Elise said, crouching by the closest husk. It must have been a newborn. Its legs were twisted and froglike, the skin on its fists was peeling, and its eyelids were sealed shut by dried yellow fluid.

James coughed wetly into his arm. He hadn't vomited at the scene of an attack yet, but the sight of a dead baby brought the flavor of last night's wine to the back of his throat.

The sound he had heard at midnight replayed in his mind over and over again. The sharp little yelp. A sound of such pain and fear.

"Good Lord," he groaned.

Elise stroked a hand down the side of the baby's unmoving face. Her brow furrowed. It wasn't sadness in her gaze—not exactly—but something else he hadn't seen before.

Then she reached behind her and drew one of the swords. Before James could stop her, she sliced the body open.

He lost his fight against the nausea. He ducked behind a shipping container, braced his hand on the metal, and vomited everything he had eaten for the last twelve hours onto the asphalt.

Elise focused on the corpse as James emptied his stomach a few feet away. The air that had been trapped inside the carcass smelled like brimstone, but there was a strange undertone to it—something familiar.

She leaned her nose close to the body to get a good whiff.

"Now that is dedication," someone said from behind her.

It was a man's voice, but not James's.

She spun on her knees, bringing up her sword, and it connected with metal. Her blade bit into the rebar and stuck.

The person standing behind her was surprisingly handsome, in that drunken football hooligan kind of way. He had bright eyes, a square face, and brown hair that stuck up in the back. His jacket bulged under the arm. He had a gun.

"See? I expected that. I'm learning." He dislodged the rebar from her sword and dropped it.

It took Elise a moment to bring a name to mind. "Malcolm. Right?"

"Bless the gods, she remembers me. It was the kiss, wasn't it? Couldn't forget that, could you?"

"What do you want?"

"Oh, I can think of a few things." Malcolm grinned, but it quickly faded. His eyes dropped to the body on the ground. He swallowed. "McIntyre called me. He said the French kopis died last month—I think by drowning. He asked if I felt like covering this territory. Good thing I agreed."

"Good," Elise said. "Right."

James came around the shipping container. "Oh, great, it's you. Just who I hoped we would run into never again."

Malcolm took a few big steps back. "Ah, the guard. Don't worry; I'm here for the same thing you are. Pig demon. Cloven hooves. Eats its kindred, then moves to the human babies, and then leaves."

"It's not a demon," Elise said.

James inched around Malcolm to her side. His face was still very pale, and he wouldn't look at the babies. "What makes you think that?"

Because it smelled like an angel.

She didn't say that out loud. Maybe if Malcolm hadn't been there, she would have shared her suspicion with James, but she didn't trust the other kopis. It was impossible to trust someone who smiled and winked that much.

"I just know." She sheathed her sword. It was going to need to be sharpened before she used it again anyway. "Check for tracks, James."

The witch hesitated, glancing at Malcolm. "Very well."

He headed down the docks, and Elise searched for a tarp. She found one covering a crate of fruit. Slicing the ropes free with her boot knife, she pulled the sheet over the three small bodies.

"How long has it been, Elise?" Malcolm asked, leaning his elbow on the fence. "A year? You certainly have... filled out."

She faced him and crossed her arms tightly. "What are you doing?"

"What?" His eyes were wide and innocent.

"I've found three dead babies. I'm trying to figure out what killed them so I can stop it. What are *you* doing?"

"Well," he said, sidling up to her, "this week, I've been hunting. Last night, I was searching. And right now, I'm hitting on you. I believe you still owe me a drink, miss."

Elise glanced at James, who was walking up and down the docks in search of footprints. His pea coat fluttered around his knees like a cape.

"Maybe some other time," she said.

After that discovery, James brooded in their apartment for hours. Elise took the time to sharpen the tiny dent the rebar had left in her falchion's blade, smoothing it into a perfect arc once more.

A pig farm was attacked near Valenciennes the next day.

"We missed it," James said dully, setting down the newspaper. "More children are going to die tonight." She kneeled on the floor by the couch and touched his arm. He covered her fingers with his hand. "Why infants?" His voice was ragged.

Why pigs?

That was the real question. She was sure of it.

Elise leaned her head into his shoulder. "You should sleep."

"We can't lose any more time."

"We won't." He glanced at her, and Elise gave him an innocent look. "Malcolm has already moved north."

"And you trust him to take care of it?"

"I trust that he'll move faster than we can, and that you need to get some sleep."

Finally, reluctantly, James nodded.

As soon as he was unconscious and didn't respond to his name, Elise wrapped her falchions in her jacket and took the train to Valenciennes.

She watched the country blur past her, mulling over infants and pigs and the slow move north. The smell of brimstone—not quite demonic—and the cloven hooves had set alarms ringing in her skull.

By the time she reached the city, night was falling again.

She didn't go to investigate the farm where the pigs had died. She didn't need to. Instead, she looked up.

Elise wandered the city all evening, searching for the sky and tracing the shapes of the buildings against the clouds with her eyes. Rain began to beat upon her, cold and harsh, but she didn't don her coat.

She ducked under the awning of a shop for shelter while she considered her surroundings. The buildings around her were all low and old, sitting on the curves of wide streets. The train station was tall, but not tall enough. The city hall was

85

impressive, too—but even though she had to crane her neck to see the top of the clock tower, it wasn't tall enough, either.

A postcard in the shop's window caught her attention. She ducked inside.

The photo was of a building with a tall spire with four tiers and grimacing grotesques. She flipped it over. Saint Cordon Church was not far, and it was apparently the tallest building in Valenciennes.

Of course.

Elise held the swords and jacket over her head as she ran the five blocks to Saint Cordon Church. It loomed out of the darkness at the end of the street like a towering scion protecting the city.

The basilica was in poor condition—the grotesques were green and the stone was crumbling. The sign said it was closed, but the door was unlocked.

She eased inside. The stained glass windows were dim, but the cross on the altar was illuminated by a single light, a point of ghostly gold among the shadows.

Darting into the loft, she took the stairs two at a time and ascended into the tower. The sound of dripping rain echoed throughout the stairs.

Elise reached the first landing before she felt the presence.

Its energy was like walking face-first into a wall. It burned over skin, twisted her stomach, and tasted like sulfur on the back of her tongue.

She had found him.

"I'm here," she said to the empty room.

A shuffling noise responded from the level above.

She unwrapped the swords from her jacket and climbed higher.

It wasn't until she had reached the top of the bell tower, with its open walls and weather-slicked floors, that she finally saw him. A dark shape crouched in the corner behind the bell. It made a huffing, wheezing noise that snorted through thin nostrils, and she realized it was crying.

A breeze sprayed her with rain as she stepped around the bell. "It's me," she said, holding out her hands to show that they were empty. "Don't be afraid."

It was too dim to make out the face as she approached, but she could see its curves silhouetted against the wall—the jagged beak, the patchy feathers, the goat-like legs. Through the darkness, she could see that the hooves were cloven.

The figure wheezed again. "*Elise?*"

All it took was the name, and the reverence with which he said it, for Elise to know who was speaking.

She had suspected it would be an angel. She never would have dreamed that it could be Samael.

He inched forward so that she could see him in the dimming light of evening. Samael was no longer the beautiful, elegant angel that had freed Elise from His garden. His body was distorted. Wrinkled red flesh hung beneath his chin like a rooster's wattle. His eyes sagged in their sockets. The bony stubs of what had once been marvelous wings twitched at his shoulders.

"Help me," he whispered in a barely-human voice.

She dropped to her knees. "Samael… what *happened?*"

He shuddered. Pain wracked his features. "I fell." The rain drummed against the tower, and the wind echoed softly within the bell. He snorted and huffed before speaking again. "It's my punishment for helping you. For speaking to you. For rallying the cherubim…" Elise said nothing, but she felt like her feet had been kicked out from underneath her. "What year is it?"

She tried to speak, but her throat wouldn't work. Elise swallowed hard. "Two thousand."

"How long has it been?"

"Two... two years."

He closed his eyes, and a line of red trickled down his cheek. "I've been killing them, Elise." His lips, hardened into the shape of a beak, clacked when he spoke.

"No, you wouldn't—"

"But I have!" He reached his hands for her, but hesitated. "I can't stop. I try to eat animals... try to satisfy my urges with inhuman flesh, but..." His eyes opened again, and the irises were red. "*I'm so hungry.*"

"Infants, Samael?"

A ragged sob tore from his throat. "It's my punishment," he repeated. "The cravings. I think of nothing but children. No matter how hard I fight, no matter how fast I run, I always succumb. I am *damned*, Elise." Even now, he spoke her name reverently. "I can't do this anymore."

"I know." She hesitated. "The others?"

"Dead. I'm the only one who survived the massacre to fall into hell. I just... I *can't...*" He reached for her again, stretching his pale fingers toward her arm. "Mercy, Elise. *Please*. Can you heal me?"

She considered his plea, resting her fingers on her knife. Wouldn't the greatest mercy be to kill him?

He hadn't killed her when she asked for mercy in the garden.

Elise peeled one of her gloves off with her teeth. Samael flinched to see the mark on her palm. "I don't know if I can heal you, but I can try."

The gratitude etched upon his twisted features was sickening. He took her hands. Elise opened her mind to him.

And then she was gone.

February 2000

Elise reached consciousness slowly, painfully. It was like trying to climb out of a muddy grave. Each time she thought she had gained traction, she slipped again, pulled back under the crushing weight of the drugs.

A rhythmic beep pulsed. Hisses and sighs surrounded her—wind rustling through leaves.

Fear clenched low in her gut. Was she back in the garden? Had Samael somehow surrendered her?

Skin touched hers—the brush of a hand on her arm, gliding to her wrist. Fingers wrapped around her hand. "Elise…" The voice was a beacon in the shadowy gloom of her mind. Something to focus on, something to grip, something to bring her back to life. "Come on, Elise…"

She ached to respond. Her pulse sped, her skin warmed, and she sucked in a huge breath that hurt her lungs. It was like she had never breathed before.

Elise dragged herself to the surface, following the voice to the world of the living. Her eyelashes were glued together, but they opened after some effort.

She was in a hospital room. The signs on the wall were in French, so she must have still been in France. That was where she had been felled.

More importantly, she was on *Earth*.

She struggled to make her mouth move, but found no words. Took a long blink. Almost fell asleep again. It was so hard to keep her eyes open.

"Here," someone said, and a cup touched her lips. Half of the water spilled over her chin, but she managed to get a few drops to slide over her tongue, bitter and sulfuric. She was so parched that the flavor was welcome.

She worked hard to swallow. Tubing rested on her upper lip. A cannula. It blew cool, dry air into her sinuses.

"Thank you," she croaked out.

James set the cup down, leaned forward, and took her hand again.

Elise may have felt terrible, but he looked even worse. Dark shadows rimmed his eyes and lines framed his mouth. He was wearing the same clothes he had been when she had last seen him. Was that gray hair at his temple? "I thought you were gone, Elise."

"The angel," she said. His hand tightened, preventing her from speaking.

"I know." His eyes searched her face. "It was my fault. If I had been there, I could have protected you from it."

Her head shook. A fraction of a movement, but it was enough to drive a spike of pain into her brow. "Samael…"

Surprise registered in his face. "You knew it?"

"Him," she said. The angel was the only reason she had escaped His grip, and he was not an "it"—even distorted, destroyed, and fallen. "Was he healed?"

"Healed? All I saw was a monster leaving the tower."

Her heart fell. "I have to help him."

James's hand stroked her arm. "He nearly pulverized your mind, Elise. Many of the bodily functions your brain unconsciously controls, like blinking and your heartbeat and— and *breathing*—he turned those off when he attacked you. You've been on life support for a week."

Her eyes rolled as she studied the room. The ward had three other beds, all of them empty. "I was trying to help him."

"And I could have stopped him if I had been there. It's my fault." James's fingers tightened.

"Not my aspis."

It was hard to speak, but she didn't need to elaborate. He understood.

Any witch could work alongside a kopis, but in order to fully protect them from metaphysical assault—especially the kind that an angel inflicted—they had to be bound.

He lifted her knuckles to his mouth and kissed them gently. "I could be."

Even if Elise could have spoken, that would have stunned her into silence.

He sat back, and she realized that he had spread pages from his Book of Shadows across the side of her bed and the table on which her lamp rested. "I'm going to let you sleep for a few more hours. I have a lot more work to do before you're well enough to be released, and we can't afford to be in the hospital much longer. Do you understand?"

She gave another dry swallow before nodding.

"James," she said as he selected a page from his Book. The spell was filled with looping lines, crisscrossing from one corner of the page to the next.

"Yes?"

"Thanks."

A smile ghosted across his mouth. "Don't thank me yet," he said, and then he gently blew on the page. The tip of it smoldered.

Sleep sucked her into its warm embrace.

The doctors, amazed by Elise's rapid recovery, allowed her to be discharged the next day. They attempted to discuss her prognosis with James, who barely understood three words of French, while a nurse disconnected her from the equipment.

There weren't any translators on the weekend in their hospital, which meant that communicating with James was mostly done via elaborate hand gestures.

"It's impossible," the doctor said with an exasperated sigh when she got tired of waving her arms around. "Three days ago, the girl had a concussion and a cranial hemorrhage. Now she's in perfect health. How is it possible?"

He gave them his best clueless face, smiled, and nodded.

Elise's mother had spoken to her in nothing but French when she was a child, so she understood perfectly. Medical terminology had been on the lesson plan because Ariane liked to describe battle injuries. But Elise didn't reveal her comprehension. When they spoke to her, she did the same as James—she looked confused and nodded.

"Cranial hemorrhaging?" she asked James as they sneaked out of the hospital that evening. They weren't supposed to leave without completing her paperwork, but they wanted to avoid the inevitable questions that would be posed once the hospital's translator arrived. "You didn't mention that part."

James shrugged. "I didn't know. I'm not a doctor; I'm a witch. I attempted to heal your entire body. Apparently it worked."

"Humble talk from someone who saved my life."

"Oh, I wouldn't take much credit for that." He yawned, and his foot caught on a rock sticking out of the street. He tripped.

Elise steadied him. "Are you okay?"

"I'm tired. Too much magic and not enough sleep."

She didn't let go of his arm. "What's happened with the killings? Have any other bodies been found?"

"It's moved north again. Malcolm is tracking it. Don't worry; I gave him the number for your answering service when he visited in the hospital, and he promised to send updates."

She blinked. "He visited me?"

"Professional courtesy, I'm sure." His voice was very dry.

They returned to their hostel, and James slept for two days straight.

Elise tried to do the same, but she slept fitfully without the assistance of his magic. Dreams of Samael, beautiful and radiant in His garden, were interspersed with the Samael she had seen in the church, fallen and wretched. She kept waking up in a feverish, frightened haze.

When she awoke for the fourth time, she gave up and decided to call her answering machine.

Malcolm had indeed left them several messages. He had tracked Samael out of Brittany, north into Belgium, and now over to Denmark. Samael must have been moving quickly.

Each of Malcolm's updates was punctuated with the reminder that Elise owed him a drink.

She stared at the phone in her hand. What was wrong with this guy?

Elise glanced at James where he slept in the bottom bunk. Their room at the hostel was intended to sleep four travelers, but they bought out all the beds, which gave them a door that locked and plenty of space. His feet hung off the end of the bunk. One arm was flung across his eyes, and he snored.

Elise wondered if his offer to do the binding ritual had been a dream.

Her father had always made it clear that he didn't want her to have an aspis, and he hadn't trained her in strategies with the help of a witch. Elise wouldn't have known what to do with one. She also assumed that James was still waiting for the opportunity to leave. He had never really *behaved* that way, but that was what she expected.

In reality, he had been dogged in staying close to her side. But binding constituted a promise that they would run together for the rest of their lives. She had heard her mother say it once:

more permanent than marriage, more fatal than family, and closer than the oldest of friends.

It wasn't a vow. It was a warning. A binding gone sour could kill both kopis and aspis. Trying to separate was impossible—until one of them died.

James mumbled in his sleep and rolled over, pressing his face into his pillow. He was still wearing that jacket. It didn't look comfortable.

She shifted him to peel off his coat and hang it from the chair. He didn't stir.

James had a life, didn't he? Didn't he ever want to go back to the coven, his family, his friends? He had already spent two years following Elise around. Did he plan on doing that until she died?

She rubbed her fingers over her gloved knuckles, pondering the new gray hairs on his temples.

And what did it mean if James wanted to bind?

Elise didn't get any more sleep after that. She took to the fenced courtyard behind the hostel and exercised, though it was the middle of night and the air was heavy with damp fog that rolled off the ocean.

After limbering her body, which had been in repose for days, she found herself in relatively good condition. Her punches were swift and her kicks were still powerful. Once she warmed up, her muscles responded as though she hadn't been damaged at all.

James had healed her well. Very well. And healing magic was among the most difficult.

A nagging voice spoke from the back of her mind. *What kopis would be crazy enough to refuse the partnership of such a powerful witch?*

When she finished, she took a knife into the bathroom and trimmed her hair, leaving the curls longer than normal.

Then Elise sharpened her swords, ran around the village, and repeated the process until James woke up.

She was waiting for him in the opposite bunk, cross-legged and jiggling one foot, when he finally opened one eye to a slit. He didn't seem startled to find her staring at him.

"Good morning, Elise. You look… fresh."

"It's evening. And I've been awake for a while." She couldn't hold back the question that had been bothering her for thirty-two hours. "Did you really suggest binding as my aspis?"

He scrubbed a hand down his face, then through his hair, and rolled over to check his watch. His eyebrows lifted. "What day is it?"

"Wednesday."

"Hold that thought." He gathered the blankets around him and stumbled into the hall to use the bathroom.

Elise waited as patiently as she could. Her toes drummed against the bedpost.

When he returned, he had splashed water on his face, and the three days of beard growth shadowing his jaw was damp.

James sank to the bed across from her and rubbed the scruff on his chin. "Binding is a serious decision, Elise. I did suggest it, and it's something I've been considering for some time, but you shouldn't feel pressured to—"

"Okay."

He blinked. It took him a moment to catch up. "Okay?"

"Let's do it."

His puffy eyes narrowed, and a knot gathered in her stomach, along with a powerful certainty that he was about to change his mind.

Then he smiled. As exhausted and haggard as he looked, it brightened his face, and the tension was instantly gone.

"Great," he said with a laugh. "That's, uh… great. Excellent, actually."

She grinned and ducked her head. "Yeah."

"When do you want to…?"

"As soon as possible," she said. "Before I find Samael again."

"Very well. Then I suppose we have some work to do."

PART FOUR

OPEN
BORDERS

V

November 2009

The red strobes in Eloquent Blood pulsed like a heartbeat, enveloping Elise and reducing the motions of the clubbers to a jerky, stop-motion play. Bass throbbed through the floor and the metal railings encircling the walkway overlooking the dance floor.

She shoved past the sulfur-crusted tables and leaped over the bar, tripping the stripper that whirled around the pole.

"Hey!" Andrea protested, barely catching her balance on six-inch heels. Then she saw who had struck her. "Oh my God, I'm sorry." Her voice was barely intelligible over the music's volume.

Elise ignored her and kept going. Anthony and Nukha'il were already in the hallway behind the bar.

She stripped off her jacket and tossed it into her boyfriend's arms. "I need you to run to the manager's office. Get your shotgun and my charms out of the closet." She faced Nukha'il without waiting to see if Anthony would obey. "Get behind the DJ booth and block the elevator. Nothing goes down without me—and don't let anything up, either."

Nukha'il swept off to follow her orders, but Anthony hesitated. "What happened under Rick's Drugstore after I left?"

She snapped her fingers. "Shotgun. Charms. Go."

Anthony's mouth drew down at the corners. "I'm not a soldier for you to order around, you know."

Elise slammed into the dressing room.

Neuma had become used to having Elise barge in on her and barely registered surprise at her entrance. She twisted her arms around to hook her leather bra.

"Water," Elise said.

"Just a sec."

"*Now.*"

Neuma rolled her eyes, dropped the bra, and poured a glass at the bathroom faucet. Elise swirled it around in her mouth and spat it out. The taste of ash was still thick in the back of her throat.

"You okay, doll?" Neuma asked.

"Someone's in the Warrens."

What little color was left in the bartender's porcelain skin drained to gray. "How?"

"I'm about to find that out."

The phone on the wall rang, and Neuma answered it as Elise dropped all the climbing equipment in the closet. It was impossible to tell the difference between Elise's rigging and the bondage gear that the half-succubus wore onstage.

She limbered her muscles, stretching her arms over her head and then touching her toes. Then she washed her hands in the sink and took another drink of water.

Neither action helped. After walking through the caverns under Rick's, she still felt… slimy.

"You got a visitor, Elise," Neuma said, hanging up the phone.

"I don't have time for a visitor. Get me a knife—any knife, I don't care." The bartender tossed her a dagger from the dressing table, and Elise rucked up her jeans to tuck it into her boot.

"You've got time for this one. I already told Cass to send him down."

"You did *what?*"

Neuma's mouth stretched into an expression that could have been a smile or grimace. "Sorry."

"Goddamn it, Neuma, I have to get down to the Warrens *now*, I can't—"

The door opened. Music from the club spilled into the dressing room.

Elise knew, an instant before she saw him, whom Neuma had decided was important enough to bring downstairs. She probably would have felt him coming much earlier if she hadn't been so distracted. Instead, James's presence rolled over her like a heat wave coming off pavement, and it shocked her into silence.

He edged into the room and shut the door again. She stopped in the middle of tucking the knife into her boot.

James seemed uncomfortable in a club filled with flowing alcohol, pulsing music, and sweaty bodies, and he wore his composure like a shield. In a white button-down shirt and dove-gray slacks, he looked professorial, which was entirely too tasteful for somewhere like Eloquent Blood.

For all that they had been glimpsing one another's lives through the active bond, it had been weeks since Elise had talked to him face-to-face. It hadn't been a pleasant conversation. Although neither of them had raised their voices, they didn't have to yell to argue anymore. She could feel his annoyance through the bond without a single cruel word being uttered.

In fact, she felt a lot when James was around—grief, fear, guilt, and all the things she normally blocked out. The bond was like a raw, open wound, and having James in the same room was as good as salting it.

That was why she had told him she wouldn't do the accounting for his business anymore. It was also why she had told him to stop calling her. He hadn't taken that well.

Elise busied herself with arranging the knife in her boot. "What are you doing here?"

"I was in the neighborhood to visit Stephanie." He glanced around the dressing room with a furrowed brow. "You haven't been coming to see me, so I thought I should try visiting you instead."

Neuma mouthed *sorry*, hugged a costume to her chest, and snuck out the door behind James. He caught her movement out of the corner of his eye and jumped away from the door, careful not to let his skin brush against hers. Elise picked up a glimpse of his thoughts—*It's that thing that kept trying to flirt with me...why does Elise always have to be around demons...smells like whiskey and pot smoke in here*—and it took all her strength to tune him out.

She didn't realize she had backed into the dressing table until her hip hit it. The dressing room was large, meant to accommodate a dozen girls at once, but standing on the opposite side of the room from James still wasn't far enough to dampen their bond.

"I told you earlier, I'm kind of busy," she said, voice strained.

James ran through a dozen options of things that he could say to her, which skimmed over the surface of the bond for an instant before he spoke. "You've been ignoring all my calls." And below that: *You're avoiding me.*

"That's because I told you not to call me." It felt stupidly redundant to speak aloud.

He ran a hand through his hair. "Listen, Elise..."

I miss you.

"This isn't a good time for that conversation."

Exasperated, James took a notebook from his back pocket. "This is too difficult. Wait a second." He flipped through the pages, and she saw the designs he had drawn sliding through the air before he picked one out.

James flicked the spell into the air and spoke a word of power. A cool mist sprinkled down her skin, from the crown of her head down to her toes. Radiating calm followed it—and silence.

Elise worked her jaw around, trying to clear her ears. Nothing happened. But she could still hear the thudding bass in Blood, could still hear her own breath.

It wasn't her ears that had been dampened. The silence was inside her skull.

She tried to listen to James's thoughts, but they were a muffled undercurrent—not entirely gone, but inaccessible. "How long have you been able to do that?"

"A few days now. I put a charm on my home office so I can do magic without disturbing you, and it's holding up well. This particular spell will only last an hour or so." James crumpled up the page and dropped it in the trash on top of an empty box of condoms.

"If a spell exists that can mute the bond, does that mean you've found someone who's been through…this?"

"No. I had to design the spell. It's the first one I've made in years." He gave a sheepish smile. "I'm a little rusty."

She tugged on her earlobe again, even though she knew the silence wasn't really in her ears. "This doesn't really change anything. I'm still too busy to talk."

James's eyes tracked over the costumes, the makeup cases, Neuma's favorite riding crop, and the knives that Elise kept on an empty vanity. He moved to touch a chain hanging by the door, but seemed to think better of it. "Busy with… what, exactly?"

"Prostitution," Elise deadpanned. "It's exactly what you fear."

He gave her a look that said he didn't think she was as funny as she did. "I would have a hard time missing that. You're not that good at shielding your emotions."

"Maybe I don't get emotional about it."

"Elise…"

"I'm working. Okay? Neuma and I have been handling administration for all the Night Hag's former businesses. It's a lot of ordering, supply chain management, and threatening to stab demons who hold out on me. I've been trying to keep new bad guys from taking the territory, too. Does that sound okay to you? Do I have your permission to have a life?"

The corners of his eyes pinched, as though he was in pain. "I'm not trying to be judgmental." Elise drummed her fingers on the edge of the counter. Of course he was. "But you do have to admit, it's strange. You're a kopis, Elise—a demon *hunter*."

"We've never agreed on that definition of the term. Kopides are meant to preserve a balance between angels and demons and humans—"

He spoke right over her. "But demons are *always* a threat to humans."

"—and that doesn't always mean killing demons. They're not all evil."

"By definition…"

"They have chaotic impulses." Elise's volume was increasing, and she couldn't seem to stop herself. "There's a difference between chaos and evil."

James let out a sigh. "And you think you can bring order to their chaos?"

"I'm doing a pretty damn good job of it, yeah."

"And how, exactly, are you making money out of this?"

The answer was tithes—a practice where kopides took a percentage off the top of local demons' dealings. But Elise didn't say that. "I'm not," she said instead. "Have you seen where Anthony and I are living?"

"No. You don't speak to me, much less invite me over for dinner."

And they were back to that again.

"I have to go." Elise tapped her knives to double-check their locations—one at her ankle, one at her hip—and then checked her back sheath. It still felt strange with only one sword. Then she tried to brush past James to exit the room.

He stopped her with a hand on her arm.

The contact was enough to split the bond open again. For an instant, she saw herself through James's eyes: her curls fraying out of her braid, her hollow cheeks, her pale lips.

When was the last time she slept?

"What happened to the other falchion?" he asked.

Elise pulled her arm free, blinking rapidly to clear her vision. "I'm not wearing it," she said, knowing that he would feel the lie. "But you didn't visit me to check on my swords."

He sighed. "Okay. I've learned some information—"

The dressing room door opened, forcing them to step quickly aside. Anthony peered around the corner before entering. He had put on his spine scabbard, and the butt of the shotgun jutted over one shoulder.

His eyes widened. "James. Hey. Good to see you." He handed the chain of charms to Elise, and she looped them around her neck. "Ready to go?"

"Just a second. I'll be right there."

Anthony glanced between them and ducked out of the room again.

James's eyes traced the charms, and the line of worry in his brow deepened. "Do you need my help tonight?" *Please let me help you.*

"I already have enough backup." She glanced at her cell phone. "I'm about to meet Nukha'il and Anthony, so you've got my attention for about twenty seconds. What do you want? Really."

James's hand stroked down her braid, and one of the curls at the bottom briefly wrapped around his finger before bouncing free. "I want you to stop avoiding me, for one thing."

"That's why you came down? Really?"

A thousand thoughts flicked across his features and vanished again. Blissfully, Elise couldn't hear a single one of them.

"Sorry to have bothered you. I'll leave."

They stepped into the hall together, and Elise hesitated before going into the club. "James? When you get home… check all your wards. Make sure you're protected."

His smile was sad. "I will."

"Where's James?" Anthony shouted when Elise finally joined him at the elevator behind the DJ booth. Her lips were thin, the tendons in her neck were rigid, and a vein bulged on her forehead. The stress radiating from her skin was palpable.

She said nothing.

Nukha'il opened the gate for the elevator, and they all piled in. It creaked to life as soon as he shut the door.

Anthony tilted back his face to watch the shaft stretching overhead. The music echoing from the club faded rapidly. The bass died first, and then the treble, until all he could hear was the occasional faint hiss of snare.

Then that, too, was gone, and all he heard was the occasional creak of the elevator's chain.

It was discomfortingly similar to Anthony's descent into the cave-in. Had the path to the Warrens always been so dark?

"What's the plan?" he asked Elise, trying to distract himself from the claustrophobic walls of the elevator cage.

She cracked her knuckles. "We find out who's gotten into the gate."

"And?"

"And we make sure that they don't come out again."

"You mean, we're going to kill them." Anthony choked on the sentence. "But Nukha'il left alive. Doesn't that mean that this man is harmless?"

Elise remained silent, but he could feel her judging him. Her stare all but screamed, *You stupid boy.* Of course someone who had navigated the Warrens to reach the gate wouldn't be harmless, and they certainly wouldn't be innocent. And of course she wouldn't think twice about killing them. She wasn't Anthony.

He shut his mouth and didn't bother trying to talk again.

They descended in silence for a few more seconds. He tapped his toes, trying to focus on the bars of the elevator instead of what was waiting for them below.

The light dimmed and buzzed. Elise shot a look at Nukha'il. He had woven his own feathers through his hair, and they shimmered with internal light.

"It's not me," he said.

Anthony spun slowly, gazing at the rising walls beyond the cage of the elevator. Or at least, he tried to see the walls—it was suddenly dark beyond the bars, very dark, and he couldn't see the smoothly hewn stone at all.

The bulb popped. Sparks rained down on them, washing over Elise's hair with a shock of yellow.

And then there was no light at all.

Anthony reached out, searching for his girlfriend's hand, and found her elbow. She shook him off. Metal rasped on leather as she drew her sword. "I thought you said the shadow hadn't reached the gate," Elise said.

"It hadn't." Nukha'il sounded worried, and that only made Anthony more worried.

The elevator grated to a stop, and Anthony held his breath. Had they reached the bottom level, or had the motor failed?

"Flashlights," she said.

He fumbled in his pockets and almost dropped it. His fingers searched over the smooth plastic case for the button. His thumb met rubber. He pressed it.

Blue light spilled into the elevator, and that tightness in his chest eased a fraction—just a fraction. Anthony shone his flashlight upon the faces of his companions. Nukha'il's eyes reflected silvery white. Elise's jaw and shoulders were tight, and all the color was sucked out of her shirt and hair, making her look ghost-like.

She shoved the door open. The elevator had jammed a few feet short of the bottom, and they had to jump to reach the ground. The metal rattled and squealed when Anthony dropped.

He had been in the upper level of the Warrens so often that it had become a familiar sight. The long, narrow shaft extended in either direction, suspended by ancient boards that creaked with the weight of the rock. It was silent aside from the occasional whir of the ventilation system that cooled the air and pumped out water.

If he went left, he knew he would eventually find himself in a structure like a honeycomb, which housed some of the territory's uglier demons; if he went right, it would go down, down, down into the depths of what used to be the Night Hag's domain.

Beyond that, deeper in the earth, awaited the gate. He had been having nightmares about it for months.

Elise headed right.

"Stay close."

He followed her, letting the angel take the rear. Even without his wings exposed, Nukha'il was disturbingly inhuman. He had to stoop to walk through the mines, and he held himself as though he were dragging those massive, eight-foot wings behind him.

But Anthony had bigger worries. It was dark down there—so dark. Hadn't the Night Hag installed lights? Where was the power?

They passed a fork that he had never explored before. A wind breezed out of the tunnel.

Anthony…

He stopped. Nukha'il almost ran into him, but the angel stepped back with a rustle of feathers, like a bird offended by the gust of a storm.

"Did you hear that?" Anthony asked.

Elise's jaw was tense. "Keep moving."

"But someone said my name."

She grabbed his arm and pulled him around to face her. "Don't listen. Keep moving."

That measured tone meant she was keeping her emotions tightly controlled. It was usually comforting. Elise could keep a cool head against anything. When things got bad, he and Betty used to joke, "What would Elise do?" and they usually agreed that the answer was, "Kick ass and yawn about it later."

But Betty wasn't there anymore. She had died in front of that gate.

Another breeze sighed around his feet.

Anthony…

"What's down here?" he asked.

Elise shoved him. Anthony stumbled but kept his footing. "Whatever you hear—whatever you see—keep moving. Guns aren't going to work on anything we meet."

"Then why did I bring the shotgun?"

"Security blanket?" Nukha'il suggested, bumping shoulders with Anthony as they strode down the corridor.

Anthony sped his pace to get in front of him. He glared at Nukha'il, and the angel stared back, calm and unsmiling.

Elise took them to another fork and turned. A few steps later, they turned again. The walls became paneled with wood on one side. A couple of them were cracked. Anthony remembered glimpsing demonic settlements on the other side—some built into narrow crannies, some built into caves.

But now, even though he shone his flashlight on them, all he saw was darkness waiting on the other side.

"We're almost there," Elise said, drawing her sword.

Anthony…

A chill rolled over him, like something heavy and wet slithering down his spine. He swatted at his neck and spun, searching for the source of the sensation.

Heavy shadow yawned at his back.

The corridor behind them had disappeared.

"Elise," he began.

His flashlight dimmed. Elise's flickered.

And then all light was gone.

He couldn't move his feet. Cold fingers brushed his face, his scalp, his arms. An icy kiss of darkness caressed the hollow of his collarbone, and he tried to brush it away.

"Stay close," Elise said, but her voice was distant, echoing.

Oh God, she was leaving. "Hey, wait! I can't see anything! Elise? Nukha'il?"

He reached his hands out, searching for walls. Shouldn't they have been right there? It was such a narrow passage. But he found nothing.

He popped the strap on his scabbard and drew his shotgun. The metal was warm, so much warmer than the tunnels, as if it had been fired recently. He hugged it to his chest.

Elise's words swirled somewhere far away. "Keep moving..."

"Wait for me!" Anthony shouted.

He hurried to keep up with her, following the occasional scuff of footstep on stone.

Anthony...

His flashlight flickered to life again.

He stood alone in the center of three divergent tunnels.

Elise and the angel were nowhere in sight.

Each of the passages was the same—wooden posts suspending sagging stone. And they all seemed to go down, down, down. But hadn't he gone *down* to get there? Shouldn't one of them have led up, back to oxygen and daylight and safety?

He held his breath, listening for a hint of motion that would tell him where Elise had gone, but he heard nothing beyond his racing heart. The sound of the ventilation was gone, too.

White flashed in the corner of his eye. He whirled, raising the shotgun to aim it down one of the tunnels.

His heart thundered in his chest.

"Is someone there?" Anthony called.

And then, in response, a tiny voice: "Help me."

It sounded like a child. His shotgun wavered.

He took a step down the tunnel. "Hello?"

"Please... someone help me."

111

He hesitated, remembering what Elise had told him. *Whatever you hear—whatever you see—just keep moving.*

Another flash of white.

Bare feet pattered on the stone.

Common sense told him that there was no way a child could be in the Warrens. But hadn't Elise found a demon lost beneath that drugstore? Wasn't there a chance that *someone* was lost and scared in the shadows of the mines—someone other than Anthony?

"It's okay," he said, sliding down the tunnel with his back to the wall. "I'm not going to hurt you."

He glanced over his shoulder. Darkness swallowed the junction and urged him forward. That voice was gone, and so was the breeze. It was just Anthony, his shotgun, dead air, and the voice of a little girl.

A few more steps, and a hazy white shape emerged at the end of the tunnel, which terminated in more wooden panels. Something small and pale was curled in the corner.

Anthony recognized the curve of a bare shoulder, stubby toes, and locks of long, golden hair.

It really was a child. Her knees were drawn to her chest, and her face was buried in her arms. Judging by her size, she couldn't have been older than four or five. She looked terrified. And who could blame her? Some guy was approaching her with a gun.

"Hey." He sheathed his firearm. "It's okay."

She lifted her head enough to peek over her arm.

Alarm bells rang out in his head. *Her eyes are black. Completely black. That can't be right.*

But she spoke before he could move away. "Who are you?" Her voice was musical and light. He almost didn't notice the undertone of a throatier, more womanly voice beneath it.

Anthony…

112

His flashlight dimmed again, but all Anthony wanted to do was pick up the girl, carry her from the Warrens, and take her somewhere safe. She was so helpless. So fragile.

He stretched out his hands as he lowered himself to a crouch.

"My name's Anthony. Anthony Morales. It's okay—I'm one of the good guys."

As he approached, she buried her face in her arms again. Her blond hair fell over her forehead. "I'm scared," she whispered.

I'm so lonely. Hold me.

"I'll get you out of here," he said, sounding braver than he felt. She drew into a tighter ball when he kneeled at her side.

"You can help me?"

He reached out to touch her shoulder. "Yeah. Of course. I won't leave you."

She lifted her head again. Her face was round, with a pointed chin and plump red lips. More of a woman's face than a child's. Tears shone on her cheeks, dripping off her jaw onto a bony clavicle. Her skin was luminous, like moonlight contained in human form. Beautiful. Truly beautiful.

"Thank you for saving me, Anthony," she said.

Her lips didn't move when she spoke.

Her mouth yawned open, sudden and wide and filling his vision. He shouted and threw himself back, landing hard on his butt. The shock of it jolted up his spine.

Anthony flung an arm up to shield his face. The back of his head bounced against the wall.

The darkness was complete.

113

VI

Elise wasn't surprised when the flashlights died again. She was more surprised that it had taken so long.

She slammed her flashlight against her hip, but the bulb didn't even flicker. She forced herself to speak calmly. "Don't worry, guys. We don't need the lights anyway. Nukha'il?"

The angel's eyes lit first, shining like daylight through blue plates of a stained glass window. A second glow followed quickly at his back. It wasn't his wings—there wasn't enough room to deploy them—but it came from the space where they should have been. The ethereal light penetrated the darkness, flooding a few feet around them in the hall.

Anthony was not there.

Elise swore, kicking a loose rock into the wall. It gave a satisfying, but muffled, *crack*.

"Goddamn it, Anthony—I told him to stay close!"

"He's most likely been taken."

Cold reality splashed over her anger to dampen it. "No. He's fine. He's probably just a couple of halls away. Go find him."

His wings drooped. "And leave you alone, with no light?" Nukha'il looked so pathetic that an ounce of something resembling sympathy bloomed within her.

"I'll be fine."

His glimmering gaze was locked upon her. "If you want me to search the darkness for him, I will search. I only want to see you happy."

"Don't talk like that."

"I have no choice. When I'm near you, all I think about is having your smile radiate on me."

She took a step back, but he responded with a step forward. Nukha'il took her hand.

"Don't," she warned.

He dipped his head, and before she could react, he kissed her knuckles. It was the barest touch, but it jolted into shoulders, elbows, and palms.

The pain was instant and all consuming. She stiffened. Tried to breathe. But all she could smell was sunrise, sunset, the moon in the sky, the heavy moisture of clouds—angel smells. It only intensified the pain. Her vertebrae locked together as if gripped by silver spikes.

Elise pushed him back. Touching him made her hands burn, but it took a moment for her brain to register the additional sensation, like briefly resting her hands on a hot stove.

"Jesus," she bit out, shutting her eyes against the shudders rippling through her. She didn't have to remove her gloves to know that the marks would be bleeding. Again. It rippled through her in waves, contracting her back muscles and making her head swim. But each ripple was smaller than the last, and after a few seconds, the pain faded.

When she opened her eyes again, there was a helpless, searching look on Nukha'il's face. "You never smile for me," he whispered.

Revulsion swirled in her gut. "Don't you *ever* do that again."

"I know, I know. It is damnation—sweet damnation." Nukha'il gave a shuddering sigh. "I love Itra'il so much. So very, very much. But it's nothing like what I feel for you, Elise. You are a forest fire, and I am the dry grass. I adore you. I want—"

"I don't care what you want," she interrupted.

His brow knitted. "I want to be rid of you. I've watched civilizations rise and fall, but I'm helpless against you because you've been marked by Him. I'm only sane when you aren't around." Nukha'il's pale eyes burned with barely-contained fire. "I think I hate you, Elise, in as many ways as I love you."

She said nothing. She hadn't asked for it—any of it. She hadn't even wanted the angel to come back to the city.

Nukha'il took a deep breath. His face blanked, and he was calm once more.

"You've made a request, and I'll honor it. Your whims are my directives."

He strode away, followed by the dim ghost of wings. He took all the light with him.

She worked her mouth around, gathering what little saliva was on her tongue, and spit it onto the asphalt. It was stained with blood.

Elise hated to be adored.

Even though her skin still buzzed, she didn't hesitate— she jogged down the mineshaft the instant Nukha'il was gone. She didn't have far to go. Elise's movements began echoing differently, and she realized she was at the end of the tunnel.

She held out her hands and moved slowly until she found the door. She ran her hands over the wood and found the metal bar that served as a handle. Even in the darkness, she could make out the faint shape of magic glimmering over it; she had used one of Craven's resident witches, Treeny, to cast a weak locking charm on the entrance. Theoretically, only she and Nukha'il should have been able to get inside.

She pressed her hand against the metal bar. The door slid open.

White light flooded the hall.

It was like falling into the sun. Elise flung up her sword to shield her stinging eyes. Tears blurred her vision.

"Who's there?" she shouted into the light.

The responding voice was cool and masculine. "Come in and close the door."

Elise headed down the ramp encircling the room with the gate, following her memories rather than her vision.

She began to make out shapes in the room—first, the high, arching stone of the gate. It wasn't the source of the light. It was no more than a shadow. But she could see the marks rimming the base, even through the specter of too-bright light in her eyes. It hummed when she approached, as if greeting her.

Then she saw the shape of the cavern stretching high overhead. She had never been able to see the roof of it before. It was always too dim. But the light filled every cranny, and she realized that the Night Hag had left tapestries suspended near the top. Dozens of them.

Finally, she saw the source of the light.

It was a man. He stood in front of the dark gate with his thumbs hooked in the belt loops of a pair of very snug leather pants. He was barefoot, bare-chested, and wore a thin leather collar with a ruby in the center. Black hair spilled down his shoulders to his lower back. His eyes were almond-shaped, and they tilted up at the corners as though he smiled, though it didn't touch his lips.

"Elise," he greeted.

It took her a moment to remember how to speak. "Thom?"

The man who called himself Thom Norrel sauntered toward her. With each step, the light dimmed, becoming more and more bearable until it was no more than a comfortable white glow.

The last time Elise had seen him, he had been pretending to be a witch in the service of the Night Hag, but he had vanished after Elise returned from the angelic city. James admitted that they had spoken once while she was unconscious, though he was vague about the details of that conversation. The only thing he would say was that he was certain that Thom was not a witch at all—probably not even human. Elise was inclined to agree.

"I was beginning to think that you might have been devoured in the Warrens. It's good to see you've survived." His voice was pure silk.

"Nukha'il told me he didn't recognize the man by the gate."

"I wasn't recognizable when he found me," Thom said.

Elise frowned. "What did you look like?"

He gave an elegant shrug. "Someone else. I wanted to get your attention. Would you have hurried here as quickly if Nukha'il had told you that I was the one waiting?"

"Maybe," Elise said. "It depends on what you're doing here."

He circled her, his dark eyes scanning her from feet to face. She resisted the urge to turn and keep him in her line of sight. "Perhaps I wanted a few minutes alone with you."

"Bullshit."

"Such language," he murmured.

"The gate is supposed to be locked. Nobody should be able to get in here."

"I don't care for locks." Thom fluttered a hand at the cavern. "I also don't care for shadows."

Elise's hand tensed on her falchion. "What do you know about that?"

"Everything, as a matter of fact." He let the sentence hang in the air as he slunk back to the gate's dais. Thom sank to the first step, lounging on it like a cat in the sunshine. He never took his eyes off of her. "You can put that away."

Reluctantly, Elise sheathed her sword. She had fought Thom once—just once. She hadn't won. He was about as impressed by swords as he was by locks and shadows.

"Tell me why you're here, and feel free to skip the cryptic crap."

He studied his fingernails. They were painted black. "I'm holding up my end of the agreement."

"What agreement?"

"You agreed that the infernal and ethereal delegations would help you guard this gateway. I have watched as you and that angel bumbled for weeks, doing your best to bluster and intimidate petty demons while an enemy emerged unseen and unopposed. She approaches now, and I'm here to stop her."

"How do you know about the agreement?"

"I am the father of all things that slink in the night," he said. "I know *everything*."

The last word slipped through the air and curled around her. Elise recalled the night of the summit, when she had stood alone in the desert with Nukha'il and a demon-possessed cat to discuss the guardianship of the gates. If Thom knew what they had discussed…

"The cat?" she guessed.

He smiled. "Come sit with me."

Elise didn't move.

"If you know what's happening, this would be a great time to share."

"We have little time. I shall make this brief." Thom held up one finger. "You know the dark gate beyond this one can lead to your greatest foe. But for a demon to pass through the door would violate the quarantine, and the Treaty of Dis. The consequences could be disastrous."

119

"Apocalypse," Elise said, and he shrugged.

"Possibly." Thom lifted a second finger. "A demon *wants* to pass through the gate. She wants to destroy the world, and everything in it."

Her eyebrows lifted. "Including herself?"

A smile quirked at the corner of his mouth. "Especially herself."

"And that's the shadow." She paced along the edge of the cavern, giving the dais a wide berth. There had once been other paths into the cave, paths that led to other branches of the Warrens, but Elise had sealed them with Neuma's help as soon as she had moved into the manager's office at Craven's. She had boarded them up and poured cement into the doorways.

They were all intact, and there was no reason to think they could have been opened. But she checked them anyway.

"Yes." He lifted a third finger. "Finally, I am the only thing that has prevented her from achieving her goals. She is at your front door now, knocking in the only way she knows how."

"Does this shadow have a name?" Elise called back to the dais.

"Yes." Thom's voice came from right behind her, and she jumped, spinning to face him. He loomed behind her. His irises were black, making his pupils seem enlarged, and he radiated heat. "She is Yatai—the oldest demon alive."

His voice caressed down her body like a warm waterfall. Elise swallowed hard and tried not to stare at his bare chest.

A shimmer caught her eye.

One of the doorways in the very back of the room had collapsed. The boards Elise had nailed in place were shattered, tearing down part of the stone wall to bare, raw mineral.

The rocks sparkled with flakes of brassy yellow pyrite. Where water dripped over the stones, they were stained with sulfuric acid.

Elise had been on the other side of that collapse not two hours before.

As she watched, the rocks shivered again. The glint of pyrite had only caught her eye because it was vibrating.

Thom followed her gaze, and he arched one eyebrow.

"And now Yatai is coming," he said, as calmly as though he were announcing his dinner plans.

He winked out of existence at her side.

Then the collapsed section exploded.

Concrete and wood showered around Elise. She jumped back, shielding her head with her arms.

Everything she had constructed to block the shaft was scattered across the ground. The hole yawned open, and there was nothing beyond it.

Silence fell over the cavern. The last of the dust and debris rained around her, settling on her hair and shoulders.

Something in the tunnel moved.

Exorcist...

Her heart leaped into the back of her throat. She held her falchion between her body and the tunnel like a shield, vulnerable without her second blade.

"You can't have the gate, Yatai," she growled.

Motion in the depths of the darkness.

The sound of scurrying was faint at first, like distant rats scrabbling in the walls. It could have been a breeze in the mines, whispering down the hole vacated by Rick's Drugstore. But it quickly grew, and it rushed toward her, approaching impossibly fast.

It became thudding as it grew closer, and then it multiplied.

Bodies. Lots of them.

Her hand tightened on the hilt.

A shape launched from the tunnel.

It was like being blindsided by a car. Her back slammed into the floor with the full force of its weight, and all she could see were wide, rolling eyes—slicked over with oil—and a gaping mouth with teeth that oozed shadows. It shrieked at the sudden light, as though the brightness caused it physical pain.

She realized with a shock that it was a fiend—one of Zohak's minions. And it was possessed by the shadow.

Elise's arm was pressed against her chest at the wrong angle for attack. She lifted her knees between them and launched the fiend into the air with a hard kick.

Before she could get to her feet, another jumped on her, and then another. They clawed at her legs. Their combined weight made her stumble.

She twisted away and danced back, jamming the falchion in the mouth of the one on her right. The blade plunged into the soft palate and erupted from the other side. Ichor splattered from the back of the fiend's skull.

Elise jerked the blade free and whirled, cutting down the second fiend with an arcing blow.

The blade bit into its shoulder and sank into bone. Elise kicked it in the chest, forced it off her blade, and then stabbed it in the heart.

Elise searched for Thom, but it was too bright in the cavern to distinguish shapes or direction. There were more fiends—so many more. Their shapeless forms were a mass of screeching flesh draped in shadow, seething around her like a midnight ocean.

She crashed into them, letting instinct move her. She launched a kick behind her, cracking the skull of one fiend and sending it stumbling into another. Elise swooped low and drew her boot knife as she thrust the falchion into the gut of her latest attacker.

Flinging her arm out straight, she launched the slender knife into the throat of a shadow and was rewarded with a strangled, bubbling scream.

Teeth sank into her arm. They were blunt, but the force crushed against her bone. Hot pain bloomed through her arm. Blood dribbled down her elbow.

She jammed the falchion into the fiend's eye. Her sword ripped free as the demon fell, taking a hunk of skin with it.

No time to stop.

Instinct kept her light on her feet. She cut down one fiend after another, and their oily blood slicked the floor beneath her boots.

It was only a diversion. Over their heads, the shadow in the tunnel seethed.

A column of darkness extended from the mineshaft beyond the collapse, as thick around as Elise's torso. It seemed to emerge from the rock itself. It was no longer mere shadow. It had taken on form, like a serpent with scales that caught no light.

The infernal power radiating from it was immense, and Elise felt it burn straight through her skull. The snake was Yatai embodied.

And she was carrying a body.

Yatai swept over her head, and Elise's heart dropped as she saw the dangling limbs, the head rolling on the shoulders. It was a man, lanky and longhaired. His wings were lifeless at his back.

The shadow clamped tight around Nukha'il's midsection and shoved him toward the gate.

Elise kicked a fiend off of her sword and ran toward the gate, but clawed hands gripped her shirt and jeans to hold her back.

The symbols ringing the gate glowed with brilliant white light against Yatai's shadow, which flung Nukha'il to the dais. He slid and bumped into the base of one of the columns.

At his touch, the humming intensified. Energy raced up the pillars. Elise's palms burned.

The column of shadow descended, ready to seize Nukha'il again.

"No," she growled, kicking free of the fiends and launching herself up the steps.

Thom got there first.

He appeared between the angel and Yatai, and he faced the darkness with no fear. Elise had never seen him angry before—she didn't think that he could be anything but detached and, occasionally, vaguely amused. But his eyes blazed, his lips were peeled back into a growl, and he flung his arms wide with his fists clenched.

The shadow blasted into his chest and deflected. He took a single step back.

Thom roared, and white light burst from his flesh, crashing into Yatai like fire blazing over the surface of water. The smell of ozone and burning hair crackled through the air.

A shockwave blasted from the contact. It struck Elise, and her feet slipped from beneath her. The steps of the dais rose to meet her face. Pain cracked through her forehead, and stars sparked at the edges of her vision.

The power of Thom and Yatai's clashing energies toppled the fiends and struck the walls of the cave.

The rocks groaned. Debris showered around them.

Yatai slithered back and struck again, pounding into Thom. Elise could only watch sideways, crumpled against the dais, stunned and limp.

Come now. You don't care about the gate. Let me pass.

That silken voice was simultaneously softer and louder than the responding shudders of the cavern.

Thom didn't respond except to take a step forward, pushing into the shadow.

Elise dragged herself over the steps, belly flat to the shuddering dais. The air grew thick as she crawled to Nukha'il, who was sprawled behind Thom's legs. The gate responded to her proximity—it vibrated harder, and the cavern on the other side of the pillars vanished, replaced by bright gray fog.

She didn't have to lay her palm on it to open the gate a second time. It was as though the stones remembered her touch, though it had been months since she was last there. Maybe the gate had never fully closed.

Her fingers fell on Nukha'il's wrist. One wing was crumpled beneath him.

The angel stirred, eyes opening to slits. His blue irises had turned to gray. "Get away," he whispered. "She's here."

Elise tried to drag him away from the gate. But he was immensely heavy, her bitten arm ached, the air was so thick, and Yatai spotted them.

This has been fun, she said, *but I will wait no more.*

"You're lost to madness." There was a quaver in Thom's normally empty voice.

And when you favor the light, you are weak.

The serpent reared. Elise saw it thicken over Thom's shoulder, becoming dragon-like and vast. It crushed the light radiating from his skin. Tendrils oozed over the back of the gate.

The white light shattered.

Yatai slammed into Nukha'il, ripped his arm from her hand, and shoved him against the gate as the gray curtain parted. Together, the serpent and the angel passed the threshold—and vanished.

A boulder dislodged from the wall and crashed into the other side of the gate. Elise rolled away from the showering detritus and slipped down the steps, thudding into the cavern floor. The floor vibrated, and a mighty *crack* rent the air.

A boulder the size of a train split from the ceiling. It tumbled toward her end over end, almost in slow motion.

Elise rolled, protecting her head and knowing that it wouldn't be good enough.

Thom blinked into existence at her side long enough to fold his arms around her shoulders. She felt reality bend and realized what he was about to do.

"No!" she shouted, but her cry never reached the cave.

They disappeared an instant before the boulder crashed into the dais.

VII

Elise blinked. The crumbling cavern disappeared and was replaced by white walls and wooden floors. The air turned from dusty and hot to air-conditioned cool, and the seething energy of angels disappeared, leaving her palms cold under the gloves.

Instead of being far below the city, she was suddenly in the entryway of a condo. Her mind bucked, rejecting a reality that could so easily shift.

Her cramping stomach was the only warning that she was about to vomit. Thom allowed her to fall to the floor and empty her stomach on the parquet. It burned up her throat and tasted ashen on her tongue. The puddle of bile was black, but not with blood.

Her arm throbbed, and she pushed back her sleeve to see the bite wound. She sucked in a hard breath.

What should have been nothing more than the imprint of a fiend's dull teeth was exposed, bleeding flesh. But she was bleeding ichor—the same shadows that had dribbled from Zohak when she had stabbed him.

The same shadows that turned him to obsidian.

As soon as she saw it, the pain intensified and swept up her shoulder. She lost balance and sat back against the wall.

Elise gasped, and every time her breath wheezed out, it was with a small cry. She hated to whimper, but it was pain unlike any other. So much worse than when Death's Hand had ripped her shoulder open, worse than having her leg shattered under falling rock, worse than getting grazed by a bullet.

SM Reine

Ice spiked through her heart, gripping her chest with cold fingers. Where the pain spread, so did shadow. Her skin grayed and hardened. She clenched her teeth and slammed her head back against the wall.

Thom disappeared and then reappeared in front of her a heartbeat later. White dust puffed around him, as though he brought the air with him when he phased back from the cavern. He held a sword in his hands—the falchion Elise had dropped by the gate. Shadow oozed over its blade.

"This won't do," he said. He peeled the darkness off of it as though it was no more than plastic, leaving her blade clear and clean.

Her instant of relief was fleeting.

"Thom—my arm—"

He set down the sword. "Is there a problem?"

Thom lifted her wrist to inspect the wound. The lightest touch shot spikes of fire into her ribcage, and her chest heaved as she fought to breathe. She couldn't fill her lungs. Elise whined through her teeth.

"Ah, I see. You would die of this." There was longing in his eyes, and his voice was husky. "It will turn your blood to oil and your flesh to stone. And it will hurt—oh, it will hurt." He traced a finger around the edge of the wound, and she kicked her leg against the floor. She couldn't wrench her limb free. His hands were gentle, but unyielding. "You should feel death marching on you now, I think."

"James," she panted, "take me to James, I need him—"

"Your witch cannot heal this."

"I'm not dying from a fucking bite!"

He hummed low in his throat. "Yes, you would. If I allowed it."

Thom lowered himself over Elise, sitting in her lap. His face loomed, beautiful even as her vision blurred and darkened.

128

He cupped her face in both of his hands. He was so close that the tip of his nose brushed hers.

"You don't know what a gift it is to die." His lips tickled against her mouth. "It pains me to watch you beg for life when I would do anything—*anything*—for the blessing you deny." His tongue darted out and wetted Elise's bottom lip. "Let me drink your death, sword-woman. Let me have a taste…"

Thom's mouth closed over hers, and there was nowhere she could go, trapped between his hands with her arm aflame and no oxygen in her lungs.

His kiss was so much more than the sensation of lips against lips. Demons held domain over the physical, and the caress of his tongue reached hands deep into her flesh, clenching her muscles and burning between her thighs.

She leaned forward despite herself, and he took it as an invitation. He deepened the kiss, pressing his body into hers, and it felt like melted chocolate dripping down her throat.

It was almost good enough that she forgot that her arm was turning into obsidian.

Almost.

Her struggling heart skipped a beat. She fumbled for her waist with her good arm, and every motion jolted her wound.

Her fingers closed around the hard hilt of her knife.

Thom's hand caught her wrist before she could draw the blade. He drew back, humor sparking in his bottomless eyes. "I'll have you know that kings have gone to war for my kiss."

"Were they *dying*?"

"All humans perpetually spiral toward oblivion." Thom lowered his lips to the graying skin on her arm. "But I cannot die of this venom. I could draw it from you into myself." The whisper of his breath across the wound rocked her as though he had slammed her arm into the wall. "Would you like me to heal you?"

129

She couldn't speak anymore—she could barely breathe. So she only nodded.

His eyes remained fixed on hers as he lowered his mouth to the bite... and licked it.

Thom's saliva sizzled on the flesh, but instant relief radiated through the muscle. She sucked in a hard breath.

His tongue laved over the wound, lapping up the blackened blood around the edges. It stained the spaces between his teeth. Then he opened his mouth wide and latched his lips onto the entire injury.

The suction felt as though he drew a silver thread from her toes to her groin to her heart, which stuttered mid-beat. Elise couldn't tear her eyes away as his mouth worked and his Adam's apple bobbed. His eyes burned as the whites swirled with shadow.

Her skin took color again. The weight lifted from her chest.

She gave a shuddering sigh as the last of the spikes drew from her ribs, receding into the wound, and then vanishing.

It only took a few minutes before he was drinking only blood, real blood, from her arm.

But Thom wasn't done. His lips traveled from the bite, still open and raw, to her shoulder. He licked a line along her collarbone, leaving a cool trail of moisture in its wake. His teeth briefly settled on the pulse in her throat.

Even with the haze of pain lifted, it took Elise a moment to realize what he was doing. She tried to pull her arm free of his grip.

He sighed into her throat. "I want to finish you so badly. The flesh of a kopis is sweet."

"You're done. Stop it." Thom released her, but didn't move from his position straddled across her legs. Elise was suddenly very aware that he was half-naked. His bare shoulders were smooth and warm under her hands. He had left a line of thin, pink blood up her arm when he licked her. "Get off of me."

"Suit yourself." The leather of his trousers creaked as he stood.

Elise got to her feet, wobbling on knees that couldn't quite seem to support her weight. She steadied herself with a hand on the wall.

He was still standing too close. "Back up," she said.

Thom smirked and took two steps away.

She finally left the hall to examine the place where Thom had taken them. It would have been a posh condo if it had had furniture. The living room was wide open, with tall windows that stared into the face of illuminated casinos. They were across the street from the downtown parking garage. In the mirrored city, the darkest gate stood on its roof. The sight gave her chills, so she turned from the window.

The only thing in the condo aside from Thom and Elise was a clay statue. It was shaped like a petite woman with a tiny waist and wide hips that tapered into a snake's tail, and her arms spread wide over a basin of sand.

Elise stepped around the statue to see its face. The eyes were empty, and the expression was peaceful. It was so lifelike.

Thom watched her approach the statue, like he was afraid she might break it. His steps matched hers as they circled the basin. "We have to go back," she said. "Yatai took Nukha'il. They're inside the city."

"You can't go back to the cavern."

"Just phase us through. I can handle it."

"I don't think you understand," Thom said. "The cave has collapsed. There is nowhere to go."

Her mouth fell open. "What? Then how…?"

"You can't save Nukha'il." Thom broke away to saunter to the window. His eyes were lidded and his lips were swollen, as though he and Elise had shared a passionate embrace. "A noble desire, I'm sure, but futile. The angel knew what he was doing. Don't mourn him."

"He's not dead," Elise said.

"Not surely, no. But very likely."

She clenched her fists. Nukha'il couldn't die—not that she cared about an *angel*, but he was Itra'il's only guardian; if she broke free of her long sleep, she would be dangerous.

Elise couldn't shake the mental image of Nukha'il trapped in the city. Alone against the darkest gate.

"I have to do *something*."

His eyebrow quirked. "I could take you directly into the ethereal city, if you wished it."

"No," she said immediately.

"Then he is subject to Yatai's mercies."

Elise paced, arms folded tight across her chest. "Okay," she said. "Fine. Let's do it." She moved for the hallway, but stopped when she saw Thom staring at his own hands. He didn't seem to have heard her speak. "What's wrong?"

He ran his hands down his chest. "You have weakened me," he said, as though this was a marvel. "I took your blood into myself and have become… less." He caught her expression. "Granted, when you are near-infinitely powerful, as I am, it is difficult to detect a modest change. But I know. I can tell."

"You were probably injured by the shadow."

Thom dismissed the suggestion with a wave of his hand. "Yatai can't hurt me." His eyes sharpened. "But you—you have wounded me."

In two long strides, Thom was in front of her. She couldn't move fast enough to get away.

132

He took her arm again and gazed at the wound. His pink tongue darted out to wet his lips.

"What if I ate you whole?"

Elise shook herself free. "Let's keep it academic."

She returned to the hallway to grab her falchion. She hadn't imagined Thom removing the shadow from the blade; it was shiny and clear, as though recently polished. Zohak had been consumed by the darkness, and he was a king among demons—so what the hell did Thom have to be in order to remove it from a sword, much less drink it down, without being hurt?

When Elise turned, he stood at her back. She hadn't heard him approach.

"What *are* you?"

His secretive smile was distinctly feline. "I am a demon. A very ancient demon. There is no word for my species, for I am almost one of a kind, and the roots from which all other demons on Earth spring. The Gray call me their father. The humans call me Satan. I am the serpent, I am temptation—and fortunately for you, I am your ally today."

"I don't understand."

"No," Thom said. "I expect you wouldn't." He extended a hand. "Are you ready?"

Elise sheathed her sword and nodded.

Thom wrapped his arm around her and touched the red stone dangling from the choker at his throat.

Nothing happened.

He blinked. It was the barest show of surprise, but given his usual blank features, he might as well have fallen over with shock.

"What is it?" she asked.

His brow furrowed.

"I can't phase."

133

James parked his car on the roof of the hospital's garage and checked his cell phone again. Nothing.

It had only been a couple of hours since he had picked up Stephanie's order for lab work and had the draw performed for his karyotype test. He knew from his not-infrequent hospital stays that even rush orders moved with all the urgency of a glacier, so it wasn't surprising. But impatience nagged at him.

James sat on the hood of his car as the engine ticked and cooled to watch the stars and wait.

It was a cold, clear night. There wasn't a single cloud in the sky. The forecast said there would be snow over Thanksgiving weekend, but for now, the stars were bright, his fingers were chilly, and he was much too wired to rest.

He took the Prophecies of Flynn from his back pocket, opening to the table of contents. His fingertip trailed over the section titled "Aspis." If there were prophecies about Elise's aspis—about *him*—then everything in that section would be about his future.

Did he want to know? Really?

All he had to do was locate page two hundred and thirty-six, and that gnawing curiosity would be satisfied.

"No," he said aloud. "That's a terrible idea."

He closed the cover.

Then he opened it again.

"Damn it," he muttered.

James started on the first page of prophecies.

The text was tiny, and riddled with codes and abbreviations that made no sense to him. He flipped to the back. There was no key.

He tried to read it anyway, but without understanding their acronyms, most of the lines were gibberish. The first paragraph of the introduction was half abbreviations such as "CEV" and half of Elise's biography, which he could tell by the dates. Her birthday was mentioned, as well as the date her parents had left her to pursue their own ambitions.

James soon found himself on page two hundred and thirty-six, which was marked with the "Aspis" header. It was the only time he was referenced in such impersonal terms. The rest of the time, his name was annotated as "JF."

He held his future in his hands—all the information that people weren't meant to know about themselves.

"No happiness will come of this," he said again.

He started reading anyway.

The entire first page was a disordered biography of James, and how he came to be Elise's aspis. Even knowing what they were talking about, it was still difficult to follow. There were massive gaps in the information, and the level of detail was, thankfully, very brief and disjointed. They had minimal information on his time with the coven in Colorado. They didn't seem to know about his connection to Elise's parents, either.

He turned to the second page. James stopped a quarter of the way down.

24 - Events precipitated by the birth of JF's offspring (V2:134:12) catastrophic; will lead to 'unraveling'—BFU.
25 - UP: RA - Explore destruction of offspring as PM.

He read that line again. *Events precipitated by the birth of JF's offspring.*

JF's offspring.

The line was embedded in observations about his studies of paper magic (lines sixteen through twenty-three) and the date the Union suspected that he and Elise bound as kopis and aspis (line twenty-six). Both of those had occurred well in the past.

SM Reine

"I don't *have* offspring," he said, as if that would change the words on the page.

His hand found his cell phone. Stephanie was on speed dial as number three.

"Hello, darling," she answered curtly. "Can I help you?"

"I was wondering if…" He trailed off. Cleared his throat. "Did you get the blood work?"

"Not yet. Darling."

Alarms squealed in the background of the call. That was never a good sign. Common sense told him to hang up, but now that he had her on the line, he had to ask. "I have a strange question."

"Stranger than wanting a karyotype test?"

"I suppose not." He hesitated. "Are you… pregnant?"

Stephanie gave a short laugh. "You have developed a strange sense of humor, my love. No. And if such a thing were to happen between my IUD and the condoms, it would likelier be the son of God than yours." Her voice softened a barest fraction. "If you would like to have children, I'm happy to have that conversation in the morning, when two of my patients are not coding. Is there something *actually* important I can help you with?"

He forced himself to laugh, too. "Sorry, Stephanie. I didn't mean to bother you."

"Okay. Talk to you later. Kisses."

"Yes," he said faintly, and he hung up.

Line twenty-three seemed bigger than all the other lines on the page, as if it was bolded and enlarged with flashing arrows aimed at it. *JF's offspring.* His eyes dropped to the next line. *Explore destruction of offspring.*

And to think that James had believed the Union might have friendly intentions.

136

He closed the book, returned it to his pocket, and fully intended on getting in his car to leave. But he didn't move.

Instead, he picked up his cell phone again and scrolled through the contact list. He was meticulous about keeping his contact information intact over the years, even when he and Elise had been living out of one backpack between the two of them, so he still had the phone numbers for his former high priest and priestess. He still had the phone number for his friend, Grant, who he hadn't spoken to in about seven years.

He also had the contact information for his ex-fiancée, Hannah Pritchard.

Before he could think too much about it, James hit the button to dial her number. He wasn't sure if he was relieved or not when it turned out to be the number for a pizza delivery place in Boulder, which was, unsurprisingly, closed for business after midnight.

After hanging up, he double-checked his contacts. James hadn't spoken to Hannah in so long that he didn't have her email address, but he did have an email for the high priestess of the coven.

James drafted a short message on his Blackberry with a subject line that said "ATTN: Hannah," and hit send.

VIII

Elise paced the length of the manager's office in Craven's with an unlit cigarette between her first two fingers. She had been trying to call Anthony for an hour and hadn't gotten a response.

When she got his voicemail again, she flung her cell phone to the desk. The back popped off. "Goddamn it," she growled, patting her pockets for a lighter.

Neuma hurried in, wearing a baggy t-shirt over her leather stripper gear, which made her look like she had just rolled out of bed. Considering that her idea of breakfast involved an hour of messy sex, she probably had. "What's wrong, doll?"

"Nothing," Elise said reflexively. She immediately amended it to, "Everything. I need you to get two teams together—one prepared to excavate a collapsed cave, and another with very bright lights and big guns to help me comb the Warrens."

"Diggers and a search party. Right. Big teams?"

"As big as you can get, and as fast as possible."

"Will do." The half-succubus frowned. Her plump lips made the expression seem more like a pout. "Only problem is, the sun's rising. We've pretty much only got whoever's in Craven's right now."

"Then shut down the casino and get everyone equipped. Have Lock's hardware store send us what we need—he owes us. They're late on last month's tithe."

"We'll lose a lot of money if we shut down." At Elise's look, Neuma's held up her hands in surrender. "All right, all right." She tucked the shift schedule for Craven's under her arm and began searching the filing cabinet. "It's going to suck getting anyone to volunteer, though—the last two never came back from dumping Zohak."

"They ran away?"

"No, I mean, they went missing." She pulled a Rolodex of phone numbers out of the drawer and perched herself by the desk phone. "Them, and the guy I sent searching for them. He called me to say he found tire tracks before his phone died. I think someone snatched them."

Elise didn't have time to worry about three employees. They were just demons anyway. "I don't care what it takes to get people moving. Bribe them, threaten them, whatever. Are you calling Lock?" Neuma nodded, pinning the phone against her shoulder. "Ask him to bring his guys with the equipment. We can use the extra help digging."

"Will do. What are we looking for when we get down there?"

She spotted a lighter that had been hiding under the Rolodex and took it. "Anthony. My boyfriend got lost in the Warrens."

Neuma blinked those heavily lashed eyes. "Oh, no, he didn't."

Her thumb paused on the igniter. "What?"

"I saw him pass through Eloquent Blood a couple of hours ago. I asked what was up, and he said he was going home." Her smile faltered. She covered the receiver with a hand. "That's not good news?"

Elise lit the cigarette and took a very long drag. It wasn't enough to calm her down.

"I still need the diggers," she said, flicking the ash into the tray and heading for the door. "As fast as you can."

SM Reine

Outside, the morning seemed darker and colder than it should have been, and Elise didn't think it was because the nights had become so long.

Anthony went home?

She dropped her cigarette in the can outside the door to her apartment building before racing upstairs.

Elise slammed into the living room. Even with the curtains open and the eggshell walls, it felt like the sun had to fight to brighten the furnished apartment she shared with Anthony. It was always dim and gloomy—always. And aside from their combined laundry spread across the floor and the dirty dishes covering the counter, it was also completely empty.

"Anthony?" she called, checking the bathroom. Empty.

Elise stormed into the bedroom.

The door bounced off the wall when she opened it, rattling in the frame, but her boyfriend didn't wake up. He was in bed, sheets tangled around his hips, with a very distinct snore coming from his mouth.

Sleeping.

The urge to rip him out of bed was overwhelming. She tightened her hand on the molding by the door until the wood creaked.

Part of her had thought—had hoped—that Neuma was lying. Anthony would never have gone home instead of following her into a fight. It was cowardice.

But there he was. Sleeping.

She left the bedroom door open and wore a path in the carpet between the kitchen and the bathroom door, arms folded tightly across her chest. The light through their window, which was barred on the outside, didn't seem to pass through the doorway. She could barely make out Anthony's shirtless form in bed.

He flipped over without waking up. His hand flexed, and relaxed.

Anthony had been having nightmares. He told Elise about them, once. He said that he was dreaming about the gateway, and the things he had seen on the other side—the things that had happened to him when Elise and James were fighting Mr. Black. She didn't want to know about it. That conversation had a way of spiraling inevitably back to Betty.

Elise kicked a pair of jeans out of her path and turned, walking back to the other wall again.

Was his fear of the city really enough to make him run? After everything they had done together? Zombies, stealing a semi from a dozen guys with submachine guns, facing down the Union…

She really wanted a smoke.

As if her thoughts disturbed him, he rolled over again and flung an arm off the side of the bed. His chest was soaked in sweat. His hair was plastered to his forehead.

She tore open the knife drawer. Contemplated the paring knives. Slammed it shut again.

After weeks of exploring the higher levels of the Warrens together, there was no way he could have gotten lost. He must have been *trying* to run. To escape the fight.

And while he slept, Nukha'il was at Yatai's mercy in the ethereal city.

The heat in her gut grew until she couldn't contain it anymore. Elise stalked into the room and flung open the drapes. Feeble yellow sun splashed over the bed. "Get up." Anthony mumbled and pulled the pillow over his face. She jerked the sheets off of him, and he pulled his knees to his chest reflexively. "Hey! I told you to get up!"

Anthony peered at her from under the pillow, eyelids puffy and his eyes red. "What?"

141

Elise swept his jeans and shirt off the floor and flung them at him. "Get out of bed. Get dressed. And get out of my apartment."

He sat up slowly. "Elise…"

"You heard me!"

He put one foot in his jeans, and then the other, pulling them to his knees. "Are you…kicking me out?" he asked, and his voice was suddenly very clear. Tension corded his shoulders.

Was she kicking him out? Elise almost laughed.

She slammed out of the bedroom to the kitchen. The apartment was too small. The walls were too close, the roof was too low—everything was too goddamn *dark*. Elise began stuffing things into a backpack without thinking about it—the daggers she had laid out on the kitchen table for sharpening, her charms, a couple of old photos from the walls.

Anthony stumbled into the doorway, jeans unbelted and shirt hanging from his hands. "I think the stress is getting to you."

"Stress isn't getting to me," Elise snapped. "*You're* getting to me."

"Excuse me?"

"The Warrens. Last night. Why did you run away?"

He looked puzzled. "I didn't run. I got lost."

"Look, Anthony, I've got one job that matters in this territory—just one damn job. I have to protect the gate. I promised the ethereal and infernal delegations that I could handle it. And what happens the first time the gate is threatened? You get *lost*."

His eyes widened, and his mouth worked soundlessly. It took him a good ten seconds to find words. "It was dark."

Was there anything else Elise wanted out of that shithole? She couldn't lay any claim to the furniture. Everything belonged to the landlord, from the couches to the television. The plates belonged to Anthony—he could keep them. All she had were clothes and weapons and the bicycle that was chained outside.

That was all that remained of her life.

"You know what? Don't bother leaving." She leaned into the bedroom to grab a handful of clothes out of her drawer and jam them into her backpack. She forced the zipper closed. "I'm sick of this place anyway."

Anthony reached the door first. He slammed his hand into it to keep her from escaping. "You can't seriously be angry at me for what happened last night. Come on, Elise, you're—"

"You don't know *anything* about what I feel!"

Her own volume shocked her. The shout tore from her chest, ragged and harsh. She faltered. Almost dropped the backpack.

So many emotions roiled inside of her. Guilt at what had happened to Nukha'il—an angel who had no choice but to obey her every word. Fear at what would happen if the darkness got inside the gateway. Longing for James's company. Anger at Anthony for screwing up her plans. And all of it knotted into her intestines, gripping her and rocking her and making her eyes burn.

"Wait," Anthony said. He laughed mirthlessly. "Are *you* trying to break up with *me*?" The look on her face made his laughter abruptly cut off. "Jesus. You don't think of it as breaking up, do you? You don't even think of me as your fucking boyfriend. We've lived together for two months. We've been dating for half a *year*…"

"You are my boyfriend, Anthony." After a beat, she added, "You *were*."

"You know what? Good. I'm so sick of putting up with your bullshit—treating me like I'm some kind of asset, like I'm

143

another demon at your goddamn casino. You only want me because I can fire a shotgun. I didn't want to leave because I had nowhere to go. But now I don't have to worry about it."

He sat on the couch. And then he smiled.

The corner of a white book caught Elise's eye, peeking out from under the couch. It was Betty's wedding album.

She scooped it off the floor and headed for the door.

Anthony's footsteps thudded behind her as he vaulted over the table to slam his hand into the door, shutting it again before she could get into the hallway.

"The hell do you think you're doing, Elise? That's mine."

"It's Betty's." He grabbed it, but she didn't let go.

"And I'm her cousin."

Bitterness spiked through her heart. "They didn't ask you to spread her ashes, did they?"

The hurt in his eyes was worth it. His fingers slipped. But it only made him fight harder for the album, and Elise had to drop her backpack to keep her grip.

She won the fight, but he stepped between her and the hall. "Betty would have been disappointed in you," Anthony spat. "She thought you were a hero. She thought—"

Elise lifted the album. "Don't you speak another word."

He fell silent, hand outstretched as though he expected her to throw it.

She opened the cover and removed her favorite picture— a photo of Betty in her wedding dress with a long train and white flowers in her hair—then shoved the book into his chest.

"Don't come to Craven's again," she said, shoving the picture in her back pocket. "I'm done with you."

He didn't stop her when she flung the door open again. Elise shouldered her backpack and marched to the elevator, down the stairs, and into the harsh light of early morning.

A shadow passed over the sidewalk.

Elise didn't think anything of it, at first. It only temporarily dimmed the sun. The breeze that followed was chilly enough to penetrate the foulest of moods, so she hugged herself tighter and quickened her pace. She kept expecting to hear Anthony calling after her, and she wasn't sure she could keep it together if he caught up with her—her temper was too short, exhaustion dragged too heavily on her, and she desperately wanted to crack some skulls.

Sunlight crossed her path again, and then faded. She punched the button for the crosswalk and squinted up at the sun.

But there was no sun. There were no clouds, either.

Something massive and gray filled the air, like a lens a shade darker than the sky had slid over the city. It shimmered and pulsed.

The traffic light changed to allow her to cross the street, but Elise didn't move.

Whatever was in the air darkened again—just a fraction. She glimpsed a street paved with white stone. She saw what looked like the roof of her apartment building, too, as though it had been reflected on the air.

And she thought she saw a tall white gateway.

As soon as Elise realized what she was seeing, it was gone again.

The sky was blue. The sun was climbing over the hills, rapidly warming the day and making the ice turn to steam as it melted.

But there was no mistaking what she had seen: a mirror image of downtown Reno, inverted so that the tops of the buildings reached for one another.

Elise glanced around, but nobody else seemed to have noticed. A man in a white tank top, oblivious to the cold, jogged past with his pit bull trailing behind him. A car cut a

SM Reine

turn too close and bumped over the opposite sidewalk, making a woman shout and wave her fist. The other cars moved along totally undisturbed. People were too absorbed in their lives to notice that anything had gone awry.

Maybe she had imagined it. Maybe it was the stress.

Then her gaze met with that of a man sitting in a parking lot on the other side of the fence. He had a sign that said "lost my job, please help," a shopping cart piled with trash bags, and wide eyes filled with fright.

"Jesus Christ," he said. "Did you see that?"

The glorious moment where Elise hoped that she was going crazy was instantly shattered.

For a few seconds—a few utterly impossible, mind-breaking seconds—the ethereal city, and its entire parallel dimension, had faded into view above Reno.

The manager's office was empty when Elise arrived. She kicked the enchanted closet door. "Let me in!"

The hinges whined with annoyance as it opened. Elise ducked in, removed the trash bag that encased her falchion's twin, and shut the door again. She ripped open the garbage bag before she could think too much about what she was doing.

What lay inside was not the falchion that Elise had tenderly cared for all those years. The ichor had eaten into the metal, coalesced, and hardened; the blade had become the same material as Zohak's skin, like shining obsidian. The symbols she had carved into it as a teenager were distorted.

Elise swallowed hard before removing it from the bag.

What used to be leather wrappings around the hilt had crumbled into dust. It felt strange in her hand, but it had a good heft to it, and the edge looked sharp enough. She didn't dare test it.

146

The falchion felt wrong to her demonic sense, like the chime of a cracked bell, but it was exactly what Elise wanted. She couldn't use her other sword, or any other weapon, against Yatai's legions—not unless she wanted them to turn into obsidian, too. But she could use her possessed sword against them.

Carefully—very carefully—she sheathed the obsidian blade in her spine scabbard beside its twin. It was thicker than it used to be, and it took some wiggling to fit it in properly. Then she pulled the jacket over her shoulders and flipped her hair out of the collar to cover the hilts.

Elise bumped into a girl on her way down the stairs.

"Hey!" The girl looked familiar, but she wasn't wearing a Craven's uniform—not the tie and vest of a dealer, nor the ridiculously short skirt of a cocktail waitress. She also obviously wasn't a stripper. She was much too ugly.

Elise slowed on the stairs. "What are you doing here?"

"I'm looking for where you guys store the uniforms. Neuma said she'd give me a job."

She blinked, trying to put a name to the face. She finally recalled the tunnels beneath Rick's Drugstore. "Jerica. Right?"

The nightmare rolled her eyes. "How nice to see that I made an impression."

"Uniforms are in the break room," Elise said. "Stay out of my office." She hurried down the stairs, and Jerica remained at the top.

"I wanted to say thanks!" she yelled, but Elise had already sprinted across the casino floor and into the daylight.

A few blocks away at St. Mary's Hospital, James's phone chimed. He sat up from the couch in Stephanie's office. His

Blackberry was on her windowsill all the way across the room. The screen illuminated, and then dimmed.

That sound meant he had an email.

James had been resting ever since Stephanie had found him pacing the halls in the emergency room and shuttled him into her office, but his mind was moving too fast for him to truly relax. The sugar-free gelatin he had bought at the hospital cafeteria wasn't sitting well, and that beep from his Blackberry made his stomach pitch. He thought he might throw up.

He stood, adjusted his clothes, checked the buttons on his shirt, and smoothed down his hair. He double-checked to make sure everything was in his pockets—the Book of Shadows he had been carrying for weeks, the keys to Motion and Dance, and a pack of cinnamon-flavored gum. Then he adjusted his buttons again.

The phone chimed helpfully to remind him that he still had a new email.

The distance between the couch and window couldn't have been more than ten feet, but it felt like it took ten minutes for him to get there. James hesitated with his hand over the cell phone. There was a strange rushing sound in his ears. His head felt light.

The mail icon was blinking.

He swallowed hard and picked up the phone.

Before he could unlock it, the Blackberry vibrated in his hand, and Elise's name lit up on the screen. The first bar of "Für Elise" tinkled over the speaker.

He deflated, sagging against the windowsill and bumping his forehead against the glass. James gave his heart a few seconds to slow before lifting the phone to his ear. "Hello?"

"Where are you?" Elise sounded out of breath.

"St. Mary's. What…?"

"Good. I need you to meet me at the Shell station, the one on Sierra. I think we've—"

The line went silent.

"Elise?" he asked.

James checked the screen. She hadn't hung up on him; there was an "x" where the bars indicating his signal strength should have been.

He swore under his breath and moved into the hallway, lifting his phone to search for the network.

He bumped into Stephanie when he passed through the door. Her strawberry-blond hair was loose around her shoulders, and she chewed on her ponytail holder in the corner of her mouth. She only did that when she was really absorbed—like when she was losing to James at a game of Scrabble, or when she was worrying about one of her patients.

She waved the lab sheet. "You're still here! Good. I have your results."

It took him a moment to remember what results, exactly, she could be talking about. "Oh. Excellent. Could I borrow your cell phone?"

"Don't you want to know what I found?" she asked, handing her smart phone to him.

"Of course. In a minute. My phone died in the middle of a call, and I think it was important." James dialed Elise's phone number from memory and pressed the button, but the call didn't connect. Stephanie didn't have any reception, either.

"Your results are a lot more interesting than I expected," she said, resuming her chewing. "Did you know—?"

"Myostatin deficiency?" he asked, tucking her phone in the pocket of her lab coat again.

The hair tie fell out of her mouth. "Yes. Exactly. How long have you known about that?"

149

SM Reine

"Roughly three seconds," James said. He held his cell phone over his head and paced to the end of the hall. Still no reception, although his email had already been downloaded, and the icon was blinking persistently. "I need to step outside."

Stephanie followed. "What's going on? Is there something you're not telling me?"

"Yes. A great many things, as a matter of fact. I'll see you at home."

He dropped a kiss on her protesting lips, took the stairs to street level, and jogged across the parking lot.

Elise was waiting at the gas station, holding her cell phone over head the same way that James had a few minutes before. As he grew closer, he began hearing her thoughts as a rapid-fire undertone. Her brain was filled with a hum of distress.

City's here…Anthony…Goddamn it, Yatai…

She spoke aloud. "Do you have any reception?"

"No. I think the network must be down."

"I think I know why that is." Elise pointed at the roof of a casino.

"Because of the Eldorado?"

She made an irritated noise. "No. *Look.*"

He scanned the sky. He still didn't see anything. But then he thought of the myostatin deficiency, and the way Elise had begun to see magic in the same way that he did, and he stopped trying to see with his eyes.

James relaxed and stretched out his senses.

Opening himself made it impossible to tune out Elise, but she was focusing on the same thing he was, so it only amplified the new sense he had recently acquired—the one that could feel the proximity of infernal and ethereal powers. And there *was* something in the sky over the casino. It made his palms itch.

"What *is* that?" he asked.

Her mouth was drawn into a grim line. "It's something bad. Really bad."

As if on cue, the sign for the Shell station buzzed and went out.

James jumped, despite himself. The lights inside the station had turned off, as well, and a trucker who had been trying to fill his semi shouted as the pump failed.

Brakes squealed behind them, and there was a loud *crunch* as two cars at the intersection connected. One of them had been making a left turn onto the street. The other had tried to progress through the light at the same time, and they had collided.

The stoplight wasn't working.

"No," Elise said, running to the sidewalk, "no, no, no—"

What could disable the cell phone network and the power grid at the same time? It had to be the same thing that had his palms itching—a powerful ethereal presence, such as the one that would be suspended over downtown Reno.

All at once, the signs along the street turned off, and the traffic signals followed.

The honking of car horns filled the air. People began stepping out of buildings onto the sidewalk, staring around in bemusement at the perfectly clear day.

"This isn't right. This can't be caused by angels." Elise showed her cell phone to him. It still had power. James felt a small jolt of surprise to see that her wallpaper was an old photo of them dancing together at a competition. "Angels disable electrical devices. We should have lost power to our phones before losing reception."

"But the ruins—"

"That's a different problem. I don't know what this is."

A man behind them spoke. "I believe I can take you to the ethereal city now."

151

James spun. The man standing behind them had long hair sleeked into a ponytail, flawless skin, and a white formal suit that was unbuttoned at the throat to reveal a ruby choker. His eyes were entirely consumed by black, from the irises to the sclera.

Elise didn't register surprise at seeing Thom Norrel waiting for them, but James felt an unpleasant lurch. She spoke first. "What's changed? Why can you phase now, if you couldn't earlier?"

"The barrier between dimensions is thinning."

She extended a hand. "Fine. Great. I'm ready to go when you are."

"Does someone want to tell me what the hell is going on?" James asked, stepping forward before Thom could give her his arm.

"An extremely powerful demon has gotten into the ethereal city," Elise said, moving around him. Thom took her gloved hand in his. "And she has an angel."

"I'm coming with you," James said, seizing her opposite wrist.

"James…" she began.

She didn't get to finish.

"Prepare yourselves," Thom said.

He shifted his weight to the side, stepped off the sidewalk, and disappeared from the dimension.

IX

Thom blinked them back into reality about three hundred feet above the street.

For an instant, they hung on the glimmering edge between Reno and the ruins. Elise had a heartbeat to realize that they had entered the ethereal city in midair, on the same level as the highest floor of the tallest casino, which was followed immediately by the second realization that the formerly bone-white streets were rotting beneath her. Ichor was slicked over the surface, and the stones crumbled into dust.

Then they began to fall.

The hotel tower blurred as they rushed through the air, and the roofs were suddenly *right there* and they were going to hit—

Thom's arm tightened around her. Elise squeezed James's hand.

She blinked.

Cobblestone connected with her knees, but it was from a fall of inches rather than hundreds of feet. The shock of the impact rocked through her legs and up her spine. Elise gave a sharp cry.

Her abs clenched, her back muscles strained, and what little remained in her stomach burned up her throat. She spit a few drops of bile onto the ground with pink-tinged saliva. It had been hours since Elise had eaten—she didn't have anything left to throw up, and it hurt to try.

Her stomach quickly settled. She rolled onto her back with a groan.

Vertigo rushed over Elise as she saw the streets of Reno inverted over her head. Everything seemed serene through the shimmering veil between dimensions. There was no way to tell that the power had failed, aside from the clogged intersections. She could barely pick out the car accident they had left behind.

She sat up and wiped her mouth clean. Thom's second jump had dropped them by the gas station's mirror image, one block from the north edge of the ruins, where gray void severed the bridge over the freeway.

The last few yards weren't made of the same white cobblestone as the rest of the street anymore. They had been devoured by shadow, and the edge of the gas station rotted, sending black ash swirling into the air. The ground was stable and untouched beneath her knees, but the line of darkness was inching—slowly but surely—in their direction.

Beside her, James was also throwing up. His vomit was red. Fear hit Elise like a punch to the gut, and she crawled to his side. "Are you okay?"

"I'm fine," he rasped, wiping his mouth with the back of his hand.

"The blood—"

James looked embarrassed. "I ate a Jell-O cup at the hospital."

Thom seized her arm and hauled her to her feet. Her pulse quickened at his touch. "What are you doing?" she demanded, twisting out of his grip.

"Look."

He pointed to the buildings surrounding them. Heavenly light had once filled every inch of the ruins, keeping the insides of each building as bright as the streets, but the empty windows were dim. Not even a hundred feet away, the mirror of the hospital was crumbling. Its supports were exposed, the foundation was sinking, and the grass was dead.

And there were shapes moving in the shadows of its towers—not only Zohak's possessed fiends, but more humanoid forms, too. Nightmares, basandere, incubi. Demons that Yatai had taken from under Elise without her noticing.

"Shit," she breathed.

Where could they run? The street was rotting only a block away. Everywhere else was void.

"The sewers," Thom said. "Go!"

James didn't wait to be told twice. He jammed his fingers into the holes on the manhole cover, levered it open, and set it aside as easily as he might have moved a skillet. The shaft that opened into the sewers was the same bone-white material as the street.

"Elise?" he asked, poised over the hole.

The line of fiends swept toward them, and Elise moved between them and the sewer. "I'm right behind you, James."

He threw his legs over the side and dropped.

Elise drew the obsidian sword. Its blackened blade was a fraction heavier than its twin, making her feel strange and unbalanced.

The nearest fiend rushed her, and she swung. The possessed blade cleaved right through it. A halo of dark energy rippled through the air, and the fiend splashed to the ground in two pieces, like a water balloon sliced in half.

Ichor gushed over the sidewalk. Elise had to jump back to keep her feet from getting hit.

"I never should have come here," she grunted, impaling another demon. "There's no way to get through the city. Yatai's already taken the whole thing."

Thom whirled and darted over the street. His bare feet touched Yatai's ichor and came away unscathed. "Not the gates. Not yet."

He slammed his hand into the mouth of a fiend. It gagged. He jerked its slimy tongue out of its mouth, and she plunged her sword into its eye to finish the job.

"Where is Yatai?"

He caught the last nightmare standing by the throat and twisted. Its head popped off. Shadow splashed over his hands. "The cathedral."

St. Thomas of Aquinas Cathedral was several blocks south of their position—and there were a lot of fiends and shadow between them.

Elise nodded, clenching her jaw. "Okay, let's go."

"I've already faced the serpent and drank her venom today. I won't be with you."

"What? Then how am I supposed to get home?"

"Take this." He tossed her a ribbon. A ruby matching the one on his choker dangled from the end. "When you reach Nukha'il—if you survive—speak my true name, and I will get you back to Reno."

She shoved it into her pocket. "What's your true name?"

The corner of his mouth twitched. "Yatam."

Yatam?

A second wave of demons scrabbled toward them, emerging from the depths of a casino's rotten husk.

Thom shoved her. She lost her footing and slipped into the open manhole.

Her elbow smacked into the edge as she fell, wrenching her arm over her head.

She tried to catch the ladder. Slipped.

She landed on a soft body—James.

Her momentum carried them both to the ground. They splashed into water at the bottom of the sewer.

The shock of hitting the ground wasn't as terrible as the shock of her body being pressed fully against his. The flimsy barrier between their minds evaporated at the contact, and everything Elise had been struggling to avoid for weeks crashed over her.

Betty with a gunshot wound in her forehead.

The funeral. Her sobbing family.

Carrying the box of ashes through the forest at Lake Tahoe.

Holding McIntyre's premature newborn at the hospital. The way Anthony had looked when she told him that she was incapable of having children.

James strolling through an orchard hand-in-hand with Stephanie, talking about marriage.

Elise gave a cry and scrambled away from him, pressing her back into the wall. He reached toward her, concern rippling through the bond, but she held up a hand to stop him. "Don't touch me!"

He froze. "Sorry."

She shut her eyes and took a few deep breaths, trying to compose herself.

Betty's face floated behind her eyelids. Not the way she used to look, slathered in lip gloss and smiling impishly, but the way she looked after she got shot. A trickle of blood down the bridge of her nose. Slack face. Colorless lips.

James hovered over Elise, hand hesitantly outstretched. She shoved him. "What the hell were you thinking, following me to the ruins?"

"I came to help you."

"You can't help me. And I can't fight with you in my head."

"But I've made a solution for that." He took a box out of his pocket. The corner was dinged, and magic seeped out of the gap. James gingerly lifted a pair of rings from the box, and Elise flinched. They were bright—too bright. "I designed the charms

157

on these. They're wards." James pocketed the box. "This one should be your size, I hope."

"What does it do?" she asked.

His response was to hold the ring out.

Elise hesitated before removing her leather glove. There was nothing underneath to protect her palm, and the symbol was raised and irritated.

James slipped the ring over her middle finger. It was too big. "Damn. I used some of the jewelry you left at the studio to size it—I was so sure it would fit."

"I've lost weight." She put it on her left thumb instead.

As soon as the smooth metal slid over her skin, the tunnel blurred, and her head spun. Everything was a little bit darker when her vision cleared. The world had fewer colors. She lifted her hand to stare at the ring, but its radiance was gone.

She couldn't see magic anymore.

Then James put the matching ring on. It was sized to fit the first finger on his right hand.

An invisible barrier smashed between them, cutting off the undercurrent of his thoughts and lifting a weight from her gut.

He vanished from her mind. She was blind, deaf, and alone.

"There," James said, looking winded. "Normal again. Well, as normal as we could ever be."

Elise turned around in the middle of the tunnel, trying to orient herself among the gleaming white stones. Everything looked different without the gleam of magic. "Good," she said, but she wasn't sure she meant it.

Above their heads, Yatai's ichor had consumed the manhole cover. It oozed around the edges and dribbled down the walls in thin lines. The sewers might have been untouched, but it wouldn't last long.

"We should hurry," James said, but she didn't immediately move.

"You know, manhole covers are heavy. They probably weigh as much as I do. You lifted that pretty easily."

"I suppose I did." He sighed. "I just had Stephanie run blood work for me. It looks like I've developed a myostatin deficiency. You aren't the only one who's changing with this bond."

Elise frowned, and irritation plucked at the back of her neck with icy fingers. What did that mean? Would he become as strong as she was?

"We'll have to arm wrestle," she said.

"Now?"

"No. When we're not in mortal peril." Elise squinted at the dripping ichor. Beyond it, she could no longer feel Thom's presence. Gone? Or dead? Only one way to find out. "Which way is the cathedral?"

"East." James pointed down the tunnel.

They started walking.

The ethereal sewers were almost beautiful. There was almost no trace of the real Reno in the tunnels—it was pure angelic architecture, from the white stone to the graceful arches embedded with silvery-gray symbols. The walls were carved with murals.

"Seems the builders got carried away," James said as they splashed through crystalline water that had puddled over an etching of an angel. They stuck to the side of the tunnel. Part of the wall was missing, and void yawned on the other side.

She hesitated over the etching. "Why would they put so much effort into a place that nobody would ever see?"

"Angels." He shrugged. "Perfectionist bastards."

She narrowed her eyes at him. Even when she focused, she couldn't hear his thoughts. The rings were good. "When we

159

SM Reine

get to the cathedral, I want you to wait for me in the sewers. I'll get Nukha'il and come back for you."

"Why? I followed you because I wanted to help," James said.

She gaped at him, unable to respond.

Help? He wanted to *help*?

She whirled without responding and stalked down the tunnel, mentally counting the arches that marked each block on the surface. After a beat, she heard James's splashing footsteps following her.

"How are we ever supposed to get through this if you walk away every time I try to talk to you?"

Elise shot a look at him. "What do you want? Really?"

The question seemed to startle James. He blinked. "Well, the rings take care of our bonding issue, so… I hoped it meant things could go back to normal."

"Normal?" She gave a mirthless laugh. "No, James. We can't be normal again. There isn't enough magic in the world to make things *normal* again." Her words came out a sharper than she intended. "You know what I did on Labor Day weekend?"

He blinked at the change in subject. "No."

"I went to Lake Tahoe. Betty never liked paying the fee for Sand Harbor—said it was too busy and overpriced. So we used to go to this… God, this really awful pile of rocks. There was nowhere to stretch out. But Betty would bring cranberry juice and vodka so we could drink warm cosmos out of plastic cups." A laugh jolted from her chest. "The last time we went, we got lost trying to climb out again. We had to swim through that icy water to Sand Harbor anyway."

She turned the corner. There was a ladder at the end. Judging by the way her palms ached, the cathedral was close.

160

"So that's where I went on Labor Day. I took Betty's remains to the lake, and I left her there. Those awful rocks. Her dad asked me to do it. They gave the urn to me and…"

Elise couldn't speak anymore. James touched her arm, but she pushed him away—probably harder than she needed to.

"I miss Betty, too," he said softly. "The esbats aren't the same—not without Betty, and not without you."

She fixed him with a hard stare. "*That* was normal life. Betty's the one who got me through college. She made me sunbathe in our front yard and dance with strangers at bars, just because it was fun. When everything was shit, Betty was still sunshine. She made me laugh, James."

"It's okay to grieve." He raked a hand through his hair. "There are other reasons to laugh."

"God, James, what's the point? My choices killed my best friend, and all I can think since then is…" She clenched her fists. "You know what? Everyone dies. I'm so sick of this— these *emotions*. I'm sick of being sad, of being in pain, of being lonely, of having to fight all the time just to survive—"

"Then why keep fighting?"

She threw her hands into the air. "What else am I supposed to do? Roll over and die?"

"If the Union took control of the city—"

Elise cut him off. "*What?*"

Deadly silence filled the air between them.

James continued, more tentative than before. "I know that the Union's been trying to get a foothold in America. Maybe—well, perhaps there's some merit to that. Think about it. I'm sure the Union could defend the territory. They have more resources and manpower than we could ever muster."

Elise stared at him, mouth hanging open.

It was almost the exact same bullshit propaganda the Union had spewed at the semi-centennial summit.

Why the hell was *James* saying it? He knew how she felt about them.

Her jaw clapped shut. "Fuck the Union."

Conversation over.

Elise scaled the ladder, swift as a spider monkey, and left James no choice but to follow.

They emerged behind the church. Roiling clouds filled the air, blotting out what little ethereal light remained in the city. It smelled like the entire world was on fire, and Elise had to cover her face with her sleeve to keep from coughing.

The cathedral was a lone light among the crumbling black buildings. A heavy black cloud swarmed its steeple, but the glossy white bricks were untouched. The shadows rippled where holy ground met street, unable to move forward.

Elise jumped from the manhole to a clear patch of pavement. James grunted behind her as he jumped.

They were the only living things in sight as they jogged across the parking lot. What used to be the Santa Fe Hotel down the street was now nothing but a crumbling mess of obsidian. The concrete holding up the traffic lights had crumbled, and the metal poles crossed the intersection, broken in their fall.

But the church remained a radiating beacon of light among the darkness. The walls stood strong. Only the roof had crumbled away, and she could make out the apex of the stone gateway inside.

She stuck close to the wall as she moved around to the front doors. Her hands burned as she approached the entrance.

On Earth, the tall doors to the cathedral were made of bronze, but they had been formed of shimmering gold in the ruins. Each panel was carved with an image of a different archangel—from Metaraon, with his unmerciful stare, to the sad eyes of the angel of death on the far left. Samael.

Elise reached up to touch the carving of his face. His peaceful, *human* face.

The door buzzed under her hand. She swallowed hard and shoved it open.

The pews were carved of the same glossy white bone as the graceful arch of the gateway. There was no sign of Yatai. No shadow creeping over the floor, no giant serpent, and none of her legion of possessed demons.

But they weren't alone in the church. Through the shimmering air beneath the arch, Elise could see the altar—and the body that lay upon it.

Nukha'il was stripped naked and stretched out on the cross, his wings pinned to the wall by spikes of obsidian. Ichor oozed from the wounds, crept over his feathers, and turned them to stone one by one. Each feather made a tiny *crack* as it broke off and shattered on the floor, like icicles falling off of tree branches.

His eyes were closed. She couldn't see him breathing.

Her heart ached. "Nukha'il," she said. She didn't have to raise her voice for him to hear her. His eyelids fluttered.

"You made it," said a high, girlish voice.

A child stepped out of the confessional. She wore her Sunday best—white stockings, saddle shoes, and a prim dress that covered her to the knees. Brunette hair fell around her shoulders. Wide red lips—the same crimson color as the Thorn's ruby—curved into a wicked smile.

She didn't have any eyes. There was nothing beyond the frame of eyelashes but the vastness of space.

Elise recognized that face. The last time she had seen the girl, she was possessed by Death's Hand and covered in black marks. Her name was Lucinde, and Elise had failed to save her.

She drew the obsidian-bladed falchion. "Yatai."

Exorcist, the girl responded without moving her lips. She gave a tiny curtsy.

Elise lunged, bringing the sword down on the child—

And the blade swept through empty air.

Yatai stood a few feet away, though she hadn't moved an inch.

You're too late. The deed is done. She swept a tiny, fragile-boned hand toward the altar. *I didn't have enough marks to open the gate, but it will surely open when his brethren retrieve his body. Angels are so protective of their own.* She smiled at James, baring white teeth. *Aren't they, witch?*

"If you pass through the gate to Heaven, it will violate the Treaty. It could destroy the world," Elise said. "Everyone will die. *Everyone.*"

The smile was frozen on Lucinde's face. *And may God have mercy on every soul.*

She vanished.

"Oh, hell," James said.

Elise didn't wait. She sheathed her sword and ran at the gate.

She vaulted over the pews and jumped onto the nearest pillar, wedged tight against the wall. Grabbing the ethereal stone was like seizing an electric fence. Her bones shook and her teeth strained against the gums. Her skull ached. Her vertebrae tried to pull apart.

Elise scrambled over the top and dropped to the other side.

"Elise!" James's voice was distorted as it passed through the gray veil of the gate.

"I'm fine," she said, scrambling to her knees, "I'm fine!" Blood seeped through the wrist of her glove. She wiped it off on her jeans before rushing to Nukha'il's side at the altar.

It was worse seeing the damage up close. Yatai hadn't just driven spikes through his wings. She had pierced his ankles, his palms, and sliced open his forehead. Stigmata trickled down his cheeks.

Her eyes narrowed as she studied the spikes driven through his flesh. They were like jagged shards of crystal, and the bite wound on her arm throbbed with sympathy. How could she remove them without getting infected?

She struck one with the hilt of the possessed falchion, but they were too deeply embedded in the cross to budge.

At Elise's touch, his eyes opened. Nukha'il's lips moved, but he spoke so softly that she had to lean close to make out the words. "I'm dying. Have mercy on me."

Her heart fragmented. Elise smoothed a hand over his brow, careful not to touch the blood. His eyelids drooped shut at her touch, as though it soothed him even as it wracked her skin with buzzing tension.

"I'm so sorry, Nukha'il." Her throat clenched tight. "I shouldn't have sent you into the Warrens. I should have—"

"Will you take care of Itra'il?"

She swallowed hard. "She would eat me, and I don't want to be eaten. You're just going to have to survive. Okay?"

The idea seemed to pain him. His face twisted. "Promise me."

Elise finally nodded.

James climbed over the gate to her side of the church, dropping awkwardly to the other side. The Book of Shadows stuck out of his pocket. She jerked it free and flipped through the pages.

"We have to heal him. Which one will do it?"

He rested his hand on her shoulder. "We can't heal this infection. I'm sorry." The second part was directed at the angel, but he didn't seem to hear.

SM Reine

Nukha'il's wing muscles spasmed. Blood slid down the feathers.

She thought of what he had said to her a moment before she sent him into the Warrens to find Anthony—*you never smile for me*—and she forced her lips to spread in an expression she hoped would look happy.

Her chin trembled and her face flushed, but she smiled.

It was as though all the pain faded from him. His eyes unfocused, and he looked right through her without seeing. "Thank you, Elise."

He spoke her name with such reverence.

The light in his eyes dimmed. The tense muscles in his wings relaxed. Slowly, his eyelids drooped closed, and the radiance seeped from his flesh until no color remained.

The gate thrummed.

Yatai's shadow oozed over the walls of the church. The stones began to crack and crumble. A roof beam fell, striking a pew and cracking it in half. Inky darkness splashed where it hit.

"We need to run," James said, pulling her away from the puddle of shadow. She let him move her without responding.

A wind rose around them, lashing through the cathedral. What was the point in running? She had failed. Nukha'il was dead—another name on the list of people who her choices had killed—and the gate was opening. She could already see figures glowing on the other side.

Shadow fell over the church. The mighty serpent rose over the crumbling ceiling, more massive than ever before, like a mighty dragon grown out of night. Yatai's empty eyes burned in its head.

The serpent arced over the wall and slithered into the cathedral, bringing the rising wind with her. It battered Elise and made her drop the Book of Shadows.

The notebook opened, and pages vortexed into the air. James shouted and dived, but half of the pages were already gone.

Yatai's darkness smashed into the gateway. The barrier snapped. Elise's mind split open.

It felt like a lightning bolt had struck her crown, cracking open her skull and ripping her body down the latitude. She screamed without screaming—her throat worked and her lungs emptied, but she had no air, no voice.

Reality peeled apart. The threads that bound everything together in burning golden lines were devoured. She saw through the buildings to the gates, and beyond. She saw the planes of Heaven, pale and glowing. And eyes looked back at her.

As quickly as everything had opened, it all slammed shut again. Elise was still standing on an island of white stone among the slithering shadows with Nukha'il's corpse spread beside her. James's back pressed against hers.

Yet something had changed. Elise wasn't sure what, at first—the consistency of the air, maybe, or the way the all-consuming glow of the city had completely vanished.

It wasn't until she looked up that she realized what had shifted. The hazy line separating the angelic city from the real city on Earth was...gone.

Wind blasted over the streets and through the front doors, whipping the obsidian dust into a thick haze. She covered her face with an arm as the debris pelted against her.

Elise flung out a hand without seeing, and fingers found hers. James yanked her into his chest. They dropped to their knees, sheltering behind a pew.

The walls fell down.

But down wasn't *down* anymore.

Her braid lifted. There was no ground beneath her feet. She felt rather than heard James shout—the cry vibrated through his chest against her cheek, and she clung to him tighter, digging her fingers into the muscles of his back.

The axis of gravity reoriented itself to the city on Earth, and suddenly, they were the inverted ones.

Elise and James began to fall.

A rushing sensation filled her stomach as they slipped into the air. James swiped a hand at the nearest pew, and even though his hand brushed the top of it, there was nothing to grasp. They slipped.

The church dropped away from them, and Elise managed to grab a fragment of wall, stopping their descent with a hard jerk that nearly ripped her arm from its socket.

James's grip around her slipped. She held on to him tighter with her other arm.

"Don't let go!" she tried to yell, but even though her throat burned with the volume, all she could hear was the wind and her pounding heart.

Elise's feet dangled over the patchwork of buildings in Reno, which was shadowed from the sun by having the ethereal city appear above. The wall of the cathedral dissolved in her fingers.

It slipped.

They fell.

Together, they plummeted through the air. The moist air froze the tip of her nose and her ears. She couldn't draw in a breath, couldn't see where they were going, could only feel the rushing air and James wrapped around her and the swords on her back.

The city grew quickly.

Red flashed past her eyes—the ruby Thom gave her drifted out of her pocket and tumbled through space.

Elise swiped at it. Missed. Grabbed again.

Her fingers closed on the choker, and she managed to squeeze out his name: "Yatam!"

They slammed into the pavement.

X

The impact shocked through Elise's entire body, like a steamroller blowing over her shoulder, her chest, and down her legs.

James landed on top of her, and there was a *crack* that might have been his elbow, or her skull, rupturing. She thought his knee drove into her gut, but with her every nerve exploding, she could barely tell.

He shouted. She couldn't do the same. All of the breath had rushed from Elise's chest.

She tried to breathe in again, but her lungs wouldn't obey. They jerked and collapsed. She wheezed. Squeezed her eyes shut. Tried not to panic.

Was she bleeding? Was she about to die?

She tried to breathe in through her nose but only gasped for breath like a fish flopping on the deck of a boat. Her hands clawed at her chest.

Her lungs drew a staccato breath before emptying again, and the second time she breathed, she almost filled them. The influx of oxygen made her head swim and the stars disperse from her vision. It hurt—*oh God* it hurt.

Yet they were, impossibly, alive.

James held himself over her on both of his arms, blood cascading down the side of his face. One of his eyes was swollen shut. She thought she heard him utter a few colorful swear words, but it was impossible to hear over the whine of her throbbing eardrums.

He flopped onto his back beside her.

There was air above. Empty air. Clouds of ash plumed overhead, as though a volcano had erupted in the nearby mountains. She couldn't see the ethereal city.

Elise finally expanded her chest fully. A spike of pain drove through her side.

Skin brushed against hers—James's hand. She clenched it tightly. He spoke, but she was slow to understand the words. "Pocket. Right side. Get the Book."

She braced herself before getting onto all fours. It felt like gravity had tripled, and Elise's muscles shook with the effort. Her wrists wouldn't support her. She rocked back on her heels and nearly fell over.

James's arm was curled against him, the hand crumpled and useless. The Book of Shadows protruded from his right pocket. It almost had fallen out.

"Last page," he gasped. "Put it in my hand." Elise did as he asked, and James squeezed his eyes closed, took a deep breath. "Take off our rings."

She pulled hers off, and then his. Dropped them on the asphalt.

James spoke a word of power. It didn't boom through them so much as whimper—more like the *pop* of a cap than the usual atom bomb of his most powerful magic. But it was enough.

Magic showered over her. The pain in her side eased. The cut on James's forehead stopped bleeding as she watched. Her muscles strengthened and the ringing in her ears subsided. When the magic faded, she wasn't healed—not completely. She was still bruised and battered.

But nothing hurt, nothing bled, and she had the strength to get onto her knees.

They hadn't fallen onto the street of downtown Reno. Instead, they had somehow reappeared in James's suburb, north of the city. His house was twenty feet away.

As far as Elise could see, all of the grass, bushes, and trees on the street had died. Tens of thousands of dollars of landscaping pulverized in an instant.

All magic had a cost. Especially the kind that saved lives.

James sat up. "Are you okay? I landed on you."

She scanned the street, using his shoulder to get to her feet. "I'm fine. I think our fall must have been broken by…"

Yatam.

A body lay a few feet away, folded into the fetal position. The ruby stone she had used to summon him was on the street between them.

She scooped the choker off the ground as she ran to him.

The entity called Yatam may have been one of the oldest surviving demons, but he wasn't impervious to damage. He had been pale the last time she saw him; now he was purpled and swollen with ruptured blood vessels, his gray suit was dirty and torn, and his hair was spread around him like a cloak.

Elise had been wrong—she hadn't taken most of the impact. Yatam had. There was a crack in his skull, and what oozed out was black.

Against her better instinct—and everything she knew from first aid training—she put an arm under his shoulders and lifted. He didn't react.

"What are you doing?" James asked, hovering nearby. She could feel him holding the golden rings in one hand. After being isolated by the magic of the bands for an hour, it was a relief to be able to hear him again within her skull.

"Getting him inside your house. We have to do something—we need to heal him."

"*Him?*"

172

"He's the only reason we survived."

"My spell—"

"Your magic would have done *nothing* if we had pancaked," Elise snapped. "You can agree or disagree—that's up to you—but you'd better get out of my way."

James pocketed the rings, took Yatam's legs, and helped her lift him. The demon sagged between them, limp and useless. Elise almost missed the step onto the curb. They took quick, shuffling steps past James's white picket fence, his dead lawn, and onto his door. The potted flowers on the patio were wilted.

She staggered inside and set him on the floor harder than she intended. His eyes remained closed. Even with half of the skin on his face stripped off, he was beautiful.

James flicked a light switch. Nothing happened. The power was out there, too.

"Damn. I'll have to find candles."

She stepped in his path before he could leave the room. "Heal him."

"I don't have it in me to perform magic of that magnitude again today. I could kill myself."

Yatam groaned. His skin shimmered, and Elise glimpsed the lacework of veins in his arm and chest, as though his flesh had turned to a transparent jelly. He was going incorporeal, like so many demons did when catastrophically weakened.

"Then give me your Book of Shadows. *I'll* try to heal him." At his stare, she went on. "You're sensing demons and growing the muscles of a kopis. I sense magic—who says I'm not getting witch muscles, too?"

He raked a hand through his hair. "Elise…" She held out a hand. He removed the notebook from his pocket and placed it in her hand, but didn't immediately let go. "I'm going to walk you through it."

SM Reine

She nodded and took the Book. "Which page?"

"Find it yourself. If you can do the magic, you should be able to see it. Hang on—we'll need a sacrifice."

James hurried out of the room and disappeared down the hall. "We don't have time for you to test me," Elise called after him.

"Just do as I say!"

She thumbed through the pages, starting in the back where the other healing spell had been located. She found one that glowed with a similar red light, like blood and roses, and removed it.

Yatam's skin flickered again. She could see his teeth through his cheeks.

James returned with a cage of mice. Living energy was the fastest way to gather strength for a spell, and they had already killed all of the flora on the street. Elise held up the page she had picked out. "This one?"

He nodded and set the cage on the floor by Yatam. "That spell is dangerously powerful if wielded improperly. It requires immense focus." James cupped his fingers around hers. His skin was warm and rough. "Words of power are not spoken, strictly speaking. It comes from the mind, the chest, your *core*—you only open your lips as a focus to direct it."

When Yatam's skin faded a third time, it didn't come back. He was a mess of twisted muscle with slivers of bone peeking through.

James folded his arm around her and pressed a fist into her solar plexus. It still hurt after their fall. "Bring it from here. Gather the power. See the magic on the paper. Speak the word."

"What word?"

"The word on the paper."

"I can't read the spell," she said. "Help me out."

"*Look.*"

At his insistence, she lifted the spell in front of her eyes. It blazed at their joined touch. "All I see is light."

"There are words within. Incantations. Pages upon pages of painstaking inscription. You only have to find it."

Focusing on it brought the magic welling up inside of her, like water overflowing in a cup. But she couldn't direct it. "I feel it, James, I do—but I can't read the words."

He spoke a word into her ear. And then she *saw* it.

The word of power rose from her throat unbidden, coming from a core that was not within herself, or within James, but somewhere between them. Her voice didn't make a sound, but it scraped her chest on the way out as though she had screamed it.

The magic unfolded.

Ropes of energy bound her—from the mice and the demon in front of her to James's arms wrapped about her body. Elise was connected to the earth and air, the fire in the core of the earth, the clouds in the sky. The house around her fell away, and she saw only the golden shimmer of life, and the gloom of impending death.

And it *hurt*. It was like peeling the veins from her forearms and tugging until it ripped at her heart.

With a sickening lurch in her gut, the magic ended.

She could see the house again. The mice in the cage were dead, and Yatam's skin had reappeared.

Elise dropped what was left of the paper. All but a scrap had burned away.

She sagged against James. "That didn't feel good."

"No," he agreed, "it often doesn't. It's worst when I perform magic that asks too much of my abilities."

"How do you survive it?"

"With a lot of practice."

An hour later, Thom was still asleep. James cleaned the mouse cage, helped Elise move him to the couch, and watched his unconscious body from the doorway. "Who is this man?" James whispered, arms folded across his chest. "I mean, who is Thom really?"

She sighed. The dark circles under her eyes had only deepened since performing her first spell. "His name—his true name—is Yatam."

Of course. Elise couldn't have made friends with a thousand other demons. She had to have somehow picked up the most ancient demon who had fathered every single incubi, succubi, and nightmare on Earth. Why wasn't he surprised?

James glanced down the hall. "Let's talk somewhere safer."

Passing through the doorway to his private office felt like stepping through a wall of pure electricity. He barely dropped the warding spells, just in case. Of course, even if James was one of the most powerful witches in the world, he was still nothing against a demon as ancient and powerful as Yatam.

James set his empty cage by the back window, moved a fallen statue of the Goddess, and picked up the books on his futon. Elise watched him tidy without moving from the doorway, and he wondered what she saw. If she was developing like a fledgling witch, she wouldn't know how to ignore the common signs of magic, and his room would be colorful. Everything his hands touched sparked, like striking a sword on the anvil. The room was attenuated to his presence.

She stopped in front of the mirror hanging over his desk. The hairs that had come loose from her braid stuck straight out in every direction. He took the opportunity presented by her distraction to scoop up a few more books on apotheosis and the concept of deity, which she didn't need to see.

"What happens now?" she asked.

"Relative to what, exactly? Having the city devoured by Yatai and brought into our dimension? The part where the oldest demon on Earth is sleeping on my couch? Or do you mean the fact that you—a kopis—just performed magic using one of my spells?"

Elise shook her head. Her curls stuck out in every direction, tacky with sweat. "Any of it. All of it."

"Well, Yatai failed," he said simply. "We're still alive, and the world is intact, so we can be sure of that. We can also be sure she'll try again." He began sorting books on his shelf. He glanced at her. "Perhaps with the help of her brother."

"Brother?"

"If he's Yatam, as you say, then he's her twin. They are ancient and immeasurably powerful."

"But he tried to keep her out of the city in the first place. He healed me when one of her fiends bit me. Yatam wants her to fail."

James shoved a book between two others with a sigh, pushed his glasses onto his forehead, and pinched the bridge of his nose. "An entity as old and as evil as Yatam is immensely clever. The route he would take to accomplish his agenda would be...circuitous."

Elise planted her hands on her hips. "I'm not easily tricked, James."

"No. I suppose you're not." He sighed. "Just because Yatai pushing through the gate didn't destroy us doesn't mean the consequences won't be catastrophic."

She peered through his window, and he leaned around to find out what she was staring at. It was hard to see through the plants growing in his greenhouse—which hadn't been damaged by their spell on the street—but they could make out the cloudy haze billowing from the city. It was creeping over the desert and blotting out the sun. James's office grew darker by the minute.

"The Treaty of Dis is a tricky thing," he went on. "Some laws are utterly inviolable. For instance, a demon *cannot* be born with the ability to use magic. But there are a few laws that simply cause reality to reform to make the Treaty hold true. Yatai seems to have found one of those."

Elise sank to the edge of his futon. "She'll keep trying. There are still eight other gates. And a reality that bends can still break." Her eyes were distant, and for once, she didn't seem to be in the mood for fighting. It was like all the strength had drained from her.

James chose his words carefully, hesitant to broach the subject of the Union again. "I don't think that we can handle her. Not a demon like Yatai. Not alone."

She didn't seem to hear him. "I should have been able to heal Nukha'il."

"We can't save everyone."

Elise's face dropped into her hands. "Some days, I don't think I can save *anyone*, James."

He moved to put an arm around her, but she slid away and shook her head. He sighed. "It's getting dark in here. I have boxes of candles in the garage. Wait here. And...don't touch anything."

She didn't look at him.

His cell phone alarmed as he stepped out the door, warning him that the battery had less than five percent of its charge remaining.

The sound was like a spike of crystal driven through his heart. Between everything that had happened in the city and healing Yatam, he had forgotten that there were other problems looming on his horizon. And with no utility power to the city, it might be his last chance to check his email.

James glanced at the living room to make sure Yatam wasn't stirring before opening the message. His phone had downloaded it before he had lost the connection.

It was from an address he didn't recognize, but it was signed by Hannah. All it said was, "I guess we should talk," with a new phone number at the bottom. There was also an attachment to the email—a photo.

In the thumbnail, he could make out his ex-fiancée's tall blond figure standing next to someone shorter, someone who barely reached her shoulder. Someone the size of a child, perhaps ten years old.

All the gravity in the world seemed to have suddenly been inverted, like when he stood in the cathedral with Elise.

James tried to download it, but a "no network connection" message flashed on the screen.

He hit the button again. The message flashed a second time. "Oh, come on!"

His battery died, and the screen went out.

Anthony was sleeping when Hell arrived in Reno.

He twitched awake and almost fell off the couch. Betty's album dropped from his lap, hit the floor, and bounced closed.

The right side of his face was tacky with drying saliva, and he winced as he tried to wipe his cheek clean. The spot where his head had been resting was a damp circle. His muscles ached, his back cracked, and it hurt to sit upright.

The apartment was dark. Even the microwave clock had gone out, which meant he didn't have power. But even without the lights, it was *too* dark, as though the sun had gone into hiding. How long had he been sleeping? It couldn't have been night yet.

179

He stumbled to the window, stiff and graceless. He had to press his face to the glass to see the sky beyond the bars and between the buildings behind them.

And he looked straight up into a city suspended over his own. Ash fluttered and wheeled through the wind. The mirror of Anthony's apartment building was decaying.

For an instant, he felt fear. He registered that something was horribly wrong, and that he needed to call Elise.

Calm blanketed him. *It's just a bad dream.*

"Yeah. I'm dreaming again." He went to the kitchenette sink and splashed water on his face. He had been dreaming of the city a lot—every night, in fact.

He dreamed of being lost among empty buildings on white cobblestone streets, of pulling the shotgun's trigger and watching brains spray against the wall, of seeing angels wheeling overhead as madness overcame them.

You should go for a walk.

He needed air. The apartment was too small.

Anthony turned to leave.

A young girl, barely a teenager, stood in the center of the room. Her blond hair was looped around her head in a milkmaid's braid, framing a face that was still round with baby fat. She wore pale blue capris and a white shirt tied at her midriff. And her plump lips were red—very red.

She hadn't been there a few minutes before, but he was certain that she had been waiting for him in the apartment for a long time.

Anthony realized she had been watching him sleep, and felt nothing.

Her mouth didn't move when she spoke.

Could you help me?

The question sent sadness lancing through him. She was so lost and alone. She needed his help—needed *him*—so much more than Elise ever had.

"Yeah, of course," he said. "Anything you need."

She followed him to the front steps of his apartment building. Cars were jammed against each other in every lane, bumper-to-bumper, with nowhere to go.

The hellish, rotting mass of the ethereal city loomed overhead. Anthony heard screams—but none of that mattered.

The blond girl held out a hand. He took it.

Together, they walked into the city.

PART FIVE

SHIELDED

February 2000

The binding spell to turn a witch into an aspis required obscure supplies—or at least, supplies that were obscure in rural France. They had to get in contact with James's old coven to have a set of crystals and holy items shipped. For the rest, they took a train into Paris, and spent several days dealing with the demon underground.

Elise had seen some strange and disgusting things in her time as a kopis, but the undercity in Paris was uniquely foul. The demons dwelled in filth dragged from the surface. She recognized a few gypsies among the black market, as well as several imps that masqueraded as children on the surface.

Buying everything they needed wiped out their francs, and the last message Malcolm left was from Denmark, so they carefully boxed up everything they needed for the ritual and headed north.

The flight to Copenhagen was mostly empty. James and Elise had three entire rows of seats to themselves. They sat together in the back.

"What are you reading?" Elise asked. His head had been bowed all morning over a book that had been sent by his coven, and she was bored of watching the frozen ocean outside her window.

He held it up so she could see the cover. It was a slender text with the graphic of a circle slashed by an arrow stamped on the cover. "It's a reference on the binding ritual. I'm trying to understand all the nuances of it before we do anything."

"But you're one of the most powerful witches in the world. I thought you were beyond learning from books."

James shrugged. "I've never done this ritual before. I'd prefer not to kill either of us."

She peered over his shoulder. He was examining a drawing of an unusually elaborate circle of power. There was an illustration of a man's forearm on the other page, and a knife digging into his skin. Inky blood dripped off his wrist.

"Who's getting stabbed?" she asked.

He turned the page, hiding the illustration. "Both of us."

They had splurged on lodgings and arranged for a small condo in Klampenborg, which had two bedrooms, a private bathroom, and relative privacy. It was on the edge of the king's hunting grounds, so they only had neighbors to the west, and trees protected their windows.

Elise pushed all of the living room furniture into one of the bedrooms. James gave an approving nod at the area left behind. "Lovely condo. Too bad we won't get our deposit back." And then he set about converting the living room into a ritual space.

Elise jogged through the park while he worked. Everything was buried in a foot of snow; crowds were sparse aside from the occasional passing carriage and wandering deer.

When she returned to the condo a couple of hours later, out of breath with the tips of her ears stinging and red, she found the air thick with incense. James had carved the circle directly into the wood floor. She had never seen such elaborate designs, and they were enlarged to fill the space from wall to wall. There was barely enough room for the door to open.

Elise stuck close to the wall as she removed her jacket. "You weren't kidding about the deposit," she said, watching as James anointed the northern point with a jar of oil.

"You can enter the circle. It's not complete yet."

Even with permission, she didn't immediately step over the line. He had set a candle in the south, a bowl of water in the west, and a wand in the east. Pretty typical supplies. But she had no idea what the rest was used for. He had spaced crystals, candles, and a few small statuettes along the edge. The center of the circle was strangest of all. He had left pillows in the center of the pentagram.

"Are you going to nap in here?"

"Probably." He finished rubbing the oil around the pile of salt and sat back, wiping his hands on a towel. "I think that does it. The circle will need a few more hours to set, but we can perform the spell this evening."

His voice was odd, as though speaking around a lump in his throat. Elise gave him a sideways look. Was he reconsidering the binding?

"I want to get dinner," she said.

They took the train into Copenhagen and wandered around while eating hot dogs. The ocean was frozen beyond the docks, too, and the streets crunched with snow. The sun had barely risen that day—it was a wobbling yellow circle on the horizon.

As they walked, James explained the spell. "It's an ancient ritual, as old as kopides themselves. Though there have been some improvements over the years, it does require that we transfuse blood directly into one another's veins."

"Do you have any diseases?" Elise asked.

"No, but it wouldn't matter if I did. Kopides are immune to most infections. I'm most worried about catching something from you."

"Excuse me? I don't have anything."

"You're a ginger," he said, tugging one of her curls. "I'd hate to discover that it's contagious."

Elise shoved him. He stumbled and slipped on the ice, but he was laughing. She found herself smiling, too.

She took the wrapper for his hot dog and threw it in the trash with hers. They walked with their heads bowed into the wind, shoulder-to-shoulder.

James stuffed his hands in his pockets. "It's not reversible, Elise."

"I know."

"The bond's integrity is critical. A kopis and aspis who fail to trust one another will find the bond souring. They become more vulnerable than they were without, and—"

"I know," she interrupted. "I've heard this from my parents before."

"It's important that you know what you're getting into."

Elise stopped on the corner and tilted her head back to study James. He had a scarf wrapped around his face, but his cheeks were pink with cold. "I know what I'm doing."

His eyes curved up at the edges. His mouth was hidden, but she could tell he was smiling. "Jesus, it's cold here. Let's go back."

The condo felt different when Elise and James returned. The air was thicker, and not just because of the incense haze. She didn't need to be able to feel magic to know that the circle was ready.

He patted his pockets, searching for a lighter. "Why don't you get comfortable while I light these candles? The spell is going to take some time."

She hung her jacket on the door and removed her boots, stripping down to her leggings and undershirt. Elise carefully stepped over the carved lines of the circle with her bare toes and settled on a pillow.

James found his lighter and shed layers of clothing until he reached his t-shirt and slacks. He flicked off the electric lights, lit the candles one by one, and muttered an incantation under his breath. Vapor spiraled toward a ceiling that was gray from the incense smoke.

He took one last glance at the book his coven sent before closing the circle with a line of salt. His eyebrows lifted. "That's quite the circle."

Elise glanced around the room. Nothing had changed. "So are we ready?"

He nodded and folded his legs beneath him. James held one of her knives. She had bought it to skin brands off of demons, but she hadn't used it yet, and the blade was razor-sharp. The flat part of the metal was dotted with red oil.

James handed the knife to her.

"We'll each need to open a cut on our arms." He took Elise's wrist and ran a finger from the inside of her elbow to her wrist. Her glove was in the way. He rolled up the end of it to expose the heel of her hand.

"You told me that before. I know what to do."

She didn't hesitate to drag the point of the knife up her arm, from the inner seam of her wrist to the joint of her elbow. The metal was sharp, and all she felt was a hot sting. A red line swelled on her pale underarm.

The pain took a moment to follow. A cold wave washed across her flesh and left goosebumps in its wake.

Elise handed the knife to James, and her arm dripped onto the circle. She put a hand under her elbow to catch it.

"Let it fall," he said.

She flicked the blood to the pentagram. It puddled in the carvings like a slick red channel.

He hesitated, considering the bloody tip of the blade. Second thoughts?

"We can stop," she said, gently flexing the fingers of her left arm to distract herself from the injury.

James's eyes flicked to hers. His irises were the same shade of blue as the frozen ocean beyond the line of the beach, but they were darkened with thought. "That's not necessary. Unless you've changed your mind?"

She shook her head.

He slashed a matching line up his arm.

"Quickly," he said, trading the knife for a roll of bandages.

Elise offered her arm. He gripped her elbow, and she curled her fingers around his upper arm. He quickly wrapped the bandages around both of their arms, then uncorked another bottle of oil with his teeth and spilled it over the cloth.

James spoke a word of power.

Elise folded inside out.

Power settled around her midsection, like a thick chain connected to her breastbone. She could see the line form between her and James, strengthening and thickening with every beat of her heart.

Their shared blood burned inside of her. It opened her skull and spilled her thoughts through the circle, dancing on the clouds of smoke.

And she could read James's thoughts.

His arm ached and his pulse thudded in time to hers. He worried about her; he didn't like asking her to spill blood. He was also totally certain that binding was the right thing to do.

So many feelings. Elise didn't know what to do with them.

The circle sparked with colors she had never seen before. It swam with power, like a swirling bubble of energy around them that built in intensity by the second.

She felt dizzy. She was going to pass out.

"James…" she began, but he had already seen the thought.

He tugged her forward, careful not to break their grip, and moved behind her. It made him twist his arm uncomfortably. He didn't really care.

James's voice spoke directly through her mind.

I have a lot of work to do on the spell, but you can sleep.

Elise sagged against him, but she didn't want to sleep. She wanted to watch the lights spark and cascade around them. She wanted to explore his thoughts and mind. But the dizziness overwhelmed her; her vision darkened at the edges, and it felt like the strength was pumping out of her arm.

"I don't want to fall," she mumbled, and she wasn't sure if she said it out loud or not.

Relax.

Her eyes drooped closed, and the magic carried her into oblivion.

After he finished the incantations, James drifted in and out of sleep for hours.

When he finally awoke, he became aware of three things simultaneously: first, that he was laying on a very hard floor, somehow having missed every single pillow; second, that the spell was complete; and finally, that they were not alone.

He opened his eyes. Malcolm was prowling around the circle's perimeter.

James lifted his head enough to see Elise resting on his chest. Her face was tilted up, her eyes were closed, and she was snoring softly.

"How cozy," Malcolm said. "Sleeping like precious babies."

His voice was enough to make Elise stir. She shifted and sighed. Her eyes opened a fraction, and when she saw James, she smiled.

As soon as she saw Malcolm, the smile vanished.

"Don't mind me," he said, feeling a hand around in the air as though searching for a wall of power. He wouldn't have known if there was anything there, but the sight of it irritated James.

Sitting up was complicated and required cutting open the bandages. James's shoulder was stiff from keeping his arm around Elise for the length of the spell—according to the clock, a good eleven hours. He inspected his arm. The cut had already healed into a raised red bump.

"Did it work?" Elise asked, ignoring Malcolm.

James closed his eyes. He could feel her as a new presence in the back of his mind. "Yes. It worked."

They were bound.

The dizzying mix of worry and euphoria was overridden by Malcolm stepping into the circle. "You lovebirds might be interested to know about what happened to all the pig farms in Denmark this week," he said, picking up a crystal and rolling it over in his fingers.

Elise plucked it from his hand. "What happened?"

"Nothing. Nothing at all."

"You lost the trail?"

"No. He just didn't bother with the pigs this time."

He tossed a digital camera to Elise. She paged through the pictures, and her expression darkened in increments as she saw each one. James stood over her shoulder to look. His stomach churned when he saw the too-familiar bodies of infants. "Where did you take these?"

"All over the island," Malcolm said. "The killer has gone mad. There are new bodies every day or two, and each cluster is centered on Copenhagen. I think it's sticking around here."

"He," Elise said as James dampened a towel in the condo's sink and wiped the blood off his arm.

"Pardon?"

"The killer is a 'he.' Not an 'it.'"

Malcolm lifted his hands in a gesture of peace. "However you like it. Something's changed. If you two are done casting epic magic and snuggling up for naps, we have some hunting to do."

When Elise didn't respond, James stepped in. "We both need a few hours and some fresh air in order to recover. We'll have to ground ourselves after magic of that enormity."

Malcolm nudged the bowl of salt with his toe. "Right. What were you doing, exactly?"

"I'll meet you at the central station in Copenhagen tonight," Elise said. "Eight o'clock."

"Fine by me."

She rolled her eyes, pushed him outside, and shut the door very solidly.

Elise and James walked along the frozen beach outside their condo, bundled tightly in multiple layers. The fjord was frozen solid, and the occasional snap filled the air as a new crack appeared. Their footprints left a wavering line in the snow behind them. "Remind me to never visit the Arctic Ocean during winter again," James said, voice muffled by his scarf.

"Why? It's nice."

He glanced at her. Elise's hair was frozen at the tips, but her eyes were bright, and she looked happier than he had ever seen her. "You actually like this?"

"It's peaceful. I feel… good."

"Are you certain that's not the fresh bond speaking?"

"Maybe." She hugged her arms around herself. "But the ice is pretty. It's sparkling."

James couldn't help but smile. "Sparkles. In the two years we've traveled together, you have never struck me as the type to appreciate sparkles."

"Only the pretty ones," she said, her lips spread in a thin smile.

James turned to walk backwards for a few seconds, watching the frigid ocean retreating behind them. It reminded him too much of the Russian tundra. "I would give anything for sunshine and a drink that has an umbrella right now."

"We'll do that next. Maybe the Caribbean…after we find Samael." The words fell flat in the cold air.

"We will find him. Nobody else is going to die."

"What do I do when I find him?"

He didn't think it was a question she intended for him to answer, so he didn't.

They wandered on in silence for a few minutes, passing a dock with icicles the size of James's arm glistening in the dim sunlight.

"I don't think anyone understands me," she said suddenly, surprising him. "Other than you, anyway."

"I'm not sure I would say that I understand you. Your layers of mystery are one of your greatest charms."

Elise snorted. "You're also the only one who thinks I have any charm whatsoever."

"Malcolm seems to find you very charming."

"He's a moron."

"We're of a mind on that subject." James cast a sideways glance at her. "What brings this up?"

She shrugged. For once, she was so relaxed, so emotionally open, that it was almost like spending time with a normal person. The distinction was probably cruel—it wasn't Elise's fault that she was terrible with people and emotions, and as she said, nobody really understood her anyway. The fact that they had been able to share moments of companionship with her inability to communicate on a level that didn't involve fists and blade was nothing short of miraculous.

But a pleasant walk along the beach was a world away from their usual dire situations. He could almost imagine life being normal.

"My arm itches," Elise said.

"Mine as well. I imagine it will do that for some time." He laughed. "Actually, I have no idea. Witches in my coven never bind to kopides. Your mother was an anomaly."

The mention of her parents wasn't enough to dampen her mood. Elise only rolled her eyes. "No kidding." She sighed. "My dad would be angry if he heard I got an aspis. He didn't want me to rely on anyone."

He hooked an arm around her shoulders and hugged her against his side. "Regardless, I can't think of anyone better to watch my back," he said, giving her a tight squeeze and dropping a kiss on her forehead.

Elise stopped walking. Before he could let go, she stretched onto her toes, pulled down his scarf, and kissed him on the lips. Her face was chilly, and so was his. He could barely feel it.

The shock of it was so powerful that he completely froze, unable to respond or register any kind of rational thought. After a half-second of utter brain failure, a single thought rose to the surface, which was along the lines of a less coherent *what the hell?*

His lack of response was apparently as good as a refusal. She dropped back. Cocked her head to the side. Her brow was furrowed, like she was only just giving thought to what she had done, and attempting to decide what James's reaction meant.

"I'm sorry," he stuttered. "How—uh, what…?"

The corners of her mouth drew down. Even Elise could tell he was not pleased.

"Forget it."

Once he was thinking again, a thousand things whirled through his mind: the fresh bond, the fact she had just turned eighteen years old (*good God, I'll be thirty this month*), how difficult it had been to earn her trust, the enemies at their back, the enemies in their future, and how that particular line was not one that he would have ever, not in a hundred years, have expected Elise to attempt to cross.

She stood out of arm's reach. He hadn't noticed her back away.

"I'm sorry, Elise," he repeated. "It can't ever be like... *that*... between us."

Her expression shuttered. The glorious moment of openness was gone, and Elise was dead-faced and distant again. "Sorry," she said. He wasn't sure if she was apologizing or echoing him.

"Elise—"

She walked up the beach toward town with long strides, putting more distance between them. Disappearing was her favorite way to end conversations, and he thought he had gotten used to it, but it suddenly filled him with powerful annoyance.

James ran both of his hands over his hair, cupped them behind his head, and blew out a long breath. He could still feel the surprising softness of Elise's lips on his.

"Damn it all," he said.

***

Malcolm wasn't the kind of bloke who got hung up on dead people. He had seen a lot of bodies since he had claimed his territory at sixteen—it was just one of those things a kopis had to deal with. It was easier to laugh about it than get upset.

Sometimes, though, those annoying, niggling feelings of fear and regret and grief crept up on him, and he found that beer helped get rid of them. Good beer helped even more. And after all the tiny bodies he had covered with blankets that week, he found himself suddenly very, very thirsty.

Fortunately, the alcohol in Copenhagen was plentiful, and there was plenty of beer to be found. But three exceptionally large drinks later, he was still thinking much too clearly.

Bloody fucking hell. Babies should have been flopping uselessly on blankets, kicking at very bright dangly toys, and getting kisses from their mums—not having their organs sucked out their noses.

That was a bad place for his thoughts to stray. Not funny at all.

Beer. He needed more beer.

He waved down a bartender with his empty mug. "Got another?"

Someone took the stool next to him. "And one for me."

A slow smile crept onto his face as he gave Elise a long look, from the melting snow on her boots, up the curve of her stockings to a loose skirt encircling her trim waist, and the blush of freckles on the back of her neck.

"Took you long enough to find me," he said. "Come to regale me with stories of being a noble, wandering force of good against evil at long last?"

"I just want a drink."

"You came to the right place for that, too. Bad day?"

She stripped off her scarf and dropped her forehead to her hands. "You have no idea."

The image of tiny bodies came to mind again. "You'd be stunned at the ideas I have," he said, tipping his glass back to try to find a few more drops. He slammed the mug on the bar. "Tell me, my beautiful lady friend—how much alcohol does it take to drown the sorrows of two very disturbed demon hunters?"

She fished around in her pocket and dropped a wad of cash on the bar. "Let's find out. This round is on the blood of my enemies, long since burned and dead." She kissed the second fistful of change before scattering it. "Thank you, Mr. Black. Hey! Bartender!"

"I fucking love Americans," Malcolm said.

They did beer for a while, and then switched to shots of akvavit. Malcolm seemed to recall the liquor having a very powerful and very offensive flavor of black licorice, but his tongue was so numb that he couldn't taste it.

Elise loosened up as she drank. She removed her sweater, which let him get a lovely peek at the impressive cleavage she usually hid under layers of clothing. But she didn't quite relax, not like most women did. Her gaze remained fixed on the door and the people around her, as if she expected an attack.

He couldn't even get her to talk to him. Of course, he didn't really care if her tongue was loose, and he didn't really care to hear what was on her mind. Mostly, he cared about her cleavage. And her legs. Definitely the legs.

The bartender kicked them out after a few hours. Or maybe they drank all the alcohol. Either way, the two of them ended up on the snowy streets of Copenhagen, gripping one another for support, and attempting to find a train station. It really shouldn't have been too difficult, but Malcolm didn't read Danish, and Elise didn't seem to care.

"Why *babies*?" he asked as they stumbled down the docks. How had they reached the docks anyway? Something about seeing the boats had triggered that nasty thinking thing again.

It was snowing, too. He didn't remember it starting to snow.

"Because it's what he fears the most." Elise's face was red, and her eyelashes sparkled with melting snowflakes. "He's fallen, and he's hungry. He tried to satisfy himself with the pigs, but he's been damned, and Samael can't resist the infants."

She was talking. Malcolm was sure she was talking. He focused on her lips and didn't pick up half the words.

"Who in this whole bloody world is Samael?" he asked, pulling her between buildings, where it was more sheltered and the snow was replaced by slick ice.

"I don't care," she said. "I don't fucking care."

"Fantastic. I don't, either."

Malcolm pressed a sloppy kiss to her mouth.

She punched him across the alley, his feet slipped, and he sprawled against the brick. He was so drunk that it took a moment for his face to explode with white-hot pain, but his eyes watered when it finally did.

Elise had good aim. He wiggled one of his loosened incisors with his tongue. "Feisty," he said, unable to repress a grin. "God, I love feisty women."

The finger she pointed at him wavered in the air. "Why did you do that?"

"What, kiss you? Again?"

"Yeah. That."

Malcolm pieced his thoughts together before responding. He liked to think of himself as a well-spoken drunk. "It might have escaped your attention, but I'm aiming to fuck you." Well, maybe not that well-spoken.

She stalked across the alley, and he braced himself to get hit again. Maybe—with enough head trauma and all the sweet alcohol flowing through his veins—he would forget everything he had seen. He could bleach every one of the infants' unmoving fist and pale, wrinkly face from his brain. Maybe he wouldn't have any new nightmares to add to his cold nights.

But instead, she seized his shirt in both hands, slammed him into the wall, and mashed her lips against his.

It wasn't graceful or all that sexy, really—or at least, it wouldn't have been if Malcolm had been a few points more sober. The number things he found arousing when he was inebriated jumped from "almost everything" to "*absolutely* everything," and he wasn't going to argue with even the clumsiest attempts at seduction.

He flipped them around, crushing Elise into the corner of the alley. Her hands were everywhere, on his neck and shirt and face, like she didn't know where to put them.

Malcolm thought he copped a feel of a very nice breast—two of them, in fact, as one always hopes for in the middle of a spontaneous drunken hook-up—but he wasn't really sure. He lifted her weight, which was heavier than he expected, and set her on a trashcan. He occupied the space between her knees and pulled down her leggings.

"I would lick your feet," he informed her, which seemed like a sexy enough thing to say at the time.

"Shut up," she said, her breath tasting of akvavit.

Malcolm thought he probably ripped her underwear trying to get them off. Something ripped, anyway. She was completely hairless underneath. Kinky little slut.

She fumbled at his waist, clumsy with his belt, and shoved his pants away. He was erect—the knob was always game for sport—and he buried himself inside of her with a single, swift stroke.

Elise made a muffled noise against his shoulder, and her fingers bit painfully into his arms. "Yeah," he said, feeling hazy and a few minutes away from falling asleep, as well as barely aware of any sensation below his navel, "that's right."

Malcolm was always down to fuck, but that didn't mean he was at his peak performance. After a few short thrusts, tension built in his balls, and he jerked free of Elise just in time to empty himself on her leg.

She gaped at him. "What the hell?"

"Ah, bollocks," he said against her neck, bracing his weight on the wall behind her. "Sorry about that. Drinking... the thing... oh, well, you know."

She shoved him off, dropped to her feet, and almost fell. She picked up her underwear. Swiped at her sticky leg.

"Oh God," she said. "That is... *fuck.*"

"You are so sexy," he slurred, trying to do his zipper again, but his hands didn't work. His vision was fuzzy, too. Maybe it was the snow. Maybe alcohol poisoning was catching up with him. Either was fine.

His knees gave out. Malcolm was unconscious before he hit the ground.

James spent his evening mentally rehearsing things that he wanted to say to Elise—apologies, mostly, along with a few very carefully worded explanations.

But when three in the morning rolled around and there was still no sign of his newly bound kopis, he had to sleep. After all the magic he had performed in the last couple of weeks, he had no choice. If he hadn't climbed into bed, James would have passed out against the window watching the empty street for Elise's approach.

His dreams gave him strange, misty impressions of a towering tree, valleys of shadow, and babbling brooks. He awoke at midmorning with rain pattering against his window.

The pipes in the wall beside him rumbled. The shower must have been running. James muttered a quiet thanks, raked a hand through his hair, and headed into the living room.

He found Elise drinking a cup of coffee on the couch, which she had dragged out of her bedroom and left on top of the pentagram. Judging by the open bottle of vodka at her side, she must have put a shot in her morning drink. Her hair was also completely dry.

And the shower was still running.

James paused in the threshold. Glanced at the bathroom door. Frowned. "Elise," he began, and everything he had prepared to say vacated his brain before finding its way to his mouth. Instead, he asked, "If you're out here, who is in the shower?"

Elise got to her feet and went into her room without acknowledging him. James looked between the bathroom and bedroom doors, his frown deepening.

That was when he noticed that her shoes and sweater—which were in the middle of a muddy puddle by the door—were not alone. A pair of brown loafers and blue jeans lay beside them. The leather jacket hanging on the hook didn't belong to him.

The shower cut off. The door opened. A very wet, very naked Malcolm stepped out. "Hey there," he said, waving at James as though greeting him from across a coffee shop. "You're out of clean towels in the bath. Got any spares?"

It took him a moment to find words. "What the *hell* are you doing in my condo?"

Elise emerged with a towel and handed it to Malcolm. James gaped at her. She stared at a fixed point over his shoulder.

"Well, I'd best put on some—you know." Malcolm wiggled his hips. "I'll be back to enjoy the awkward tension in a

202

minute." He kissed Elise on the shoulder, pinched her ass, and went into the bedroom.

The door shut behind him.

She did not move.

James had practiced the things he wanted to say. Lots of things. But he didn't want to say any of it.

"McIntyre called Malcolm this morning," Elise finally said. "He has a lead on Samael. We'll be leaving in a few minutes."

"I think we should talk," James said.

She grimaced, picked up her coffee, and followed Malcolm into the bedroom. The lock gave a very loud, very clear *click*.

Concealing two heavily armed kopides on public transportation was easy in the winter. James had watched Elise strap on her twin falchions, and he still couldn't see any bulges underneath her long leather jacket. The yellow scarf did a good job of concealing the swords' hilts.

Malcolm was slightly more conspicuous. He only had two pistols, but his pockets were heavy with magazines. "If you need to shoot more than twenty-six rounds at an enemy and reload, you're probably already dead," he had informed James cheerfully, despite the witch's best efforts to ignore him. "But I like to be prepared. You never know, with a fallen angel."

Between the three of them, they could have killed everyone on the train—probably everyone on the railroad, really, given the power in James's Book of Shadows. But the riders were totally unaware.

A man read the newspaper by the window. A woman whispered to a toddler chewing on the nipple of a bottle in his stroller. Two bicyclists chatted by the doors.

203

And Malcolm had his arm around Elise's shoulders.

A pleasant noise chimed over the speakers, and a polite female voice announced that they were approaching Herlev.

"Next stop's ours," Malcolm said.

The bicyclists moved aside so that they could step onto the platform, and the trio walked through heavy snow to Herlev Hospital. It was truly a marvel of modern architecture—the tallest building in the Copenhagen region, and majestic with all of its bright glass and bronze aluminum.

A nurse met them outside the front doors. She looked relieved to see them.

"You're Malcolm?" she asked in accented English. At his nod, she glanced around and pulled a silver pentacle necklace out of her shirt. "My coven put me in contact with McIntyre. My name is Karolina."

"What's wrong, Karolina?" Malcolm asked. He hadn't dropped his arm from Elise's shoulders, but he was still leering at the young nurse. Foul excuse for a human being.

Karolina lowered her voice. "There's a demon hiding in the hospital. I've only seen it on security footage, but it's large, and it smells like rotting eggs on the roof."

"Where did you last see it?"

"Last night, in the maternity ward—" Her beeper chirped, and she checked the number. Karolina's eyes widened. "I'm being called to an emergency. The number indicates a lockdown. Missing patient."

"And you work in the maternity ward?" James asked, but he and Elise were already jogging toward the doors.

Alarms were going off inside the hospital, and it took three swipes of Karolina's security badge to get them inside the locked down maternity ward. A security guard met them at the swinging doors.

He shouted at them in Danish, but the sight of Karolina stopped him. James noticed a silver pentagram pinned to his lapel—another witch.

"An infant has gone missing from the nursery," he said, switching to English. "The demon has gone to the roof."

Elise didn't need to hear anything else. She ran for the stairs.

Malcolm drew a pistol.

"Is there another way up?"

Karolina twisted her hands together. "The elevators, but they're automatically disabled when one of the infant bracelets triggers the alarm. You could take the south stairs." He gave a sharp nod to James and left. "There will be hysteria if this gets out, and if it kills the baby—"

"That won't happen," James said, hoping it was true, and then he followed Elise.

He had to sprint to catch up with her. She was already four floors up, sword unsheathed and fire burning in her eyes.

The air did smell like rotten eggs. Elise staggered when she reached the landing at the top of the building, pressing a fist against her stomach. Her cheeks were pale.

"Samael," she said.

Elise moved to push through the doors to the roof, but James stopped her. "Wait. We need to... you know. Piggyback."

The idea didn't seem to have occurred to her. "What do I do?"

"Hold still," he said.

James wished he had more time to recall what he knew of joining in an active bond—he hated to perform his first piggyback under duress. He turned inward, as though meditating, and sought out his core of power. That part was easy. Stretching out to join with Elise, as though with a heavy chain of energy—that was more difficult. He lost his concentration twice before finally succeeding.

She gasped.

Her thoughts, feelings, and emotions crashed over him. For a dizzying moment, he could see himself as though looking up from Elise's position, a good head and shoulders shorter— was he really that tall? The power of the fallen angel was overwhelming. Elise felt like she was on the verge of throwing up, or passing out, or maybe both. And her palms burned.

The worst part was her mind—it was a pit. She was so angry. James had never experienced that emotion at such depth, and it was almost crippling.

Yet she wasn't thinking about Samael. She was thinking about kissing him on the beach, and how much Malcolm pissed her off, and that she blamed James for the previous night's drunken sex. What little she remembered of it. And that only made her angrier—that she was still thinking about sex and kissing and struggling with embarrassment when Samael was on the roof with his next victim.

It would have been so much easier if you loved me.

He didn't need to hear that.

James tried to tether off the binding. He fumbled and almost lost it—then caught firm.

Her thoughts dropped to a low murmur in the back of his mind. The seething anger faded. She didn't show any indication that she knew that James had heard her most private thoughts.

"Elise—" he began.

A muffled gunshot rang out on the other side of the door.

She slammed through the door to the rooftop. The sky seethed with heavy gray clouds. Malcolm was crumpled on the concrete with a gun six feet from his outstretched hand.

But Samael was nowhere to be seen.

James kneeled to check Malcolm for a pulse. Cold winter air lashed over the rooftop, making his fingers cold as soon as he extended them toward the kopis's throat. The other man wasn't dead. Just unconscious.

Elise slipped on a patch of ice, caught her footing, and slid around a shed.

"Wait!" James called, hurrying to follow her.

He almost ran into Elise. She had stopped on the other side of the shed.

The fallen angel was at the corner of the roof, crouched on the ledge like a massive, gothic grotesque. His back muscles twisted. The stumps of his wings twitched. A low moan rose from his throat, more like a sob than a growl. He cupped the infant between his clawed hands—a tiny bundle of striped blankets that wasn't moving. It was too dark to tell if it was alive, but the silence made James's heart plummet.

"Samael!" she called. "Put the infant down!"

He looked over his shoulder, and hope sparked in his eyes. "Elise. You're alive." His wing stumps twitched again. He pulled the baby closer to his chest. "I was so sure that I killed you."

"I'm fine. Put it *down*."

He teetered on the edge of the roof, and James stepped forward. Elise barred him with her arm.

"I'm hungry," the fallen angel whispered. It should have been impossible to hear him over the blasting wind, but his voice drove through James's mind like a spike of ice. "Maybe—maybe this will be the last one. If I can't satisfy this gnawing *need…*"

"No, Samael," she said. He lifted the baby. "Wait!"

She stripped one of her gloves off with her teeth and held it out. The fallen angel froze, staring hungrily at her palm.

"You couldn't help me before," he said.

SM Reine

"But I can now. I promise."

He swayed. Hugged the infant tightly. Elise moved to his side, adjusted her grip on the sword, and took a deep breath. He gazed at her with wide, trusting eyes. Her attention was locked on the baby.

She buried the blade in his back.

Joining with him, flesh to flesh with a bridge of steel, made ethereal power explode over Elise and James. The fallen angel screamed. His mind beat uselessly against them, and James could feel Samael slip against the barrier of their fresh bond, slipping and sliding away.

He unbalanced.

The angel dropped from the side of the roof.

"No!" Elise shouted, flattening her belly to the concrete barrier and flinging out a hand.

She over-balanced. Her fingers snagged Samael's tattered sleeve, and her hips began to slip over the side, too.

James grabbed the back of her jacket.

The combined weight of the kopis and the angel was almost too much, and his feet slipped on the ice. But then his knees hit the wall, his feet found traction, and he dragged her back with a groan.

Elise's hand remained tight on the angel. She hauled Samael back onto the roof and dropped him. He was still twitching, still shaking, still not quite dead.

And his arms were locked around the bundle of blankets.

She sheathed her sword and pulled the baby free. She lifted it awkwardly—mostly because it was squirming, crying, and *alive*. Its face was purple. Its chin trembled with the strength of its screams.

"Shh." She bounced it gently with one hand under its neck and the other under its legs as though it were a football.

"You're okay. Stop crying." She turned panicked eyes on James. "*Is* it okay? Is it hurt? What's wrong?"

He took the baby and held it against his chest. A tiny pink cap had fallen to the roof. A girl, then—not an "it."

"I think she's just startled." He offered his pinky to the infant, and she closed her toothless mouth around it. She fell silent and began to suck. He couldn't help but smile. "There we go."

Elise climbed to her feet, legs shaking. "What did you do to it? Is it dead?"

Her gums pressed into his knuckle. Her face scrunched. Fairly typical baby business. "She's just fine."

Satisfied, Elise turned to study Samael. He twitched on the ice. Blood bubbled over his lips. "Mercy," he whispered.

"Mercy," Elise agreed.

She stabbed him again—through the eye, this time.

He stopped twitching.

James felt a surge of vindication as he bounced and swayed over the body of the fallen angel, cradling the last baby Samael would ever try to kill. It didn't bring back all the children who had died in Africa, Egypt, or France. But for the parents who would get to take their child home that day, everything was going to be just fine.

"We need to get rid of him," Elise said.

He had a spell for that, but James's hands were still occupied, and the little girl didn't seem to show any inclination to release his finger. "Book of Shadows. Front jacket pocket."

Elise tugged it out. He directed her to remove a page about halfway through and hand it to him. The infant didn't stir when he whispered a word of power and carefully flicked the spell at Samael.

His feathers caught fire, and the flames crept over his flesh, which dried and curled like flakes of paper.

"Close the piggyback," Elise said.

He silently terminated the bond, severing his thoughts and emotions from hers.

It was a relief—the burning of her palms immediately vanished, and so did her rage. He felt empty, and was glad for it.

She bowed her head over the smoldering remains of the fallen angel. Her expression didn't change, but she closed her eyes and rested her chin on her hands as though in prayer.

He waited until the baby began to fuss, grunting and kicking her legs, and then he said, "We should go."

Elise straightened. Her cheeks were dry, and Samael was nothing but cinders.

She went to Malcolm and slapped his cheeks a few times. It didn't wake him up, but he was breathing. She pulled him over her shoulders in a fireman's carry. "What's the baby doing?" she asked, hefting Malcolm's limp body.

"Judging by those noises? Probably trying to fill her diaper."

Elise gave him a very, very wide berth as they headed downstairs.

They turned the infant over to the nurse. Karolina wept to see her unharmed, and then gave them a private room for Malcolm to recover in. He snored softly as Elise dropped him on the hospital bed.

"I don't think he's even unconscious," James said, exasperated. He shoved the kopis's legs onto the bed. "I think he saw Samael and fell asleep." Elise flopped into the chair by the door and covered her face with her hands. He hesitated, wondering if he should try to comfort her, or apologize, or say anything at all. "Samael…"

"I don't want to talk about him."

"Are you all right?"

"Fine." She rubbed a hand over her bandaged forearm. Seeing her scratch at the new scar made James's itch, too. "It's too late to change your mind now, you know."

"I wouldn't, even if I could." He sighed. "I'm sorry, Elise. About the beach. I hope you don't… well. You know. It's not you." She didn't say anything. After an awkward moment, he repeated, "Sorry."

She gave him a steady stare that told him nothing about what she was thinking.

That was the closest thing they would have to a discussion on the subject for quite a few years.

PART SIX

GODSLAYER

XI

The ethereal city hung suspended over Reno, defying gravity and common sense. James could see it from the hill behind his house. A helicopter buzzed through the ash-fogged sky, and he shielded his eyes against the sting of dust to watch it approach the city.

The buzzing faded quickly, but the ash kept blowing like an early snow on the hillside.

"I have a son," James said aloud into the cold wind, just to test the sound of it.

He had never been so frustrated to be without a phone or internet in his life. The fact that he couldn't see what the news reports said about the ethereal city didn't bother him so much as his inability to call Hannah, or his parents, or the high priestess of the coven.

What was the child's name? Was he a Faulkner or a Pritchard? Was he a witch, and was he powerful?

What about him made the Union think that he needed to die?

The questions he couldn't ask overwhelmed James. He shivered and rubbed his hands together.

He went inside, which wasn't much warmer without a functioning heater. He had set candles around the kitchen, and some of the tapers were burning to their final inches. If the power didn't return soon, they would be without light and heat.

Elise stepped into the room, and her eyes met James's from across the counter.

She looked as exhausted and emotionally destroyed as he felt. She set the toothbrush he had loaned her on the counter. Crossed her arms. So many unspoken things ran between them as she toyed with the ring on her thumb using her forefinger.

I have a son. The words were still on his lips.

He swallowed it down.

As if on some silent cue, Elise shed her jacket and pulled off her t-shirt to reveal the tank top underneath. Grief had burned away more of her body fat since the last time he saw her; she was wiry again, like she had been when they used to travel together. The lines of her bicep and shoulder were emphasized by the deep shadows of candlelight.

She turned one of the dining room chairs around, rested its back against the table, and straddled the seat. She propped her elbow on the agarwood-topped table.

James's eyebrows lifted. "What are you doing?"

She held out a hand. "Don't you want to know who's stronger?"

If the situation hadn't been so bleak, it might have been laughable. Elise and James had tried to arm wrestle once after a few too many drinks, more as a joke than anything. She had flattened his arm to the table with zero effort and left before he could think of words that might soothe his wounded pride.

He considered her outstretched arm, and finally unbuttoned his sleeve, rolled it above the elbow, and sat down. "Just remember that if you injure me, my chances of survival in the demon apocalypse aren't going to be very good."

Elise wrapped her gloved hand around his. She had traded the winter gloves for fingerless weightlifting gloves, and the matching rings glimmered on their fingers in the candlelight. "Then you'd better beat me."

At his nod, they began.

Her chest and shoulder muscles tensed, her bicep flexed, and his hand strained against hers.

The corners of her mouth drew down into a tight line. James took a deep breath and let it out, focusing all his energy on their joined hands.

His arm trembled. Elise's jaw tightened.

He slammed the back of her hand to the table. She grunted, like he had hurt her.

"You let me win," he said.

"No." She sat back, rubbing her arm, and she sounded as surprised as he felt. "I didn't."

He flexed his fingers, watching the tendons in his hand ripple. Unease crept through him. "What does that mean?"

"Not much. I couldn't beat most kopides at arm wrestling. I'm strong—very strong, for a woman—but I'm small. Mass usually wins out."

"You're saying that I'm as strong as an average male kopis."

"Possibly." Her hand dropped. "If you're not yet, it wouldn't be hard for you to get there."

"Hell," he said. "Maybe that means you'll be out-witching me in a few weeks."

She stood without responding and stepped into the formal dining room. Elise looked shrunken amongst the darkness.

He heard a *click* and saw a brief flare of fire.

James pushed his chair back and followed her into the dining room. From the doorway he could see through to the den, where Yatam's still-sleeping form lay. He hadn't moved since they had put him there.

Elise was trying to make a silver Zippo lighter produce flame, but was only getting sparks. She swore as she flicked it again.

"What are you doing?" he asked.

She flung the lighter to the table. "What does it look like?"

Elise took what remained of the Book of Shadows from the belt of her jeans. She flipped to a candlelight spell and ripped it out. He noticed a white box sticking out of her pocket, and James felt a small jolt when he recognized it as a box of cigarettes.

She waved the page through the air. "How do I make this work again?"

"Elise…"

She blew on it. James's stomach lurched, and the corner ignited.

Before she could light a cigarette with it, he crossed the room, plucked the paper from her hand, and stomped it out on Stephanie's bamboo flooring. "That's not what magic should be used for."

She scowled and popped the end of a cigarette into the corner of her lips. "Then do you have a lighter? Mine's busted. Zippos are such pieces of shit."

"Since when do you smoke?" She ripped a second spell out of the notebook, and he took that, too. Then he plucked the cigarette from her lips. "What the *hell* do you think you're doing, Elise?"

"It's none of your business."

"You're my kopis. Everything you do is my business." He grabbed her wrist when she took out the pack of cigarettes again. She smelled of stale tobacco. How hadn't he noticed that earlier?

"Let go of me, James."

His hand only tightened. "Why? So you can continue to act like—God, Elise, I don't know what you're doing. You're

SM Reine

drinking like Prohibition's coming back, you've avoided me for weeks, and now you're smoking, too?"

"Why do you get to judge me? You want me to perform exorcisms, but only when you ask. You want me to save the world, but only if it doesn't mean helping demons. And now you won't let me have a goddamn cigarette when I'm seriously on the verge of snapping."

"I'm not judging—I'm trying to take care of you."

Her eyes flicked to his hand. "You're hurting me."

James released her. His fingers had left red imprints on her forearm. "Stephanie is in danger," he said with forced calm, flattening his hand at his side. He wasn't used to being that strong. "We should return to Reno, find her and Anthony, and get them to safety."

He watched helplessly as she pulled out another cigarette. "We can't leave before Yatam wakes."

"Don't you care about what happens to Anthony?"

"No." Her brow furrowed. The candlelight spell in James's hand ignited. The tip of her cigarette flared, and she put it to her lips, taking a long draw before speaking again. "I left him." Smoke curled out of the corner of her mouth.

"You left him? As in…"

"I broke up with Anthony." She held up a hand to keep him from speaking, the cigarette trapped between the first two fingers of her hand. "He can take care of himself. But I have other business to take care of in the city. We do need to head back—once Yatam wakes up."

James's lip curled. "I don't want you smoking in my house."

She brought the cigarette to her lips again, sucked on it hard, and blew the smoke in his face. He coughed and waved his hand to clear the air. "Fine." She tried to put the Zippo

218

back in her pocket, but met resistance. There was already something there.

Elise pulled out a photograph. It was of Betty when she was young and smiling and newly married. Elise hesitated, thumb tracing over the bouquet. "You know, Betty thought I was a good person. She trusted me to be a hero and make the right decisions. What she saw in me..." Elise put the photo back in her pocket. "I wish I was that person, James."

"You are. You can be."

She gave him a look that clearly said she disagreed. He didn't need to break through the bond to know it.

"I'll be outside," she said, and she left.

***

Elise finished her cigarette on the patio. Clouds were gathering beyond the haze drifting off the ethereal city—real clouds— and their gray weight hinted at oncoming snow. She twisted the cigarette in her fingers and watched the smoldering tip crumble onto the step. It tasted horrible, but the smell was so relaxing.

Elise.

The voice whispered around her, and for a heartbeat, she thought Yatai had arrived. But it sounded a little deeper and more masculine. Yatam must have been awake.

She ground the cigarette butt into the cement and headed inside. A few of the candles had gone out, leaving the entryway gloomy and dim. She would have given the rest of her cigarettes for a working light bulb.

Elise stepped through the archway to James and Stephanie's den... and found herself in the middle of a throne room.

A hot wind blew through open windows, blasting dust over a floor hewn from sandstone. Silken curtains hanging from the ceiling fluttered. A potted frond swayed beside a tall, bejeweled chair. Elise spun, seeking the entryway behind her. It was gone, replaced by an arched doorway.

If the throne room was an illusion, it was a convincing one. She smelled incense and oils. The wind was as hot as the worst day in Nevada's summer. She lifted a hand to shield her eyes from the sand as she stepped cautiously to the window. There was more sand beyond the wall—endless, waving stretches of it, sculpted into peaks and valleys by the wind. Directly below the window sprawled a small town built of sandstone and clay. Elise's vantage point towered over them.

"It certainly is desolate," said Yatam from behind her. "But an impressive sight nonetheless." He sat where the throne had been empty before. He wore a woven wig, a necklace of gold and gems, and held a wand in one hand and a hook in the other. Kohl rimmed his eyes. He looked like the painting of a pharaoh come to life.

"This is a dream, isn't it?" Elise asked.

"It's a memory. My memory."

"You were never a pharaoh."

Yatam stretched out, throwing a leg over one side of his throne. He seemed as comfortable on it as he would have been on a couch. "No?"

"I went to college. I've read history books. There was no King Yatam."

"Of course not." He lifted his arm to study it. The sight of it seemed to satisfy him. "You healed me, and for that, you are likely due thanks. But it was wholly unnecessary. I would have survived."

"Then you do a really good impression of someone who's dying."

"The body would have died," he agreed, "but the soul cannot. As you can see, I have lived for a long time. I am cursed with the gift of eternal life—I would have been reborn elsewhere, somewhat weaker than before, but otherwise unharmed. I have died hundreds of times. Thousands. Yet I always return."

Elise folded her arms. "Weaker, you say?"

"Yes."

"Then you still owe us thanks. I need you to be strong if we're going to kill Yatai together."

"She is the same as I am—eternal. She cannot be killed." Yatam inclined his head. "And she is insane."

"Great," Elise muttered. She glanced around the throne room again. It was as tangible as it had been when she first arrived.

But there was one other thing she hadn't noticed: the statue of a woman whose body was a serpent's, with her long tail curled under her and a benevolent smile as she extended her hands over a basin of clay. She was veiled behind filmy white curtains. It was the same statue Yatam kept in his condo.

"Who is she?" Elise asked, brushing aside a curtain.

"Her name is Nügua." Yatam almost sounded wistful. "Her hands sculpted the clay that became my form. She is my mother, and as such, is the grandmother of all demons."

She traced her eyes over the serpent's body. "The mother of both you and Yatai? You're siblings, aren't you?"

"Indeed."

"Your sister is still out there." Elise let the curtain fall. "She's going to try again, and we have to stop her. If you really are the most powerful demon—"

"Second most powerful," he corrected. "My sister is stronger."

She rolled her eyes. "If that's true, then why pretend to be a human witch? Why save me from the ethereal city and fight Yatai?"

"You want to know?" He gave a small smile. "Very well. Watch."

The sun sank lower to the horizon, and for an instant, the wind blew hotter. When it faded, a new man strolled into the throne room.

His confidence was that of a king, but his clothing was nothing more than plain white linen. He had a long beard, brown curls, and a hooked nose, but his lips were as full as a woman's, and his eyes were a paler shade of blue than the sky itself.

The newcomer surveyed the throne room with obvious disdain. He didn't look at Elise even once, but he did look at Yatam, and it wasn't with a friendly expression.

"Do you like my humble home?" Yatam asked, addressing the man directly.

"No," he responded. "It sickens me to think of you so deeply enmeshed in the affairs of mortals." The motions of his mouth didn't match the sounds Elise heard. It was like watching an interview on the news that had been dubbed over.

Yatam studied the wand in his hand. "I am wounded by failing to meet your approval. Truly."

Elise stepped forward. "What's going on?"

Neither of the men acknowledged her.

"What brings you here, my friend?" Yatam asked.

"An utter lack of remaining alternatives, believe me. We're lost as to what comes next."

"And so you desire my counsel? The angels attempting to appeal to the better nature of a demon. I am charmed."

An angel? Elise tried to see the man with fresh eyes, but he didn't make her palms itch, and she couldn't sense him at all the way she could Yatam. He wasn't there—not really. A memory. "I don't need your counsel. I need a favor," said the angel.

"Oh?"

He paced, linens fluttering around his ankles. "You must know by now that He's gone mad. The things He's done—it's sheer insanity. He has no regard for the lives of the humans descended from Him. He has no regard for the Treaty. His interference worsens by the day."

Yatam twirled the wand over his fingers, apparently unconcerned by this pronouncement. But his voice was hard. "I would take care speaking of your Heavenly Father in such a fashion."

"He is no Father of mine," the man snapped. "It doesn't matter. He's not even listening. That's part of the problem!"

"Then perhaps you should pray," Yatam said.

He scoffed. "We need to kill Him." Elise felt a dull jolt of shock, which was echoed in the way that Yatam arched an elegant eyebrow. "My brothers and I are helpless against him, but we can't allow His behavior to continue unchecked. You are the most powerful that Hell has to offer now. Rally your children. March upon the garden and take what remains of His sanity and life!"

"You want me to commit an act of deicide," Yatam said.

"Essentially, yes." He spread his hands wide in a helpless gesture. "What else are we to do? No angel or mortal can harm Him."

Yatam pushed off of the throne, strolling across the floor with his wand tucked under one arm. "I find it fascinating that the first solution that comes to your mind is one involving bloodshed, Metaraon."

Elise recognized that name. He was the highest of angels—the voice of God on Earth. Immensely powerful, absolutely terrifying, and talking about killing his master.

Metaraon followed Yatam as he walked to the window. "It's not our first solution. It's *far* from our first. But it's our best."

"Pathetic," Yatam said, and he winked at Elise.

Metaraon's fists clenched. "And you have a better suggestion?"

"Indeed I do. The solution is simple: You must fascinate Him. Give Him reason to live, and live well." Yatam snapped his fingers. The doors beyond his throne opened. A bald man shuffled in, eyes on his feet. "Bring the women."

The slave left.

"What in the world could *fascinate* someone as mad as He has become?"

"Isn't it obvious?" Yatam slunk toward the angel with a seductive slant to his shoulders, and Metaraon stepped back, lip curled. "Give Him a wife."

Elise tensed.

Metaraon frowned, oblivious to her anger. "A wife?"

"Indeed. How long has it been since Eve died?"

"Thousands of years. Millions. Damnation if anyone knows—I can never be certain of how time flows on the planes of Earth."

"A mortal mind in an immortal body is unprepared to accept the rigors of eternity. A man needs love to survive." Yatam's lips curled, catlike and smug. "Angels are born immortal—cold and without mercy—so you will have to take my word on that."

The slave returned with a line of five women. Three of them wore beaded dresses made of fishnet with their lips painted red and tattoos on their breasts; the other two were utterly naked aside from their golden sweat. All of them stared at the floor.

Metaraon lifted his chin to survey them with cold disdain, but Yatam trailed his wand over their backs as he circled the room.

"Take one of mine. They are all beautiful and worthy of being adored. Put her in the garden and see how quickly your problems subside."

"A human woman? She wouldn't last long. Even drinking the waters of Mnemosyne—even with the strange way that time flows—she will eventually die. And then we will have a God who grieves for His wife, as well as a mad one."

"Then when she dies, replace her. There is no shortage of them. Humans love to breed."

Metaraon considered the suggestion. "It would save us a lot of trouble," he said after a long moment. "And it would be much easier than killing Him."

"Take one. Take them all."

Still, the women did not react. They remained frozen until Metaraon strode up to the one in the center. He rested his hand on her bare shoulder.

Her eyes lifted to his.

"What do you think, human?" Metaraon asked, but her lips remained sealed.

"They are dumb, of course," Yatam said.

"As are all mortals," the angel sighed. "Very well. We shall try it your way. But if it fails, and more plagues strike this earth, the blood of His victims will be on your hands."

"And such a woe that would be to me."

Metaraon took the arm of the slave and unfurled his wings. They appeared behind him with a shimmer of light, and he swept them wide, sending golden feathers showering over the dusty floor. Elise stepped back reflexively.

He vanished, taking the concubine with him. The room grew dark.

When Elise could see again, the women were all gone, and she was alone with Yatam.

She felt numb and empty. It took a long time for anger to come creeping to the surface, but when it did, it struck her like a burning fist. "So it's your fault. You're the reason I was sent to the garden. You goddamn *bastard*."

Elise reached back for her swords, but she wasn't wearing the sheath. She settled for clenching her fists.

"I never chose another wife," Yatam said, unbothered by her glare as she stalked toward him. "The selection of a sacrifice was deferred to humans, whom you have to thank for your particular situation."

Elise swung. Yatam disappeared before her fist could hit, and he reappeared by the throne.

With a roar, she dived for him and swung again.

He was too fast. Yatam flashed behind her, trapping her arms at her side and burying his face in her neck. She shouted, but his grip was iron. She couldn't escape.

The skin of his cheek was warm and smooth on her neck. "You forget that I read your body as easily as a poem," he murmured. "Your biochemical reactions are of fear, not anger. But you need not fear me. I have no interest in sending you back to His loving embrace—not yet."

She drove her elbow into his gut. It was like striking a brick wall. He didn't let go.

"That is not the last time I spoke to Metaraon," Yatam went on. "Indeed, my plan was successful. Giving Him wives certainly created the desired fascination, and it allowed mortals two thousand years of respite. But it did nothing to His sanity." He inclined his head. "As you know."

"I barely remember it," she said, her voice hoarse.

"How fortunate for you. To be able to forget your life must be... pleasant." He sighed, breath hot on her skin.

"Eventually, I became bored of playing with humans. As my sister lived on and her madness grew, I slept—and some centuries elapsed."

Yatam waved a hand. The throne room dissolved around them, replaced by a narrow room built of gray stone. It was almost pitch black inside, aside from a single sliver of moonlight that fell through a narrow window set high in the wall.

A plain stone sarcophagus stood in the center of the room. Yatam released her and perched himself on it.

"Even in sleep, rumors drifted to me, carried in the minds and hearts of my children. I heard suggestions that they were going to attempt to kill Him after all. It didn't take long for Metaraon to come again, after that."

The door groaned open.

Metaraon's face hadn't changed over the long years; his nose was still hooked, his eyes still cold. But his hair was short, and he had no beard. He wore a plain t-shirt and jeans that fit him as though tailored. He was so...ordinary. "The conversation was long and boring, I'm afraid," Yatam told her, ignoring the angel. "We'll skip to the interesting part." He addressed Metaraon. "Aren't you happy? The wives have occupied His time. His influence on Earth wanes."

Elise felt the strange disconcertion of stepping into a conversation halfway through. But the angel didn't mind. He wasn't aware that anything had been skipped at all.

Metaraon paced the room, obviously frustrated. "Yes. It's worked fine. But the last child... well, she escaped. He's unwedded."

Yatam smiled at Elise, whose stomach churned.

"Is that so?"

"Try not to sound so satisfied. This is catastrophic! Our binding on the garden frays, the quarantine won't last much longer, and He fights to free Himself. I don't need to remind you of the unholy terrors He wreaked upon us all last time, and He is madder by a thousand-fold now." Metaraon stopped pacing and faced Yatam. "And *angry*."

"Then find the child and take her back."

"That's not the point." Working up the ability to elaborate seemed to cause Metaraon physical pain. "She was meant to be an assassin."

Yatam laughed. "An assassin! A human girl against a god? The idiots." He winked at Elise again. "Angels have dominion over the mind. One would think that they would have the brains to match it."

The angel went on without reacting to the mockery. "We couldn't trust Him anymore. He's unstable. So we forged a weapon and put her in the position to be taken as the next sacrifice. Everything seemed to go as planned, until her escape."

"You want me to go find her for you."

"Yes."

"No," Yatam said.

Metaraon flung his hands into the air. "If I can't appeal to your absent good nature, then allow me to address your selfishness. We call her the Godslayer. She can kill anything— including you."

The angel froze where he stood, like a movie put on pause.

"'She can kill anything,'" Yatam mused, drawing a leg to his chest and resting his chin on his knee. "You were the first to escape, and you did it as a child, before becoming wedded and embedded in the fabric of the garden. When they planned for you, they did not anticipate that a weapon powerful enough to slay a god would likewise be powerful enough to elude him."

"And you've only helped me because I can kill you?" Elise asked. It was absurd. Ridiculous. And yet...

Metaraon sprung to life once more and spoke. "But she's not ready. As with all weapons, a blade must be honed. She can't kill a god—not yet. If you find her, if you *complete* her, she will surely kill you."

Yatam snapped. The angel vanished.

He hopped off of the sarcophagus and faced Elise, now utterly expressionless, but expectant.

"Complete me?" Elise asked.

"You are my death," Yatam said, his voice heated, "if only I can discover how to hone and wield you, sword-woman. So tell me—how do you kill a god?"

"It's not possible. They're eternal."

The mausoleum disappeared, leaving Elise surrounded by all-consuming darkness.

Yatam's body was gone, too, but she could still feel him there. Waiting.

His voice echoed from the shadows. *If you want to prevent Yatai from killing all that you know and love, that is a question you will need to answer. We are eternal, but we can be slain, if only you discover how.*

"If you're so bent on death, why not let Yatai succeed? It would kill you as surely as everyone else."

A chuckle rose out of the darkness.

Fascination. I am fascinated with humanity, and the thousands of children I have spawned. I want them to live on. His breath sighed around her. *I suppose even I am not willing to lose that vestige of immortality...*

Elise woke up.

She lifted her head. She was kneeling beside the couch with her arms folded and her head resting on them—she could tell by the trail of drool connecting her lips to the back of her wrist. Her mouth felt sticky, and her eyelids were hard to open.

Yatam wasn't on the couch anymore. It was empty.

She got to her feet, muscles stiff and sore. The clock said that no more than ten minutes had passed since she finished smoking outside, but it felt as though she had been on the floor for hours.

With a wince, she stretched and popped her back. The candle on the coffee table sputtered as the wick entered the puddle of wax, and went out.

Shadows fell. A breeze wafted through the room.

Sword-woman...

Elise shivered.

"How do you kill a god?" she asked the empty room. There was no reply.

XII

Elise and James departed with a quarter tank of gas, which would be more than enough to take them into town and back—but not enough to escape.

He plugged his cell phone into the cigarette lighter to charge it before setting out on empty streets. "Our priority should be evacuation," James said, heading for Vista Boulevard. The headlights cut two bright circles into the night. "We should get our friends to safety and regroup. Considering what has appeared over downtown, I'm expecting hysteria. Even if Yatai hasn't attacked again, it will be dangerous."

"I need to get to Craven's," Elise said. "I have people there. They can help me control the panic."

"People? You mean demons."

She glared at him. "Loyal demons."

His phone chimed.

James's heart jumped. Before he could reach for it, Elise turned on the screen. "We've got a signal. Just barely." She dialed a number and lifted the phone to her ear, but after a moment, she shook her head. "But it doesn't matter if nobody in the city has a signal."

"Too bad," he said faintly. He had brought Hannah's phone number with him.

They blew around a bend going seventy miles an hour. His headlights reflected on the back end of a stopped car, and James slammed on the brakes.

He squealed to a stop inches from the bumper.

Elise flung open her door and stepped out. "What the hell…?"

Cars had been stopped heading into town. Their windshields glimmered in the night for miles down the road. It looked like the worst traffic jams in Los Angeles, but the cars were empty. Nothing moved.

James stepped onto the street, leaving the engine running. There was an accident on the shoulder of the road, and vehicles were piled up all the way to the fences at the bottom of the hill. There was no way around.

Elise climbed onto the car in front of them for a better view. "I don't see an end," she said. "And they're all turned off. I don't see drivers or passengers. Whatever happened, it must have been hours ago."

"Where could everybody have gone?"

"Home?" she guessed, hopping down. "It's hard to tell with no power or lights. Guess we're walking."

She grabbed her jacket out of the front seat and pulled it over her spine scabbard.

They weaved in and out of the cars. James and Elise weren't the only ones on the road—they glimpsed a woman trying the doors of several cars, and a young couple retrieving their belongings from the bed of a pickup.

"Excuse me," James called, jogging toward the couple. They turned wide eyes on him, dropped a box on the bed of the truck, and fled into the night. "Damn. They're scared."

"Who is this?" Elise asked, her face illuminated by James's cell phone. She must have pulled it out of the car when she got the jacket, and she had opened the attachment on his email so that the image filled the screen.

She didn't fight him when he took the phone.

The world around him vanished as James drank in the details of the photo. Hannah was older than he remembered, but still so beautiful. There was a hint of a smile at the corners of her eyes, which were marked with crow's feet.

But it wasn't her face that he lingered over. It was that of the boy at her side.

His hair and eyes were dark brown. His jaw shared the same curve as Hannah's, but his lips were the exact same bow curve as James's favorite aunt. Thick-framed glasses sat on the bridge of his nose. He looked very serious, like he had never smiled in his life. James recognized that serious expression. He saw it in the mirror every morning.

"James?"

The boy would be roughly ten years old. Maybe eleven. Hannah had to have known she was pregnant when James left. Why hadn't she *told* him?

Elise was speaking. "James," she said again.

He realized he had stopped walking, and he pocketed his phone. "What?"

"Is there something you want to tell me?"

He gaped at her, trying to decide how she could have known about his son. But she wasn't looking at him—she was looking beyond the stopped cars to a row of flashing lights and a barricade of orange barrels.

It was the Union. They had blocked off the road ahead using a line of SUVs that blended into the night.

Elise drew her sword. "You already knew they were here, didn't you? That's why you brought them up in the sewers. You've been talking with them."

The change in focus was too fast for him to catch up. He stuttered. "Just the once, but—Elise!"

She stormed through the cars, jumping on the hood of an El Camino by the barrels.

A man with a gun on the other side of the barricade spotted her and shouted. He aimed the rifle at her. Elise didn't

233

seem to care. "What the hell have you people done?" she shouted.

James ran to the side of the vehicle. There were two guards now, and another was running from farther down the line. "Get *down*!" She shook his hand off her calf.

"Drop your sword and back away from the barricade," the nearest man shouted.

"Is this Gary Zettel's unit? Where is he?"

Three guns aimed at her chest.

James stepped in front of the bumper, holding his hands out in a gesture of peace. "Wait, please. Don't shoot. Contact the commander. Tell him it's James and Elise." The man who yelled put a hand to his ear and spoke softly into the earpiece. The other two didn't waver. "Now get down, Elise!"

"Do you see what they've done?"

She pointed over his head and beyond the SUVs. James couldn't see from his position on the ground. He climbed onto the roof beside her—with the armed kopides tracking his motions very closely—and squinted past the bright lights.

The road was destroyed. They had blasted the pavement open, turning a hundred-foot swath into rubble. There was another barricade on the other side, and more stopped cars.

The Union had killed all traffic entering or exiting the city on that road.

"The commander is on his way," the armed kopis said finally. He addressed the other two. "Drop your guns. We're not allowed to shoot."

Elise glared fire at James. "You have been in contact with them."

"They approached me. I spoke to them once. Don't look at me like that."

"Why didn't you tell me?"

"When was I supposed to mention that, exactly? When the oldest demon in the world dragged us into another dimension? When we fell a few hundred feet and almost died? When you decided to become the first kopis in history to cast magic?"

"How about when you were taking all my cigarettes?" Elise snapped.

James clenched his jaw and dropped off the side of the car. The men let him climb onto the other side of the barricade.

"He'll land down there," one of them said, gesturing toward a cul-de-sac that was cordoned off at the bottom of the hill. "I'll escort you."

Elise stalked after them.

There were few signs of life in the neighborhood. People peeked through their windows. Some sat on their front lawns. A truck at the end of the street passed out bottles of fresh water to a line of civilians, many of whom wore pajamas, and its idling engine powered a single spotlight.

"Are you guys invading Reno? Seriously?" Elise asked.

"We're helping," the kopis replied.

She seemed to have more to say—a lot more—but she didn't get the chance to speak. A helicopter roared overhead, flying low to hover over the cul-de-sac. Its propellers kicked up dust and blew James's hair off his forehead.

It settled gently in the center of the street. The engine slowed, but didn't stop.

The door opened. Malcolm hopped out.

"Darling," he said, grinning at Elise's shocked expression.

She punched him.

Even though he had to be expecting it, he was still flattened on the pavement. The armed guard cried out and whirled to aim the rifle at her again, but James stepped between them before he could fire.

SM Reine

Elise stared at James. "This is who you've been talking to? *Malcolm*?" She didn't give him the opportunity to respond. She shoved Malcolm in the chest as he tried to get to his feet. "What are you doing?"

"Elise—"

"What have you done to my *territory*?"

"I'm doing my job, that's what," he said. "Calm down; we're on the same side!"

She moved to attack him again, but James grabbed her arm, holding her back. The look she shot him was pure venom. "The Union's not welcome here. I've got a handle on the situation."

"Oh really?" Malcolm asked. He didn't have to say anything else to make his meaning clear. The snowing ash was more than enough.

"The agreement at the summit—"

"Totally circumvented us." She lifted her fist again, and he stepped back quickly before she could strike. "I know, I know. But give me a chance. The Union's a whole different company under my command."

Elise barked a laugh. "You're the *commander*? What happened to Zettel?"

"Demoted."

"Then you have the authority to let me back into Reno."

"I do, but—"

"I need to speak with you, Malcolm," James said. He glanced at Elise. "Privately."

He walked a few short feet away, and the commander sauntered after him. Malcolm dropped his voice low to speak under the thumping engine unheard by the others. "That's not a woman prepared to surrender her territory to the Union right there, is it?" he asked with a frozen smile and clenched teeth.

"We haven't had an opportunity to discuss it," James said. "I've been somewhat distracted by the impending apocalypse."

"I bet you have. And you've had plenty of reading material to keep you distracted." His voice sharpened. "What did you think of the Prophecies? Good reading?"

"You want to kill my son."

"You're a smart guy, Jim, but you lack context. There are a lot of Union codes in there—you have no idea what any of that says."

James took the prophecies from his pocket and opened it to the page he had dog-eared. "'Explore destruction of offspring.' That's what it says, verbatim. If I misunderstand that, I would certainly appreciate enlightenment."

"Well, yeah, I can see how that would *sound* bad." Malcolm grabbed for the book, but James held it away. "That's Union property."

The witch shook the book at him. "This is my life. This is *Elise's* life."

"You know what the Prophecies of Flynn say about me?" Malcolm asked. "Nothing. Nothing at all. And you know what that means? Nothing! Prophecies are uselessly incomplete. A man could drive himself to madness worrying over that kind of thing." He suddenly lunged and ripped the book out of James's hand. Malcolm touched the butt of his gun when James moved to take it back. "Watch it."

"I want to take my son and his mother to the Haven," James said.

"You do, do you?"

"Yes. I want you to arrange transportation for me to Colorado, and then for my family from Colorado to the Haven."

Malcolm rubbed a scar that protruded from the side of his eye patch. "The terms are the same. You can take the Easter Bunny with you for all I care, but Elise has got to go, too."

"Of all the idiotic—"

"Not my choice. It comes from Union HQ."

James glanced at his partner. Elise was having a conversation with an armed kopis by the generator, and whatever she was saying didn't look nice. She pointed at the guard's gun, the people in line, and the houses around them. Her shouts were drowned out by the helicopter's beating propeller. Her hair and jacket buffeted around her.

"I can convince her," James said finally.

"And what a fun conversation that will be." Malcolm stuffed the Prophecies into his pocket and strode back to Elise's side.

Her yells became more distinct as they approached.

"—children in those houses, and you idiots are so fucking trigger happy—"

"Let's go for a ride, Elise. We'll have a chat," Malcolm interrupted. He planted a hand in James's chest to keep him from approaching the helicopter. "Not you. We're getting people out of Reno, not letting them in. You're going back the way you came."

"And what am I supposed to do? Go home? Twiddle my thumbs?"

Malcolm tapped the side of his nose and pointed at James. "Spot on." He waved at the kopis Elise had been yelling at. "I need transport. Take this gentleman wherever he wants outside the barrier." He jumped into the helicopter again.

"Elise," James said as she followed the commander. She paused with a hand on the door, and he tucked the remnants of his Book of Shadows in her pocket. "Watch out. Don't do anything stupid."

A smile ghosted across her lips. "Stupid? Me?"

The helicopter lifted off.

It was a harrowing ride through the black sky. The usual collection of Union monitors were spread across the cockpit, but they couldn't be precise enough to guide the pilot through such perfect darkness.

Yet the helicopter ascended steadily, the houses fell away beneath them, and it blew through the clouds as briskly as though it was the brightest of days.

Malcolm buckled himself in, and Elise followed suit. Another man was already harnessed near the opposite door, feet on the skid with a gun trained on the neighborhood. She didn't recognize him, but judging by the nasty look he shot over his shoulder, he knew her. "You were with Zettel's unit at the summit, weren't you?" Elise asked.

"I guarded McIntyre when he was in custody." She might not have known his face, but she knew his New England accent.

"Oh, yeah," she said. "I remember now. I kicked your ass."

He swung the muzzle of his gun around, but Malcolm leaned forward to get between them. "Remington, Elise—relax. We're all friends here."

She scowled. "I'm not friends with the Union."

"Not yet," he said. "But I told you things are different with me here."

"I'm not friends with you, either."

He put a hand to his heart. "I'm wounded. I thought we split on good terms."

"I checked out of a hotel while you were at a bar and left a note with the clerk. James and I were halfway around the world by the time you sobered up. *If* you ever sobered up."

Malcolm's eye sparkled. "I've had worse breakups."

"I believe that." She almost smiled. Damn if he wasn't still a funny bastard. "What happened to Benjamin Flynn? The precog kid? Is he around?"

"He's not with the Union anymore," Malcolm said. "He escaped."

He wouldn't be collared anymore. He was free. Probably on the run—but free. "Good," she said forcefully. Which only left one very large, very frustrating item of business. "You guys cut out the phones and power in the Reno area, didn't you?"

He shrugged. "This is the internet era. The Union had to act fast to keep the information contained and prevent—you know—panic. Mayhem. General hysteria." He reached into the cockpit and grabbed a clipboard. "I'm going to have to ask you to sign a non-disclosure agreement, actually."

"A non-disclosure…?" Her jaw dropped. "You need me to sign *what?*"

He handed it to her. Elise flung it out the open door of the helicopter.

"Oh, come on," Malcolm said. "What if that hits someone in the head?"

"You can't isolate an entire city from the rest of the world."

"Actually, we can."

"You don't think having no power is going to cause more mayhem and hysteria?"

"Reno's somewhat of a lost cause anyway." The helicopter swung through a bank of clouds, and the city became visible under them again. They were flying low to the streets, just over the train tracks.

She grabbed his shirt in a fist. "That's my home you're talking about."

Thumping explosions echoed through the air. A tank rolled down the road, firing on a cluster of inky-black fiends that scrabbled in front of it. Elise glimpsed them for only a moment before the helicopter lifted again.

Carefully, Malcolm dislodged her hand. "We're doing what we can to make this go smoothly. The Union's been preparing for this event for weeks—ever since Flynn saw it. It came earlier than we expected, but it's going smoothly."

"You call this smooth?"

"We've evacuated fifty thousand people to Fallon. Another twenty thousand are headed over the pass to Sacramento. That's pretty good, you've got to admit."

"You don't need to evacuate if I can stop this. And I can."

"You've done really well so far," Malcolm said. "Hear me out, Elise. Some things are too big for a single kopis to handle. Remember the Grand Canyon? You never could have done that one without McIntyre. And this event is easily triple that. Quadruple. This is a mess, and the Union's uniquely equipped to handle it."

"Like with the summit?"

Malcolm grabbed the side of the helicopter as it banked hard. "We can save lives. A lot of them. But you've got to let us." He put a hand on her knee. It was more of a fraternal gesture than a sexual one. Their days of angry sex were long gone. "You don't trust the Union, but you once trusted me to watch your back. We traveled together for, what, three months? Four? We had a good time. Nobody died. I seem to remember saving you once or twice."

Or three times. Malcolm was a good fighter, strong, and fun—but unreliable. Elise would have kept him around longer if she could have trusted him not to disappear and get drunk on a whim. "What's your point?"

"If you can trust anyone to watch your territory, it's me. I've got this. You have to believe me."

The helicopter abruptly began to descend. Elise gripped a handhold as her stomach rose into her throat. "Where are we?"

"North Reno."

"You're letting me back in the city?"

"A gesture of goodwill," Malcolm said. "Finish your business. Find your friends, if you've got any. Keep away from my teams. They're doing damage control, and it's terribly dark out there. And once you're done, then get your ass back out again."

"This is my home. *My* territory," Elise said. "I'm not going to leave it."

"I hope you'll see us in action and change your mind."

The helicopter touched down gently on an empty street. Darkened apartment buildings stood around them.

He handed Elise something heavy off of the seat beside him. It felt like metal panels covered in cloth, but she couldn't make sense of the straps. "Bulletproof vest. There's a lot of gunfire."

She almost didn't put it on. She didn't want to wear anything in that absolute shade of Union black with the bright UKA logo across the chest. But after a moment of consideration, she stripped her jacket and donned the vest over her spine sheath. She had to tighten the straps completely to get it to fit.

Elise felt dirty putting it on, but if it kept her from getting shot by a confused kopis who shouldn't have a gun—fine. Whatever it took.

He offered her a Union earpiece. "Here."

"Not a chance."

"Take it. Then you can call me when you're ready to be extracted."

"Malcolm…" Elise blew a breath out of her lips. "I don't hate you."

He grinned. "That's a glowing recommendation."

"But I hate the Union. I'm not taking it. And I'm not going to be extracted."

Elise dropped out of the door. It felt good to have her feet on solid ground again, even if the cold wind tasted like fire and she couldn't see beyond the end of the street. "Avoid downtown if you can. It's messy." He grinned. "We'll have to get a drink after this, if you survive."

She didn't smile back. "Not a goddamn chance, Malcolm."

XIII

The Union escort only took James as far as his car. It was up to him to pull it out of traffic and drive it over the median to head in the opposite direction.

He passed a few optimistic cars attempting to enter the city and wondered if the Union would bother turning them away personally, or if those vehicles would get jammed in traffic like everyone else. The road was empty heading north.

James ran out of gas on the edge of his neighborhood.

Muttering profanities, he unplugged his cell phone again and walked the remaining distance. The houses were stirring with motion; the family on the corner was loading their minivan, and James was almost run over by another car on its way out.

He spotted a neighbor—who he only knew as Mrs. Patrick—standing on her front step in a bathrobe and slippers. "What a night," she called to him. "Are your phones working?"

"No, Mrs. Patrick."

"What about your water?"

"It's still running, as far as I know. If you're having problems, I can bring a few gallons to your house."

Her thin lips drew into a frown. "That won't be necessary. My water is still running, too—for now. But just you watch." She cast a final glance at the sky. "I think I should go stay with my son in Susanville."

"That might be a good idea."

Mrs. Patrick shuffled inside, and James went into his house as well.

There was no sign that anyone had been there since he and had Elise left. He sank to his couch, which still had the impression of Yatam's sleeping body on the cushions and smelled faintly of myrrh.

The Union expected him to wait. Do nothing. Contact nobody.

James pulled the grocery list out of his pocket. It was short; they only needed eggs and milk. It felt strange to realize that they now needed to replace everything else in their freezer, since it would have begun to thaw. Of course, that was with the expectation that he and Stephanie could escape a Union evacuation in the first place.

His phone barely had any reception, but he got a dial tone. Taking a deep breath, James tapped out the phone number from the bottom of the list.

It rang twice. Two very long rings.

"Hello?"

It had been eleven years since James had spoken to Hannah, but he still recognized the musical undertones in that single word. Her voice was high, a little breathy, and it always sounded like she was on the verge of singing.

He realized that he had been silent for too long, and he said, "It's me. It's… it's James."

"You got my email," she said, sounding resigned.

He closed his eyes to savor the sound of her voice. "Yes. I got your email."

"How did you find out?"

"Do you really think that's the issue here?" he asked with a small laugh. "You're wondering how I found out about something as monumental as having a son?"

"*I* have a son." Hannah's voice was hard.

"Well, is he mine?"

"He's *mine*. But… yes. You're the father."

245

James's head dropped into his hand. Discovering that his ex-fiancée had cheated on him after a decade would have been so much easier than discovering he had a son.

The receiver rustled. She lowered her voice. "Hang on. I'm switching to the line in my bedroom." She covered the mouthpiece, but James could still make out her muffled shout through her hand. *Do you know what time it is? Get back to bed. Right now.*

It fell silent for so many long moments. He took deep, measured breaths as he waited, trying not to let the thumping of his heart consume him.

Eventually, she picked up again.

"Are you still in Reno? It looks bad."

"Yes, I'm in Reno. What does the news say?"

"Channel two says there's no information yet, but some of the news sites are claiming volcanic eruption. It's not a volcano, is it?"

He sighed. Volcanic eruption. Of all the harebrained claims the Union could think up…

"No. It's not a volcano."

"Demons?"

"What do you think?" he asked. "It doesn't matter. It's under control. I didn't call to discuss the news."

She huffed. "Okay. Fine. Tell me what you already know."

"Only that I have offspring. And that's a vast increase in the knowledge I possessed prior to yesterday." James swallowed hard. Hannah remained silent. "What's his name?" His voice came out much weaker than he intended.

A long pause.

"Nathaniel."

Nathaniel. That wasn't one of the names they had discussed for future children when they were engaged. Or was it? It had been too long. "Is he like me?"

"He's a witch. Showing signs of being powerful. Probably the strongest in the coven." It didn't sound like that made her happy.

"Who's teaching him?" James asked.

"Landon is working with him directly." That was the high priest, who had been in charge for as long as James could remember. He was an old man with skin like beef jerky and a passionate love of herbal magic.

"He'll need a better teacher than that."

"No," Hannah said.

"I wasn't trying to—"

"Don't forget, James, I know all of your secrets." She didn't sound angry. She sounded tired. "Every single one of them. I know who you are, and what kind of man you are, and the oaths you've made. And I know you are not the person I want to be in my son's life."

He felt numb. His skin was flushed and hot. "It's been ten years. You don't know me anymore."

"Some things don't change. They *can't*." She sighed. "You're famous now. I've heard of the things you've accomplished with Ariane's daughter, and—well, you should be proud of yourself, in that respect."

"Has Nathaniel heard these stories?"

"Not many."

"Does he know I'm his father?"

"He knows he's not the immaculate conception," she said, a hard edge to her voice. "Tell me, James. Ariane's daughter. Elise. Does she know the truth about you?"

James's hand clenched on the receiver. "I'm her aspis. We've fought hundreds of battles together. The things we have seen, the things we've done—whatever you've heard of us is barely the beginning. She is..." He let out a breath. "Elise is more than a friend. More than family."

SM Reine

"But does she *know*?" Hannah pressed.

He bowed his head. "No."

"Like I said. Some things really don't change."

It took all of James's self-control not to throw the phone. Instead, he focused on the reason he called. "I'm coming to Boulder. Nathaniel is in danger."

Her voice sharpened. "How so?"

"I learned of him through a prophecy which speaks of the end of the world. He's somehow connected."

"Of course," Hannah said with a bitter laugh. "Of course."

"What's that supposed to mean?"

"It means that trouble follows you, James. I don't want you in Boulder."

"Even to protect Nathaniel?" She didn't reply. He went on, struggling to keep the anger out of his voice. "I know somewhere safe to take him—to take both of you."

"And leave his school? Landon? Our family?"

"Be rational, Hannah. He can't go to school if he's dead."

"You're an asshole."

James closed his eyes. He couldn't think of an argument. He didn't really disagree. "I'll depart as soon as I can. I think I can be there by Monday, and you should be prepared to leave when I get there."

"We can talk about it," she said in a tone that made it clear she had already decided not to go anywhere with him.

But she would let him talk. He could see his son. It was a start. "I can protect you," he said. "Both of you."

Someone knocked on James's front door. He glanced up at the clock. It was after two in the morning.

Hannah was speaking. "We don't need your protection, and we're not going to run."

"We'll discuss it when I get there. I'll email you when I know what day I'll be arriving."

"I can't wait."

She hung up.

Another knock on the door, louder than before. He dropped his cell phone on the desk and grabbed a notebook. It wasn't his normal Book of Shadows—that was with Elise in Reno—but the dozen or so spells were better than none.

He slipped through the dark house to the front door, using only the moonlight and his memory to navigate. James peered through the window beside the door without ruffling the curtains. There was a man slouched on his doorstep with brown skin and a tribal tattoo on his bare shoulder.

Anthony swayed out of view long enough to punch the doorbell, which didn't make a sound without electricity. He knocked again.

James opened the door. Anthony focused bleary eyes on him. "I didn't know where else to go." The sentence slurred together so that it sounded like a single semi-coherent word.

"Have you been drinking?" James asked, leaning forward to sniff the air around Anthony. "Have you been *driving*?"

He gave a hiccupping laugh. "Of course not. I sold my fucking *Jeep* for her. What would I be driving? Sunshine? A unicorn? Happy thoughts?"

James glanced around the dark houses around him. It was hard to tell if anyone was watching when none of the lights worked. "All right, Anthony, relax. Come inside." The younger man stumbled in, and James shut the door behind him. "How did you get through the barricade?"

The younger man blinked. "Barricade?"

"The highways have been demolished," James said, lighting one of his remaining tapers. "Nothing is getting in or out."

249

"I didn't take the highways." That line of conversation didn't seem to interest him. He shuffled through the gloomy house toward the kitchen, leaving James no choice but to follow with his candle.

"Care for some tea?"

"Tea?" Anthony scoffed. "*Tea*?"

"You're very drunk, so you should drink water. You can have it plain or you can have it in the form of tea. It's your choice."

"You kidding? This is hardly the time for tea."

"Having one's heart broken is the perfect time for tea," James said, patting him on the shoulder. Anthony's skin was slick with sweat, even though he had been walking outside in the cold wearing nothing but a tank top.

The younger man's mouth fell open with shock. "How did you know?"

"I'm a very good guesser." It was better than admitting that Elise had told him about it. There was no need to add the fuel of embarrassment to Anthony's meltdown.

James sat him on one of the stools at the kitchen island, then ducked into the garage to find the camping stove. He set it up on the counter.

"She never loved me," Anthony said.

He filled a pot with cold water. At least that was still working. "I'm not sure if that's true. Where emotions are concerned, Elise can be somewhat of an enigma."

"Screw that. She's not an enigma. She's a heartless fucking harpy."

James tried not to smile as he lit the propane flame. It wasn't funny. It really wasn't. But he had thought of Elise in similar terms once or twice, and it was cathartic to hear someone else share the complaint.

While the water heated, he lit a few more candles. The room brightened with dancing flames reflected off the stainless steel surfaces and the hallway mirror.

The teapot boiled. James poured two cups, and Anthony curled his lip at the infuser. His face was gray, his eyes were shadowed, and it looked like it had been days since he had last shaved. "Would you like to tell me what you're doing at my house?" James asked.

Anthony fished the metal ball out of his cup and set it on the counter before trying to drink the steaming tea. He winced and set the mug down again.

"I couldn't go to my mom. She's in Vermont with the rest of my family this week, and there are no flights in or out of Reno, so I can't join them. And I couldn't go to Betty, because she's…" He trailed off, but anger clouded his eyes. "Elise didn't even cry for her. Her best friend."

James stirred milk into his tea, watching the swirling white clouds billow. Elise *had* cried. Once. She had also spent every day that followed trying not to think about Betty.

He chose his words carefully. "Grief is very personal."

Anthony got off the bar stool, pacing the kitchen.

"Why the hell am I trying to talk to you about this? Of course you're going to be on Elise's side. Everyone's on Elise's side. My family—my own *family*—even had her spread Betty's ashes. Can you believe it?"

He didn't give James a chance to answer.

"People are so patient with her, but why? She's a bitch. She doesn't care about anyone." He stopped and braced his hands on the counter, staring hard at James with bruised eyes. "That's not rhetorical. Why do you put up with her?"

James sipped his tea before responding. "Anthony," he said quietly, "I'm not in the mood for this. Any of it. Not this conversation, not your presence in my house, and certainly not

251

your mood. So sit down and drink your tea before I do something you'll regret."

Shadow flashed through Anthony's eyes. A shudder ran through him.

The older man frowned.

"Are you all right?"

Before Anthony could respond, the candles in the hall guttered and snuffed out.

James put a hand to his Book of Shadows. There was no breeze in the house, and the tapers had only been half-burned. But the hallway was suddenly dark—very dark—and he knew that all the candles had gone out in the living room as well.

He went to the mouth of the hall, slipping the notebook of spells from his back pocket. There was a strange texture to the air, as though it was filled with water and he had to swim to reach the darkened area.

Even though it was nighttime outside, it shouldn't have been completely dark. There should have been moonlight. A glow reflecting off of the clouds.

But his house was utterly lightless.

He reached out to feel for his warding spells around the house.

They were gone.

"Yatai's here." His voice fell flat in the air.

The candles in the kitchen flickered.

Anthony stood beside him. "What are we going to do?" he asked, lifting his fists as though he could punch a shadow.

The house trembled as though stirred by an earthquake.

Wood squealed. Cracked.

The window in the dining room shattered, exploding inward with showering glass. A thick serpent of shadow punched through the hole and landed on the floor in an inky puddle.

Anthony jumped back. "Holy shit!"

"To my office. Run!"

He took a deep breath and plunged into the darkness, dragging the younger man toward the only room he knew to be protected enough to withstand Yatai. It could withstand anything.

"She's coming!" Anthony yelled, and even though he was right behind the witch, his voice sounded distant and muffled.

James pounded a fist into the doorframe. The charms disengaged.

He threw Anthony through the door and jumped through, slamming it in time for the serpent to strike into the other side. The charms engaged with a shower of silver sparks.

"Jesus," Anthony said, searching the room with his eyes. "What is this place?"

The door jumped and rattled in the frame.

"It's my workspace," James said.

Anthony stepped carefully over the edges of the incomplete circle, gaping at the bookshelves and hanging poultices. "It's strong enough to keep her out?"

"Yes, of course." Silently, he added, *Probably.* "At least for a couple of hours. But we can't stay long—I don't have supplies or weapons."

James pulled out his cell phone. He only had one bar of reception, and nobody to call.

The door stopped shaking.

"Did she give up?" Anthony asked.

James hurried over to the window between his office and his greenhouse, double-checking the locks. "Yatai is ancient and as powerful as a god. She won't let us go easily if she wants us." He raised his voice. "I don't have anything you want!"

The younger man stopped in the center of the circle. "I wouldn't be too sure of that."

"What do you mean?"

But Anthony wasn't talking to him. He was watching a fixed point in the corner of the room. It was darker than the others—too dark, considering the moonlight that streamed through the window.

James's heart sank.

"Why do you want his spells?" Anthony asked the empty corner.

Even though James couldn't see anything, he was shocked to hear a voice respond.

I have to deconstruct them. His paper magic is preventing me from accessing the gates.

It was her—Yatai. She had possessed Anthony.

Which meant she had followed him through the wards into the office.

"Damn," James said.

Anthony turned. His eyes were completely black.

James didn't wait for him to attack.

He swung, putting his full strength behind the blow. His knuckles connected with Anthony's face.

His head snapped to the side. But he didn't fall.

The younger man grabbed the back of James's head and slammed his face into the bookshelf. Bright stars of pain flashed in his eyes, through his skull, and books scattered across the floor.

He grabbed for shelves and missed. Fell to the futon.

Anthony dived, but James lifted his feet in time and caught him in the chest, kicking him back.

The witch stumbled to his feet, holding out his hands to try to calm him. "Don't do this," James said. "You've been possessed. I can help you."

Anthony swiped at his head, like flies were buzzing around him. His hands raked down his face and hair. "She didn't mourn for you," he growled. A shoulder twitched. "She doesn't have a soul."

He lowered his head and threw himself into James like a linebacker, lifting him off his feet. He was airborne.

White-hot flames bloomed down James's back as he hit the window into the greenhouse. Glass cracked.

Digging his fists into James's sides, Anthony pulled him back and smashed again.

The glass shattered. Shards sliced the back of James's head, his arms. He lost his balance and tumbled through onto aromatic soil with Anthony's weight crushing him.

James was dizzy with pain, and every motion made tiny glass fragments dig into his skin, but he was not as weak as he had once been. He recovered quickly. Flipped his weight over to get on top of Anthony. "Control yourself!" he snapped, trying to pin down the younger man's arms.

There was no recognition in his face—no sign that he had heard James. His eyes swam with ichor.

The voice whispered, *Kill him if you must.*

Anthony flung dirt into James's face. His eyes burned and stung as he fell.

James rubbed the dirt out of his eyes in time to see Anthony snap a fragment of glass off the window and dive for him.

He threw himself behind a planter. The makeshift knife swung over his head, whistling through the air.

James grabbed a potted tomato plant and smashed it into Anthony's skull. He fell. James scrambled over the windowsill into his office again.

Something snatched at the hem of his pants. He twisted to see Anthony's fingers grasping for his ankle. James kicked him in the face, freeing his leg.

He rolled over the futon, covered in sparkling fragments of glass, and hit the floor.

James didn't have a spell to exorcise Anthony—if only Elise had been there. What herbs could he use? Lotus? Nettle leaf?

He tore open the drawers on his desk, searching the labeled compartments for supplies.

Anthony launched through the window and slammed them both to the floor. The younger man was so much stronger than he should have been—even with James's newly developed muscles and extra height, he couldn't get him off of him.

He struck at Anthony's arms, ripped with muscle from his work at the mechanic's shop, and found them like bars of iron.

Yatai's voice slithered through the air. *Take what we need.*

"I'll take what I need," Anthony agreed.

Demonic energy built and crackled around them, sudden and choking, forcing itself down James's throat. Power battered his heart against his ribcage. His spine arched as he roared.

Be quick. We're out of time. They're coming.

"What am I looking for?" Anthony asked.

Give me his secrets.

James knew nothing but the fire—it burned through his veins, coursing over his muscles and skin and leaving nothing but blistered charcoal in its wake.

He twisted and thrashed. Beat his fists against Anthony.

Nothing helped. Nothing made the pain end.

The shadow spread over both of the men and sank into them.

Let me see... ah. There we are. For an instant, Anthony's face vanished over James's, and all he saw was a boy—black-haired and brown-eyed, with thick-framed glasses and a grave

256

expression. The child spoke with Yatai's voice. *I understand now. We're finished here.*

Anthony's hands lifted, and the crushing weight went with it.

James rolled onto his side. His vision sparkled. His chest felt like it had been stuffed with the broken glass from his window.

The other man's feet crossed in front of his vision.

"What now?"

Kill him.

James crawled for the end of his circle. Anthony stepped in front of him. "Sorry," he said, fist gripping the fragment of glass so tightly that his own blood ran in a line down the edge.

The witch reached blindly over his head. He found the open drawer and a fistful of salt.

Anthony raised the glass.

James scattered the salt over the circle. With a mighty clap of thunder, the circle sealed.

Light flooded the room. Yatai shrieked. The shadows retreated. Anthony shouted, his voice mingling with the demon's, and he dropped the glass. It shattered by James's head.

He threw himself at the window, crashing through it to the safety of night outside. James didn't wait to see if he would return. He broke the circle, ripped away the wards, and fled.

XIV

St. Mary's Regional Medical Center was in chaos. Elise had to fight her way through the crowd in the emergency room's foyer to get inside.

A man was huddled against the wall, crying. Children were screaming. A couple argued with the triage nurse in Spanish. An old woman was slumped in a chair with a young man pressing an oxygen mask to her face as he shouted in her ear. The stench of sweat and effluence dripped from the walls. Police were spread throughout the room, trying to get control, but three men and a woman in uniform meant nothing to the panicked patients.

Elise stepped over a man on the floor. His thigh had been bitten, and his gray skin oozed ichor. She hesitated, considering the injury. That man was going to die, and he wasn't the only person who had been infected—there was another body by the admission desk that had already turned to obsidian.

She pushed past a teenage boy behind the triage nurse's desk and slammed into the ER. Someone shouted at her to stop. She ignored them.

It was just as hectic on the other side of the doors. Every chair in the waiting room was filled. Elise didn't pass a single empty bed as she searched for Stephanie's familiar strawberry-blond hair.

She spotted the doctor working on a man with a bite wound on his chest. She was elbow-deep in blood—all of it, thankfully, a normal shade of red-brown—but the shadow was creeping up her scalpel.

"Stephanie!" Elise burst into the room. "Drop that!"

The doctor took one look at her and the bulletproof vest and returned her attention to the patient. "Whatever you want, I don't have time for it."

Elise knocked the scalpel out of her hand as the shadow spread up the handle. It swarmed with ichor. "Don't touch that with anything you aren't prepared to lose. And don't let it get on your hands. It's infectious."

"Who are you?" asked a nurse in blue scrubs, stepping into Elise's space, as though he was going to force her out of the room.

She shoved him. "Listen to me! The black stuff can kill you with a touch. Don't get near it!"

The nurse looked askance at Stephanie over his medical mask. The doctor reluctantly nodded. "Spread the word." The man on the table whimpered and thrashed. Shadows pulsed from his chest wound and dribbled over his body. "How do I save him?"

"You can't," Elise said.

Stephanie let off a colorful string of curses and led her out of the room, pulling the curtains around the man. She lowered her voice. "First of all, don't talk like that where the patients can hear you. Second of all, that's not the right answer. There must be something I can do for them."

"You can keep the infection from spreading. That's it. Tell your staff to quarantine anyone who's been bitten or has a black wound. Focus on the people they can save—the ones with other traumatic injuries. And once you've spread the word, we need to get out of here," Elise said.

"I'm not going anywhere. Where's James?"

"Safe. You can join him if you come with me."

"Thank God for small mercies," Stephanie said, heading down the hall. She stripped off her gloves, removed her apron,

259

and washed her hands in the sink. "This attack has caused thousands of injuries. We're overwhelmed."

"And there's nothing you can do."

"That's pessimistic for a kopis." She put on a fresh apron. "You should know that there's always something to be done for someone." Stephanie took a moment to close her eyes and take a few deep breaths. When she began moving again, it was with newfound resolve. "Now, if you'll excuse me, I have patients to treat."

Elise caught her arm. "Come on. Please. James is worrying about you."

Stephanie's eyes filled with fire. "And these people need me."

They shared a long stare. Elise dropped her hand. "Evacuate as soon as you can."

"Don't hold your breath."

Stephanie hurried off to intercept a stretcher with a young man missing his leg from the knee down.

Elise slipped out of the hospital again in time to see a fleet of Union SUVs coming around the corner. They escorted several large vans, which were filled with dusty, wide-eyed civilians. A witch was arguing with a paramedic beside the open doors of an ambulance.

"We need to evacuate the entire hospital," the witch said. "We have medical facilities—"

"And who the hell are you?" the paramedic interrupted.

Elise rushed to the sidewalk, squinting through the mixture of ash and snow whirling through the air.

The situation had gotten worse since she and James had fallen from the ruins. Parts of the crumbling buildings in the ethereal city had collapsed and destroyed sections of downtown. She could see a restaurant that had been turned to obsidian by Yatai's fiends at the end of the street. Now the ichor was spreading through the real casinos as well.

The only bright places remaining were the gates, still protected by Alain's magical ribbons, still glowing in the darkness with ethereal energy.

The popping of gunfire broke the air.

Elise jumped behind a gas pump, watching from around the corner as one of those massive tanks rolled past. It was herding a cluster of limping fiends. It wasn't firing with the cannon—there were two kopides sitting on the outside with submachine guns, and a handful of humans screamed and ran into the nearest parking garage when they saw it.

"Under control?" Elise muttered. "I am going to kill you, Malcolm..."

She waited until they were gone and made a break for Craven's.

There were more demons possessed by ichor around the corner—more than Elise thought could have come from Zohak. They weren't all fiends, either. A dozen of them milled in the alley.

Elise thought she recognized a few of them. The two basandere who volunteered to dump Zohak's body—they were there. And so were a couple of nightmares. Yatai had been busy.

She skirted around the alley before they could spot her, sprinting full-speed down the street.

Elise passed under one of the gates, which hung from the mirror of the train trench. A mixture of silver and crimson light sparked in her vision as Alain's magic mingled with ethereal energies. Her skin buzzed and her palms ached when she passed underneath it.

Craven's looked like it had been closed and condemned, but then, it always looked like that. The neon sign was dim. No light came through the boarded windows.

Elise jiggled the front door. Locked.

Sudden energy built behind her. Lightning split the night. She spun, pressing her back to the door.

The gate in the train trench flared with light. Crimson sparks showered on the street, dancing over the buildings as the magic ripped free and splashed over the sidewalks. The light emanating from the pillars of bone intensified. The marks around the base flashed white.

And then the shadows began oozing up the sides.

Yatai had torn open the warding ribbons.

Elise gaped. "How…?"

She almost fell when the door opened behind her. Pale hands shot out, grabbed her shoulders, and dragged her into Craven's.

Neuma wrapped her in a tight embrace that made Elise's skin feel like it was going to crawl off her bones. Light from the gate poured through the cracks in the boarded window, and the half-succubus's pale flesh glimmered in the darkness. "Elise!" she cried, gripping her shirt in both hands. "That shadow, that thing—it took Treeny!"

"Wait, slow down," Elise said as Jerica hurried to chain the front door again. She was pleased to see the nightmare armed with knives and wearing a biker jacket and chaps. One other demon was waiting nearby—a squat, hideous door guard called Ed. "Who's Treeny?"

Neuma was hyperventilating. Her impressive chest rose and fell with every breath. "The waitress, the witch! I called her into work, but when she was down the block—the black thing—the screaming—"

"A giant snake," Jerica interrupted. "Blacker than shadow. It came down from the ruins and grabbed her."

"Treeny must have opened the wards," Ed said, peeking through slits in the boards at the gate.

He was right. A demon wouldn't have had the requisite abilities. But how would Treeny have known what to do? Alain could only perform rudimentary paper magic because he seized some of James's spells. Nobody else knew how to do it— certainly not a weak witch that worked for her casino.

Unless Yatai had somehow gotten the information from James.

Elise's stomach flipped. "Where's the team I asked you to collect, Neuma?"

"Downstairs."

"Okay. Forget the excavation. Ed, I want you to take everyone into the Warrens. Find somewhere safe from Yatai and wait for me. I'm going to need your help getting the city back under control once I kill her."

Ed wasn't just the scariest-looking bastard on her team; he was also one of the most obedient. He nodded and headed downstairs.

"What about us?" Jerica asked.

"If the magic keeping Yatai out of the gates is failing, she'll still need an angel's mark to open them. So we've got to keep her from getting one."

Neuma's brow furrowed. "Nukha'il?"

"He's dead." She swallowed the lump that rose in her throat. "That means Itra'il is unprotected. We've got to get to her before Yatai does. Find weapons and get ready to move."

Neuma scurried away, taking tiny steps in her four-inch boots—which were modest, by her standards—and vanished into the darkness of the empty casino floor. "Who's Itra'il?" Jerica asked.

"An angel. She was driven crazy by enslavement to a human master, so another angel was keeping her in hibernation. But he's dead now."

"Where is she?"

"Locked in the vault beneath a former bank. It's about four blocks from here."

Jerica glanced out the slats in the boards. "Four blocks? Out there?"

Elise drew her obsidian sword. "Yeah."

"Great," said the nightmare. She blew a big bubble of gum and popped it.

As they waited, Elise felt the wards around another gate open. She couldn't see it from inside Craven's, but there was no mistaking the pulse of magic, the flush of ethereal energy.

Three gates unprotected. Six to go.

Neuma returned a few minutes later. She had traded out the boots for high-tops and worried a leather whip between her hands.

"That's your weapon of choice?" Elise asked, arching an eyebrow.

She looked at the whip. "What's wrong with it?"

"Nothing. Never mind." She unchained the doors again. "We're going to the bank on Center. We have to reach Itra'il first—whatever it takes. Don't let anything touch or bite you. Assume everything out there is infectious. Got it?"

"Let's rock and roll," Jerica said.

Elise flung the doors open.

Lightning danced through the sky, arcing between the street and the gate above. It leaped from the gate in the trench to the gate in the cathedral—exposed by the missing roof—and lit the city with crackling white light.

"Move," Elise yelled, "move!"

She ran west, and Jerica loped at her side, butcher knife in each hand.

Energy split the air. The gate suspended from the mirrored roof of Harrah's Casino's hotel tower flared with light and magic. The serpent of Yatai's energy lashed through the clouds, darting from one gate to the next.

When they reached the next intersection, Elise leaned around the corner to check for fiends. There was a tank positioned under the Reno arch.

The cannon thumped as it fired. Fiends shrieked.

Elise gestured, and they darted to the old bank.

She almost thought they were going to make it unscathed.

The entrance to the vault was in the alley, and her heart plummeted to see that the other demons had gotten there first. The door was untouched, but the wall was melted away by ichor, and quickly eating into the foundations. A van was tipped on its side, and the red Turtle cases from its back were spread across the asphalt.

Elise's feet crunched on CDs and tape media as she hurried to the hole in the wall. The demons had eaten through layers of cinderblock and steel to reach the vault's entryway. Inside, fiends were digging and clawing at the door of the bank vault. Shadows made the paint peel.

She stepped inside and clambered on top of a desk that had once belonged to the intake officer. "Hey!" she barked.

The fiends turned, bulbous eyes bulging with inky shadow. They were being supervised by a possessed nightmare—a tall, slender man with yellow claws. Rick—from the drugstore—was barely recognizable.

Jerica gasped.

"It's not him anymore," Elise said. "You can't—"

She didn't get a chance to finish. The fiends rushed at them.

Elise whirled through the possessed demons. There was no room to fight, and the fiends could climb walls—they scurried to the ceiling and dropped on her. She jumped off the desk and kicked a fiend into the metal cage protecting the elevator.

"Duck!" Jerica yelled.

She threw herself to the ground as the nightmare flung a butcher knife. It hurtled through the air with terrifying precision and buried into one of the fiend's skulls with a *thump*.

Rick lunged for Jerica. Neuma lashed out. The whip curled around Rick's throat and held firm; she jerked, and he fell to the ground.

She loosed it with a flick of her wrist and lashed again. It sliced open his cheek. Ichor spilled over his mouth and down his jaw, dribbling to his chest and soaking his shirt.

"No!" Jerica cried.

Elise hacked him in half. He collapsed in two pieces, splattering wetly on the concrete floor.

She made short work of the remaining fiends, which fell under the possessed blade like water evaporating on a heated skillet. She flicked ichor off her blade onto the ground and went to check the vault's door.

There was a hole the size of a small child halfway up the wall. It was still growing.

Jerica sobbed over Rick, hands covering her face. "Get her off the ground, Neuma. We have to move," Elise said.

The bartender's eyes widened. "Right now? Can't you see she's grieving?"

"She can grieve when we aren't in mortal peril."

"But Elise—"

Her argument was cut short by a groan in the building above them. The walls cracked. Shadow seeped through the fissures. "Take cover!" Elise shouted, shoving Neuma for the door.

It was too late.

Sudden light flooded the basement. Cold air gushed over Elise's skin.

Pain flared in her shoulder as a chunk of concrete struck it, and the ground rushed to meet her face. She rolled onto her back in time to see a steel I-beam fill her vision.

She flung her arms to shield her face from the blow— which never came.

Elise lowered her arms.

The debris was frozen, suspended in a black fog. It looked like Yatai had clenched the building in a massive fist of darkness. And with a single blow, she scattered it, leaving Elise and the entire basement vault bared to the open air.

Above, Elise could see the mirrored bank: only half of the building remained, which was twice as much as the building on the ground. Ash snowed on her, turning her bulletproof vest and braided hair a dull shade of gray.

Three fiends scrambled over the debris from the street. They ignored Elise's army and plunged through the hole in the wall to vanish inside the vault.

Elise struggled to her feet. Her shoulder ached. She slipped.

A hand caught her elbow and helped her to her feet. Jerica's face shone with tears, but her eyes blazed with hatred.

"Come on, Godslayer. Let's get your angel."

She gave Jerica a thin-lipped smile and clasped hands with her for an instant. Then she jumped through the vault's door, and the nightmare darted after her.

Beyond what remained of the door, the vault was a huge, concrete room with shelves, smaller safes, and iron bars. It was big enough to fit an entire office inside. But ripping away the building hadn't touched the reinforced walls of the vault, and it was too dark to see a few feet beyond the door. Elise could only hear the scrabbling of fiends' feet and claws ringing flatly on the cement.

Jerica didn't seem to have any trouble seeing through the gloom. She darted into the depths of the room, and Elise followed the dim glow of her skin.

They jogged down the hall and turned a corner. Pale light emanated from a cage at the end of the hallway, though it struggled against Yatai's shadow to brighten the wall. The fiends pawed at the door, trying to melt away the bars.

Jerica flung her second butcher knife. It buried itself in the back of a fiend's skull.

Elise attacked the other two, letting rage and instinct move her through the dance of flailing limbs.

Dull nails slashed through the air. She twisted and parried.

With a thrust, she impaled one of the survivors. It shrieked. Splattered. Jerica sidestepped the ichor that oozed forth.

An impact rocked through her side as the remaining fiend struck her in the small ribs. It felt like a knife to the kidneys, and it left behind a smear on her jacket.

Elise stripped it off and flung her coat in the fiend's eyes.

Before it could see again, she buried the sword in its gut. She kicked her jacket to dislodge its corpse from her blade.

"What in all the hells possessed these guys?" Jerica asked as Elise's coat turned brittle and began to break apart.

"You don't want to know."

The answer seemed to satisfy her. The nightmare shielded her eyes with a hand, squinting into the glow through the bars of the cage. "The angel is in there, isn't she?"

Elise responded by taking out her keys and unlocking the door. She and Nukha'il had been the only people with copies—

even the owner of the vault, a cambion named Ricardo, hadn't been able to get in.

She stepped inside.

Itra'il was stretched out on her stomach on a metal table, cheek resting on her folded arms and coppery hair spilling down her shoulders as she slept peacefully. Although she was naked, her long wings concealed everything to the ankles. A layer of downy feathers covered the floor around her. They radiated a dim golden glow.

Elise skirted around her. She was uncertain what might stir the angel—Nukha'il had been the one to help her sink into a restful coma, and now that he was dead, there was no way of telling what was keeping her there, if anything.

"What's the plan? Are we going to move her?" Jerica asked.

She had shown mercy to an angel before. It hadn't gone well.

Elise approached Itra'il and stood at her side, gazing down at her sleeping face. Nukha'il wouldn't have wanted his lover slaughtered. He loved her with all of his heart, and hoped that she could heal and live out eternity with him.

But now he was dead. Itra'il had no future.

Elise swallowed hard and lifted the blade, heart thudding in her chest.

The angel's eyes opened. They were a pale, crystalline shade of blue, with an internal light like sunshine. Her lips parted in a sigh.

Elise buried the sword between her wings.

Itra'il jerked. Blood spilled over her lip.

She mouthed a name. *Nukha'il.*

"Sorry," Elise said, even though she wasn't sure she meant it. She definitely didn't feel it. She didn't feel anything.

She stabbed again, making certain to pulverize the chest cavity. Itra'il didn't jump a second time. She deflated against the table, her wings sagged, and her eyes fell half-closed.

The light faded from her skin.

Jerica watched from the doorway. "You would have done well as a demon."

Elise's mouth twitched.

She ripped a page out of the Book of Shadows and laid it on Itra'il's immobile body. Even when an angel was dead, their limbs had terrible powers. The marks on their wings could be used to operate ethereal objects. Their flesh and bones could be turned into artifacts themselves, like the gateways. She couldn't risk Yatai retrieving her corpse.

Elise pulled off her ring. James must have still worn his— she couldn't feel his thoughts, and was glad for it. The magic around the page brightened as soon as the metal left her finger.

She sought her core of strength and collected her energy.

Help me, James, she silently prayed.

And then she spoke a word of power. The chain of magic jerked under her ribs. Fire leaped out of page.

It consumed Itra'il's feathers, spreading over her back as quickly and surely as the ichor devoured the bodies of the possessed. It flared with heat that scorched Elise's eyebrows.

She stepped back and sheathed her sword. It took two tries to get it in.

Watching the angel shrivel inside the flames, popping and twitching with the heat, jangled her nerves. And Nukha'il— what would Nukha'il have thought, if he'd seen it? "He wouldn't want her to be alone," Elise whispered, sliding the ring onto her thumb again.

"What did you say?" Jerica asked.

"Nothing." She pulled out a box of cigarettes and extended one toward the pyre, catching the tip with the flames. "Want a smoke?"

The nightmare took a drag. "Thanks."

The smell didn't settle Elise the way it usually did, so she watched Itra'il smolder until her cigarette was burned down to the filter, and then flicked it at the charred remains.

"Let's go," she said.

Anthony walked for some time. Somehow, James's neighborhood had turned into an empty highway, and then main street. He wasn't sure how he got there—he guessed he must have walked all those miles.

He met nobody in the hallway of his apartment building, and his door was ajar when he arrived. The lock had been smashed, but nothing inside had been touched.

"I should wash my hands," he told the darkened apartment.

He squirted a dollop of soap into his hands and used the back of his wrist to push the faucet into the hot position. Anthony massaged his left thumb with his right, scraping off blood he couldn't remember bleeding. Brown clouds swirled down the drain.

He flipped his hand over. There was blood on the heel of his palm too, crusted around a deep slash and under his fingernails. There wasn't much to do about that. If it hadn't been blood, it would have been engine oil instead.

The scalding water sent ripples of half-pain, half-pleasure down his spine. It felt purifying in more ways than one.

Leaning down to bump the faucet off with his elbow, he flicked the water from his hands into the sink and grabbed a towel. Anthony's hands were bright red, but clean. It felt good. Great, even.

Now the gun.

Anthony grabbed the Teflon oil and sat on the foot of the bed with his shotgun. He slid the action back, unscrewed the tubular chamber, and twisted off the barrel of the gun. He ran the rod through the barrel and pushed it out the other end. His motions were stiff, mechanical. He didn't quite see the gun as he worked on it.

A woman sat beside him. Her weight didn't make the bed sink.

Thank you for helping me, Anthony, she said. *The knowledge you retrieved has told me so much. I know what to do next.*

It felt like a hand had reached into his gut and clamped down on his stomach.

"Wait... what did I do?"

He almost put his finger on it—almost drew the memory of what he had done from the murky depths of his mind.

The woman rested her hand on his knee. A dark fog settled over his brain again.

You've been helping me, she said, her crimson lips curled into a smile that didn't touch her empty eyes. *Very bad men are coming after us. They're not happy. They're going to try to kill you.*

That statement barely stirred him. He reassembled the shotgun. "Why?"

Because you tried to kill someone. And failed, I might add. He survived.

"Oh," he said.

He jacked a round into the chamber.

They will be at your door soon. Don't let them take you. I don't want you to tell them anything—not when I'm so close to finishing here.

"What should I do?"

Kill them, she said. *Or kill yourself. Whichever is more convenient. But don't let them take you.*

There was something wrong about that, but Anthony couldn't think of what.

His finger slipped over the trigger.

"Kill myself," he said, facing the woman at long last. He recognized her face, the blond hair bobbed around her chin, the joyful smile. "Betty... it's you."

Who is Betty? Do you love me?

A hot tear slid down his cheek. "I've missed you so much. It hasn't been the same since you died."

This seemed to amuse her. *Am I so important to you?*

"I killed him. The man who shot you—I shot him back." Anthony reached out to touch her, to hug her, but the woman was suddenly out of his reach.

The men are here. It's not too late for you to make amends. Protect me. Kill them.

"Kill them," Anthony echoed.

Anger knotted inside of him. He marched into the living room with his gun at the ready, and the woman drifted behind him.

He heard footsteps thudding in the hallway an instant before the door slammed open.

Anthony shouldered the rifle and fired.

BLAM.

The shot rocked him back on his heels. The first man through the door took it in the chest.

Crimson misted the wall. People shouted.

"Man down!"

"He's armed. Spread out!"

Too much motion. More gunshots.

Anthony took cover behind the wall. He pumped the shotgun. Stepped out. Fired again.

273

An elbow drove into his side, and he fell. "Get the gun!" someone yelled.

Pain flared in his temple, sudden and bright and sharp.

For an instant, Betty stood over him again, arms folded and face twisted into a scowl of displeasure.

Then he saw nothing at all.

XV

Neuma was waiting outside the vault when Elise and Jerica emerged. She was picking through the rubble and tossing aside empty cases, as if searching for something valuable to pawn.

When Itra'il didn't step outside with them, her stenciled eyebrows lifted.

Elise spoke before she could ask. "You don't want to know."

Her sentence was punctuated by a pulse of energy. A silent gong resonated through the city, shaking the buildings around them and making the debris jitter. The wards surrounding another gate fell with an eruption of light, and every gate blazed with angelfire as bright as daylight. It drove away all but the blackest of Yatai's shadows.

Elise flung up a hand to shield her eyes, but by the time she reacted, it was already over.

Another gate exposed.

"She's going to open them all and kill us, isn't she?" Jerica asked, bracing a foot on a chunk of concrete to rip a piece of rebar free. She hefted it in her hand like a sword.

Elise shook her head. "Yatai needs two marks, and there are no angels left here. She can tear down the wards all she wants. She can't get through the gates."

"So what now?" Neuma asked.

"Now I've got to kill her before she thinks of a way around that." And she had to do it before the city was destroyed by tanks. She could have strangled Malcolm. "Reconvene with the other demons in the Warrens. The

Union's not going to distinguish between Yatai's legion and the two of you. If they catch you on the streets, you'll get shot."

As if on cue, a car rounded the end of the alley—a big black SUV with the windows rolled down.

"Get down!" Jerica shouted.

A gunshot cracked through the air. Something sledgehammered into Elise's chest.

She staggered with a cry, and her foot slipped on a piece of cement. She tumbled. Hit pavement.

Oh God.

With a moan of pain, she rolled over, curling her knees into her chest. It was like being crushed underneath an anvil. The throbbing in her ribs and chest blinded her.

Her fingers traced over the place she had been hit. A flat metal disc was pressed into the bulletproof vest, and it scorched the tips of her fingers when she traced its edges.

The Union had shot her. They had fucking *shot* her.

A hand seized her arm. "Elise!" Through the haze of pain, she recognized Neuma's touch and voice.

She pushed the bartender away and struggled to her feet. "Run!"

Neuma and Jerica bolted. Gunshots sprayed through the alley, smacking into brick and pinging into the van.

She took the distraction of the other women fleeing to move into the spotlight and reveal her branded ballistics jacket. Elise lifted her hands over her head. "Don't shoot!" she yelled. "I'm human!"

A masculine voice responded. "Witch on the ground! Stop shooting!" She jogged to the SUV unharmed. "Who are you?" asked the driver, lowering his gun. He had been steering with one hand and popping off shots with the other.

Elise reached through his window and jerked him halfway out of the SUV. "You shot me. You *asshole*!"

He kicked and struggled as she hauled him to the pavement. Supporting his weight hurt her bruised ribs, but his exclamation was satisfying enough to make up for it.

The backdoor opened, and a familiar woman with red hair and broad shoulders jumped out: Allyson Whatley. She was Gary Zettel's aspis, and was equally intimidating without her partner present.

She leveled a pistol at Elise. "Watch yourself."

Elise didn't drop the driver, though he beat against her arms. She shook him by the coat. "You guys can't blow through here shooting at everything that moves. You're going to kill the wrong demons!"

"We've got orders to secure the area for the safety of the citizens," Allyson said.

Elise tossed the driver to the ground. He rolled. "These *are* citizens!"

"I'd heard the rumors, but I didn't think it would actually be true. You're with the demons now." Allyson holstered her gun and took handcuffs off her belt. "I'm going to have to take you into custody."

"Like hell you are. Malcolm sent me back into the city," Elise said. Allyson faltered. Doubt flashed across her face. "Check with him."

The witch turned away, putting two fingers to her earpiece. "Malcolm?" She lowered her voice so Elise couldn't hear her. The driver scrambled into the open door of the SUV.

After conferring with Malcolm, Allyson faced her again. Her mouth twisted like she had gotten shit on her tongue. "I'm under orders to give you any... *assistance*... you might want."

Elise shielded her eyes, seeking the remaining gates warded in the city above. The ones Yatai had exposed were rapidly darkening, but a glow emanated from the north, where one of the casino gates would still be standing. "I need an escort to that gate." She pointed. "I have to get to the roof."

Allyson climbed in the driver's seat. "Walk. I'll follow you."

Elise jogged down the street with her path illuminated by flashes of lightning and the SUV's headlights. Another one of those black tanks blew past a block away. Distant thuds suggested another blasting its cannon to the south.

There was no sign of the demons Elise had taken from Craven's, but as they approached the casino with one of the remaining gates, signs of Yatai's other demons quickly began to appear. The sidewalks were black with ichor.

She passed a hole in the ground where a pawnshop used to stand, and recognized it as one of the Night Hag's businesses.

The fiends themselves were destroying a casino.

They climbed the outside of the hotel tower, claws digging into the walls and leaving ichor in their wake. It began to crumble in the same way that the mirrored casino had, and as Elise watched, a fragment the size of a car broke off near the roof and tumbled toward Earth. It bounced off the side of the building, struck a fiend, and dislodged its claws. The demon fell with a shriek to splatter on the sidewalk.

Above, the white gate pulsed with light as a thick shadow serpent whirled around it.

"I'm going in," Elise told Allyson through the window. "Careful where you shoot. I'm going to be pissed if I get hit again."

The witch immediately peeled off, circling around the street. Elise moved for the entrance, skirting a patch of ichor on the sidewalk.

The automatic doors didn't react to her approach. She wiggled her fingers into the crack between them and tried to force them apart.

The gate pulsed with energy. Sparks showered around her as the wards opened.

Burning ribbons drifted to the street as Elise watched. The symbols stitched into the cloth were aflame as the spells unraveled.

Broken.

White light flooded the street again. Elise flung an arm over her eyes.

The shadow serpent plunged through the roof of the casino tower with a *thump* that shook the entire building. "Oh, shit," she muttered, stumbling backward. The ground beneath her feet trembled, and she felt a thudding that could only mean that the floors above were collapsing.

She abandoned the doors and ran.

Halfway across the street, asphalt rose underneath Elise. She lost her balance and slipped to her knees as a spike of earth erupted from the road. She clung to its side.

It shoved higher and higher and jerked to a halt twenty feet in the air.

Her gloves lost traction. She slid, scraping her chest down the rock. Elise landed on broken fragments of pavement, which had been reduced to rubble beneath her feet, and she stumbled off of the asphalt hill. Yatai had ripped through the ground underneath the street like an earthworm through soil.

Sharp cracks rent the air. Windows in the hotel tower shattered, and glass showered down the sides of the buildings.

The remaining fiends scattered, scrambling around to the other side of the building, and the sound of gunfire a block away was drowned out by the roar of the casino's collapse. One by one, the floors of the building began to fall in like a house of cards. Clouds of dust rushed through the street, blasting over her face and turning everything to white.

The street pitched underneath her. Pain flared in her knees and shocked up her hips. She landed on all fours, and her stomach rose into her throat as the pavement split and fell.

She jumped onto the sidewalk just in time for the place she had been standing to collapse.

Debris showered around her, pounding into the street and exploding like small bombs. The glass doors into the casino burst, and white clouds of plaster and concrete gusted over the entire block like a sandstorm.

She threw herself over the hood of a truck and rolled onto the ground. Her side hit hard. Her breath rushed from her mouth. A chunk of concrete the size of a couch smashed into the sidewalk behind her, and Elise scrambled under the truck, belly to the ground.

Elise watched as the casino crashed around her, bracing herself for the blow that would crush the vehicle on top of her.

But it didn't come.

The earth yawned open to devour the building first.

The ground was falling away—sucking in the casino the way Rick's Drugstore had been taken. And a line of darkness swept toward her hiding place under the truck.

"Fuck, fuck, *fuck*," she cursed under her breath, digging in her fingers to wiggle free again.

The highest floors of the casino vanished. Emptiness roared toward her, and she scrambled to her feet to run. Yatai's ichor licked at her heels.

Her shoe caught on a rock.

She fell.

The ground disappeared beneath her.

Elise shrieked as the pavement crumbled away, scrabbling at the rocks with both hands and finding nothing to grip.

Her weight jerked on her shoulder as the ground disappeared. Her feet dangled over void.

But she wasn't falling.

She looked up. Yatam's fingers were closed around her arm, and his beautiful face was peaceful and calm. "Do you need assistance?"

Elise searched for traction with her other hand, but the road crumbled away everywhere she tried to grab, and her feet couldn't seem to find rocks that weren't falling either. She swallowed hard. The hole was so deep that she couldn't see the bottom—it must have opened into the Warrens.

"Sure," she said through hard, heaving breaths. "Assistance would probably be good."

The demon hauled her up with a single arm, stepping back until she was on solid earth.

He wrapped an arm around her waist. Yatam's eyes traced over her face, and his lips curved into a half-smile that was more reminiscent of hunger than friendliness.

Elise pushed away to stare into the hole.

The casino was completely gone. All that remained was an empty, gaping chasm in the street and some fragments of glass sparkling on the pavement. Hot air and a sulfur stench gushed from the earth.

It felt strange being able to stand on the main street and look past the block to the hospital beyond.

Elise clenched her fists.

She took a mental tally of the body count. Anyone who hadn't evacuated the casino would be dead. Depending on the hole's depth, hundreds of demons might have died with them. She had told the Craven's employees to hide down there.

Maybe thousands dead, all because Yatai didn't want her to reach the gate.

"Goddamn it!" she yelled into the chasm, voice echoing down the depths of the earth. "*Goddamn it!* Mother of all fucking demons!"

"My sister doesn't do things halfway."

She spun on him. "You *asshole*. This is your fault—you and your sister's, and your goddamn suicide wish!"

Yatam arched an eyebrow. "You're welcome." His hand was covered in blood from holding her arm, and he licked one of his fingers. "Delicious."

She groaned. "Don't do that." She flung an arm toward the suspended ruins. "How the hell am I supposed to get up there now?"

"There are other ways to reach the ruins. Follow me."

The path to Yatam's condo was clear, and they didn't encounter anybody on the way. There were no signs of normality remaining—all the demons and humans had fled, leaving the streets vacant aside from the occasional Union SUV chasing fiends.

The bell desk in the condominium lobby was empty, and the elevators didn't work. Elise took the stairs two at a time.

His condo was on the highest level of the building, close enough that they could have touched the its mirror if they had a ladder. Nügua smiled benevolently at her basin of clay, unaffected by the chaos.

Elise shielded her face from the wind, gazing up at the crumbling black apartments. Only a block away, the Union was erecting scaffolding between the parking garage and the dark gate. A helicopter buzzed between the Silver Legacy and its mirror. "What happened to your ceiling?"

"I spoke with Yatai. We had a disagreement."

Some disagreement. She paced between the walls, studying the mirrored ruins. They didn't look stable, and the

Union's scaffolds were too far away. "How am I going to get up there?"

"What do you plan to do?"

"I don't know," Elise said. "Maybe I can destroy her with the obsidian blade."

He waved a dismissive hand. "Highly doubtful."

"Do you have a better idea?"

"Perhaps. Let me tell you a story, Godslayer." Yatam circled Nügua. "Over five thousand years ago, two children were born in what would become Myanmar. They lived a modest life, ruled by the passing seasons. To them, wealth meant many animals flush with milk, and good rain that became good crops. Until a woman visited."

He nodded toward the statue.

Nügua continued to smile.

"She was a wealthy traveler with no interest in farmers, but the children caught her eye. She was as enamored with the twins as their parents were with her jewels, and so she offered a trade. For the price of her necklace and a basket of spice, she took the children as her slaves."

"What are you telling me?" Elise asked.

"I am telling you that I did not become a man through the natural cycles of life. I became a man because Nügua purchased me, sculpted a new body for my sister and I, and breathed our souls into the new forms."

"You were born human."

"Both of us were, Yatai and I." He stroked Nügua's shoulder. "Mortal minds in immortal bodies."

"So she made you into demons," Elise said. "That's a violation of the Treaty of Dis."

"It didn't exist at the time. Nügua did as she willed. And she willed for us to be her eternal companions."

She eyed the statue. "Some companions."

"Like me, Nügua grew tired of living. And, also like me, she could not die. Instead, she crafted a new body for herself— one that is eternally asleep. And I have guarded her for countless years."

"Why don't you destroy it?" Elise asked.

"Because she would be reborn." He lowered his lips to one of her outstretched hands, and his voice dropped. "I don't hate her so much." She wasn't sure she was supposed to hear that part.

Yatam bent and scooped clay from the basin, letting it fall through his fingers. His eyes were distant, as though he were reliving thousands of years of life.

"I thought she left this clay for me so I might follow her into eternal sleep. So I could sculpt one more body for myself and bleed my life into it. But who would guard us? Who would ensure we never awoke?"

"She must have known that," Elise said.

His fist clenched on the clay. Yatam turned his burning eyes on her. "Yes. She must have known."

"I can't turn Yatai into a statue."

"That's not what I'm suggesting. The legends say that Nügua breathed souls into her creations to make them live, but this isn't true," Yatam said. "She opened her veins and *poured* life upon my sister and I. Blood, sword-woman. It's all about blood."

He rose, swift and sudden, and seized her wrist. His grip was painfully tight.

"Let go of me," Elise said, voice level.

"I know what it means to be the Godslayer now." His arms encircling her back to press her chest against his. "The angels intended you to be His wife. To be with you is death. Consuming your blood weakened me, so consuming more—

consuming your flesh—would draw your mortality into me. I could become human again."

Elise's heart pounded. So that was Metaraon's solution to the God problem—giving him a tainted bride. And using her angel-crafted blood to kill demons would have probably infuriated the ones who meant for her to assassinate Him.

She pushed against Yatam, leaning back in his arms. "But if you drink my blood and eat my flesh, then who's going to take care of Yatai?"

"I will take us only to the brink. I shouldn't need to kill you."

"But Yatai—"

"She is my sister, and where one of us is damaged, we both shall fall." He pressed his pelvis into hers. He was growing aroused, and it pressed painfully against her stomach. "Trust me, sword-woman."

"That's not going to happen," she said, even as her body disagreed by flushing with heat.

"I can make this painless." He stroked his hand down her throat. "As angels have dominion over the mental, so do demons over the physical. This does not need to feel like dying."

He tipped her head back gently, and his lips brushed down her chin.

"Get off of me," Elise said. "Your suggestion to give Him wives is the whole reason my life is ruined. I should hate you."

His tongue flicked over the pulse in her throat. "Yet you don't."

"Yeah, I do." Her gasp made it sound less than convincing.

"You're attracted to me," he said, circling the button on her jeans with a finger. "Don't be ashamed. I'm the father of demons—incubi and succubi inclusive—and my touch is sinful

Heaven on Earth." With a flick of his thumb, he popped her fly open. His fingertips dipped behind the waistband, stroking the smooth skin below her navel. "You want to surrender your blood and body to me. You want my touch."

"No," she said, but then his hand slid into her underwear, and her ability to say anything else fled. She sucked in a hard breath.

But he didn't move further. His eyes were burning coals, and he looked so serious. Deadly serious. "Let me bleed you, Godslayer. Make me human."

His lips brushed over hers.

She barely breathed as she nodded.

He lowered her to the rim of the basin in a single smooth motion and gestured for her to lean back. Elise braced her hands on the edge.

"What are you doing?" she asked.

Yatam's hand stroked down her calf to her ankle and removed the dagger from her boot. He slashed the hem open to bare her leg. "I will drink from your femoral."

She tensed. "You could drink from my arm."

Yatam's breath was hot on the inside of her bare leg. "Most likely. But don't you think this is so much more fun?"

Before she could respond, he sliced open her thigh. The cut was shallow, and it only hurt for an instant. Fresh blood, so thick that it was black, dripped down her thigh.

His mouth closed on the wound.

He drank deep, and every draw of his tongue on her thigh sent warm sensations rippling through her core. It was not painful, although the initial suction was so powerful that she struggled to breathe.

Her fingers gripped the basin. "Careful," she said, feeling light-headed.

Yatam didn't seem concerned. He slid his hand up her leg, cupping the back of her thigh as his mouth worked over the wound.

When he lifted his mouth, his lips were stained red, and he was breathing hard.

"It hurts," he said, as though it was a revelation. "In my chest—I can feel my heart failing."

"Is that enough?"

He laughed. "No."

Yatam tugged her pants to her knees, pulling them over her feet to render her naked from the waist down except for her boy-cut underwear. He removed her boots. Even through her dizzy haze, it made her feel exposed, and she put a hand on his shoulder. "Wait."

He smirked and said again, "No."

Dipping his head between her knees again, his hot breath burned over her skin. His tongue darted over the back of her knee and slid higher.

His deft fingers opened the belts on the bulletproof vest and spread them open. Relieving the pressure over the bullet wound hurt as much as getting shot for the first time. She gritted her teeth.

He removed the spine sheath next, letting the falchions clatter to the ground, and stroked his hand from her navel to her breasts. Yatam cupped her throat. Her blue veins were visible under the translucence of her peach skin, brighter than she had ever seen them before. "So much blood waiting to be tasted."

"Not all that much."

Yatam slid up her body, covering her cold skin with his warmth and abandoning the wound on her leg. For an instant, she was actually disappointed—but that must have been the blood loss speaking.

His weight settled over her, and he bit her shoulder gently. His teeth were sharp enough that the lightest of nips drew blood. Arousal flushed between her legs.

"I'm going to devour you. You, and every drop of your dire blood."

She burned. Before she could think to say anything else, a single word slipped from her lips: "Okay."

She surrendered.

Her fingers dug into his shoulders as she levered herself against him, pressing her lips to his. His tongue danced over hers, tasting of copper pennies and ash.

Yatam supported her with a hand splayed over her back as the other explored her breasts and abdomen. Everywhere he touched, she lit with flame.

He leaned back long enough to remove her vest and shirt, then pressed himself to Elise again, kissing her so hard that it hurt. She felt it all the way down her throat, into her gut. It was like dying.

His fingers, slick with blood, tugged her underwear aside and traced the dampness between her legs for an instant before plunging inside. She gasped. "Cut me," he groaned into her neck as he worked his fingers in and out of her. His other hand pressed hard metal into hers—the knife he had used to cut open her leg.

It took her a moment to realize what he had said, but even when her brain managed to process the words, she couldn't grasp the meaning. "*What?*"

"Cut me. I want to see how I bleed."

He kissed her again, harder than before. He nipped her tongue and caught her bottom lip between his teeth. The pain was brilliant and delicious.

She dug the knife into his shoulder, dragging a line down his chest. Blood dribbled down his pale skin, crimson on white.

The wound didn't close.

Yatam gave a low groan and pressed himself against her.

Elise's balance slipped with his weight. Her back sank into the clay, and she gazed up at the smiling face of Nügua as Yatam's slick, bloody chest rubbed across hers. Her pulse thudded between her legs.

"You have rendered me mortal," he said, voice husky and deep.

Her hands moved of their own volition to push down his leather pants, baring his body to hers, and Yatam chuckled with his mouth against her breast. His teeth sliced open the skin over her pectoral, and his tongue massaged the wound.

Blood upon blood. Her fingers gripped his shining hair and dug into the back of his neck.

Yatam settled his weight between her legs. "Cut me," he said again, face hovering over hers. His eyes were brown. Truly brown.

She slipped the sharp edge of the dagger over his hardened nipple, and at the same moment, he drove his body into hers.

It was tight and uncomfortable—it was always uncomfortable—but it was a kind of ecstasy that Elise had never known. Drawing his blood as he forced himself inside, the heat of him against her, the satisfaction of being filled.

She lost herself in the rhythm, grasping at his shoulders, unaware if she was damaging him with the knife or if she was even holding it anymore. She had been reduced to a sum of parts—exposed breasts, cold in the air, her bared legs, and the place between them where Yatam buried himself.

Her knees were pinned tightly to his sides. Each thrust rubbed against the wound on her femoral artery and ached in just the right way. They were both slippery with her blood. His mouth sucked hard on her wounded shoulder.

289

SM Reine

Elise's head swam. Her vision was blurry.

How much blood had she lost?

It took Elise too long to realize that the pounding she heard wasn't her fading pulse. Someone was beating against the door to the condo, trying to get inside.

Yatam's tongue laved along the side of her neck. "You taste like mortality and my death," he whispered before pressing his lips to hers. "For this, I will love you for the rest of my life—may it be only hours."

She tried to lift a hand to his face, but her arm was too heavy. Her pulse was too fast, too weak.

The door smashed open.

Yatam was suddenly gone, and she was cold. So very cold.

Elise rolled over, trying to collect her senses, but moving only made her heart struggle to beat. Her vision darkened at the edges. An ocean roared within her skull.

Somehow, she threaded her feet through the scraps of her jeans and pulled them over her hips. She found her shirt, but couldn't get it over her head.

And then there were people there, surrounding the basin. People with guns.

Goddamn Union.

"We've got a survivor!"

Someone kneeled beside her. Elise could just barely make out his nametag when it hovered over her face, which said that he was named Bellamy. "God, what a mess—but check this out. She's got a Union vest."

"Don't touch me." She tried to push him away, but her muscles were liquid, and blood slicked her hands.

A familiar man loomed nearby. His neck was as thick as his jaw, his shoulders were broad, and he looked like an angry gorilla. "She's not Union," said Zettel. "Trust me. We don't want to take her back to the compound."

290

Elise reached blindly, hoping that his throat would be close enough for her to grab, even if she couldn't see him clearly.

A hand caught her swiping arm.

"I'm going to follow regulations. I'll let Malcolm work it out when we get there," Bellamy said, restraining her gently. "Allyson. Yates. Bring the gurney." His face was kind and sympathetic. "What happened to you? Did you get mauled by a fiend?"

She was falling, spinning, struggling to breathe.

"Don't touch me," Elise whispered again.

Bellamy lifted her out of Nügua's basin.

"Don't worry. The Union's got you—you're going to be fine now."

XVI

Bellamy informed Elise that the Union had established a temporary hospital northeast of Reno where they processed the injured before evacuating them. The ride felt like it took hours. She drifted on the edge of consciousness the entire way.

Every time she almost passed out, sharp pain would rouse her—hands applying pressure to the injuries on her neck and thigh. They gave her IV fluids. It didn't seem to improve anything.

Bellamy delivered her to the ward with minimal fanfare. A witch wrote down Elise's name, and then he wheeled her into a long room full of beds—all occupied.

Lights slid overhead. It made Elise dizzy.

A familiar voice spoke, distant and hazy.

"Elise?"

Footsteps. James's face swam into her vision. She didn't realize she had reached out until he caught her hand. "What are you doing here?" she asked.

"I was injured. The Union provided medical care. Forget about that—you're so pale," James said, pressing his hand to her forehead. "Jesus, you're clammy. What's happened?"

If she'd had any blood left to blush with, her face would have turned red. It was Bellamy who responded. "Significant blood loss. Looks like a pretty bad attack."

"Is she all right?"

Elise pushed his hand off. "I'm fine." To betray the lie, she immediately shivered. The room blurred.

How quickly could blood be drawn through the femoral artery, anyway?

James lifted the sheet to inspect her for wounds, and Elise was trembling too hard to stop him. He saw her missing jeans, which had been cut off by a paramedic, and the bandaged leg. His eyebrows lifted toward his hairline. "Battle wound?"

"Sure," Elise said.

James kept pace as they wheeled her gurney to an empty space in the infirmary, which was next to an unconscious man whose arm terminated at the elbow with a bandaged stump.

"I'll alert the doctor," Bellamy said, disappearing.

The corner in which he left them was quiet, if not private; the curtain wouldn't completely enclose them. "What's happened in Reno?" James asked, still grasping her gloved hand.

"We lost a casino. And I killed Itra'il."

Surprise flicked across his face. "Why?"

She struggled to think of an answer. Elise knew there was a good one, but she couldn't remember it. "No mercy."

His brow lowered over his eyes. "What of Yatai?"

"Opening the gates," Elise said. No, wait. That wasn't right. Her eyes were so heavy. "I don't know."

James's voice faded in and out of her ears, carrying over the quiet bustle of the ward. "Where are the doctors?"

"I'm cold. I want another blanket."

"You're sweating."

Where was Yatam? What would he be doing, now that he was mortal? "He said he wouldn't kill me."

James's hand tightened. "Who said that?"

The curtains opened.

"There you are," said a woman, and James's hand disappeared.

"Stephanie! Thank God."

Elise's ears rang. They were talking—something about evacuating the emergency room, transferring patients, the collapse of a hospital tower. Yatam's face loomed in the foggy place between asleep and awake. He was smiling. His lips were dripping blood.

And then cool, dry fingers were probing Elise's skin, opening her eyelids, pressing a stethoscope to her chest. Stephanie's clinical briskness was comforting, for once.

She only listened for a moment before pulling the blanket over Elise again.

"Based on your symptoms, I'm going to guess you've lost two to three units of blood. Ideally, you should get intravenous fluids and a transfusion. I can't imagine we'll have access to donor blood here, but that should be all right. You're hardy. You probably won't die. A few days of rest—"

"Days?" Elise tried to sit up, but her vision dimmed at the sudden change in posture, and she almost slipped off the side of the bed. Stephanie pushed her back with an irritated huff.

"We don't have days." James took the chair beside her and rolled up his sleeve. "I'll donate."

The doctor's lips drew into a thin line. "Are you compatible?"

"More than you know. We've done it before."

"Far be it from *me* to attempt to give medical advice to either of you, but blood diseases…?"

"Kopides don't contract them."

"Have it your way. I still need equipment. I can't magic a blood transfusion."

"Find a man named Malcolm," James said. "He's the commander."

Elise had no idea how long it took Stephanie to find him. She was pretty sure that she fell asleep again. The rasp of the curtain opening stirred her at some point, and Malcolm's face filled her vision, replacing Yatam's.

The commander took one look at Elise, pale and limp on the gurney, and laughed. "Have fun in Reno?"

"Come closer so I can hit you again," she mumbled.

"Don't make promises you can't keep, darling. Hey, you!" Malcolm snagged a passing nurse. "See these lovely people here? Get them whatever they want."

"Donor blood," Stephanie said promptly. "And access to labs so I can perform analyses."

"Anything they want, short of that," Malcolm amended. "One of the blood banks has been destroyed, and we don't have access to the others yet. Sorry."

She huffed again. "Then I'll need a few supplies."

"This way," the nurse said, leading her away.

Malcolm peeked under Elise's blanket. She kicked weakly at him. "You've had a fun night. Where was my invitation?"

"Thank you," James said in the least grateful tone possible, which seemed to be all the cue the commander needed.

Malcolm winked at Elise. "Enjoy the party." He followed another kopis out of the infirmary.

If nothing else, her annoyance at her ex-boyfriend was enough to briefly clear her head. She looked over at James. His face was bruised, his glasses were missing, and there were bloody handprints on his shirt. "What happened to you?"

"Anthony. He's under Yatai's influence."

She craned her head around to get a better look at his wounds. "Possessed?"

"That's my guess. Yatai wanted information from me, but to what purpose, I'm not certain."

So that was where Yatai had learned to open Alain's wards.

SM Reine

James's girlfriend returned, and, with the help of the nurse, quickly prepared Elise for the transfusion. Stephanie had two bags of saline, an IV pole, and some tubing. "Are you sure you're up for this, James?" she asked as she hung the saline from the pole.

"Always."

"Well, in order to transfuse a unit of blood, which is all I dare to take, we'll need seven or eight hours," Stephanie said, tying a rubber tourniquet around Elise's upper arm and swabbing the inside of her elbow with alcohol. "There's no way to speed it up. You two better get comfortable. It would help to sleep through it."

He adjusted himself so he was leaning against her gurney. Elise watched as Stephanie attached the saline, and then the other tube. James's eyebrows furrowed as she inserted the needles.

Then it was Elise's turn. The needle slid into her skin with an instant of pain, which was immediately lost among the mess of other aches and bruises. It was nothing in comparison to having Yatam drink her life out of her thigh.

She relaxed against the bed, the flow of saline cold against her arm.

Sharing James's blood was enough to bypass the wards on their rings, but she was far too tired to worry about his thoughts, or what he might get from her. Words faded in and out of the back of her mind like trying to tune into a distant radio station.

So tired... city destroyed... Anthony... why her thigh? What's she not telling me?

She wanted to tell him not to worry about it, but gravity was so heavy.

Exhaustion sucked her under.

Hours passed in the darkness.

Stephanie's return was heralded by the swift patter of footsteps and the rattling of metal curtain rings.

Elise didn't open her eyes. She felt much more alert as soon as consciousness hit—her head was clearer, thinking wasn't so difficult, and she was aware enough to realize that she was mostly naked under the paper-thin blanket. But she remained still as Stephanie addressed James.

"How do you feel?"

"Thirsty," he said. "Thank you for the water."

"They've offered me a place on the next convoy out of here," Stephanie whispered over crinkling paper. Plastic snapped. The tubing tugged against Elise's arm. "They want my assistance providing medical care at the receiving area in Sacramento. Considering the situation here, I thought… maybe I should stay in California."

James was quiet for a long time. "You mean, stay with your family."

"Yes. I hoped you would come with me, but…" She sighed. "You won't, will you?"

Cloth rustled against cloth. "I'm needed elsewhere, Stephanie."

"Of course." Elise opened her eyes to slits. Stephanie bent over James, giving him a long kiss. When she righted herself again, she was smiling and holding the bent needle that had been in his arm. "That's the problem with trying to date a hero, isn't it?"

He traced the line of her jaw, smiling sadly. "I'm not a hero."

"Well, if things change, you'll know where to find me. And I hope you will."

She taped gauze to his arm. James rose to use the bathroom.

Elise finally opened her eyes when Stephanie's blue-gloved hands touched her arm. "And how do you feel?" the doctor asked. The usual bite was missing from her tone.

"Like I could wrestle oxen," Elise said. Her voice croaked from her dry throat.

"Done with angry badgers, hmm?" The needle pinched as Stephanie removed it and pressed gauze over the pinprick. "There. Leave that on for about ten minutes, please."

She dropped everything in bag marked with a hazard symbol. Elise sat up, hugging the blanket to her bare chest to watch Stephanie tidy up. The doctor wore white sneakers and carried a duffel bag over one shoulder.

"Leaving?" Elise asked.

"Yes. In about an hour." She glanced at the clock. "Well, half an hour. I should get going." Stephanie paused with a hand on the curtain. "Malcolm brought your belongings, which they recovered from the scene of attack. He also dropped off fresh clothing for you. It's all in the bag on the chair."

"Thanks."

The doctor gave her a final, appraising look. "Try not to kill James."

Elise snorted. "It's not in the plan."

"Good."

She departed, leaving the curtains open. Irritation spiked through Elise. She was only wearing underwear and the blanket—some privacy would have been nice.

Then a gurney passed the other side of her curtain, and her irritation quickly dissipated.

A man thrashed on it, strapped down at the shoulders, hips, and feet by rope. The muscles in his neck strained as he fought. His skin shone with sweat.

Anthony.

298

Elise climbed out of bed, finding her shirt in the black bag. It was bloodstained, but preferable to a Union polo shirt. They hadn't given her what remained of her jeans, so she had no choice but to wear the cargo pants. They were loose and rode low on her hips.

James returned, holding a fresh glass of water. He seemed surprised to see her standing. "What are you doing? Be careful—you might still be weak."

"They just dragged Anthony through here."

His eyes widened, and he didn't stop Elise when she hurried to follow the gurney in her bare feet.

She stopped when she stepped into the hall.

The door from the infirmary opened into a huge warehouse. She stepped up to the railing and found she was only on the third level—several more floors stretched above and below, and there was a garage at the bottom with more of those hulking black SUVs. The Union bustled around her. She had never seen so many kopides in one place before, even at the semi-centennial summit.

They had a base outside Reno. An actual outpost.

How the hell had the Union built such a thing without her noticing?

The gurney continued down the hall. Elise stepped back from the railing and followed.

Anthony was wheeled into an unmarked room, escorted by two kopides. The door swung shut behind them. She moved to open it.

Malcolm appeared seemingly from nowhere, blocking the door with his body. "Doesn't anything keep you in bed? I thought you were supposed to be on the verge of death."

"I got better. Let me in."

"Why?"

"I know that guy."

299

Malcolm laughed. "I suppose I shouldn't be surprised that you know him. I can't let you in there, though. For your information, 'that guy' blew away three other guys with a shotgun. You're a tough bitch, but are you *that* tough?"

A chill washed down her spine. "Anthony killed three men? That has to be a mistake."

"I'll let you judge."

He led her further down the hall, down a flight of stairs, and into a dark room with a bank of monitors. A witch sat in front of them, typing rapidly. Malcolm perched on the desk next to her.

"Cue up the arrest footage we pulled off Jack's camera, please?"

A low-resolution image appeared on the main monitor. There was no audio, and she could barely make out the eggshell walls. It wasn't until she saw the darkened chandelier and the barred window at the end of the hall that she recognized the location.

It was her apartment building.

She watched with sick fascination as the swaying image approached her door. Another man moved into view to kick it open.

The camera went wild, and red mist sprayed. The man in front dropped.

Anthony stood in the apartment's living room. He pumped his shotgun and stepped behind the wall.

The man with the camera entered the apartment, and Anthony faced him. His motions were mechanical as he stepped forward to fire again.

A rifle swung into view, held by the kopis with the head-mounted camera, but he didn't get a chance to shoot.

The camera fell. It bounced off the floor.

Anthony's feet took another step. Another body fell to the carpet.

Elise could only see them from below the knees as men swarmed him, slamming him to the ground. A woman delivered a few swift punches, and the sliver of Anthony's face that was visible in the image didn't seem to register pain.

"That's good," Malcolm said. "Thanks, Carradee."

Elise watched the monitor for a few long seconds after the screen froze on a single frame—a shot of Anthony's impassive face, and a bloody limb on the carpet. She wasn't sure if it was an arm or a leg.

When James told her that Anthony had attacked him, she hadn't imagined anything quite so... fatal.

"He's been possessed," she said. "There's no other reason he would do that."

"Psychotic break?"

"Anthony isn't crazy."

"He is definitely showing signs of possession," Malcolm admitted. "We're not equipped with an exorcist right now, though, so the best we can do is keep him from hurting anyone else. In case you're worried, we have regulations for this. He won't be punished for what he's done under the influence."

Elise traced a finger over Anthony's face on the monitor. He must have been taken in the Warrens—and she thought he had been running away.

Another one of her friends' lives destroyed by her decisions.

She sighed. "Don't send him to a priest. Just get someone to bring my belongings to me."

"Why?"

"Because I'm going to exorcise him."

SM Reine

Elise met James in a darkened observation room. She studied Anthony through a one-way mirror into Anthony's cell. The Union had strapped him to a heavy wooden chair, and the only things holding him up were his bindings. He was slumped over with his head hanging from his shoulders. The ropes at his wrists had rubbed him raw and bloody.

"Can I get you anything else for the exorcism?" Malcolm asked as she took her belongings from James and pulled the spine scabbard on like a backpack. "Holy water? Bell, book, and candle? Young priest and an old priest?"

"Privacy," she said.

"That's a good one. You know the Union records everything, right?"

"Exactly. Turn off your cameras. Leave this room. Don't watch us."

"We have regulations against that."

"Of course you do," James muttered.

Elise caught the commander's gaze. "Please."

"Oh, bugger. Why not?" Malcolm pushed a chair into the corner, climbed onto it, and plucked wires out of the back of the camera that pointed at the window. "If I get demoted, I expect you to make room for me on your couch."

She snorted. "You'll have to buy me a couch first."

Malcolm laughed and clapped a hand on her shoulder. "God, I don't like you. I don't think I've ever liked you. But you are fun as hell. Try not to kill this guy, all right?"

He left, and the door into the hall gave a solid, satisfying *click* as it closed behind him.

It left Elise with nothing but the door into Anthony's room, a chain of golden charms, and a sick sense of inevitability.

"The sooner we do it, the better, I suppose," James said, moving toward the cell.

302

Elise stepped in front of the door. "Actually, I wanted total privacy." When he only looked at her blankly, she added, "Including from you."

"But we've always piggybacked before you performed an exorcism."

"I know."

"That means I would see everything that happens in that room anyway." James dropped his warding ring onto the table and waited expectantly.

She sighed and twisted the ring off her thumb.

The magic wore off, and Elise's mind blossomed like a flower facing the sun. His thoughts and senses washed over her. There was magic threaded through the fiber of the room, from the wards on Anthony's chair to the light hanging from the ceiling. It dazzled with crystalline energy.

Elise didn't really want to see herself through James's eyes, but she had little choice. She always looked awful, and that day was worse than usual. A unit of James's blood hadn't completely restored her color, and it had done nothing for her shadowed eyes and bandaged shoulder.

After a minute of deep, controlled breathing, she was back in her own head again. She entered the cell before his emotions could hit.

Anthony didn't react to their presence, but Yatai's energy was palpable in the room. It made the air feel thick, as though she had to swim to Anthony's chair. James felt it, too, but he wasn't as accustomed to forcing his way past infernal energy. He hesitated to cross the threshold.

Elise kneeled in front of Anthony, getting low enough to see his face underneath the veil of his bangs. His eyes were closed. His skin was soaked with sweat. She reached up to smooth the hair out of his face.

Anthony's eyes opened.

He grimaced with pain and lifted his head. "Oh *man*, my neck hurts," he groaned. His fingers twitched, like he was going to try to rub away the aches, but he could barely jiggle his arm within the restraints. Anthony's eyes fell on the ropes.

Panic flashed over his face. He shook his seat, making the legs scrape against the floor.

"Relax," she said. "Don't fight. You'll hurt yourself."

His eyes flicked from Elise, to James, to the door, to the mirrored wall. "Where am I?"

"We're in a Union warehouse."

"Why am I...?" He pulled on his wrists again. Fresh blood welled under the ropes, and he hissed.

Elise glanced at James, uncertain of what she should tell him. There usually wasn't much point in talking to someone who was possessed. If they were conscious enough to understand, they wouldn't believe it. And once the demon took over, it didn't matter, anyway.

"We're trying to help you," James said.

Anthony gave a harsh laugh. "Help me? By tying me to a chair? Let me go, guys." Elise looped the chain of charms around her fist. He froze. "What are you doing with those?"

She circled the chair silently. It was James who responded. "Remember that we're your friends. We aren't trying to hurt you, and this will be over quickly."

"What is 'this'? Elise?" He craned around, trying to see behind him. "Elise!"

"*Crux sacra sit mihi lux.*"

The chain of charms flared with power. And just as they had during Zohak's exorcism, they immediately grew warm. She focused on the strength she shared with James.

"You can't exorcise me," Anthony said. "I'm not possessed!"

"*Non draco sit mihi dux.*"

304

His mirthless laughter turned to panting, and then small cries. He twisted his fists.

A ragged cry ripped from his throat.

"Elise!"

"*Vade retro, Satana,*" she went on in a low voice as the chain grew hotter.

James's thoughts ran underneath hers—*what is she doing, she isn't focusing her energy at all, this isn't going to work*—and she pushed it away.

Elise's spoke softer than before. "*Nunquam suade mihi vana. Sunt mala quae libas—*"

Anthony screamed. He flung his head back, smacking it against the back of the chair, and his biceps strained as he tried to lift his hips. The harder he fought, the brighter the warding symbols on the wood burned.

"*—ipse venena bibas,*" she finished.

He stopped fighting. Anthony slumped again, his head hanging over his shoulders as he sagged.

Elise flung the burning charms to the ground. Heat turned the metal molten white.

"That can't be it," James said.

She stepped back. "It's not."

The demonic energy hadn't left Anthony. In fact, using the prayer of St. Benedict had only intensified the fire burning over his skin. The tension in the room heightened. Her blood felt slow in its veins.

Anthony's head lifted again.

This time, he didn't struggle. His face was slack, his mouth hung open, and his drooping eyes were no longer brown—the irises had turned as black as the abyss that Yatai had tunneled through the earth, except that she had burrowed through his mind.

The lone light bulb in the center of the ceiling flickered.

Yatai had come.

Shadows slithered from Anthony, extending tendrils to each corner of the room. The eggshell white walls dimmed. *Trying to exorcise me again? I thought you would have learned that it's impossible by now.*

"I did."

Then you waste your time as well as mine.

"Not exactly. I thought you might let him go."

Her chuckle was identical to Yatam's. It poured over her skin like a cold kiss and stirred deep within her belly. *Why would I do that?*

"Because I can give you what you want." She struggled to take a deep breath in the thick air, steeling herself. "I can kill you." James's gaze fell on her. She felt his silent incredulity, and ignored it. "You don't have to destroy the entire city to die. There are other ways."

Yatai was silent for so long that if Anthony's eyes hadn't been so dark, she might have been certain the demon was gone.

When she spoke again, she wasn't quite so confident.

I am eternal.

"And I'm the Godslayer."

Yes, but how is such a weapon wielded? Consider it. The figure of a child stepped out from behind the chair. Lucinde was still wearing her Sunday best, but there was still no mistaking her red lips and hungry eyes for anything but Yatai's. *Do you think you were meant to return from the abyss of the garden? You are a sacrificial lamb. A life for a life. You may be able to kill me, but surely not without surrendering yourself.*

Yatai strolled toward her, slinking with a sway to her hips that was unnatural for such a small child. She circled Elise, trailing an icy hand over her back.

Your life is your weapon, and it can only be wielded once. The question is… how badly do you want me to die?

306

Elise thought of Nukha'il, and Itra'il, and the casino sinking into the earth.

"Very badly."

But not badly enough. You have no resolve, Godslayer—you aren't prepared to die.

"You should ask Yatam what I'm willing to give to kill you," Elise said. "Both of you."

Uncertainty flickered over Lucinde's innocent features. *He is enamored with what you represent.*

"I know."

He doesn't love you. He only loves his death.

Elise had to laugh at that. "I'm not worried about love. Trust me."

Yatai faced her, and the darkness in the room grew until Elise couldn't see beyond the length of her arm. Anthony and James vanished, sinking into fog. Only the girl remained visible—a ghostly figure in the void.

Her hands smoothed over her blue skirt. She looked… nervous.

"Yesterday, I fed your brother my blood and my flesh. And when I drew my knife across his chest, he didn't heal. Do you know what that means?" Elise asked. The demon didn't respond. "I can kill you. You just have to abandon the gates and let the city go—you have to let *Anthony* go."

The girl's mouth drew down into a frown. *My brother lives. I feel him. I think you're lying to me.*

"I'm not."

You are prepared to die to bring death upon us both.

Elise opened her mouth to say, "Yes."

But she hesitated for a heartbeat. Just a heartbeat.

It was enough.

The room reappeared around Elise. Yatai stepped back. *Your love of this life is still too great. You will not die for us.*

"Wait—"

If you change your mind, come and find me. I will lay my life at your mercy feet, spare your city, and surrender this man to you for the low cost of your blood and soul. Otherwise…

She disappeared, taking the shadows with her.

Anthony arched in the chair. He roared, throwing his head back and kicking out both feet.

The thrashing was so sudden that the chair tipped. It cracked against the floor. He screamed and strained his arms against the wrists, beating his feet against the legs.

Elise dropped by Anthony's side, but the seizure wracked his entire body, and he didn't respond to her touch.

James hovered by the door, eyes wide circles.

How much had he seen?

She felt him probe her mind, and Elise shoved the warding ring onto her thumb before he could see anything.

"Get Malcolm or a doctor or—*something*," Elise said, grabbing one of Anthony's hands. He was ripping his wrists apart trying to get free. James didn't immediately move, and she shot a glare at him. "Go!"

He flung the door open and ran.

A Union doctor with a syringe full of morphine wasn't enough to sedate Anthony. It took an entire unit of kopides to strap him to a bed and wheel him to the infirmary, where they had more drugs and more staff to hold him down.

Elise paced the empty hallway outside the ward, arms folded tightly across her chest. James hung by the railing overlooking the warehouse. He hadn't looked at her once since they had left the containment cell. He watched the teams move on the floor below as though his gaze could set them on fire.

Malcolm emerged from the infirmary.

"Well?" Elise asked.

"He's finally unconscious. He bit a witch's hand, though, and we're not sure if he's spreading the ichor yet. Might have to amputate."

Her back hit the wall, and she slid down to sit on the floor. "Damn it."

"We've got an exorcist on staff who can fix him. Don't worry about it."

She didn't feel like explaining that there was no time for that. Exhaustion weighed heavily on her. "Yeah. Thanks."

Malcolm glanced at James. "Just so you two know, the helicopter is making its last trip out of here in an hour—we'll be making our final assault after that, and we can't promise the safety of anyone who doesn't evacuate. I hope you'll both be on it."

James nodded silently, and the commander left.

Elise hugged her legs to her chest and bowed her head to her knees.

The doors to the ward swung open, and then shut again. A stretcher rolled past, escorted by two nurses. Another followed a few minutes later. The helicopter wasn't the only transport leaving soon; another convoy was about to depart, and they were taking as many civilians as they could.

"Is it true?" James finally asked, staring out at the activity in the Union warehouse. "That you would have to die to kill something like Yatai?"

Elise let her head fall back against the wall with a soft *thud*. "Yeah. Probably."

He was quiet for a long time, rubbing his left forearm with a knuckle. Beyond him, the team was mobilized for the assault. Vehicles emptied from the garage in a long train. Survivors began boarding long black buses.

"What do you plan to do?" James asked.

"If I can't kill Yatai, then everyone in the territory dies," Elise said. "Including Anthony. Including me. If it's my life against everyone else's... well, it's not like there's a question."

He came to kneel at her side. "There's another option."

She let her head fall to the side so she could see him. James looked thinner and younger than ever before, but the gray at his temples had begun spreading to the back of his head, and the stubble around his jaw was turning silver, too.

His bright eyes locked on hers. "Leave with me. We'll evacuate on the helicopter. Together."

"And the city? Anthony?"

"Let the Union take care of it all."

Elise barked a bitter laugh. "Like they protected everything downtown?"

His hand fell on hers, and he rubbed his thumb over her knuckles. "Better than choosing to die. That's no choice at all."

"The Union can't slay a god."

"Yatam and Yatai aren't gods. You can't listen to them making those claims. They're demons, nothing more—and it doesn't require a sacrifice to destroy them."

She stared at his hand on hers, shoulders tight and stomach churning.

Her blood flowed through Yatam's system. It had been enough to destroy his regenerative abilities. Maybe he was weak enough to be killed without having to empty her veins completely—though she doubted it.

What would it take to kill Yatai?

Was Elise really willing to die for it?

James rested his chin on her hair. "Most people have been evacuated now, and you've already given everything for this city. It's not worth sacrificing yourself for whatever remains." His hand stilled, fingers tightening. "Not even for Anthony."

310

"But if the Union can't take care of Yatai—if I trust them to do this, and they fail—we'll lose him."

He pulled back, cupping her cheek in a hand. The lines deepened between his furrowed eyebrows. "And if I lose you… that would kill me, Elise."

She buried her face in his shoulder. James smelled familiar and warm, like home should have. But what was home anymore? Every place where she had ever known that illusion of comfort and security was gone.

Her city was going to go next. She could save it, or fall with it.

Or she could run.

"Fine," she mumbled into his arm.

"Fine?"

"You're right. It's not worth it." The words had weight as they fell from her lips. Each syllable made her heart sink lower. "I'll leave with you."

XVII

The helicopter's landing pad was on a hill overlooking the freeway. From the top, Elise could see everything—the sprawling Union warehouse, the glimmering line of buses evacuating the area, and what remained of Reno. It was cold and dark, and she wasn't sure if it was day or night anymore.

Snow was falling on Reno, but it wasn't white; it formed a sludgy mess of brown and yellow with splatters of crimson on the ground, and she didn't want to know where the colors came from.

The Union bustled around them. A steady stream of injured civilians headed into the facility, and a steady stream of trucks exited. Maybe by the end of the night, Reno would be evacuated. Nothing would be left behind but a ghost town, the Warrens, and the rotting remains of an ethereal city.

Even from that distance, she could hear the occasional, distant *pop* of gunfire as Union men slaughtered demons who had spread into Sparks. The vehicles that returned were splattered with ichor.

Her hometown was a stranger to her.

And she was abandoning it.

James was a warm, looming presence at her side. He held her hand, even though her fingers remained slack, and she would have preferred not to be touched at all. She watched the city, and he watched her.

The whirring of a helicopter approached. Half-melted puddles rippled. A wind kicked up around Elise, and she stepped backwards into a slushy mess of mud and snow. It soaked through her shoe and made her toes cold.

The helicopter landed, and the door slid open.

"Get in," shouted Malcolm.

James moved forward. Elise didn't have a choice but to follow; he hadn't let go of her hand. He climbed inside, and she took the seat by the door.

A few other kopides got in with them. Elise didn't recognize any of them. She focused on her knees.

Malcolm stepped onto the skid.

"This is goodbye," he said, his grin weaker than it had ever been before. "You two kids take care of each other, all right?"

Elise rolled her eyes, but James said, "Thank you." It almost sounded like he meant it.

Malcolm started to step down, but paused. "Hey, did one of you drop this?"

He handed a piece of paper to Elise. It was the wedding photo of Betty, eternally smiling, forever happy. It must have fallen out of her pocket.

Anthony looked more like the Mexican side of his family than Betty's, but they had the same smile. Maybe it was the innocent eyes. Maybe it was the abandon with which she smiled, the "you only live once" attitude, the easy way she let herself be happy.

Betty trusted Elise to make the hard decisions. The heroic ones. She had trusted Elise enough to follow her into a deadly battle, and not return.

And so had Anthony.

Spotlights slammed on, illuminating the opposite side of the landing pad. It drew Elise's attention over Malcolm's shoulder.

Someone screamed. "Let me go! I didn't do anything!"

313

It was Jerica. The young nightmare was only wearing a tank top and underwear, which revealed bony knees, sharp elbows, and bruises mottling her colorless skin.

They were dragging her out of a van. Jerica was putting up a pretty good fight, but not good enough. There was only so much she could do with that much light on her.

"Let me go!"

A powerful sense of wrongness struck Elise. Her hand tightened on the wedding photo as the commander stepped off the skid and waved to the helicopter pilot. "Put on your harness," James said. "We're going to lift off."

He was holding one of the straps out to her. Elise stuffed the photo in her pocket.

"Sorry," she said, but she didn't take the strap.

Elise used James's hand to pull his head down, and she kissed him fiercely. He tried to draw away. She grabbed the back of his head and held him in place. The rushing in her ears could have been nerves, or the rotor, or the wind. The folded corner of Betty's photo jabbed her in the hip.

When she released him, James looked stunned. "Still?"

She suppressed a swell of sadness. "Always." Elise rose from her seat and grabbed the strap over the door. She only managed half of a smile. "Bye, James."

"Wait!"

Elise stepped onto the skid, took a deep breath, and jumped to the pavement.

The helicopter hadn't risen far, but an eight-foot drop was still painful with all of Elise's injuries. She grunted and rolled to her knees.

"What are you doing?" Malcolm asked, stepping back so she wouldn't hit him. "You agreed to leave."

She shielded her eyes to glance up at the ascending helicopter. "Change of plans."

Damnation Marked

James was leaning out the helicopter door, but his features faded as he quickly ascended. She was glad for that. She didn't want to see the confusion and anger.

Malcolm put a finger to his ear.

"Commander to pilot—"

She grabbed his wrist. "Don't call them back."

"You have to leave, Elise."

"I don't *have* to do anything. Except this."

She strode across the landing platform to Jerica. A kopis restrained her by the back of her shirt. The nightmare had lost her footing, and he dragged her through the spotlights to the side of the hill.

Elise grabbed Jerica's arm. Her fingers sank into the girl's sallow flesh as she pulled her away from the other kopis. "Don't you know anything about nightmares? She's young. This much light could *kill* her."

"We have containment procedures!" Malcolm ran to her side. "We're not going to injure it."

"Screw your procedures. Get out of here, Jerica. Run!"

The nightmare took three steps to escape the circle of light. The kopis raised his rifle, and Elise shoved the muzzle down.

"Thanks," Jerica said. "Seriously."

She phased into shadow and disappeared.

"Give me a car. I'm going into Reno again," Elise said.

Malcolm sighed and ran a hand over his stubble. "This is crossing a line. Sorry, Elise." He gestured to the rifleman. "Arrest her."

She didn't wait for the kopis to attempt it. She slammed her foot into his face, wrenched the rifle from his hands, and aimed it at Malcolm.

Instantly, a dozen other guns were aimed at her.

315

She backed toward the edge of the landing platform without dropping her aim. Elise glanced over the side. The ground was twenty feet down, but there was sagebrush at the bottom. She lowered her voice so only Malcolm could hear her. "I'm going to kill Yatai before she opens the gates. You can help me, or I can do it alone. I don't care."

"I'm under orders not to let you return. Don't make me take you out."

She barked a laugh. "You're welcome to try."

Elise threw the rifle at him and jumped off the platform.

Bushes rushed at her. She missed them.

Her side connected with the dirt, and she rolled into a bush. The hard branches stabbed at her face and hair. She staggered to her feet, using her momentum to carry her down the hill.

It was too dark to navigate gracefully. Her foot caught something—a rock or a root, it was impossible to tell—and she tripped, falling head-over-feet to slide down the slope. Grit and ice scraped up her side, her arm, her cheek.

People were shouting. Gunshots thundered overhead.

Elise slid to a stop where the hill leveled off, entrenched in mud and sludgy snow. Her body burned with friction, but she didn't stop to nurse the wounds.

She could just make out a trail winding toward the highway. Scrambling through the sagebrush, she broke onto the clear path.

Her breath tore through her throat as she fled, pumping her fists and dodging the muddiest puddles. The hill steepened again, and she slid a few more feet. Ran another handful of yards. Slid some more.

Spotlights began scanning a few yards uphill. She dug a hand into her pocket and found the ruby choker. "Yatam. I need you."

The answering pause was long enough that she thought he might not show up at all. But then he flashed into life at her side.

He wavered on his feet, clutched his stomach, and fell to his knees in the mud. Then he threw up. Ichor splashed onto the dirt.

Elise pushed his hair over his shoulder, but touching him didn't fill her with a sense of overwhelming power. In fact, she felt nothing from him at all—no more than she did when touching Neuma.

Yatam gave a low moan. "This... I had forgotten this."

His head lifted, and Elise felt a shock as a light swept over them, briefly illuminating his face. His eyes were brown. Not black. Crow's feet marked his eyes, and the slightest lines framed either side of his mouth.

The light vanished again, and she was grateful for it. "Don't take this the wrong way, Yatam, but you're looking very... human. My blood did this to you?"

"I said it was delicious, didn't I?" His brow furrowed. "Feel this."

He took her hand and pressed it to his chest.

Elise's eyes widened. There was a heart beating underneath.

"I am failing." His eyes gleamed. It was the same look he had given her while his head was between her legs. Even with his aging face, it made her ache with remembered heat. "A heart beats a finite number of times before death."

She didn't have time to fully absorb the implications of it. There were spotlights tracing the sagebrush at the top of the hill—the Union was approaching.

"Can you phase us into the city?" Elise asked.

He took her hands. Closed his eyes.

Nothing happened.

"No," Yatam said. "I started losing the ability after the first touch of your blood. Now, it seems to be gone entirely."

An SUV crested the hill. Light splashed over them.

"Great time to lose it," she said. "Fantastic. Okay. We've got to run. Can you move?"

He got to his feet. "Yes."

They fled over the trail together, gripping one another's hands to keep close, and the SUV pursued. Elise could imagine Malcolm driving it, grinning that manic grin he got when he was drunk on excitement instead of alcohol, and she kind of wished she had shot him before jumping.

Sagebrush flashed past them in the night. The desert was a blur of motion, and Elise moved purely on instinct.

The SUV began closing the distance between them.

"This way," Elise said, taking a fork that narrowed and twisted through rocks too large for the SUV to climb over.

The highway waited on the other side.

"There!" Yatam said, dragging her around a boulder to a crevice under the road. It was small—barely big enough for both of them lying down.

They squirmed inside, shoulder-to-shoulder.

The SUV roared toward them. The spotlight slid over their hiding place—and moved on.

Elise held her breath as the engine noise grew. Tires splattered mud on her arm as it rushed past, but it didn't stop. The Union hadn't seen them dive into the hole.

Yatam moved to climb out, but she held him back. "Wait."

Her heart pounded as she waited to see if they would circle around. The sound of the SUV faded into the distance.

"Now," he said, and they scrambled onto the empty highway.

The SUV was still searching the hills, but it was going in the wrong direction. They stayed low to the median and continued to run.

It was a long way back into town.

"Were you in Reno before I summoned you?" Elise asked, the words choppy and short through her heaving breaths. He nodded. "What's going on?"

"The wards around all the gates have fallen, but my sister has yet to open them," Yatam said. "I'm not certain why."

"I spoke to her earlier—told her I could kill her. Maybe she's waiting for me."

He shook his head. "She would not wait if she knew another choice was available. She must not yet have what she needs to open the gates."

"There are no angels to open the gates for her."

"I know."

"But *you* can open them. If you had left, she wouldn't be able to open the gates and destroy the city. She wouldn't be able to kill herself. Instead, you are giving her exactly what she needs to achieve her goals," Yatam said. Elise clenched her jaw and nodded. "Then why did you stay?"

"She's possessed my boyfriend, and I can't exorcise him. Yatai is too powerful. He'll die if I can't kill her."

"But you'll have to die to accomplish that," Yatam said.

She released his hand and ran faster.

Under her breath, she muttered, "I know."

The Union had been using the freeway to evacuate people, so they hadn't destroyed I-80 heading east out of town. But their barricades were still in position, and they were well guarded. Spotlights illuminated the road, guards paced along the barrels, and someone had clearly told them to watch for Elise, as they were scanning the night with binoculars.

A few hundred feet away from the barricade, well beyond the edge of lights, Elise and Yatam stopped.

She dragged a motorcycle out of a truck stopped on the westbound freeway. It was an older model Kawasaki, and it made a strange popping noise when it started, but it did start. Better still, it had two helmets.

"Get on," she said, tossing one to Yatam.

He held it away from him with a finger hooked under the strap. "What is this?"

"It's protective gear."

"I am five thousand years old," he said.

Elise pulled her helmet over her hair, lifting the mask so she could see him. "And now you have a mortal skull that can get crushed. Put it on."

Yatam reluctantly obeyed and climbed on the bike behind her, hands wrapped around her waist. "Are you skilled in operating motorcycles?"

She had ridden dirt bikes with Anthony before. It couldn't be that different.

"Sure. Why not?"

Elise avoided the Union barricade by backtracking a mile and taking the Lockwood exit. She didn't have problems balancing on the heavy motorcycle, but the tires were slick and wide in comparison to a dirt bike's. They wobbled on the turns, the engine protested when she shifted, and it was a jerky ride down the exit ramp. Yatam's arms locked tight around her midsection.

They drove through the quiet, empty night, skirting Union patrols and winding toward the waiting ruins of the city.

The air grew thick as they drove down the main street. Every inch of the ethereal ruins had turned to shadow, half of the buildings had rotted, and the smooth white bone of the gates was now obsidian. Elise paused at an empty intersection and pushed up the mask of the helmet again.

It was quiet—too quiet, considering the way that the Union teams had been mobilizing. There should have been a fleet of SUVs and tanks and gunfire.

But nothing moved.

Yatam lifted a pale hand and pointed at his condominium. The top floor was ripped open, and dark energy radiated into the air. "My sister is waiting for us."

Elise dismounted and dropped the helmet. "Then let's get going."

Her legs felt heavier with every step toward the condo.

She was sore. She was tired. She was weak. And she didn't want to go into that building.

Elise stopped in front of the glass doors and tipped her head back to look at the top of the condominiums. The shadow was greatest there, like the crux of a gathering storm. The dark gate that she had fought so hard to protect was suspended over the parking garage across the street.

She put a hand on the door to the lobby, but she didn't open it.

Elise closed her eyes and took a deep breath. *I'm not ready to die.*

But Anthony's family had shed enough blood for her.

She lifted her chin, straightened her back, and stepped into the building.

The lobby still had all the hallmarks of a high-class establishment—nice floors, the bell desk, fancy geometric paintings. But it was so much darker than the last time she had gone inside. The shadows were so deep as to be tangible, and Yatai's presence dripped from the fashionably tan walls and the desert mural by the elevators.

321

It took Elise's eyes a moment to adjust. When they did, she realized that it was darker along the walls because there were corpses piled there—corpses in cargo pants and polo shirts. At least a dozen Union kopides.

So that was where they had gone.

She had to step over a boy who couldn't have been older than seventeen to push the elevator button. It didn't work.

"Guess we're walking," she said.

They found the stairs covered in ichor. It trickled down the steps like a waterfall, oozing off the metal banisters and sliding across the floor. Yatam climbed onto the first step, and the shadow parted to allow him to pass. "Stay close."

She followed on the step behind him, her face all but pressed between his shoulders, and the ichor closed behind them as they ascended.

The climb was slow. More Union members had died in the stairwell, and they obstructed the landings. Elise tried not to look too closely at all the hardened obsidian skin as she passed. Her boots rung out on each step, muffled and flat.

What did criminals think of on their way toward the executioner's chair? Did they think of their crimes and the people they loved? Did they feel regret?

Elise didn't dare consider any of that. Instead, she counted the floors as they passed. She lost count after ten. And then she counted breaths, heartbeats, the blinks of her eyes—quantifying the gestures of her last moments.

It felt like they climbed among the bodies and shadow all night, but it couldn't have been longer than half an hour. Eventually, Elise's foot sought out the next step, and didn't find it. They had reached the topmost landing, and all that waited for them was a short hall and the door at the end.

She stared at it, feeling numb.

Something touched her hand. Elise looked down. Yatam had curled his fingers around hers. He gave her a smile that might have been comforting, coming from anyone else. "Five thousand years, Elise. It may be difficult for you to understand, but what we are doing is a blessing. You should be filled with joy."

She shook off his hand. "Sorry if I'm not dancing."

"You can face death with reluctance and tears, or you can greet it with a warm embrace," Yatam said. "Either way, we are both about to die."

He pushed the door open.

The condo was the way they had left it—roof torn open, Nügua poised over the basin, and the darkest gate across the street. The Union's scaffolding had spread across the block and formed a honeycomb of metal over their heads. The ashen night smelled like fire and death, and a haze drifted over the wooden floors.

But there was someone new standing there, too. Her skin shimmered with translucence, more like a specter than a woman. Her face had the same pleasant curves as Yatam's. A satin dress the color of rubies hugged her curves.

Yatai was wearing her true face for once. But the lone wing hanging from her shoulder blade didn't belong to her. Half of the feathers had fallen off to bare glistening bone.

She had affixed one of Nukha'il's wings to her back.

Yatai stepped forward to greet them. *Brother, you look unwell.*

"Thank you."

I've waited so many years for this. Let's be quick to greet oblivion.

And that was it. Time to bleed.

Elise drew one of her knives and bit back a grunt of pain as she slit open her wrist.

SM Reine

Yatai's fingers were delicate on her arm as she lifted it to her plump red lips. Her tongue darted out, sleek and slimy, as though an amphibian lived behind her teeth.

The caress of Yatai's flesh against hers wasn't as sensual as Yatam's had been. Nausea crept down Elise's spine, and it took all her strength not to pull away as the demon tasted her.

"Do you feel it?" Yatam asked.

Sudden fury blanketed Yatai's features. *What is this deceit?* She dropped the arm and stepped back. *I feel nothing! I am unharmed!*

Her brother faltered. "Impossible. A mere taste of it weakened me perceptibly."

That is not the blood of a kopis. It is mundane, as flat and flavorless as dirt!

Elise stared at her bleeding wrist.

What had changed? Why had her blood damaged Yatam, and done nothing to Yatai?

An image flashed to mind—the needle in her arm, and James leaning against her bed as he poured life into her veins. He might have been acquiring her abilities as kopis, but he hadn't become a Godslayer, too. And she had taken on his blood.

Which meant her veins ran with his power—not hers.

"Shit," she said.

Yatai laughed, high and chilling, but it quickly turned to sobs. *The Godslayer cannot slay gods. Am I greater than God, or is she too weak? It is the same result—I live on!* She staggered toward the edge of the condo.

"Wait!" Yatam said, stepping in front of her. "Look, sister. Look at my veins! Listen to my heart! Do you see?" But she didn't seem to care. She gazed up at the gate with tears streaming down her cheeks. "You can't open the gates with only a wing. It takes two marks—two angels—to open a gate.

324

Be at peace—we can resolve this without destroying all our children!"

Yatai turned the endless pits of her eyes on Elise.

I do need two marks. That's true, isn't it?

She threw out a hand, and shadow erupted from her fingertips.

Darkness engulfed the side of Elise's body. It overcame her in a rush, swarming from her fingertips to her shoulder.

She shouted and tried to pull free, but there was nowhere to go. Yatai's ichor clung to her like spider webs.

Frost washed over her skin. Pain, swift and sharp, drove through her forearm.

Something snapped like celery.

It took Elise a moment to realize that it was her bones.

She wrenched herself backward, and the shadow let her go. A terrible sensation ripped through the muscle and shot fire over her nerves. The tendons stretched, then tore. Elise stumbled and fell.

Her right arm did not go with her.

She stared at her elbow. Below it, there was nothing but a ragged stump gushing blood in time with the beating of her heart.

Elise could move her elbow, and it made the remaining inch of arm wiggle.

Her forearm, her wrist, her hand—all gone.

It didn't hurt. Nothing hurt.

Yatai stretched out her arm. The cloud of shadow briefly drifted over her, opaque and amorphous. When it dispersed, her right hand was gloved.

Elise's stomach lurched. That glove matched the one that was still on her left hand—black and fingerless. But Yatai hadn't just stolen her glove. She had affixed the entire forearm to her body like Nukha'il's drooping wing.

325

There we are. Two marks, Yatai said. *Thank you.*

She flapped the wing and rose into the air, perfectly balanced, as though she had a matching set.

The pain finally caught up with Elise.

She cried out and fell to her knees, gripping the stump tightly. It hurt—*oh God*, did it hurt—and she needed it to stop—but pressing her hand into the wound only made it burn worse, and letting go made it feel like she was dying, and Yatai had taken her goddamn *arm*—

"We must move," Yatam said.

That was a lot of blood.

Elise's vision fuzzed. Yatam's arm scooped her from the ground before she could fall.

"You're in hypovolemic shock. You're without at least twenty percent of your normal blood volume."

"I can't breathe," she gasped. Her fingers gripped the ragged stump, slick and raw.

"You *can* breathe. As I said, it's only shock." Yatam wrapped an arm around her waist, keeping her on her feet as they lurched toward the edge of the roof. "You'll likely survive, with medical treatment."

"My arm—"

"Yes, very unfortunate."

"*Unfortunate?*"

Her pulse was fast but weak. Her vision blurred. She stumbled.

James. She needed James. He could fix anything.

Her knees gave out.

The room flipped upside down as Yatam threw Elise over his shoulder. The rush of blood from her injuries to her skull made everything darken. "Keep the limb elevated and try not to fall," he said. It sounded like her ears were filled with water.

I'm drowning.

Yatam's body shifted under hers, and she clung to his shoulder with her good arm as he climbed the rubble that used to be his ceiling to reach the roof. Her stump smeared blood down his spine.

The view of the ethereal ruins was excellent from the top of the condo, and hanging from Yatam's back oriented her so that the black cobblestone streets were below her. The ruins seemed dizzyingly distant.

Yatam approached the Union's scaffolding and gripped one of the metal poles for balance. "Yatai!" he shouted.

Elise twisted and saw the mother of all demons floating toward the darkest gate, her body seemingly inverted.

Yes, brother?

He set Elise down gently. Rolling over almost made her lose consciousness.

Yatam stepped to the edge of the roof, arms spread wide. "I am mortal! Her blood is what I claim! You must listen to me!"

Yatai's crying laughter whipped over the wind.

Are you certain?

"Allow me to share my blood with you. We can die together!"

She returned to him. Elise lurched to her knees, preparing for Yatai to attack again, but the demon didn't seem concerned by the writhing of a one-armed kopis.

Yatai wrapped her arms around Yatam, embracing her brother. Her skin was moonlight and milk against his darker flesh. He buried his face in the shadows of her hair as her hands stroked his neck and back.

"It's been so long, sister."

Indeed it has, Yatai said. *So let's see if you're right.*

She wrenched her arms apart.

Yatam's upper half severed from his hips.

327

Elise wasn't sure what she expected to be inside of him. Nightmares didn't have organs—not like humans did. They were built of sludge and shadow. Given that Yatam had fathered all nightmares, she wouldn't have been surprised to see him simply gush black fluid.

But he wasn't black on the inside. He was red—so very red.

Viscera spilled over the cement like that of a butchered steer. His legs rolled several feet away. His upper body splattered at Elise's feet.

Panic surged through her. She stumbled and failed to catch herself. She slammed onto her side on the stump of her arm.

Elise cried out.

My brother, Yatai murmured, her voice filled with sadness and pride. *My love.* She kneeled in front of his torso, smoothing Elise's gloved hand down his face. *Mortal indeed, Yatam. Mortal indeed.*

She jerked his head off his shoulders. It severed with a wet *crunch*.

Yatai placed his head over hers, replacing her ghostly, incorporeal face with his. Yatam's features were so similar to hers as to be nearly indistinguishable. As soon as his ragged neck settled on her shoulders, his eyes blinked, his mouth twisted, and he smiled.

"Good," Yatai said in her brother's voice. It was only a touch deeper than hers. "My brother and I will end this the way we came into the world—together. That's the right way to do it. Don't you think so, sword-woman?"

The world swirled around Elise. She tried to sit up, and failed.

Yatai swept away without waiting for a response, ascending once more on Nukha'il's broken wing.

328

Elise struggled to focus. *He's dead. She's still opening the gates. She has two marks. I'm alone.*

The pain didn't matter. The blood didn't matter.

She couldn't let Yatai reach the gate.

Elise crawled to the edge of the scaffolding. The ladder reaching toward the dark gate looked impossibly, nauseatingly difficult to climb with only one hand. She couldn't do it—not with the red haze of agony clouding her mind and sight.

She took the notebook James had given her out of her pocket. "Please, please, please," she whispered like a mantra, focusing on the word to keep her consciousness.

There was nothing powerful enough to restore a limb in the Book, but there was one more healing spell. She tore the page free. It was harder with one hand than she had expected; she had to lean her knee on the notebook to hold it still.

Elise pressed her clammy forehead to the bar of the scaffold, clamped her teeth down on the thumb ring, and wiggled the gold band off. James must have still been wearing his ring. She couldn't feel him, which meant he couldn't feel her, either. Small mercy.

It took three tries to utter the word of power. The magic sputtered rather than spilled—it pulsed like the flow of blood and showered yellow sparks down her body.

The wound blackened, then began to pale, and new skin inched over the edges. It wasn't much—she was still bleeding, still hurting, still without one of her arms—but it was enough to clear her head.

Enough to stop Yatai.

Elise abandoned the Book and stood on trembling legs.

The darkest gate hummed as Yatai circled it. Lightning leaped to life within the archway, making Elise's palm burn with fresh pain. She ignored it and grabbed the ladder leading up to the scaffold, hooking her elbow over a rung and climbing behind it.

She inched up the ladder one step at a time and rolled onto the scaffolding's platform. The street could have been miles away, for all she knew. She couldn't focus that far beyond the grates.

Yatai hovered by the base of the gate, tilting her head to examine the symbols lining the bone. Energy haloed her head with darkness.

Elise crawled through the battering wind.

Only another twenty feet.

The demon peeled the glove off of her stolen hand and wiggled her fingers. "To think He would be the vehicle of our liberation," Yatai murmured, her voice carried on the electric wind.

Belly to the platform, Elise slid until she was underneath the demon—only five feet away. She levered herself to her feet using the scaffold and climbed that short distance toward the chimeric demon, who only looked more and more amused as she approached.

Yatai smiled with Yatam's lips. "What do you think you're doing?" Elise drew her knife. "Charming."

Stretching out her arm, the demon prepared to press her splayed fingers to the dark gate.

Elise threw the knife.

It buried in the back of Yatai's hand an instant before she could touch the gate. She reared back with a cry and wrenched the blade from her flesh.

The wound didn't close.

Yatai froze, marveling at the injury. Elise's aim was good, despite the blood loss—she had driven the knife straight through the center of the mark on Yatai's palm. Blood dripped down her wrist.

Red blood.

Bracing her knees against the scaffolding, Elise inched higher, drawing level with Yatai, and she pulled the obsidian falchion from its sheath.

"My brother made me mortal," Yatai said, gazing upon the wound with wonder. "His face—he carried your blood—"

Elise drove her sword into the demon's gut.

Her brown eyes went wide. Blood dribbled from one nostril.

The corner of her mouth lifted in a smile.

Elise pulled the sword out and stabbed again, and again. It made a meaty sound, like hacking at steaks.

Nukha'il's wing wilted. Yatai's expression slackened.

She drooped, her head rolled back, and her arms swept wide.

Like a feather, she fell.

The light of five thousand years blinked out, and Elise felt a great emptiness open in her senses where Yatai had been. The places her energy pervaded—the ichor that devoured the ruins, the darkness in Reno, her spirit within Anthony—vanished in an instant.

Elise clung to the scaffolding and watched as Yatai, with Yatam's head, Nukha'il's wing, and her own arm, hit the pavement.

A sob tore from her throat. She pressed her face to the bar.

The gates weren't open. The city was safe. Anthony would be safe.

And she was still bleeding.

She slid down slowly, the metal slicked with blood from her climb. Breathing was so hard, and she wasn't sure if it was due to the elevation or her exhaustion or the blood loss.

Elise made it across the scaffolding—a few levels and a ladder away from safely reaching the condominium. But holding her balance on the metal bar without a hand was too difficult. Even with James's magic healing her, she couldn't keep her balance.

Her foot skidded on a slippery bar.

Elise felt the rush of falling.

She didn't feel the landing at all.

It took her a long time to process what had happened. She had been looking at her fingers curled around the scaffolding one moment, and then suddenly she was staring up at the statue of Nügua; how she had crossed the hundreds of feet between the ruins and the condominium, she wasn't sure.

She couldn't feel anything below the neck, including her severed arm and what must have been a broken leg. Elise could see her foot twisted strangely out of the corner of her eye, though she couldn't move her head to inspect the damage. That was probably a bad sign.

Come to think of it, she couldn't feel her chin, either. Or her throat as she tried to breathe.

Maybe she wasn't breathing.

Everything was so distant.

Her eyes closed on Nügua's benevolent smile. Elise's last breath drifted from her lips, and her lungs didn't fill again.

XVIII

By midnight, the energy pouring off of the gates died down enough for Union witches to contain them. It took about six hours to construct the warding spells and execute them properly. An hour after that, a kopis reported that all of the possessed fiends were dead. And when the sun rose around eight o'clock in the morning, it was on clear streets and a silent city.

Once Bellamy confirmed that all the demons were contained or dead, Malcolm finally entered what Union HQ was already referring to as Ground Zero. His unit combed Reno for survivors, and he wanted to be there to see what they found. It was against Union regulations for a commander to take point in recovery efforts, of course, but HQ couldn't get mad about what they never discovered.

Trackers noted activity at a condominium downtown when the gates closed, so that was the first place Malcolm visited. He took his sidearm. Not that he didn't trust Bellamy's detecting spells, of course, but being paranoid had kept him alive to see thirty. Not many kopides could say that.

Malcolm limped across the top floor of the condominium to meet his aspis. "Report?"

Bellamy's spine straightened. Military instinct was impossible to beat out of a man. "We lost more than two dozen good Union men and women, sir. And we also recovered three other bodies."

"Three?"

"Two demons and a human." He hesitated. "An unassociated kopis."

Oh, hell. Malcolm scrubbed a hand over his eyes. "Which two demons?"

"Heather blew her magic out trying to identify the bodies," Bellamy said, referring to a witch on staff whose sole expertise was demonology. "They were more powerful than anything she's ever seen. Maybe the most powerful demons on Earth. Not much left of them, though."

At least they were dead. The names weren't too important. "And the human?"

Bellamy gestured to the edge of the condo.

There was only one thing in the otherwise empty room: a statue of a snake-woman atop a broad stone basin. The entire thing was made of baked clay, and perfectly untouched by the destruction.

Except for the corpse inside.

Malcolm knew who it would be before he looked, and he gave brief consideration to ordering the body's transport without confirming his fear. But his curiosity won out.

It was Elise, of course.

He kneeled by her body to gaze upon her face, slack and calm in death. There was no hint of the cold fury he had once found so sexy. Her head had been cracked open on the side of the basin, and brain matter leaked from the back of her skull, making her auburn curls clump together with glossy gray fluid. That was probably what killed her, but he doubted she would have survived bleeding out from the artery in her arm, either. The fall just got to her first.

Gary Zettel brought over a stretcher. "Sir?"

Malcolm stepped back to let him lift her onto a gurney. Gary was actually smiling—the bastard.

Malcolm stopped a passing witch. She was new to the Union, and wouldn't know who Elise was. "Bring the truck around and take this body to the medical bay. They'll want to autopsy her."

"I can take care of it, sir," Gary said.

"No, you can't. Go find something better to do." The former commander glowered at him, but moved on, leaving Malcolm alone momentarily with Elise.

He was surprised to find no sadness within himself at her death. Some part of him liked to think of her in a warrior's heaven—a Valhalla where she could battle eternally without the troublesome complications of reality and relationships.

Her eyes were still open a fraction. He smoothed his fingers over her eyelids to close them, and then pulled the white sheet over her face.

The intact left arm hung out from under the sheet. Her hand was still gloved.

Malcolm had never seen what was under those gloves before. She wore them all the time, even when they had sex, and she had traded them out for bandages when she showered. He had seen every other inch of her, but that specific area was a mystery to him.

"Why not?" he asked her shrouded profile.

He peeled off Elise's glove and turned the palm over.

Nothing. Her hand was utterly unremarkable. A little scarred, a few too many calluses on her knuckles. But it was only a hand.

"You were one crazy bitch," he murmured, sliding her arm under the sheet.

The witch initiate returned a few minutes later, and he watched as she carried the gurney away. Malcolm heaved a sigh.

He felt his aspis approach. The slender man stood by his side silently for a few long minutes as Malcolm watched the rising sun inch toward the ethereal ruins. "So Elise Kavanagh died last night," Bellamy said. It almost made Malcolm laugh to hear him say her name with such unfamiliarity, like she was a celebrity—or legend. "You had a history with her, didn't you?"

"Ancient history." He walked around the statue. There wasn't a single drop of blood to be seen.

"Need me to do anything for you, sir?"

"Nah." He kneeled by the basin and ran his hand over the smooth stone. It left a faint residue of dust on his fingers.

When he turned his hand to study the sandy residue on his hand, the recent scar from his binding to Bellamy caught his attention. He rubbed his fingers on his forearm.

"Actually, scratch that. Get me James Faulkner's phone number."

James had a long time to study the destroyed region on his way out in the helicopter.

They flew low over Sparks and buzzed the edge of the ethereal ruins, using it as a windshield as they headed for the pass. The snow was becoming too thick to tell what the Union was doing downtown, but he made out a few things in the darkness.

His heart ached as he spotted the empty pits that used to be familiar landmarks, but were now destroyed—casinos, the new ballpark, and even Rancho San Rafael park, where the fields had caved in from Yatai's merciless tunneling. They were scars on the face of the land, black areas of blight, as though she had dragged razors through the earth.

There was no sense to any of it. It was the embodiment of Yatai's suicidal despair, and nothing more. She had left so little behind.

They passed on, flew higher, arced over the mountains. Aside from the empty freeways, there was no sign of destruction once they reached the thick trees and ski resorts. Empty and peaceful.

There was sunshine on the other side of the mountain. A thick yellow haze turned the sun red where it splashed on the asphalt, and it smelled of forest fire, but everything was otherwise normal—untouched by the evil across state lines.

They touched down in an industrial area north of Sacramento. Everyone, aside from James, wore Union black. The trucks were even UKA branded. He stepped onto the tarmac and gazed at the sun, trying to remember the last time he had seen it.

"James Faulkner?"

He turned. A young man with red hair waited behind him. "Yes?"

"I'm Remington Boyd. I'm under orders to hold you until I get further instruction."

"Malcolm agreed to send me to the airport so I could get to Colorado," James said. "The flight is already arranged."

"This order comes from HQ. Your evacuation was conditional on Kavanagh going with you, and she's still in Reno. Until she's contained, I have to keep you here." Remington shrugged. "It's nothing personal."

"I'm sure."

James spent a few hours pacing in an empty room with a locked door, twisting the gold band on his finger, probing the magic, considering reaching out to a silent Elise. But what if he distracted her at a critical moment?

He sat down and occupied himself by copying spells on blank pages of his new Book of Shadows. He tried not to think about Elise. He tried not to think about frozen beaches, smooth lips, or sad smiles.

But he thought about nothing else, really.

When Remington returned, it was only to move him to a private room in the barracks for the night.

James thought he would never sleep, but he must have passed out at some point, because he was jolted awake by a knocking at the door. He was surprised to find that the time had somehow jumped from midnight to nine in the morning.

Time wasn't the only thing that had changed as he slept. Remington entered, freshly shaven and smiling. "Morning! I'm here to take you to breakfast."

"Has Elise been secured?"

"I don't know. But we won last night—that demon is dead, the city's safe, and you're heading out this afternoon. Come on, aren't you hungry? We're having a party in the mess hall!"

James's cautious optimism didn't last long. "No. Thank you. I'll wait here for now."

Remington shrugged. "Suit yourself." He turned to leave, but stopped before he could close the door and put two fingers to his earpiece. "Boyd here. Yeah… Understood. Yes, sir." He refocused on James. "There's a phone in the cabinet by your cot. The operator's forwarding a call in here."

"From whom?"

But the young kopis was already gone.

The bedside table chimed. James pulled open the drawer and found a plain black cell phone. Did everything the Union made have to be so damned black?

James answered it. "Yes?"

"Hey, this is Malcolm." His tone was unusually muted. All the humor had gone out of his voice, and it immediately put James on high alert.

"What's wrong?" he asked, even though he knew there was only one reason that Malcolm would call. James held the phone between his shoulder and ear as he twisted the golden band off his finger again.

The commander let out a sigh. "Listen, I hate to be the one to tell you this, but... How do I say it?"

James slipped the ring free, and felt... nothing.

A gnawing emptiness gaped in the back of his skull. It was like losing an entire hemisphere of his mind—or half of his heart.

"We recovered Elise's body this morning. I knew you would want to hear immediately. I'm sorry, mate. If it makes you feel any better, it looks like she went out fighting. Can't imagine she'd want to have it any other way."

James tried to sit down and missed the chair. His back struck the wall. He slid to the floor.

The phone bounced and landed near his foot.

Malcolm's voice, tinny and small, continued to speak.

"Hello? You still there?"

James turned the phone off and sat in silence.

December 2009

After too many long days of panic and blood, the Union's infirmary was finally getting quieter. Anthony awoke from his drugged haze with a nurse standing by his bed and Christmas lights wrapped around the foot of his bed.

"What date is it?" he asked when he could finally speak.

"December third," said the nurse. "Don't move." She left him and didn't return. A dour witch whose nametag read "Allyson" replaced her.

"Do you know why you're here?" Allyson asked without preamble.

Anthony struggled to remember, but his recent memory was blank. "No."

So Allyson told him. She told him everything. That he had been demon-possessed and killed people. That they had been keeping him under sedation until they could be sure he was safe. She also told him that Reno was destroyed and he wasn't going to be able to return.

And then she left, too.

He was stunned. But that didn't last very long. Bound to his bed by the wrists, Anthony had no way of entertaining or distracting himself. Once he confronted the horror of waking up a homeless murderer, it got kind of boring.

A day passed slowly, and then another. So he watched people move through the ward instead.

He caught a couple familiar faces, covered in soot with bruises and lesions, but they were just classmates or old customers. Nobody he cared to talk with. And none of them stopped to look at him. They probably didn't recognize him with two weeks of beard growth and crazy hair—he didn't recognize himself in the reflection in the steel table beside the bed.

Nobody but Anthony lasted long in the infirmary. One short check-up, and each patient moved on—either to a hospital, or to another Union facility, depending on the type and severity of the wound.

A lot of corpses passed him, too. Apparently, the morgue was just beyond his bed.

Anthony tried to catch glimpses of them, but most were covered in sheets or zipped into plastic bags. Sometimes he saw a bare shoulder, or a foot. He saw a couple of unfamiliar faces as doctors checked the identity and moved them along. If Anthony had killed any of them, the memories weren't accessible to him.

So he wasn't surprised—not really—when he saw Elise.

It happened late in the evening. A woman in Union gear stopped a few beds away with a gurney leaving the morgue. She spoke briefly to a doctor. She lifted the sheet to reveal the body.

Anthony saw red-brown curls. A bloodless face with freckles across the bridge of her nose. Full lips that he had kissed more than a few times. Skin blue with cold and eyebrows frosted with ice.

Elise seemed pretty peaceful, for a dead woman.

The exposure lasted only an instant. Then they put the sheet over her again.

"Do you have the autopsy results?" asked the doctor. The nurse gave him a clipboard, and he looked it over. "Hmm… this one's getting a formal service. Guess she was a friend of the commander. Take her to be prepared."

Elise was wheeled on.

He craned his neck around in his bed to watch the Union team member take her away, but there was nothing to see. Elise didn't sit up, push the sheet away, and climb down. Given her stubbornness, he half-expected it…but only by half. He knew death when he saw it.

Anthony stared at the ceiling.

He tried to imagine her cremated, reduced to ashes, and spread over the lake, like Betty had been.

A new nurse approached Anthony's bed. She wore the Union slacks and a scrub top patterned with white flowers. "How do you feel?" she asked, unlocking the handcuffs that bound him to the bed.

"My girlfriend is dead." He couldn't seem to make himself sound like he was grieving, but the nurse looked sympathetic anyway.

"Poor dear," she murmured. "No more symptoms of possession? Any unusual time lapses? Strange voices or urges?" He shook his head at each question. "You seem to have recovered well. You can get up and use the bathroom if you like, but stay in the ward until we can have someone discharge you." She checked his chart. "You haven't had a meal yet. Hmm. I'll find you something to eat."

Anthony sat up, rubbing his wrists. His mouth tasted like ash. The idea of eating sounded ridiculous. "Yeah," he said, "thanks."

After she left, he hobbled to the bathroom, which was a curtained room with a few basins people had been using for toilets. The nurse was right about the weakness; he could barely support his weight long enough to piss standing up. His urine was orange and filled the curtained area with the sour tang of ammonia.

When he finished, he hung in the hallway to watch the quiet bustle. Nobody seemed to notice his absence from the ward.

But he went back to his bed anyway, and sat down to give his legs a break.

It wasn't like he had anywhere to go. Anthony's family was all in Vermont. There was nobody to talk to about what he had seen, or the things he had done. What little of it he remembered, anyway. Everything after taking the elevator into the Warrens with Elise was a blur.

And if Reno were wasted, he wouldn't have a job anymore. As if he hadn't screwed up his grades enough already, there definitely wouldn't be a college to attend for the rest of the semester.

Without a job, family, or Elise—or hell, even James—Anthony had no idea what to do.

A man finally approached him. He had an eye patch, hair shorn so short that his scalp glistened underneath, and knuckles that looked like they had punched a thousand faces. His bent and scarred fingers held two small bags. "Anthony Morales," said the man with a thick Irish accent. "You're looking healthy."

"Who are you?"

The man tucked the bags under his arm and held out one twisted hand. "Malcolm. Union commander. I'm in charge of all this." He tipped his head toward the wall, which didn't have anything of particular interest on it, so Anthony understood it to mean the base at large.

He gave the proffered hand a brief shake. "What did I do to rank a visit?"

"You mean, besides killing four of my best men?"

His stomach lurched. "You're going to arrest me, aren't you?"

Malcolm laughed. "Union regulations say that victims of demonic possession can't be held accountable for what they do under the influence, so you're good to go once the doctors give their permission. It's your lucky day."

He thought of Elise being wheeled past him on the gurney, and what Allyson had told him about Reno—buildings toppled and streets ripped from the earth.

"Sort of," Anthony said.

SM Reine

The commander seemed to understand. His shoulders sagged. "Yeah. Sort of." He coughed. "Here." Malcolm gave him one of the bags. It was a plastic sack with the UKA logo on it. "You can have your belongings back. It's just your clothes, but I'm sure it'll feel nice to get back to normal, eh?" He hesitated, toying with the plastic edge of a second bag. "You were dating Elise, weren't you?"

Malcolm spoke her name like he knew her, but his face gave nothing away.

"Yeah."

"I left a message for James. Asked if he wanted to claim Elise's belongings once we had them sorted. He never returned my call, so I thought you might want them. We'll incinerate them if nobody makes a claim."

"Oh," he said. "Sure."

Anthony took the second bag. He peeled open the tape and peered inside.

There wasn't much. While the Union's commander hung nearby, Anthony pulled out a glove—just one—and a cell phone. There was also Betty's wedding photo.

And that was it. Anthony's throat closed as he looked at Betty's smile.

"Nothing else?" he rasped.

Malcolm lifted his shoulders. "Two swords. Can't have those—sorry. Our witches are studying them. There was also an enchanted ring, but the forensics department kept it. They can't figure out what the hell it's for. Is it yours? I can try to put in a request to get it back."

He pocketed the glove and Betty's photo. "No. It wasn't mine." He swallowed, and Anthony closed the sack again. "Thanks."

Malcolm set a hand on his shoulder for a moment.

Anthony watched his retreating back as he walked away. As soon as he was alone again, he turned the cell phone on. The battery still had half a charge.

He tapped the photo icon and started with the old pictures. Elise had been using the same phone for a couple of years, so the first few pages mostly showed Motion and Dance—photos of recitals, some pictures of James playing the piano, a nice shot of Elise in a dress she must have worn for a performance. She also had a few snapshots of fancy dinners that Anthony couldn't imagine her having actually eaten.

She had taken pictures of wine glasses. Lots of wine glasses. Why? Because she liked the wine, or because she liked the glass, or because she liked the lighting? He had no guesses.

Betty started appearing a couple pages into the shots. He went through those slowly. Beach photos, lifting weights at the gym, dancing together at a bar, a shot where they were both making that stupid duckface outside of a club.

He had picked on Betty for making that face. A lot.

Around the spring, Elise seemed to have stopped taking so many pictures. The wine glasses disappeared. His abs clenched as he noticed the one picture she had taken on their camping trip together—and it was of a dead spider-demon.

The last photo was of some random rocks up at Lake Tahoe. Just a month old.

And that was it. That was all Anthony had from Elise's life: one glove and a cell phone with two hundred pictures.

The phone beeped. He almost dropped it.

When his grip was good again, he saw the "new text message" icon blinking, and he dreaded seeing what James would be trying to send her. He opened the inbox.

The new text wasn't from James. It was from a number she didn't have saved to her address book.

39.107619,-120.028424. 00:54 tomorrow. say hi for me. -Ben

Anthony only knew of one Ben who might text Elise—Benjamin Flynn, the teenage prophet in the Union's employ. He looked up, half-expecting to see the boy in the ward with him, but he didn't recognize anyone strolling around the beds. They were all doctors, nurses, and witches.

Anthony read the message again.

Those digits were coordinates.

He used Elise's map application and found them centered over Lake Tahoe.

Say "hi" for me.

A spark of hope bloomed within Anthony. Say "hi" to whom, exactly? Was the text meant for Elise—or did Benjamin know that Anthony would have it?

He had to have known. That kid knew *everything*.

Anthony checked the time. It was getting late. If he wanted to reach the lake by one in the morning, he would have to hurry.

He pulled his pants on, stripped off the paper hospital gown, and headed out of the room as he pulled a Union sweater over his head. Nobody stopped him.

It wasn't easy to find a working car, but after an hour of searching, Anthony located a pickup with a full tank of gas and the keys abandoned on the dashboard. He only had to run into a few cars to free it from the jam on the freeway.

Boat rentals weren't much easier to come by in the middle of the night in December. He pounded on windows until someone woke up, and then he gave them the money that had been in his pockets when the Union had stripped him—all eight hundred dollars of his last paycheck.

The lake was black under his boat as he steered toward the middle, not quite sure what he was searching for. Freezing water slopped over the sides.

He shivered in his jeans and jacket, trying to keep his feet out of the puddle at the bottom of the boat. Anthony kept one hand on the rudder and the other on Elise's cell phone, closing the distance between the dot that indicated his location and the coordinates sent by Benjamin. There was a spotlight mounted on the front of his boat, but he didn't need it to see. The sky was filled with lush purple snow clouds. The mountain's icy peaks were a darker shade of gray against the steely clouds.

A freezing wind blasted his hair around his forehead. He crested an arcing wave, and his stomach lurched.

He checked the phone again. It was confused by his position in the middle of the lake, but it looked like he was getting close.

Anthony traveled a few more yards and cut off the motor.

Almost one o'clock.

He was in the right place. It was the right time.

More water slopped over him, splashing his jeans and chilling him to his core. "This is crazy," he said aloud, jaw chattering. "What was I thinking?"

As if in response, the wind blew harder. He seized the sides of the boat as snow whirled over the water.

Damn it, he hadn't brought gloves. His fingers were stiff and useless.

Another wave swelled under his boat, and for a moment, all he could see was the gray-purple depths of the water.

When the boat righted itself again, he saw something pale bob to the surface of the water.

SM Reine

His hands weren't working well enough to get the motor running again—he had to stick his fingers in his mouth for a few seconds to limber them first.

Anthony steered the boat closer. Turned on the floodlight.

It was a body, facedown in the lake, with masses of inky black hair spread around its head. Judging by the shape of the waist and legs, it was a woman.

A naked woman.

Probably a *dead* woman.

"Oh, Jesus fucking Christ." He rubbed his hands on his frozen jeans. "What the hell, Benjamin?"

Snow swirled harder around him as he struggled to bring his boat alongside the body. There was a pole and net underneath the seats. He used it to drag her closer. Careful not to capsize, he snagged a limp arm and dragged it over the side.

The skin was shockingly warm on his cold fingers. It felt more like he had pulled her out of a bath than Lake Tahoe in December. And she weighed nothing—it was easy to drag her legs into the boat. Masses of wet hair stuck to her face and chest.

Something dark marred one of her palms. Anthony grabbed her hand and uncurled the fingers.

There was a mark on her skin—an intricate design imprinted on the palm, more like a brand than a tattoo. A few centimeters below the base of the mark, a long red scar stretched all the way into the corner of her elbow.

It wasn't the first time he had seen that mark, or that scar.

Anthony's heart pounded as he drew her shoulders into his lap and shoved the hair out of her face.

She looked like Elise.

Rubbing his eyes and shaking his head didn't change anything. He wasn't imagining the resemblance. He wasn't

348

going crazy. Those were the same lips, cheekbones, and arched nose—except this woman didn't have the twisted bridge from having her nose broken in a dozen fights. She also had black hair. Black eyebrows. White skin, no freckles.

She coughed. Her chest jerked. Anthony almost dropped her.

Water spilled over her lip, cascading down her chest in waves, too much to have been in her lungs and stomach. Buckets of water.

She gurgled and choked on it, and it was more instinct than rational thought that made Anthony prop her up against his shoulder so that she could vomit into the bottom of the boat.

Her hands bit into his biceps. It hurt. She was too strong. He tried to push her off, and her eyes flew open with a gasp.

They were black. So very, very black.

"Elise?" he asked tentatively, pushing more hair off of her forehead.

She screamed. It was a shrill, piercing sound. She threw herself away from him, slipping and falling over the bench. She bumped into the spotlight. It spun on its base.

"Whoa! Wait, be careful—"

She jerked, staring out at the water as if she couldn't believe the sight of it. Pulled her knees into her chest. Covered her face with her hands, and kept screaming.

Then she held her hands away from her, as though she was frightened of them, and the shrieks cut off.

She lifted her right arm. Stared at the empty palm in the reflection of the spotlight off the water. Ran her fingers down to her elbow, as if she couldn't believe it was there.

And then she looked past her hand to him.

Recognition sparked in her black eyes.

"Anthony?"

ABOUT THE AUTHOR

SM Reine is a writer and graphic designer obsessed with werewolves, the occult, and collecting swords. Sara spins tales of dark fantasy to escape the drudgery of the desert where she lives with her husband, the Helpful Toddler, and a small army of black animals.

Enlist in the Army of Evil!
Be the first to hear when a
new book comes out! Visit
smarturl.it/armyofevil